Chasing Petalouthes

Book Three in The Gift Saga

Effie Kammenou

Printed in the United States of America

First Edition: June 2018

10 9 8 7 6 5 4 3 2 1

ISBN 13: 978-0-692-12059-0
ISBN-10: 0-692-12059-9

Library of Congress Cataloging-in-Publication Data TXu 2-092-076
Kammenou, Effie. Chasing Petalouthes

Cover Design by Deborah Bradseth – www.tugboatdesign.net
Cover Photography by Ioanna Chatzidiakou
Author photo by Daniel Krieger

This book is dedicated to my daughters, Eleni and Alexa—my very own beautiful and colorful *petalouthes*. Watching you both grow into the accomplished, lovely young women you've become has been my greatest privilege. Spread your wings wide. The sky is the limit and the possibilities, endless.

A Note to Readers

Chasing Petalouthes is the final book in *The Gift Saga*. Now that the series is complete, I feel a sense of satisfaction having brought these characters to life and in sharing their experiences, heartaches and triumphs with you, the readers. But, if I'm completely honest, I'm also a little sad. Anastacia, Sophia and all their loved ones and friends have become a part of my family, almost as if they truly existed. And in my mind and creative sensibilities, for the last several years, they did. So, it will be difficult to put the pen down (or stop tapping away at the computer) and say goodbye to these families that I've come to love so much.

Each book was born from very personal influences in my life. My mother's passing put me on the path to writing *Evanthia's Gift*, and I felt her presence beside me throughout the process. My childhood friends inspired *Waiting For Aegina*, ones who I still hold dear today. And *Chasing Petalouthes* had the younger generation in my family in mind as I developed the story—my daughters, nieces and nephews as they make their way from adolescence to adulthood. We live in an ever-changing world, in many ways so different than the one Anastacia grew up in, yet fundamentally the same in their simple desires. Each generation is looking for love, personal success and security.

Titling this book perplexed me until I was entirely finished with the manuscript. Once the idea came to me, I never questioned myself or changed my mind. *Petaloutha* is the Modern Greek word for butterfly, and this is a story of self-discovery and finding personal inner beauty. Interestingly, the ancient Greek word for butterfly is psyche, pronounced psee-hé. Its literal meaning is soul. In Greek mythology, Psyche was the goddess of the soul and married to Eros, the god of love. She was often depicted in ancient artwork as having the wings of a butterfly, and so, this is how, through the ages, these beautiful, metamorphic creatures became associated with the human and spiritual soul.

And that's what I hope you recognize in this conclusion to *The Gift Saga*—the spirit and soul of each character—the younger ones taking lessons from the past and understanding their connection to their family history and heritage is part of who they are, ingrained and imbedded in the fiber of their being. But the grander lesson here is for individuals to become who they are meant to be, to follow their dreams and let their butterfly wings carry them as far as their dreams will take them.

Acknowledgments

To my husband, Raymond, and my daughters, Eleni and Alexa, for all your patience, love and support. I couldn't have done any of this without your encouragement and confidence in me.

To Valerie Gildard, the first person to set her eyes on my books and offer helpful feedback. You're the best unofficial editor an author could hope for and a great friend.

To my editor, Katie-bree Reeves of Fair Crack of the Whip Proofreading and Editing for an open and comfortable working relationship. Your diligence and eye for detail speaks for itself.

To Deborah Bradseth of Tugboat Design for always providing the most professional inside formatting and the most beautiful covers.

To Ioanna Chatziadiakou for your breathtaking photography. Your ability to convey the heart of a story with one image is a special talent.

To model, Christiana Katsimpraki, for gracing the book cover.

To Estate Anastasia Triantafyllou for the use of their vineyard during the bookcover photo shoot.

To Dr. Jonathan Lown for answering my sometimes odd questions about injuries and illnesses. Thank you for always getting back to me in great detail.

To Krystina Kalapothakos for sharing, in depth, a difficult time in her life with me. Your experience inspired me to shape a storyline in *Waiting For Aegina* and it now continues in *Chasing Petalouthes*.

To Pamela and Daniel Krieger for my author photo and for showcasing my books in Mount Sinai Optical. Your enthusiasm and encouragement has not gone unnoticed.

To Joanna Martin Barouch for providing me with information on traditional Greek-Jewish customs and traditions. You are always a wealth of information on many subjects.

To Rett Tyler for beta reading and being one of my head cheerleaders. I look forward to our 2 AM conversations when it's the middle of the day for you in Australia.

To Elizabeth Monteadora for beta reading. Your edits and feedback were very helpful. As a side note, Elizabeth was one of my very own 'Honey Hill Girls.' We grew up on the same street along with several other girls our age. (No, none of the characters are based on her)

To Josephine Grisafi, Pam Krieger, Maureen Nolan and Liz Capuano for being my unofficial PR agents. Thank you for your support.

To Loreley Habran of Vine Escapes, who provided me with all I needed to know about the making of Champagne. It was a wonderful and informative experience.

To Sylvie Lancelot from the House of Lancelot-Royer, who graciously opened her home and Champagne Vineyard to me. It was an experience I will never forget, as was my time in all of Épernay, France.

To my fabulous Greek ladies in the 'Greeklish' and 'Just Me' Facebook groups. Whenever I had a question or wanted to hear about a personal experience that related to one of the topics in my story, you were all so helpful. Sometimes the chats went on for days. I especially liked the *Krevati* memories you all shared with me.

To Aphrodite Papandreou for commenting on one of my Instagram posts with a quote so beautiful that I just had to use it in the book. Thank you for giving me permission to. I can see what made you a special educator of youth for so many years.

To my Father, Nicholas Kameno, for his endless string of inspiring stories and for being the moral and spiritual support for our family.

To my mother, Eleni Debonera Kameno, who always supported my dreams. *Evanthia's Gift* was written because of you. I can feel your loving presence and graceful spirit as I write about our culture and heritage. Still, I will always miss you.

To you, the readers, for all your messages, emails and reviews. I love hearing from you and chatting on Twitter, Goodreads and on my Facebook author page. You inspire me to keep writing by expressing how connected you are to my stories and characters. There is no greater reward for a writer!

"Nature's message was always there and for us to see.
It was written on the wings of butterflies."

—Kjell Bloch Sandved

Chapter 1

Aegina

July 2005

Twilight cast an incandescent glow over the Saronic Gulf, as the sun slowly began to peak over the horizon. The reflection of porch lights from homes surrounding the shoreline glimmered like stardust on the water. In less than an hour, the sun would assume its full magisterial position and, as though gifted from the Gods themselves, another day would dawn on this enchanting island.

Two by two, a contemplative assembly of young adults leisurely walked along the momentarily vacant main road to Aegina Town. Once daylight broke and the ferryboats pulled into the harbor, the streets would be cluttered with tourists, and it was for this very reason they'd set off at the early hours of the morning. For what they were about to do required solemnity—privacy—a place to pay tribute and share deeply personal remembrances.

Evvie had left a note for her mother on the kitchen table before exiting her great-grandmother's beach house with the rest of the group. She rolled her eyes thinking of how her mother, Sophia, seemed to have the need to know where she was every minute of the day. She

1

and her twin brother, Nicky, were nineteen years old and, in Evvie's mind, their mother sometimes treated them as though they were nine-year-olds.

It was the last few days of the 'extended family' vacation Evvie's stepfather, Dean, had arranged for the entire family and Sophia's closest friends to spend some much-needed bonding time together. The past year had been a difficult one. Dean had almost lost his life in a car accident, and Sophia's friend, Amy, had been in jeopardy of losing her career and family. But it was RJ and Donna who had suffered the most dreadful tragedy of all. Donna had lost her younger son, and RJ, his only sibling. But RJ was not alone, Evvie thought. They were all brothers and sisters of the heart. After all, they were the children of the 'Honey Hill Girls,' and those girls—women—were now fifty years old and still the best of friends.

As they approached the harbor of Aegina Town, their destination came into view—a tiny, whitewashed chapel standing proudly at the edge of the dock known as *Agios Nikolaos*. It was Nicky and her cousin, Stella, two people with the softest of souls, who'd suggested this sojourn. RJ had been overwhelmed with emotion when they'd asked his permission to memorialize his brother, Anthony, who had taken his own life ten months prior in response to the emotional cruelty he could no longer suffer. This was to be their own requiescat inside the near-ancient walls they were about to enter.

As Kristos, Stella's older brother, pushed open the heavy entrance door, a light breeze blew by. A pinging rattle of rope slapped against the high, metal poles standing on either side of the double-domed building, each one waving its own flag. The blue and white banner of Greece and the double-headed eagle emblem representing the Greek Orthodox Church fluttered high above the pristine structure.

The chapel was small and the space empty, devoid of pews like many traditional Orthodox churches in Greece. The floor was made of gray marble, with a narrow pathway leading to an altar where images of saints, dulled from time and candle soot, separated themselves from worshippers. Beautifully painted icons painted above the archway had chipped in random spots, as if to remind newcomers of the many generations that had come to pray before they had.

"It doesn't look how I expected it to," RJ said, shoving his hands in his pockets and scanning the space before him. "The outside is so ... white and clean, as if it's been continually maintained."

His furrowed brow and assessing expression advertised his confusion. "I'm surprised to see the inside a bit neglected."

"No, not neglected. Naturally antiquated and respectfully permitted to uphold the beauty of its age," Sam, the eldest of the group, said with admiration. Gently, he ran his fingers over a disintegrating portion of a wall etched with dulled and faded icons. As a graduate student of Hellenic studies, Sam appreciated the beauty of the artwork before him, though it held no religious inspiration for him as a Greek Sephardic Jew.

"It's much smaller but very much like the churches I've been to with your family," RJ said to his friends. "I suppose I'm just used to everything being much newer in the States."

"The iconography is pretty much universal," Paul said. "But this church was built in the fourteenth century and they upkeep it as best as they can."

Kristos led the group further inside and gestured for everyone to sit on the floor. Melancholy hung in the air as they formed a circle.

"RJ, Anthony was your brother. Would you like to begin?" Kristos asked after a moment of silence.

Evvie could see the jump in RJ's Adam's apple and the tightening of his jaw. She reached her hand across the circle to make contact with his. "This is as much for you as it is for Anthony. We're here for you," she reassured him.

RJ nodded and forced a smile. "My brother—" He coughed, choking on his words. "This is hard," he said, clearing his throat. "My brother was a good person. The best. Kind, smart and sensitive. He never hurt anyone. I can't understand. I just can't understand ..."

Closing his eyes, RJ hung his head.

Stella slipped her hand into his, lending her support.

"I don't think any of us can comprehend what drives someone to take his own life unless we've experienced the feeling of hopelessness Anthony must have," Nicky said sympathetically.

"That's not the part I don't understand, although I can't fully grasp that either. It's the torment. Why? Why would anyone be so cruel? I found messages on his computer that were so disturbing. He'd never once mentioned them to me. He was living in a solitary hell and I had no idea." RJ huffed and shook his head in disgust. "I would have tried to do something about it. At least I would've tried to find out who was behind it."

"I don't think we'll ever understand hate or what drives it. But all you have to do is look at history to see it's ever present, always lurking like an insidious evil plague," Sam said, with more than a hint of bitterness resonating from his words. "It seems a part of the human condition, I'm sorry to say," he added.

RJ fisted his hands. "And he got no refuge at home either. My father—our father … he was awful to Anthony."

Paul, the middle child between Kristos and Stella, spoke up. "I wish he had confided in at least one of us." He and Anthony were born within months of each other and had been fairly close.

"I'd spoken to him a few days before," Adam, Sam's half-brother muttered. "I was distracted and didn't pick up on any signals that might have warned me something was wrong. If I'd only paid more attention …" He lowered his eyes in shame.

"This isn't why we're here," Stella said softly. "It's not about guilt or blame. We're here to remember what we love about Anthony and to remind ourselves never to forget him. This is to pray he's at peace."

"He was a good friend," Paul continued. "He'd want us to remember the fun we all had together."

"I wish that I'd had the opportunity to meet him," Sam said. He'd only recently become part of this tight-knit clan when he met his birthmother, Amy Jacobs Rosenfeld, for the first time. Amy had fallen pregnant just before her college graduation and wasn't prepared to care for a child. Sophia and she had spent the summer in Greece where she gave Sam up for adoption to a lovely Jewish couple in Thessaloniki. "If you each share one thing about Anthony that stands out in your minds, I can get to know him a little through all of you," Sam suggested.

"He was an amazing artist," Adam said suddenly. "Once, I told him that sometimes when I'm in D.C. I miss my home and friends in Westchester. A few weeks later, I received a package in the mail from Anthony. He'd painted my home and the surroundings just as it looked in autumn, which he knew is my favorite time of year. The attached note he sent said, 'So you won't be quite so homesick.' It made me feel much better."

"RJ, you and I hung out more," Kristos said. "We'd kick the soccer ball around one of our backyards and Anthony would come over and join in for a few minutes until he got bored."

"Sports just weren't his thing," RJ added. "But when all of us got together," he explained to Sam, pointing to the entire group, "he tried his best."

"That's because spending time with us was important to him," Stella said. "We accepted him unconditionally. We loved him."

"And he knew that," RJ reassured them.

"No one knew how to make milk come out of his nose better than Anthony," Paul blurted.

After a moment of stunned silence, laughter erupted, echoing around the chapel.

"What? It's the truth. It was one of his unique talents," Paul chuckled.

"Anthony and I had a lot of common interests," Nicky said. "He loved to paint and I like to take photographs. We both captured the world around us with our own personal perspective."

"When our dad died," Evvie whispered, meeting her brother,

Nicky's, gaze, "all of you were so supportive." She turned her focus to Sam. "Nicky and I had just turned ten when Dad was killed in a plane crash. Anthony was so kind. I could see the compassion in his expression and through the tears that welled in his eyes on our behalf. There were so many people hovering over us—assuring us everything was going to be all right. But it was never going to be all right, never again, and I wanted everyone to stop lying to me." Evvie sniffled, trying to hold back the tears that welled up behind her eyes. "Without saying a word, he came over and put his arm around my shoulder, guiding me outside, away from the well-meaning adults."

Evvie dabbed the corners of her eyes with her fingertips. The memory of that sorrowful time still stung like a fresh wound. Kristos draped a consoling arm around Evvie's shoulder; very much like Anthony had on that awful day. "We just sat there on the porch steps, you know?" Evvie continued. "Anthony didn't say he was sorry for me, or tell me it would get better. He gave me what he knew I needed—silence and understanding. He was just a little kid himself, but he instinctively knew the right thing to do."

"My brother was selfless. If he were here right now he would ask us what we were each planning on doing with our lives. I'm certain he wouldn't want us to spend one second crying over him." RJ looked around the circle. "In his name and in his honor, we have to use this time on Earth to live life to our full potential. I've decided to go back to school to get my Master's degree in counseling psychology."

"Wow!" Evvie exclaimed. "Are you planning to help your mother at the suicide hotline she founded?"

"That's the goal. And hopefully, I can expand it beyond a hotline. I want to offer counseling and group therapy." RJ sighed deeply. "I'd like to prevent what happened to my brother from happening to others."

"I would say that's the best way to honor your brother's memory." Sam patted RJ on the back. "I, too, will finish school," Sam said. "I have a little over a year left to complete my PhD and I hope to acquire a position as a professor in Thessaloniki."

"So, you're planning to stay there?" Adam asked with a tinge of disappointment in his voice.

"It's my home, but now that we've found each other, distance won't separate us. We'll always be brothers." Sam's eyes lit up. "And there's a young woman …"

"And?" Stella asked, her eyes flying up to meet Sam's.

"And, maybe you'll all be returning to Greece for my wedding one day. If she'll have me, that is."

"Of course she'll have you!" Evvie said. "Any girl would be lucky to."

"Just tell us when and where," Kristos said. "We wouldn't miss it."

"I'll be there with my camera," Nicky added. "But do it before I go off to some remote corner of the world. I want to be a photojournalist, immortalizing moments—the good as well as the bad."

"Why would you want to capture the bad ones?" Stella asked.

"The good moments should be celebrated. We don't have enough of those. But there's a hard lesson to be learned by revealing the ugly side of humanity," Nicky explained.

"And a horrifying image sparks the fire for change," Stella completed.

"Exactly," he nodded.

"I'd like to do what Uncle Dean has done," Kristos said. "Building a business from the ground up—running it and making it grow. I want to work alongside him and brainstorm new ideas on how to put the Carriage House on the map as a prestigious event destination." He looked at his cousin. "It's not as important as saving the world, but it's what I'm interested in."

Stella brushed her bangs down over her eyes and sighed.

"What is it?" Evvie asked her. She knew her cousin well and had sensed her shift in mood.

Stella shrugged. "You're all so talented and self-assured. Each of you know what you want to do with your life and you all have a definitive passion. I don't." Stella pointed to them one by one. "Sam, you're a brilliant scholar, and RJ, you're heading to a career that will make a difference and probably save lives. Nicky has his photography and Evvie is a talented and passionate ballerina."

Evvie lifted her eyebrows. "Talented, maybe. Passionate, I'm not so sure about."

"What do you mean?" Stella asked. "You have your whole future mapped out before you. In a few days you'll be studying at the Paris Opera Ballet School."

"Yup, just like my mother did. But that's her dream, not mine." Evvie's tone held resentment. "Stella, I don't want to be a ballerina. I want to work on the vineyard. I want to make wine."

"But you're so talented."

"Nicky won MVP in last year's soccer tournament for the entire state but he doesn't want to play professionally. Why can't I simply make dance a hobby and not a life choice?"

"But the vineyard?" Stella made a disdainful face. "I would give anything to have an ounce of your talent. I'm not really good at anything. I have absolutely no talent whatsoever."

"You're very young, Stella. At sixteen, I didn't know what I wanted to do with my life," Sam said. "Don't put such pressure on yourself."

"You were the only child in your family," Stella said to Sam. She glanced at Adam apologetically. "Well, you thought you were, anyway. Unlike me, you didn't have swarms of brothers and cousins around you all the time who were smart and confident and gorgeous. It's a lot to live up to."

"I never knew you felt this way," Evvie said. "We never meant to make you feel of any less worth than us. I don't think you realize how amazing you truly are."

"And beautiful," RJ added. He tucked a lock of hair behind her ear and pressed a friendly kiss to her temple.

"There's a world of possibilities out there. Give yourself a chance to explore it and find out what you love," Sam said. "Sometimes the answers we're looking for are simple. Our insecurities complicate our lives more than they need to."

"It's getting late," Nicky interjected, looking at his watch. "The morning ferry will be here soon and tourists will be sure to stop in."

"Can we each say a little prayer for Anthony before we go?" Paul suggested.

RJ nodded. "That would be nice. I'd like to go first." He looked at Sam. "My family is Catholic. I'm not sure if you knew that."

Sam smiled. "No, I didn't."

RJ began to recite the rosary. "Hail Mary full of grace, the Lord is with thee. Blessed art thou among women and blessed is the fruit of thy womb Jesus. Holy Mary Mother of God, pray for us sinners now and at the hour of our death. Amen." A sob caught in RJ's throat. "Do you think he's with God?" He looked around the room hysterically. "We need to pray for him. What if he can't go to heaven … because he …"

Stella's response was immediate. In an instant she wrapped her arms around RJ, embracing and comforting him. She shook her head emphatically. "Don't even think that. Anthony was the kindest, sweetest soul. We're taught that God's mercy is infinite. But we really don't understand what that means, do we? To me, it means you must have faith that God loves every single one of us, even when we disappoint him. Even when we make a mistake. Even when we hurt so much we can't stand to stay in this world another day."

RJ clutched Stella like a lifeline, sobbing into the crook of her neck. "Thank you for that," he whispered as he calmed down.

"I'd like to recite part of the *Kaddish*," Sam said. "It's our prayer for the dead." Sam stood and motioned for Adam. "Join me?"

Adam rose and stood by his older half-brother. He let Sam take the lead, as he wasn't sure of all the words. Together they began to recite the prayer. "Glorified and sanctified be God's great name throughout the world which He has created according to His will. May He establish His kingdom in your lifetime and during your days, and within the life of the entire House of Israel, speedily and soon; and say, Amen."

Spotting a large pebble in the corner of the room, Sam bent down to retrieve it. He pressed the pebble into RJ's palm. "It's an ancient Jewish tradition for a mourner to place a stone on the grave of the deceased. When you get home place this one on Anthony's grave for me. Though I can't be at the gravesite physically, I'll be there spiritually."

"I will. I promise." RJ said.

Affixed to the wall of the chapel was a gold encrusted icon of Christ with his right hand blessing those who came to venerate him. Evvie took Stella's hand and motioned for her cousins and brother to follow. One by one they made the sign of the cross and kissed the icon. Standing before it, they recited, in triplicate, a common Greek Orthodox prayer called the *Trisagion.*

"Holy God, Holy Mighty, Holy Immortal, have mercy on us."

Evvie turned back toward Sam, Adam and RJ. "At my yiayiá's funeral and all her memorials we sang a hymn. We asked that her memory be eternal. We came here today to remember Anthony, and we ask God not only for his memory to be eternal, but that his life and death not be in vain. May his memory be eternal."

"May his memory be eternal," they chanted together.

Quietly, they exited the church. They had come to say their final goodbyes to a sweet soul, to pay homage to him, remember him and mourn for him. Now it was time to do what Anthony would have wanted them to do—carry on and find what he never could—true happiness.

Chapter 2

Evvie

August 2005

"Quality! Precision!" Madame Rousseau commanded, pacing about the practice room scrutinizing each student's technique one by one. "Mademoiselle Evanthia, this is not the United States. More is not better here."

Evvie stared at the stern woman blankly, her lips tightly pressed together. She'd been singled out more than the others for her mistakes and, as a consequence, the other dancers steered clear of her.

"For now, two perfected pirouettes with a higher leg in passé are sufficient and more impressive than three poorly executed ones. Have I made myself clear?"

"Yes, Madame." Evvie said, making an effort to sound contrite.

"Class is dismissed." Madame Rousseau tapped a finger on Evvie's shoulder. "Not you. I'd like a word."

As they waited for the other students to file out of the room, Evvie wondered why she'd let her mother talk her into this. The schedule was grueling. Every morning she woke at the crack of dawn, greeted by a full day of warm-ups and classes, with only a short break for lunch. There was time for little else, and by the end of the night when she finally arrived back at her tiny, rented flat, exhausted, she collapsed onto her bed and fell sound asleep.

"You need to adjust your attitude."

Evvie's eyes widened. "Excuse me? Have I been disrespectful somehow?"

"By adjust I mean soften. Blend. Stop trying to outdo." Madame Rousseau arched an immaculate eyebrow. "This isn't a competition or an audition. It's a workshop for you to master your craft." She pursed her ruby-painted lips. "Naturally, that can't be done in a couple of weeks. Normally, our students train year-round and have been with us from a very young age."

"What are you trying to say?"

"Evanthia, you're a talented girl. Quite talented, actually. That is why I bother to correct you so fiercely. But I don't see a hunger in you that tells me dance is your life—your one and only priority."

She lifted Evvie's chin with her fingers, forcing her dropped eyes to meet her steely glare, and Evvie sucked in a deep breath, holding it.

"Find that passion and lose the arrogance. You could have a career—not here in Paris, of course. New York perhaps, if you put your mind to it."

"New York is just as competitive." Evvie didn't want a career as a ballet dancer, but she would not allow this woman to insinuate the ballet companies of New York were less than extraordinary.

Madame Rousseau gave Evvie a patronizing smile. "You are dismissed, for now."

In the dressing room, Evvie quickly unraveled her pointe shoes and changed into street clothes. Margot, the only girl who bothered to speak to her, came up behind Evvie, tapping her on the shoulder.

"Free day tomorrow!" Margot exclaimed. "Some of us are going to Paris-Plages along the Seine. Come with us."

"I don't know, but thank you for asking."

"It will be fun. Later in the evening we will go to le cinéma au Parc de la Villette."

Evvie pulled the hairpins from her bun. "Should I know what that is?"

"It is an outdoor movie festival."

"That does sound nice. Maybe another time. It was nice of you to think of me, but I've already made plans."

Margot seemed surprised. "You have? What are you doing?"

"I'm taking the train to Champagne." Evvie's face lit up. Finally, something to look forward to, she thought.

Chapter 3

Evvie

August 2005

Evvie's entire body tingled with excitement as she pulled into the Épernay Railway Station. The moment she was out of Paris, viewing the rolling hills and lush green landscape, her body relaxed. The fact that she didn't have much of a plan for the day didn't disturb her. She'd Googled the town and had an idea of what she was looking for.

Flinging her black, lightweight backpack over her shoulder, Evvie exited the train and breathed in the fresh country air. With her barely passable French, she asked a train conductor where she might find a bicycle rental station.

"*Office de Tourisme*," he answered.

"*Merci. Où est ce?*" Evvie looked around, but she didn't see a tourist building. The conductor pointed to a bank of taxis and Evvie thanked him once again. She was anxious to see the town and visit the wine cellars. With an eagerness to explore the house of Moët et Chandon, she intended to pay homage to Dom Pérignon, the brilliant monk who created the very first champagne. But first she had another mission—to see the workings of a family owned, French vineyard where she might learn a thing or two about producing fine champagne.

Evvie hadn't even left the station and already was squealing with delight when she saw the tall, ornate, domed tower of Champagne de Castellane. It was an image she'd only seen in pictures and now, viewing the grandness of the structure herself, she assumed it was one of the bigger houses.

Sliding into the backseat of the taxi, Evvie directed the driver. Her eyes grew wide as they passed through narrow streets with centuries-old buildings. Three minutes later, she was in front of the center for tourism. Pulling out some euros, she paid the driver and anxiously scooted out of the cab.

From her backpack she removed a scrap of paper she had scribbled on the night before during her website research. "*Bonjour*, do you know how I can get to this address?" Evvie asked the impeccably dressed young woman seated behind the counter.

"*Oui, oui*! I know it well." The young woman took the scrap of paper from Evvie and wrote on the blank side. "*C'est facile*. Follow these directions out of town."

"*Merci*. I'd like to rent a bike to ride there."

"*C'est difficile*! You have no automobile?"

"No," Evvie said. "I would like to rent a bike and see the vineyards."

"A little thing like you will never make it! The hills will be impossible," the woman insisted.

"No one has ever done it?" Evvie challenged.

"*Oui*, of course, but I would not recommend it."

She thanked the woman for the warning but happily rode off on the generic, gray mountain bike that was the same as every other bicycle in the lot. She'd had romantic visions of a pale green one with a basket filled with flowers and a baguette but they weren't to be fulfilled.

As she began to ride, she found herself in the middle of a vintner's paradise—her very own Eden. A large, round sign resembling a champagne seal was nestled in a perfectly manicured garden boasting

Épernay's claim to fame as the capital of Champagne. Charming, anti-quated buildings lined the narrow streets before opening onto the majestic Avenue de Champagne where many of the greatest labels have dwelled for centuries.

Ignoring the temptation to wander in and out of each historic building, Evvie continued on, riding toward a rural area surrounded by hills and grapevines. She was but an ant in a giant maze of vines, or so it seemed. The topography of Long Island was, for the most part, flat, and each vintner's property was clearly defined. But here she had no idea where one vineyard ended and the next began.

The air was slightly cooler than it had been in Paris, but Evvie had been warned and she was prepared for it. But after cycling for almost an hour up and down steep, rolling hills, she became overheated. She stopped by the side of the road to remove her cardigan and stuffed it into her backpack. She was about to swing her leg back over the bike seat and continue along the path, but the faint scent of grapes and the lure of the clusters hanging from the vines stopped her in her tracks.

With irrepressible curiosity, Evvie floated by the vines at the road's edge, gently taking some low hanging fruit in the palm of her hand to inspect them closer. She didn't recognize this variety. It was similar in color to the Pinot Noir, but the grapes were smaller and upon rubbing a leaf between her fingertips, she discovered a powder-like substance coating the foliage. The taste was also slightly different, she decided, as she plucked a grape from the bunch and popped it into her mouth, savoring the juice.

"Do you normally steal the grapes off of others' vines?" A young man, standing approximately ten feet from her, barked sternly to Evvie.

She jumped, startled from her thoughts, and shrieked in surprise. "I'm sorry. I didn't see you."

With arms folded across his chest and feet planted firmly on the ground, he stared at her, his eyes narrowed. "That doesn't answer my question. My being here or not doesn't make it right for you take what's mine."

16

"You're so right." Evvie's heart was pounding. "I meant no harm," she said, stumbling on her words.

His reprimanding tone and imposing stance were meant to intimidate her, but the glint in his eyes and the smile he unsuccessfully repressed revealed he was not as angry as he tried to convince her. Slowly, he strode down the row of vines until he was beside her.

"*Pardon*, I was riding and I stopped for a minute to catch my breath and rest my legs and when I saw them, I couldn't help myself," she explained. "I only tasted one. I wanted to see what kind of grape it was."

"And you think you would know one grape from another?" His mouth curved into a mocking smile.

"Most of the time." She ran her fingers over a leaf, intrigued by the mysterious white substance it held. "Not this time. It almost looks like a Pinot Noir."

"Pinot Meunier," he corrected.

"Excuse me?"

"That's the variety. Pinot Meunier. It's one of the grapes used to make champagne. The white powder on the leaves is a natural characteristic of the variety."

"All of this is yours?" Evvie took a good look at the young man. At her estimation he couldn't be more than twenty-four or twenty-five. She noted the hints of gold in his chestnut brown hair as the wind ruffled it and his azure colored eyes reminded her of the bright sky on a cloudless day. She hadn't noticed how very handsome he was at first—her attention had been elsewhere—but now as the hardness left his expression, she dared to linger on his penetrating stare.

"It belongs to my family." He pointed across the road. "That side over there are our Chardonnay vines and we have the Pinot Noir closer to the chateau."

"Wow! I live on a vineyard also. It's much smaller than this one though."

"Do you?" He creased his brow. "Napa?"

"No," Evvie laughed. "Long Island."

He shrugged.

"New York," Evvie clarified.

"I know little of New York. The Big Apple, *oui*? And Brooklyn." He pointed a finger in her direction. "Oh! And the Hamptons."

Evvie laughed. He seemed so proud of himself to know of three places in New York. "Our vineyard is closer to the Hamptons, not the city."

"And now, *voilá*! Here you are, stealing my grapes."

"Back to that, huh?" she crossed her arms, mimicking his earlier position. "I came to explore the area and learn how to make champagne. I want to convince my uncle to let me develop a sparkling wine. We don't currently produce one."

"And where are you going to learn this?"

"I Googled family owned vineyards—ones that I thought might be comparable in size to ours." Evvie pulled out the scrap of paper with the directions and the chateau name. "I thought I would take a tour at this one and see if the owners would be kind enough to speak to me." She handed it to him.

His broad smile turned into a hearty laugh. "Let me introduce myself. My name is René de Contois."

"Your—this—" Evvie stammered. She waved her arm, gesturing wildly around her. "This is the vineyard for the Chateau de Contois?"

René nodded smugly.

"I pictured it smaller—a boutique vineyard."

"It is, but we sell a good portion of our grapes to the larger houses. And this stretch of land is only for our Pinot Meunier. As I said before, the Chardonnay and Pinot Noir vines are in different locations."

"Oh, my! Would you consider showing me your process?"

"I'll give it some thought; however, I need to know a few things first." He narrowed his eyes and stroked his clean-shaven chin as if to consider her request. "Your name?"

She blew out a sigh of relief. Reaching for his hand, she shook it enthusiastically. "Evvie. My name is Evvie. It's short for Evanthia. My great-grandmother's name," she rambled nervously. "Oh, sorry," she said, realizing she still had hold of his hand.

"Don't be," René said. He drew her hand to his lips and kissed it. "A lovely name for a beautiful girl. Italian?"

"No, it's Greek. Born in America, but my blood is Greek." *And reminded of it every day*, she wanted to say.

"How long do you plan to stay?"

"I only have today."

His eyes widened. "You can't learn how to make champagne in a single day!"

"I know, but it's all I have. I'm due back in Paris tonight."

He sighed. "We will have to see what we can do then. Follow me. We can put your bicycle in the back of my truck and I'll take you to the house. It will be quicker for you that way, *non*?"

"That's very nice of you."

Evvie bent down to retrieve the bike she'd let fall to the ground earlier at the precise time that René reached for it. Their shoulders gently collided and his hands wrapped around hers as they both gripped the handlebars. Evvie's heart skipped a beat as she turned to find him staring down at her. Their lips were only inches apart—or perhaps merely millimeters. Either way his proximity made her tingle inside, though it also made her uneasy—and happy and excited—and very confused. She had never felt this turmoil running havoc through her before, and certainly not for a stranger. It was the grapes, she decided. It had to be the grapes she was excited about.

"I've got that," René smiled, taking the bike from her.

Evvie followed him to the pickup truck and helped him lift it into the back.

He opened the passenger door for her, helped her in and moved around to the driver's side. As they passed rows and rows of grape-vines, Evvie asked René about the property, the soil and the weather conditions. She'd done her own research, but hearing it directly from the owner's mouth was far more informative and interesting than reading about it.

Open black iron gates welcomed them and they rode through onto a long, gravel driveway. On the left was a small parking area for visitors. On the right, round tables and a few larger rectangular ones were situated in a nicely manicured garden, overlooking the vineyards spread out below. Many of the seats were occupied with patrons enjoying smooth wine, quiet conversation and the beautiful view.

Evvie had barely noticed the chateau. Instead, the minute she opened the door to the truck, she hopped out and ran to the edge of the hillside. Seating herself atop a sturdy, wooden table, she stared out over the acres and acres of lush green vines before her and admiringly soaked in the expansive view.

"Did you not say you live on a vineyard?" René raised an eyebrow and smirked. "You act as though this is the first one you've seen," he teased.

"It is—I mean, I've never seen one like this." Evvie swung around to look at him. "Where I live the land is so flat. This is so much more impressive. It's like admiring a beautiful painting."

Evvie normally wasn't this animated. She usually reserved her large hand movements and expressive facial gestures for the stage. But here she'd dropped her guard and couldn't help but expose her enthusiasm. Her mouth formed an 'O' as she moaned out a sigh, finally noticing the grand structure she'd previously ignored. "We definitely have nothing like that where I live. I'll bet your home is older than my country!"

René laughed. "For certain that is true. The chateau was built in 1750. Would you like a tour?"

"Yes!" she said a little too quickly as she propelled herself from the table.

He guided Evvie by the small of her back, and when he settled his hand ever so slightly lower, she didn't notice. Her mind was on the thousands of questions she longed to ask as she looked about the property. Not sure as to where the entryway led, she only hoped for the chance to see the house in its entirety. Black iron gates, similar to the ones they drove past earlier, were open for visitors. On either side of the building, sweeping stone staircases covered in ivy led to a second floor balcony.

"In here we offer wine tastings and house a small retail shop. It, of course, was not always like this. At one time it was a ballroom."

"It's gorgeous." Evvie ran her hand along the tan marble counter-top of the bar. The wood below was old but well maintained and the inlay design of fleur-de-lis was a craftsman's work of art. On the opposite wall, a smaller bar area mimicked the larger one, next to it the largest and most decorative limestone fireplace she'd ever seen. A row of French doors etched with the family crest caught her eye and René noticed her interest.

"Come." He led her through the arch-shaped glass doorway. "This is a private tasting room."

"Do you rent it for private parties?" Evvie asked.

"Not exactly. We hold tastings amongst other vintners, or some-times we have special events for our repeat clients. On rare occasions a dignitary or two has been allowed to use this space to entertain their guests."

The room was narrow but very long, and a table that could easily seat thirty guests occupied most of the space within. As René squeezed past her, Evvie once again felt that nervous thrill, and she smiled up at him tremulously, in an attempt to regain her composure.

"Where do you keep the barrels?" she asked.

"We're getting to it, my impatient girl." He led her out a back door-way where another building was situated far enough from the chateau to keep the public from intruding. "Everything is done in here: the pressing, first fermentation and blending."

Evvie inspected each piece of equipment. "It's all very much the same as what we use."

With a smug expression, René gestured for Evvie to follow him. He led her through another doorway. Her brow creased and she looked to him for an explanation.

"I don't think you have one of these," René said. "It's a press," he continued, answering her unasked question.

The large, wooden vat took up a good portion of the small room. From what Evvie could tell, a pumping system fitted with pipes ran from the ceiling to the tightly sealed cover of the antiquated press. She couldn't help but think that if the cover and pipes were removed, the structure would resemble the large wooden tub used to stomp grapes in her favorite episode of *I Love Lucy*.

"Is it still functional?" Evvie asked. She ran her hand along the weathered wood.

"Most certainly! We still use the old ways for special blends. Particularly ones my grandfather developed."

René gestured for Evvie to follow him.

"The bottling, corking and labeling is done here." He led her to another room crowded with crates of unused bottles. "One of the differences between wine and champagne is in the method of creating and keeping the bubbles in the bottle. And the corking, of course."

"Yes," Evvie said eagerly. "This is what I need to learn."

"It's an art and a very complex one. It cannot be taught in a single day."

"Are you purposely trying to discourage me?"

He brushed a finger across her cheek. "No. Maybe I am encouraging you to stay."

His touch sent a shiver through her. "I can't. I—I have other obligations."

René winked. "We shall see." He took her by the hand. "Let me show you where the bottles are stored during the aging process." He opened an old, creaky door that led to a steep staircase disappearing into the cellar below.

When they reached the bottom, Evvie noticed the lights were very dim and the air much cooler. Earlier she had wrapped her cardigan around her waist after exiting the pickup, but now, chilled by the drop in temperature, she untied it and slipped it on. As she walked down the narrow corridor, Evvie sensed she was deep within a carved out tunnel. When they reached a room lined with rows upon rows of wooden barrels, Evvie's eyes lit up with appreciation.

"The walls are made of chalk, which provides the ideal condition for soaking up humidity. That, plus the absence of light and the constant cool temperature, is what the champagne needs in order to age and ferment properly."

Evvie laid her hand on the wall. "Chalk?" she asked, examining the residue left on her fingers.

René nodded. "It's in our soil too. It helps to control the irrigation."

"Our soil is comprised mostly of clay and sand," Evvie said.

He waved for her to follow. "In here we have the exact same conditions for the champagne that is already bottled and aging. Bottles are kept in these mechanized crates at a seventy-five-degree angle and each day they're rotated an eighth of a turn."

"So I would need this machine and a chalk cave to make a sparkling wine in the *méthode champenoise* back home?"

"Maybe. I had to convince my father to perform this process by machine operation. Before that, riddling or, as we say, *remuage*, was done by hand."

"Wow! That must have been time consuming."

"Yes, it was," René agreed. "The wine was not compromised by modernizing this part of the method." He took Evvie's hand and guided her to the other side of the room. "Let me show you the old way. We still use it for some of our cuvées. When we use the old press for a blend, we follow through by using the traditional method to turn the bottle in this *pupitre*."

The wooden rack was weathered from age and looked to hold over one hundred bottles. Evvie tried to imagine spending hours each day turning bottles in a room filled with these specifically designed racks.

"And why do the bottles need to be turned?" she asked.

"To bring the sediment to the neck of the bottle. As I said before, you cannot learn all there is to know in one day. And as for the caves ... well, I'm not sure how you can do it, but you'll have to simulate the conditions in some way if you want a superior product." René rubbed his hands up and down Evvie's arms. "You're cold. Let's go back upstairs and I'll show you our home."

After they'd climbed the narrow staircase and exited the building, René walked her to the front door of his home, located on the second story of the chateau above the tasting room. Once inside, Evvie stopped to appreciate the beauty of the rolling hills spread out before her, lined with perfectly symmetrical rows of grapevines that could be viewed from the floor to ceiling foyer window. Sighing, she admired the landscape.

Warm breath tickled her ear as René held Evvie by the waist and grazed her lobe with his lips. "You love it, *non*?" he asked.

Evvie turned to reply and found herself nose to nose with him. "I do," she admitted. Before she could say another word, he kissed her lightly, and a jolt of both pleasure and fear ran through her. Suddenly, she wondered if she was alone in this massive house with this man she'd only met a few hours before. Evvie hoped it wasn't so.

As if reading her mind, René broke the kiss, took her hand in his and brushed a kiss across her knuckles. "I believe my maman is in the kitchen. Would you like to meet her?"

Searching for her voice, she uttered, "That would be very nice."

An hour later, Evvie and Sabine had become fast friends. Snapping peas, they chatted away like schoolgirls as René returned to the kitchen after excusing himself earlier when his father had requested his assistance.

"It looks like I've left you in good hands," René smiled, looking at his mother fondly.

Evvie smiled up at him.

"I was trying to convince Evvie to stay with us like other students have from time to time. She'd be such an asset with her knowledge and experience," Sabine explained.

"I asked her that very thing earlier, but, regrettably, she said it was impossible."

Sabine waved her hand dismissively. "Ah, but nothing is impossible. Perhaps when you've completed your program at the ballet school?"

"Ballet school?" René looked bewildered.

"Yes. That's why I need to be back in Paris tonight. It's nothing, really."

"Nothing! Nonsense. Only the best attend the Paris Opera Ballet School," Sabine exclaimed.

"Why didn't you tell me?" René asked.

"It's only a two-week workshop. I don't attend the school." She sucked in a deep breath. "It's not very important to me. I don't want to dance in a professional company."

Sabine stood up and hugged Evvie. "You will do what makes you happy. We only have one life, *oui*? Live it the way you wish."

"*Merci*, Sabine. I really needed to hear that."

Chapter 4

Sophia

August 2005

"A refund?" Sophia repeated, her brow creasing. "Why would you think I might ask for a partial refund?" Sophia tightened her grip on the cordless phone. "She what? No, she didn't call me. I had no idea." After listening to the little information Madame Rousseau had regarding Evvie's whereabouts, Sophia briefly thanked her and hit the end button furiously.

Seething, Sophia stood in place, her lips tightly pressed together, shaking her head in disbelief. Angrily, she punched in Evvie's cell phone number, but after four rings it went to voicemail.

She tried the number again, hoping this time she'd pick up, but when she didn't, Sophia listened to Evvie's recorded message and waited for the beep. "Evvie," she said sternly. "I just received a call from Madame Rousseau, who has informed me that you've left the school. I expect a call from you immediately with an explanation. I need to know where you are and why you left with a week still left in your program."

She killed the call with a vengeance before guilt and concern washed over her. Exhaling loudly, Sophia redialed. "It's Mom again.

Most of all I need to know you're safe. Please call me," she pleaded.

"Cia," Sophia called to her six-year-old daughter, "come downstairs. We're going to the Carriage House to see Daddy."

Cia skipped down the staircase, meeting her mother at the front door. "Mommy, why do you have that mean look on your face? Are you mad at Daddy?"

"No, not at all. Not with your daddy, Cia."

They walked briskly from their home, past the wine production building and down the path that led to the Carriage House—the catering venue that her husband, Dean, operated on the vineyard property.

She found him in the foyer speaking with his sister, Demi, who ran an event planning business out of the venue offices. Sophia released Cia's hand and threw her own up in the air in exasperation. She opened her mouth to speak but a grunt of frustration was the only sound that escaped her lips.

Dean, oblivious to his wife's anger, lifted his daughter into the air when she ran to him and kissed her plump, little cheek.

"What?" Demi asked. "You look like you could take an axe to someone!"

"I just might do that. It's Evvie."

"What about her?" Demi asked.

"She's missing!"

"What do you mean missing?" Dean exclaimed.

"She's gone. Evvie left the ballet school. I don't know where she is."

"She left without telling you?" Demi asked. "That doesn't sound like Evvie."

Dean put Cia down and massaged the back of his neck. "Doesn't it, though?"

"What do you mean by that, Dino?" Sophia snapped.

"She didn't want to go in the first place. I can't say I'm surprised."

Sophia glared at him and Demi intervened. "The question is, where is she now?"

"Madame Rousseau said she's gone off to work at a vineyard in

27

Champagne. Why would she give up the opportunity of a lifetime to pick grapes? She can do that when she gets home."

Dean and Demi flashed a brief glance at one another. Before either could respond, Kristos and Stella, two of Demi's children, came barreling through the door, arguing with each other.

"What's going on? Why are you all standing in the foyer?" Stella asked. She stretched her arms out to Cia. "Hey, cutie. Come give me a hug."

"Apparently," Sophia said, placing her hands on her hips, "your cousin took it upon herself to leave the ballet school and take off to God knows where."

Kristos and Stella looked at each other with frozen expressions plastered on their faces.

"Kristos? Stella?"

"We know," Kristos admitted guiltily. "She texted us in the middle of the night. I guess it was already morning where she was."

"And you didn't think to tell us?" Demi reprimanded.

"Where is she?" Dean asked.

"She went to a family-owned vineyard on her day off and the people invited her to stay with them," Stella explained.

"So she went back to Paris, collected her things and told the school she was leaving," Kristos added.

Stella saw the infuriated expression on her aunt's face. "She said they're really nice people and to tell you she's very safe."

"That's not the point! "Sophia hissed through gritted teeth. "Evvie is not answering her phone—at least not my calls. Text her and tell her that I want to speak to her or I'll be on the next plane to France and I will track her down and drag her home."

Stella nodded repeatedly. "I'll tell her."

"You need to calm down," Dean told his wife. "It sounds like Evvie is safe. Let's talk about what to do next in my office."

"Before you go, Uncle Dean," Kristos said, "do you still need me tonight?"

"Yes. We have that corporate event scheduled. Short cocktail hour, dinner, soft background music. I'll need a dais set up with a podium for the speeches. The staff has their instructions, but I need you to oversee them and make sure it's done the way the client requested."

"I'll stay to ensure the correct linens are used and the centerpieces are set," Demi said.

"Aunt Sophia, I know you said you didn't need me until four o'clock, but, if you want, I can watch Cia now."

"That would be a big help, Stella." Wearily, Sophia smiled at her niece and thanked her. She needed some time alone to decide what to do next about her unpredictable daughter.

In his office, Dean held Sophia in his arms, momentarily wiping away her anger and fear. But as he pulled her far enough away to look into her wounded eyes, all the emotions came rushing back.

"What am I supposed to do now?" Sophia sighed. "Does she have any idea what ran through my mind when I received that call? How I felt not knowing where she was or if she was safe? What was she thinking?"

Dean guided her to the couch adjacent to his office desk. "What's done is done. At least she's not in any harm."

"As far as we know!" Sophia exclaimed.

"Look, she's nineteen. Evvie has a good head on her shoulders and at that age kids sometimes do things they don't tell their parents." Dean looked as though he was contemplating his next sentence. "If you remember, I kept a secret or two from my parents at that age."

"Do I remember? Seriously, Dino, that's not the best example to convince me she's doing the right thing. Do I need to remind you how that turned out?"

Sophia didn't like to think about the mistakes they'd made back then. He'd hurt her terribly by keeping their relationship a secret, as though it was a clandestine affair, and eventually it was their undoing, leading to many years of heartache. Even now, after rekindling their love and seven years of marriage, there was still a tiny piece of her heart that had not completely healed from the memory of the pain she'd endured from their breakup.

"I'm sorry." Dean brushed his fingers across her cheek. "But think about why I did what I did. I'm not saying I was right, but I was thinking like the teenager I was, and that's what Evvie's doing."

"It's a completely different situation, Dino."

"No, it isn't. Not really." Dean stood and ran his fingers through his hair in frustration. "I've tried to stay out of this one, but I don't know why you're insisting that Evvie does something she doesn't want to do?"

"Insist? What am I insisting?"

Dean sighed. "How many different ways does she have to tell you she doesn't want to dance anymore?"

"That's ridiculous. She has a gift that shouldn't go to waste."

"I'll agree. She's talented. But she's had her day. She's spent the better part of her youth in a tutu and pointe shoes," Dean said. "Now her interests have changed."

"Oh, for heaven's sake!" Sophia popped up from her seat in outrage. "She has all the time in the world to do anything she wants. A dancer's career is short-lived. It would be a waste for her to throw away what she's worked so hard on for all these years."

"But she doesn't want to," Dean said firmly. "Why can't you see that?"

"I don't want her to have regrets years from now. I'm her mother and I know what's best for her."

"Do you? You don't think she's capable of knowing what's best for herself?"

"Why are you taking her side?"

Dean grunted. "I'm not taking her side," he said, trying his best to remain calm. "I'm not taking sides at all, but you're behaving a bit like my father did back in the day."

"What is that supposed to mean?" Sophia snapped.

"It means that you're acting as stubborn as he was. Pushing, insisting until it drove me away. Is that what you want? To drive your daughter away?"

Sophia crossed her arms over her chest and turned away from Dean. An uncomfortable silence filled the room.

"Hey, talk to me," Dean said. He laid his hand on her shoulder but she jerked away. "Turn around and look at me," he demanded angrily.

Sophia whipped around, shooting him a death stare. "What do you want me to say to you? You're not seeing my side of this at all."

Dean scrubbed at his face with his hands. "Yes, I am," he sighed. "I'm thinking of you and of Evvie. You don't even know where to find her and she's bound to rebel even further if you're not careful. And when she does, it will kill you. You're going to lose her if you keep this up, and I'm telling you right now, I won't let you repeat this with Cia. If she wants to dance—great! But the moment she wants to stop, she's done—over!"

Sophia felt as though she might spill tears, but she wouldn't give in. Her Dino was usually so loving and understanding, but his temper was flaring, and it was aimed at her. And where in hell was her daughter? She still hadn't heard from her.

"Cia's career plans are a long way off," Sophia said. "Why are you giving me attitude over Cia when it's Evvie I need to worry about right now?"

"I'm trying to make a point. There's more to life than your dance universe, Sophia. If Cia wants to join a friggin' circus, or orbit space, or become the best damn sales clerk in New York, then I'll support her choice."

"I think you've made your point loud and clear. I'm a bad mother who forces her children to do things they're amazing at, but want no part of." Sophia turned to walk away, heading for the door, but Dean caught hold of her arm, stopping her. "Sophia *mou*, listen to yourself." He guided her back toward the couch and gently pulled her down next to him. "You are not an unreasonable woman. You're kind and fair. Extend that understanding to your daughter."

Sophia leaned back against the couch and closed her eyes. "It's hard to be objective when it's your own child."

"I know." Dean took her hand in his, lifting it to brush a kiss across her knuckles.

"I'm scared. I don't know where she is."

"We'll find her." He pressed a kiss on her neck just above her collarbone.

"I just want Evvie to be happy."

"Me too." Dean moved in for a deep, passionate kiss. Skimming her body with his fingers, his thumbs stopped to graze over the thin, cotton material covering her breasts.

"Don't do that! I'm mad at you."

"Are you?" Dean's lips curled upward into a slow, intoxicating, if not slightly smug smile. "Your body is telling me otherwise."

"Well, I should be mad at you." Sophia's breathy pants were unconvincing.

Dean slid the thin strap of her shirt off her shoulder and slipped his finger down the edge of her lace bra until he reached a pebbled nipple, proof of her arousal. A groan rumbled from deep within him as Sophia closed her eyes, shuddering at his touch. "Tell me why."

"Why what? I forgot the question," she mumbled. He'd unsnapped her bra and held both breasts in his hands.

"Why you should be mad at me."

"You were mean … and, maybe a little bit right."

A wide grin broke out across his face. Dean brushed his lips over hers and then continued trailing tiny kisses down her neck, collarbone, chest, until his lips found what they were looking for.

"Are you trying to seduce me into forgetting my troubles?" Sophia whispered.

"Is it working?"

"Lock the door and I'll let you know."

Chapter 5

Evvie

August 2005

At the end of her third day on the Contois vineyard in Épernay, Evvie, sweaty and coated with dirt from working in the hot field after a rain-soaked morning, peeled off her clothing and sank into an oversized, white tub embellished with gold-tone, claw foot legs.

She'd worked diligently, side by side with René, learning everything she could absorb related to the growing and harvesting of grapes specifically for the production of champagne. The sugar, acidity and pH levels were different for the sparkling wines than for the still and, although she had tested for those levels at home, there was so much more to learn.

If only Evvie could stay for the harvest, fermentation and bottling processes, she'd be able to experience firsthand how to properly create bubbles with the authentic method the French have been using for centuries. But she knew that wasn't possible. Still, she would have enough information to present to her Uncle Michael in the hope that he'd agree to produce a sparkling wine on his vineyard.

She closed her sleepy, brown eyes and let her dark hair fan around her as it floated in the bathwater. A content sigh escaped her lips—for the hot water relaxing her muscles, for the tender kisses she'd shared with René, and for being exactly where she wanted to be at this very moment.

Dreamily, with thoughts of him playing on her mind, Evvie finished her bath and dressed, slipping into a golden, poppy-colored sundress that complimented her bronze, tanned skin. She tied her hair up into a messy bun, letting a few tendrils loose, and applied a scant amount of mascara on her already thick lashes. With her pinky she added a touch of natural gloss and, with a final look in the mirror, was ready to head down to dinner.

But first she had to call her mother. The few texts she'd sent wouldn't suffice any longer. She spotted her cell phone on the nightstand, flipped it open, and sat down in the ivory barrel chair tucked in a corner of the bedroom.

"Evvie!" Sophia answered on the first ring.

"Hi, Mom."

"I'm so glad you called. Are you okay? I've been worried sick."

"I'm fine, Mom. Never better. I'm happy here."

Evvie heard a deep sigh of relief hiss through the receiver.

"Really, I am. I'm sorry. I didn't mean to disappoint you. I'll pay you back for the money you lost on the ballet school."

"Oh, Evvie. It's not about the money. It's about your future and what I know you can achieve. More than that, it's about the fact that you went behind my back and took off without my permission. Do you have any idea how frantic I was?"

"I didn't mean to worry you," Evvie said with sincerity. "And I didn't intentionally go behind your back. It just kind of … happened. I went for a day trip and, once I was here, I just knew it's where I need to be."

"You're really not going to pursue a career in a dance company, are you?" Resignation and disappointment lingered in her mother's words.

"No, Mom, I'm not. I loved my years of ballet training, and I wouldn't have traded it for anything. But it's not what I want to do with my life."

"And you prefer working in fields and harvesting grapes?"

"Mom," Evvie said reprovingly, "you know it's more than that. It's not just the land and the grapes. The thrill and challenge of creating an exceptional wine is rewarding to me."

After a moment of dead silence, Evvie spoke again. "Mom? Are you there?"

"I'm here, sweetheart."

"Say something," Evvie pleaded.

"There's nothing to say. If that's what makes you happy, and you're sure, then that's what you should pursue."

"Thanks, Mom. I was wondering if I could stay longer … at least until the harvest?"

"Absolutely not! You need to be on the plane in ten days. You've already changed your flight once without telling me. School begins a week after you get home."

"But I'm taking all core classes. No oenology or viticulture classes. I could learn so much more by staying here."

"You'll take those classes eventually, but not until you take the preliminary ones. I'm not having any arguments on this," Sophia finished firmly.

"But, Mom, I have good reasons for wanting to stay."

"Reasons other than the harvest?" Sophia asked.

Evvie heard a dash of suspicion in her mother's voice. "Yes, mainly the harvest, but you see, there's this boy—a man, really." She realized how that must have sounded. "A young man, that is," she corrected. Evvie heard her mother mutter under her breath.

"And this boy is worth delaying your future for?"

"I'm not delaying anything. He's the vineyard owner's son. I've learned so much from him, and he's been very kind to me."

"But it can't go anywhere, you know this. His life is in France and yours, clearly, is not. Don't get too attached. I don't want to see you get hurt."

"Mom," Evvie said with a hint of exasperation, "you know how

I am. I've never been like Stella who crushes over every cute guy she meets."

Sophia laughed. "Like mother, like daughter, on both counts! But sweetheart, when we *do* fall, we fall hard."

"I'm fine, Mom. I have to go. I'll call again in a few days. Love you."

"Love you too," Sophia told her daughter. "Take care of yourself, and please be careful."

Evvie thought about what her mother had said. At nineteen, Evvie had never had a boyfriend—not really—not unless you count a game of Spin the Bottle at a pool party she'd attended in ninth grade, or kissing her date at the junior prom—and he was only just a friend—one who had the delusional thought that taking her to the prom came with benefits.

René stirred up not only emotions but a physical response that she'd never experienced before. No one had ever consumed her every thought, or made her shiver from his touch, or had her hanging on his every word—not until she laid eyes upon René.

She floated down the winding staircase, thinking of him still. As if he knew she'd be coming, he was at the bottom step waiting for her. Her deep brown, hopeful eyes met his bright blue ones. René held his hand out to her as she approached, then took her in his arms and kissed her breathless.

"My parents are waiting for us in the dining room."

"I hope I didn't hold them up. I called my mother and, I must admit, I stayed in the bath longer than normal."

"Evanthia, bare under a thousand fragrant bubbles." René slid his hands up and down her back until he settled below the small of her back, holding the round of her bottom in his hand. "That must have been quite a sight. Maybe next time I will join you?"

Evvie didn't know what to say. His comment and the hand on her backside made her uncomfortable. It was too soon for this. She'd only known him for a few days. Common sense was shouting, 'No!' but her body was giving off an entirely different signal. It was as though she had an angel on one shoulder and the devil on another, and a battle was raging between them. The question was, which one was going to win? The answer terrified her.

Evvie smiled timidly and took his hand in hers, removing it from her *derriére* and evading his question. "I'm starved! I wonder what your maman made for dinner."

"Sabine this is delicious. You must have been cooking all day," Evvie exclaimed, eyes wide in wonder at the meal laid out before her. Platters of food holding mushroom tartlets, crispy golden potatoes and chicken in a wine sauce made her mouth water with anticipation. "I would be happy to come back early to help you cook tomorrow."

"*Non, ma chére.* You came for the champagne. Learn all you can while you are here."

"I'll need you both in the field tomorrow," Antoine, René's father, said. "We need to go vine by vine to make sure the grapes are not crowding each other."

"Will we be using ties to pull back the vines and separate them?" Evvie asked.

"You've done this before?" Antoine asked.

"Many times."

"Good. That will save time then."

After they'd consumed every last morsel of food, Sabine brought out a platter of Biscuit rose de Reims, a regional favorite, twice-baked, pale pink cookie that resembled the ladyfinger. Antoine popped the cork on a bottle of champagne—one from their very own label, naturally. The biscuits, she was told, when dipped into the champagne, enhanced the aroma. Evvie had not heard of these delicate biscuits before, but she followed the lead of her hosts and was taken by the pleasant bouquet wafting upward as she sipped the vintage cuvée.

"It's a beautiful evening," René commented, setting down his champagne flute. He extended his hand to Evvie. "Would you join me for a walk?"

Evvie looked to Sabine. "I should really help clear the table first."

"*Non.*" Sabine shooed them off. "Go, it's a beautiful night."

Hand in hand, they stepped out into the night. Tranquil and serene, the surroundings were motionless but for the twinkling stars in the sky shining brightly against its blackened canvas. René seemed to read Evvie's mind and remained silent, allowing her to enjoy this rare moment of serenity.

Guiding her, they walked away from the house, far enough that the only illumination was the moon, which seemed to follow their stroll. René stopped at the entranceway of an old barn. Slowly, he backed Evvie against an outside wall, bracketing his hands on either side of her as he looked into her eyes.

"You are so fascinating. As beautiful covered in dirt as you are now smelling of lavender." He ran his thumb across her lips and she closed her eyes at the erotic sensation he evoked from his breath teasing her neck and his fingers kissing her. Evvie's body tingled and thrummed. Blood was pumping through her veins at a rate so fast every pulse point throbbed.

He was taking his time, watching her intently, reveling in his effect on her and enjoying her sweet torture. Evvie ached to be touched in places she had never considered allowing anyone close to before, and somewhere deep inside she knew that caution should take hold. But her slight intoxication from the champagne and the slow seduction from this striking man might have been stronger than any shred of willpower she had left.

René stepped into her, erasing what little space there was between them and kissed her—hard and deep, coaxing her tongue to tangle with his. Evvie brought her hands up to run her fingers through the soft, sandy blond curls of his hair and sighed into his mouth. Breaking the kiss, René took her bottom lip between his teeth and nipped it before trailing kisses from her neck to just below her cleavage.

Both arousal and alarm flashed at once as he dropped one of the straps of her sundress and slipped his hand inside to fondle her breast. *Danger! Danger!* Common sense and self-preservation flashed through her mind like the blaring lights from a fire alarm when she felt the hard length of René pressing between her thighs. But the way he rubbed his thumbs over her nipples sent electric currents through her and it felt so, so good—too hard to resist. Until he released one breast and slid his hand down to the edge of her lacey panty.

"No!" Evvie exclaimed as she suddenly came to her senses. "I'm sorry. No. I can't do this."

"You don't want me?" René asked, continuing to run his finger along the edge of her delicate undergarment.

"It's not that. I just don't think it's a good idea." Evvie flattened her hands on his chest, creating some distance between them. "I'm only here for a short time."

"I know. Let's make the most of it." He wrapped his arm around her waist but she unwound herself from him.

"I mean that I can't get involved in that way when it's only temporary."

"Evanthia, everything in life is temporary."

"Huh! Don't I know it!" she muttered under her breath.

"You want me as much as I want you." He played with a loose tendril hanging from the nape of her neck. "I can see how your eyes glaze over when I touch you. And when I do this ..." He kissed her neck, just under her earlobe. "... your breathing quickens. Don't let American convention get in your way."

"What does that mean?"

"You all seem to think sex comes with a promise and commitment."

"That's not true," Evvie defended. "Certainly not everyone I know expects that."

"I can make you one promise—that you will enjoy our time together if you'll only allow yourself to."

"It's late and we have an early start tomorrow. I think it's time to head back to the house," Evvie said firmly.

~Biscuit roses de Reims~

4 large eggs, whites and yolks separated
2 teaspoons pure vanilla extract
1 cup sugar
¼ teaspoon cream of tartar
1½ cup flour, sifted
⅓ cup cornstarch
1 teaspoon baking powder
Red food coloring, approximately 6 - 10 drops
Confectioner's (powdered) sugar

Preheat oven to 300° F

In a bowl, mix together the flour, cornstarch and baking powder. Set aside.

Mix the egg yolks, sugar and vanilla in a large bowl using an electric blender for 5 minutes, increasing the speed every few minutes. Beat in half of the egg whites and then continue to beat for an additional 2 minutes. Beat in the remaining egg whites and the food coloring and beat for 4 more minutes until the mixture begins to form stiff peaks. Start with 5 drops of food coloring and add drop by drop until you reach the desired medium pink coloring.

Fold the flour mixture slowly into the egg mixture until fully blended. Pour batter into greased financier pans or fill a pastry bag and pipe 3 inch strips onto a parchment-covered baking pan. Dust the tops with powdered sugar.

Bake for 12 - 14 minutes. Sprinkle with additional powdered sugar and bake for another 12 - 14 minutes.

Remove from the oven and, while they are still warm, cut the edges to make the biscuits uniform in size and shape, if desired.

Biscuit roses de Reims are a nice accompaniment with tea or coffee; however, traditionally, they are served with champagne. Placing the biscuit in the glass is said to bring out the aroma of the bubbly wine.

Yields 3 to 4 dozen depending on the size.

"Just like the butterfly, I too will awaken in my own time."
—Deborah Chaskin

Chapter 6

Evvie

August 2005

D awn had broken, replacing the black, star-speckled sky with ribbons of pink and lavender as the sun slowly appeared on the horizon. But today, the calm and stillness of daybreak held no comfort for Evvie. Sleep had eluded her and, for the first time since she had arrived here, her enthusiasm was at a low.

She dragged herself from bed and began to dress appropriately for a morning of fieldwork, all the while mulling over the same thoughts that had kept her awake all night. Evvie shivered when she remembered a sweet, almost forgotten voice in her head—a memory—and it made her want to weep. *'Don't let anyone talk you into anything you don't want to do. Be strong.'* That was the advice her grandmother had left her with. "Yiayiá," Evvie whispered, hugging herself. A hint of her Yiayiá's scent lingered and Evvie felt an unexplainable energy—a presence—a familiar comfort, and it filled her heart simultaneously with both joy and emptiness.

Evvie wasn't going to be here for much longer and she had a life back in the States. If she gave her heart away—gave her body away—it would just be another painful loss for her when it came time to leave.

Yet, she had never contemplated this step with any other boy before. Maybe it was time to let her guard down and allow herself some genuine affection. But to feel that, to experience that moment and then have to rip herself away? Was it worth it?

Evvie had decided to seek out Antoine rather than René that morning. His advances and comments had made her uncomfortable and she was still at odds regarding what she wanted to do about him. It wasn't in her nature to have a free and casual attitude like the one he possessed. Antoine had a task for her and, after all, her reason for being here was to work and learn all she could. For now, that was her priority.

"René is already in the field. If you'd like to work side by side, I'll point you in his direction," Antoine said.

Evvie tied a garden apron around her waist. "I think I should start at the opposite end. That might prove to be more efficient." She took a handful of vine ties and stuffed them in the apron's pockets.

Antoine's eyes glimmered with amusement. "Yes, I believe more will get accomplished that way."

Evvie worked tirelessly all morning, untangling vines and tying them back for support. It was tedious but she loved every moment, and as she lost herself in her work she almost forgot what had her in turmoil the night before.

"There you are!" René exclaimed. "Have you been hiding from me?" He strode over to her, picnic basket and blanket in hand. "You must be hungry."

Evvie was startled by the sound of his voice. She had hoped to avoid him for the better part of the day, but knew that was unlikely. She'd spent a sleepless night sorting through her emotions and, as much as she tried to resist him, she simply couldn't.

"I am actually," she replied casually as if nothing intimate had transpired between them the night before. She took a step toward him and opened the basket flap. "What did you bring?"

René pulled the basket away from her reach. "*Non, non,*" he teased. "First a kiss." Dropping the basket to the ground, he drew her in by the waist, pressing his lips to hers, deepening the intensity and devouring her.

An involuntary sigh escaped her lips as Evvie's heart raced. Collapsing into René's embrace, her knees weakened and her body tingled in places it had never been touched.

Breaking the kiss, René reached for the blanket he'd discarded on the ground. "Come. I don't want to be accused of starving you." He laid out the blanket, inviting Evvie to sit. He poured two glasses of champagne while she filled their plates with fresh tomato wedges, thin slices of cured ham, wedges of brie and crusty slices of baguette.

"Your champagnes are delicious. Each one I try is better than the last."

"We've had generations to perfect the art." René took the glass from Evvie, set it down and pulled her across his lap. She braced her hands on his shoulders and stared into the expanse of eyes as blue as the sky on a bright day, trying to understand what it was she saw reflected in them.

Dizzy from the wine and intoxicated by his earthy scent, and the feeling of his hands sliding up and down her thighs and the kisses he was planting between her breastbone, Evvie hadn't realized he now had her lying down beneath him, the weight of his body pressing into hers.

She was floating, enjoying every moment, her body responding to every touch, every sensation. Arching her back, she met his arousal and Evvie didn't stop René when he slid his hand under her t-shirt to find her breasts. Raising her shirt to expose her bra, he dipped his head down to take a nipple in his mouth, flicking the nub with his tongue.

Evvie groaned, continuing to levitate from the erotic sensation. But when René unzipped her shorts and tried to pull them down her legs, she froze.

"No, no, René. Please."

"*Ma chérie*, let yourself go. If you like what I'm doing now, think how it will feel for me to make love to you."

She pushed René off of her and sat up, pulling her shirt down. "I'm sorry. I am, really. I'm not as free as you are. I'm not ready for this."

Letting out a frustrated sigh, René scrubbed his hands over his face. "Have it your way," he said, annoyance coating his words. "If you insist on staying a girl rather than becoming a woman, you'll miss living life to its fullest." He got up, collected the blanket and picnic basket and walked away from her without so much as a backward glance.

Evvie went back to work, embarrassed, confused and disappointed at René's attitude.

When Evvie arrived back at the chateau, she found Sabine. She told her that she was tired and would not be joining them for dinner. Shortly after she finished her bath, there was a knock on the door and Evvie found Sabine on the other side with a tray of soup and bread.

"*Soupe à L'ail.* I always make this for René when he's not feeling well."

"You're too kind. *Merci*, Sabine."

"Rest, and if you're not up for working tomorrow, sleep late."

"I'll be fine. Goodnight."

Evvie set the tray down on the desk and reached into her bag for her phone. Taking a sip of the brothy garlic soup, she closed her eyes, savoring the mixture of flavors—garlic, chicken broth and cheese.

Right now, what Evvie needed most was a friend—someone she could talk to and confide in. Not her younger cousin, Stella. Who knows what she would say. Certainly not her brother, Nicky. He would either cringe at the details or want to kill René. Kristos. She would text her cousin, Kristos. They had always been close.

Evvie texted out a brief rundown to him.

Kristos: *If he cares about you, he won't pressure you.*

Evvie: *He's been great otherwise.*

Kristos: *Not sure about that.*

Evvie: *Am I being a baby?*

Kristos: *No! You have the answers. Follow your instincts. Don't do what you're unsure of.*

Evvie: *<3 U.*

Kristos: *Come home soon or I'll come kick his ass.*

Evvie: *LOL goodnight.*

Follow my instincts. Evvie blew out a deep breath and shook her head. It wasn't her instincts that were confusing her. It was her body and her heart.

~ Soupe à L'ail ~

2 heads garlic
2 quarts chicken broth
1 tablespoon Herbs de Provence, wrapped and tied in cheesecloth
1 teaspoon salt
2 medium potatoes, peeled and diced
2 tablespoons cornstarch
¼ cup of water
4 tablespoons extra virgin olive oil
3 egg yolks
2 tablespoons butter

Topping
Thin slices of baguette, toasted
Swiss or Gruyère cheese, shredded

Bring the chicken broth to a boil. Break up the garlic into individual cloves, leaving the skin on. Add the cloves to the boiling broth and lower the heat to a simmer. Add the diced potatoes. After five minutes, remove the cloves, which should be floating on the surface, from the pot. Let the broth continue to simmer.

Remove the garlic from the peels and mash before adding them back into the broth. With a handheld immersion blender whisk until the solids are pureed.

Mix the cornstarch and water in a small bowl and add to the soup, blending thoroughly.

In a separate bowl, whisk the olive oil and egg yolks together. Slowly ladle approximately a ½ cup of the soup into the egg mixture to temper it. Add the egg mixture to the soup and stir. Melt in the butter to finish, adding a silky texture to the dish.

Garnish with cheese topped toasts.

Chapter 7

Evvie

August 2005

The next morning, Evvie lingered in bed until she was certain the family had finished breakfast and begun their day. Tip-toeing into the kitchen, she took a croissant from under a glass dome sitting on the marble countertop and exited out the side door.

The ground was dewy from the previous night's rain and Evvie found herself zigzagging around puddles as she made her way to the barn where she was certain to find Antoine.

"Ah, there you are," Antoine smiled as Evvie entered. "Are you feeling better this morning?"

"Yes, thank you. More rested. Do you have time to answer some questions?"

"For you? Of course! What is it you need to know?"

"Since I won't be here for the bottling, I'd like to understand a little more about how to create bubbles and control the amount of pressure."

"Hmmm. That's taken generations of experience and centuries to perfect," Antoine pondered. "But essentially, when yeast molecules break sugar molecules down into alcohol and carbon dioxide gas, most of the gas escapes into the atmosphere. I suppose you know this already?"

Evvie nodded.

"At that point, we transfer the wine into tightly sealed bottles where the carbon dioxide creates pressure, which forces the gas into the liquid. The amount of pressure as well as the proper storage method and conditions is vital."

Evvie huffed out a frustrated breath. "There's a lot to know. René has gone through it with me over the last few days. Learning the process isn't the problem. But knowing just the right time for each step will be the key to success or complete doom."

"But, *ma chére* isn't that true of all wine?"

"Yes. It's just that I want to convince my uncle to take on this project and it seems like he'll have to invest money in equipment without any assurance we'll produce anything drinkable."

"I'll tell you what we will do. I need you to check the pH level in the soil for me. After you're done, I'll give you an in-depth lesson on how we make our champagne." Antoine winked at her. "I'll even throw in some old family secrets on blending."

Without hesitation, Evvie threw her arms around Antoine. "Thank you, thank you, thank you!" she said with great appreciation.

For two hours Evvie went from field to field, checking the soil for each of the different grape varieties the Contois family grew. Perfectly lined rows of vines were full with large, hearty leaves. Clusters of grapes hung, drooping from the branches, revealing the time for harvest was fast approaching.

Evvie reached the end of a section she'd finished testing. Turning the corner to head down the next row, she came to a sudden halt, and without thinking, she clung to a vine for support. It was as though the wind had been knocked out of her—as though she'd been punched in the stomach and all the blood had drained from her head.

Her mind screamed at her. *Walk away—run!* But Evvie couldn't move. It was as if her feet were made of lead and her eyes were unwillingly fixed upon what was before her. She was a voyeur, watching a private, intimate moment between two lovers. Watching what she couldn't bring herself to do with the man who was now doing it with someone else.

And it was a good thing she hadn't—hadn't given herself to him. She wasn't special after all. On the very same crimson blanket, picnic basket strewn to the side, René had a young woman pinned beneath him, in very much the same way she had been the day before. Only it was evident, unlike with Evvie, from the way René's bare behind moved over the woman, he was making love to her.

She needed to turn and walk away, so why were her feet planted to the ground as if she was stuck in quicksand? Was it curiosity for what could have been? Did she even want that with him? Or was she still disbelieving what she was seeing? What did Kristos say to her? If he cares he won't pressure you and he'll wait until you're ready.

I'm such a fool. And with that thought, the spell was broken. Quietly she slinked away until she was far enough away from the lovers' earshot. Once she was, she ran back toward the chateau as tears rolled down her cheeks.

"You're back. Ready for your lesson?" Antoine asked.

"No, Antoine," Evvie said, shaken. "I'm afraid I won't have time for that. Unfortunately, I must leave right away."

"Leave?"

"Yes. I need to return to the States immediately. My family needs me."

"*Ma chére*, you look so pale. Is it serious?"

"It's a personal matter. I'm sorry to leave you this way after all you've done for me, but I have no choice."

"Of course."

"Would you mind taking me to the station?"

Antoine looked at her with deep concern. "I would be happy to."

I'm going to miss you," Sabine told Evvie, hugging her tightly. "Here." She handed her a small basket of food. "This should hold you until you arrive back in Paris."

"Thank you for welcoming me into your home. I really loved my time here with you." Evvie kissed her on both cheeks. "I'll never forget you, Sabine."

"I should hope not! This won't be the last time we will meet. You must come back for a visit one day."

Evvie forced a slow smile. "Maybe one day."

"I don't know where René is," Sabine said, hands on hips. "He'll be quite upset when he discovers you've left."

Evvie felt the knots in her stomach tighten. She said nothing. After all, what could she say? She hugged Sabine one last time before looking around the chateau, committing the home to her memory. So many talks had been shared here between herself and Sabine. "Antoine is waiting by the car," Evvie said. "I don't want to take too much of his day from him. Thank you again."

Tears welled in her eyes as she walked out the door. In spite of it all, she would miss this place. She had learned so much, loved this land and the people who live here.

"Let me take that from you." Antoine took Evvie's suitcase and hauled it into the backseat.

"Hey!" René called out, sprinting in the direction of the car. "Evvie! Where are you going?"

"I'm going home."

"And you were leaving without saying good-bye? Why would you do that to me?"

This boy had her all churned up inside. Why was he doing this to her? She was feeling things for him she didn't want to feel—things she knew she shouldn't feel. Her throat was dry, her chest tight. She tried to take a deep breath but found she couldn't find the air.

"I'll give the two of you a minute," Antoine said as he walked away.

"Why are you leaving now?" René asked.

Her sad, chocolate eyes examined his mysterious, sky blue ones. Mysterious because she had no idea what he was thinking or what he wanted from her.

"I saw you," Evvie breathed, her voice nearly inaudible.

He shrugged. "What?"

"I – saw – you," she repeated, staring daggers at him.

"You're not making sense. Saw me where?"

"In the vineyard. With the girl."

"Oh, that. I didn't know you were there. It was nothing."

"It was nothing! It looked like something to me."

René laced his fingers through hers, but Evvie pulled them free. "That should have been you and me. I wanted it to be."

"So your solution was to find someone else? I told you, sex is not casual with me."

"This could have been a beautiful time for us, if you only wanted it to be. If you only let yourself enjoy it." He took her face in his hands and she flinched at the contact. "This is not my fault." He kissed her cheek, his lips lingering a moment longer than necessary before backing away. Turning, he said, "You're a lovely girl, Evanthia. I will miss you."

Evvie crawled into the car before her tears could spill and waited for Antoine to return and drive her far, far away.

Chapter 8

Sophia

August 2005

Evvie flung herself into her mother's embrace when Sophia opened the front door to their home. She wrapped her daughter tightly in her arms, rocking her back and forth. "Shhh," Sophia whispered. "It's going to be okay." Sophia looked over her daughter's shoulder to Kristos, who had picked Evvie up from the airport and was now dragging her heavy suitcase into the foyer. Kristos nodded a frown in answer to Sophia's worried expression.

"I'll carry this upstairs for you and then I'll let the two of you talk," Kristos said.

Sophia nodded her thanks to her nephew. Pulling her daughter from her embrace, she examined her puffy, red eyes and wiped Evvie's tears with her fingers. "Come, let's go up and get you into a warm shower. I'll make you something to eat and together we can sort all of this out."

Evvie's lip quivered and she shook her head.

Sophia gave her a sympathetic smile. "Problems seem to be less drastic with a little food and the comforts of home. You'll see." She took Evvie by the hand and led her up the staircase.

A half hour later, when Evvie emerged from her bathroom, Sophia had a tray waiting for her—baked chicken and potatoes with lemon and oregano—comfort food her own mother, Anastacia, would cook for her whenever she needed an extra dose of love.

"You know you can tell me anything, sweetheart. Believe me, you can't say anything that I haven't heard or done myself at one time. It wasn't *that* long ago when I was your age."

"I don't know, Mom. It's hard to live up to your standard of perfection." Evvie's tone was sad, but not snippy as she often could be.

Sophia choked out a quick laugh. "Perfection! Is that what you think? Hardly." Sophia stroked her daughter's hair. "Besides, you don't need to live up to anyone's standards except the ones you set for yourself." She cut a piece of meat off the chicken breast and handed it to Evvie on a fork, urging her to take a bite. "Tell me what happened with this boy."

Evvie started from the beginning, recounting how she met René, how lovely his family was to her and how much she had learned while she was there. Her face brightened as she spoke of working on the vineyard, but as she continued, her eyes glazed over with tears.

"Evvie, you did the right thing. Never, ever do what doesn't feel right to you. Don't fall prey to anyone's pressure. If he had true feelings for you, he would respect your boundaries and wait for when and if you were ready."

"There were true feelings there. I know there was, and we had so much in common. No one has ever made me feel the way he did."

"I have no doubt that *your* feelings were real."

"His were too. I'm sure they were. The problem is with me. My attitude toward sex is not the same as the European girls he's accustomed to."

Sophia raised an eyebrow. "Was he feeding you that line of crap?"

"He might have said something like that."

Sophia blew out an exasperated sigh. "Evvie *mou,* people are people—individual and with their own set of morals. Cling to yours. Look how it turned out. At first chance he was off with someone else. What if you hadn't caught him? What then? What if he'd convinced you to do something you weren't ready to do? And then a day after, or even that very day, he had gone and done it with someone else. If you think you're crushed now, think of how much worse you would have felt."

"You're so right. But … it hurts so much. Mom, I think I loved him."

Sophia took her daughter into her arms. "Oh, sweetie. I know how much that can hurt, but you only knew him for a couple of weeks. Something much better is waiting for you."

"No—I'm done. I'm tired of losing people. It's too painful."

Sophia's heart ached for her daughter. Grief consumed her when Ana had left this world too soon. The bond Ana had formed with Evvie was unbreakable, and no one could fill the ever-present void in her daughter's heart. Losing her father was another blow Evvie had not recovered from, and now a different type of ache stomped on her child's heart. How much was a mother expected to share? Sophia could tell Evvie she understood the stab of pain running through her entire being—having experienced it more than she'd ever know. But she couldn't. Confessing the breakup with Dean and the heartbreak she'd never recovered from, even during her years of marriage to Will, Evvie and Nicky's father, would shatter her world a little more. So there was nothing she could do but try to place a sensible slant on the situation.

"Let's look at this another way. Maybe René wanted to get caught. He knew your time with him was limited and it would have hurt both of you to become more involved. Even if that wasn't his intent, it was for the best."

"That could be it," Evvie sniffled. "Mom, do you think I'm child-ish? In the end he made me feel as if I was nothing but an immature girl he should have never bothered with."

"That was nothing more than a mind game." Sophia took Evvie's hands in hers. "Listen to me. You're home now, where you belong. You can't control your emotions. But do what you have to do to get him out of your system and then go back to being my strong girl." Sophia flashed her a wide smile. "You'll be back at school very soon. You have so much to look forward to."

"Thanks, Mom," Evvie said, squeezing her in a tight embrace. Releasing her, she lifted the food tray. "I've had enough. I'm so tired. I think I'll go to sleep."

Sophia kissed her forehead and left the room, shutting off the light and closing the door gently behind her. Deep in thought, Sophia crept down the stairs, remembering how, so long ago, her broken heart had been consoled by her own mother's wisdom. It all comes full circle. A mother's revenge she supposed—the child now becoming a mother herself—and only now truly fathoming the desperation and overwhelming need to rid her daughter of the venomous sting of emotional pain.

"How is she?" Demi asked, standing at the bottom of the stairs, scaring Sophia out of her reverie.

"Oh, my gosh! Demi, you startled me," Sophia exclaimed. "Where did you come from?"

"Where did I come from? I've been right here. The question is, where did you drift off to?"

"The past," Sophia sighed. "When I was just about the same age as Evvie, with my own crumbling heart."

"I don't think you can compare the two situations."

"No, Dem, but to her it's just as brutal. What can I tell her except that I understand? I have to let her play out her grief. For me there was never anyone I loved the way I love Dino, but I can't tell her that. It'll destroy her. But for her, someone much better will come along. The right person. This was her first … love? Crush? Boyfriend? I'm not sure how to define him."

"She'll be fine. Look at my Stella. Only sixteen and in and out of love all the time. Or should I say that she's been in and out of crushes since she's never dated any of them." Demi lifted her shoulders, shrugging. "She bounces back quickly though."

"Like mother, like daughter," Sophia laughed.

Chapter 9

Stella

September 2005

"Stella Angelidis," Mr. Ross called out from the front of the classroom.

It was the second day of school and Mr. Ross, Stella's biology teacher, insisted on assigning seating by alphabetical order.

Raising her hand, Stella squeaked out, "Here."

Her good friend, Danielle, shot an incredulous glare in her direction and mouthed, "WTF?"

Stella nervously motioned with her eyes but didn't move a muscle. She was self-conscious. The boy sitting directly behind her with a view of her head was none other than Joey Ardis.

"Joseph Ardis," Mr. Ross called.

"Here! Same place I was yesterday," he said, standing at attention and taking a bow.

Giggles erupted from the girls in the class.

"That's quite enough, Mr. Ardis. I expect respect in my classroom. Is that clear?"

Yes, Stella thought, this is the boy that made her nervous. Why, oh why did his name have to begin with an A? She wondered if he scrutinized her every move. Was her hair in place? Did he even like brown hair? God, she wanted him to like her.

Joey didn't walk, he strutted, in the way a guy did when he knew he was good looking. With dirty blond hair that was spiked and pushed forward, each strand was strategically placed to appear disheveled. His polo shirt was two layers deep, the popped collars revealing contrasting colors, and his one-hundred-and-fifty-dollar pair of jeans was purposely torn to shreds at the knees.

Stella wouldn't have been surprised to see his picture displayed on the Abercrombie shopping bags bulging with her latest purchases or, at the very least, modeling at the store's entrance, shirtless, spraying their signature cologne to passersby.

Mr. Ross gestured to the black slab lab tables located in the back of the classroom. "In groups of three, as I call your names, please head to the tables. These will be your lab partners for the entire year," he said before calling out the students' names. "Stella, Danielle and Joey, head to table number four."

Blood rushed to Stella's head, leaving her warm and lightheaded. This was what she both wished for and dreaded—working side by side with Joey Ardis. He would have to notice her now. But what if he hated what he saw? What if she made a complete idiot of herself in front of him?

"Hey," Joey said, addressing both girls.

"Hey, Joey," Danielle said flirtatiously.

Stella's eyes widened like a deer caught in headlights, but she didn't utter a word. Danielle elbowed her, smirking mischievously. "Hi, I'm Stella," she spluttered.

"I know." Joey smiled smugly.

"You do?" Stella said, sounding utterly surprised.

"Um, it doesn't take much to figure it out. I already know Danielle, so ..."

Flushing with embarrassment, Stella willed the lesson to end so she could make her escape.

Gathering her books, Stella bolted from the classroom as soon as the bell rang.

"What is wrong with you today?" Danielle asked, catching up with her.

"Oh, God! I'm such an idiot. He must think I'm a complete moron."

"Who?"

"Who? Joey, that's who! *'You know who I am, Joey?'*" Stella mimicked herself. "I must have sounded like some pathetic fan girl."

Danielle's mouth dropped open. "Stella! Do you like him?"

"Please don't tell anyone."

"Of course not. It'll be our little secret. But girl, you're aiming a bit high."

"Well, thanks for that," Stella said sarcastically. "Tell me something I don't already know."

"You've been in a quiet mood tonight," Demi said to her daughter. "Help me get dinner on the table and tell me what's bothering you."

Stella wasn't sure how to explain what was going on inside her. Everyone in her family, including her mother, seemed to exude an air of confidence. She'd be happy with a fraction of their self-assurance.

"How'd you do it, Mom? I've heard Aunt Sophia say that you'd gone out with a ton of boys. You even asked some of them out yourself. How did you get all those boys to like you? Where did you get the nerve to do the asking?"

Before Demi could answer her, Michael entered the room. "Don't let your mother's false confidence fool you. She couldn't talk to or look at the one boy that counted."

Stella waited to hear who that boy was.

Michael threw his head back and laughed. "Me! Is that so hard to believe?"

"Is that true, Mom?"

Demi handed her the dinner plates and Stella set the table as she listened to her parents' story.

"It's easy to flirt comfortably around a boy you have no true feelings for, but even just being close to the important one is an entirely different story. Suddenly all that ease disappears."

"So there's a boy at school I have to worry about?" Michael asked. "He better watch his step or I might have to kick his ass."

"Oh, Dad, you know you don't mean that. But you have nothing to worry about. I doubt he'd be interested in me."

"The prettiest girl around?" Michael pinched her cheeks and pressed a kiss to her forehead. "Even more of a reason to kick his ass."

After dinner, Stella went up to her room to finish her homework but found herself daydreaming instead—ridiculous, fantastical scenarios that would never in a million years happen to her—someone else possibly, but never Stella herself.

Stella was always told she was pretty, but that didn't matter if she didn't believe it herself. The tall, slim teenager with round, brown eyes the color of rich caramel and a mane of thick, dark hair framing her face, barely grazing her shoulders, was not the reflection that registered in her mind as she stared into her full-length mirror. A shy, flat-chested, twelve-year-old with braces and a uni-brow was forever branded into her psyche.

Bending to retrieve her bag, she withdrew her pink RAZR phone and flipped it open, but the number she dialed rung out. Texting a message, she waited. Nothing. Sitting down at her desk to get some work done, she stared at her books, turned on her laptop and opened the IM box.

Stella: *Hey*

Evvie: *Hey!*

Stella: *What's up?*

Evvie: *Nothing. Homework. You?*

Stella: *Me, too.*

Evvie: *What's on your mind?*

Stella: *Wish you were here.*

Evvie: *Code for boy trouble. Whoever he is, he's probably not worth the worry. But I've sworn off boys, so don't go by me. Not worth it.*

Stella: *But he's cute.*

Evvie: *There needs to be more to him than just being cute. Just remember that he should be the lucky one and if he doesn't see that then someone else will.*

Stella: *Not so sure about that … thx ttyl <3*

Over the next few days in science class Stella tried as hard as she could to not act like a complete dork around Joey. The clear goggles pressing against her face, distorting her features, didn't help, but both Joey and Danielle were also wearing them so she guessed in that, at least, they were on an even playing field.

She envied the relaxed approach Danielle had with Joey and with all the other boys they knew, and Stella was a bit intimidated by their easy banter. He must have thought she had no sense of humor at all. No personality. No appeal. Nothing.

When they were finished at the lab table, Stella removed her goggles and went to her desk to gather her books and bag.

"Hey! Wait up," Joey called out to her. "I want to ask you something."

Danielle's eyes met Stella's and a grin crossed her friend's face. "I'll see you at lunch, Stella."

Joey walked alongside as Stella clutched her books tightly against her chest in anticipation. "I was wondering if your dad had any job openings at the vineyard?"

"Oh, of course." Stella tried to conceal the disappointment in her voice. "I'm not sure. I can ask him. What are you looking to do?"

"Whatever he has. Do you work there?"

She nodded.

"What do you do?"

"I float around. I help out wherever I'm needed. Sometimes I give wine tours or help out with a special event."

"I'm up for whatever he needs," Joey said. My dad says that I have to get a job until basketball season begins."

"Did you work over the summer?"

"Yeah, I was a lifeguard at the town beach. Come to think of it, I've never seen you there. Most of the kids at school hang out there. Don't you like the beach?" he asked.

"I usually spend part of my summer in Greece and the rest of the time I help out on the vineyard."

"Awesome! I bet the beaches are sick there."

"Yup, they are. You know, I can ask my uncle if he has anything at the Carriage House too. They always seem to need waiters and busboys. Too bad you don't have your license yet. The valet parking attendants come home with a ton of tip money."

"Good to know. So you'll ask for me?"

"Sure."

"Thanks! You're the best."

"So … did he ask you out?" Danielle asked, sneaking up behind Stella on the lunch line.

Rolling her eyes at the ridiculous thought, Stella gave her friend a resounding, "No."

"What did he want then?"

"He wanted to see if I could get him a job at the vineyard."

"You're kidding?"

"Nope." They slid their trays down the line, making their usual lunch selections of French fries and pizza.

"Maybe he wants to work close to you," Danielle said wiggling her eyebrows.

A humorless laugh rolled from Stella's throat. She paid the cashier and found an empty table. "His father told him he had to find a job."

"Well, you can make the most of this opportunity."

"No, that's something you'd be good at. Not me. Drop it, okay?"

But Joey never left Stella's mind that afternoon. She wondered what it would be like to have him on her property on a regular basis. She promised herself she would speak to her father and her Uncle Dean as soon as she got home.

Chapter 10

Stella

November 2005

Stella ran out of Sophia's front door when she saw the Jeep Wrangler pull into the driveway. "I'm so happy you guys are home!" she called to Evvie and Nicky.

"It's good to be home," Nicky said, hugging Stella. "I missed you."

"Not as much as I missed you." She teasingly punched him in the arm. Turning, she bent down to hug her cousin, Evvie. "I'm so happy you're here."

"You have to fill me in on all the news," Evvie said.

"Not that much to tell," Stella shrugged.

"Will 'the boy' be here tonight?"

"He's working, yes. No progress in that department though."

"I'll just have to check him out and see what his deal is. I texted some friends and we have a decent group coming this evening," Evvie said. Whose idea was this karaoke night anyway?"

My mom's," Stella giggled. "She said it would be a fun way to attract the college kids now that they were home."

"Evvie! Nicky!" Cia screamed, running up to meet them.

"Hey, pumpkin!" Nicky grinned, scooping her up.

"I'm not a pumpkin. That was last year," Cia drew out the words. "I was a pwetty butterfly this year."

"I'm sorry I missed that," he said. "I bet you were the cutest butterfly ever."

"Do I rate a kiss hello?" Evvie asked.

Cia pressed a finger to her cheek. "Let's see," she laughed. "Only if you let me sleep in your bed tonight."

"You've become quite the negotiator," Evvie laughed.

"I'm not a go-she-ate. I'm a big girl."

They all suppressed a laugh, guiding Cia back into the house. It would be a wonderful Thanksgiving weekend.

Dean and Michael made horrified faces behind the Angelidis tasting room bar as they listened to the pair of tipsy college girls shriek out 'My Heart Will Go On.'

"Make it stop!" Demi begged, squeezing in behind them.

"Babe, it was your idea."

"And a good one. This place is packed," she boasted. I just sent Joey and Paul to bring up a couple more cases of the Cabernet."

The entire family pitched in that evening. Sophia was stationed by the front door greeting patrons as they entered and seating them at their appropriate tables, Stella and Nicky were bussing tables, and Kristos and Evvie were controlling the karaoke machine and announcing the lineup of singers.

Golden string lights hung from the rafters, mimicking the stars in the sky. In each corner of the space sat a seasonal arrangement; cornstalks, gourds and pumpkins; a haystack and a scarecrow; a miniature wheelbarrow filled with brightly colored potted mums; and a grapevine with ripe fruit weighing down the branches.

Every seat was occupied, and the bar was crammed with chatty, enthusiastic wine drinkers of various ages. Michael had stocked up on a variety of craft sodas for the underage crowd his kids brought in, many of whom he recognized.

When the night finally began to wind down, only a few of the kids' friends were left. Paul and Nicky grabbed the mics and, goofing around, laughed through a few songs.

"You kids have nothing on us," Michael told them, snatching the mic from his son. "Get up here, Dean, so we can show up these clowns."

"Let me guess," Stella shouted out, taking a seat and putting her aching feet up to rest on another chair, "'Bohemian Rhapsody.'" Evvie came to sit down beside her.

"Good idea! I was thinking of a different song, but since you mentioned it …"

Stella groaned.

"Do you have a problem with Queen?" Dean asked.

"Nope. Not at all. Just with you and my dad imitating them."

Danielle, who had come with a group of friends, joined them at the small, round table to watch Stella's dad and uncle as they took to the stage.

"They're so awesome. I can't picture my dad doing that," Danielle said.

"Where's everyone else?" Stella asked.

"They left. I wanted to stay longer, so Joey said he'd give me a ride home."

Stella looked down into her lap, her voice barely audible. "Oh, that was nice of him."

Evvie's eyes darted back and forth between Stella and Danielle, assessing the dynamic between the two.

"Hey, are you ready?" Joey asked as he approached the table.

"Sure," Danielle said, flashing him a bright smile.

"It was so crazy in here tonight. I barely saw, Stella," Joey said.

"I know, it was!" she agreed. "Have you met my cousin, Evvie?"

"Not really, but I saw you calling up the entertainment tonight. Nice to meet you." Joey extended his hand to her.

"Well, goodnight," Danielle said as she rose from her seat. "Are you coming out with all of us tomorrow night?"

"No, we have that family tradition thing we do," Stella reminded her.

"Seriously? You still do that? Can't you get out of it?"

"Maybe, but I don't want to. It's a tradition."

"Whatever," Danielle said, marking her disapproval with a blended expression of boredom and exasperation. "I guess I'll see you in school on Monday then."

After Joey and Danielle left, Evvie turned to Stella. "Sweetie, watch out for that one. I don't trust her."

"Danielle? She's one of my best friends."

"Just keep your eyes open. You have a tendency to be too trusting."

"Ev, maybe it's you who needs to be a little more open." Stella looked up when the music stopped and her Uncle Dean began to speak into the microphone.

"This one's for my girl." Dean crooked his finger, motioning for Sophia to approach. Gently taking her in his arms, they swayed softly to the music while Dean sang the words to Barry White's 'You're The First, The Last, My Everything.'

"Aw, they're the cutest. That's what I want someday," Stella said. "To be that much in love."

"Don't get your hopes up, Stella. You're more likely to find a unicorn first," Evvie said bitterly.

Demi came up behind them. "That's because your generation has lost the art of dating. You hang out in groups or, God help us, hook up, but dating seems non-existent with you kids."

"No one hooked up in your day, Aunt Demi?" Evvie asked, challenging her. "Aunt Mindy told me otherwise."

"Aunt Mindy needs to learn to be quiet."

"Get up here, Dem!" Michael insisted. "It's time for a group effort."

"It's late, Michael. Time to wrap things up."

"Play it, Kristos." Michael dragged his wife to him; the playful gleam in his eye causing her to laugh.

With their children as a captive audience, Michael and Demi, Sophia and Dean sang out and bopped to 'You're the One That I Want.'

"You see, my parents have the magic too. It's not that rare."

"I just don't think many people find that. The divorce rate statistics prove it. But, I hope, someday, you do, Stella." Evvie put her arm around her cousin. "Me, I'm never putting myself through that. Way too much drama and too much to lose. Look at my pappou. He hasn't been the same without my yiayiá."

"So you won't let yourself fall in love?"

"Not in that way. Not like them." Evvie pointed to the stage. "It's too ... consuming."

Stella frowned. "I don't think that's something anyone can control, Evvie. It just happens. And I can't wait until it happens to me."

Evvie picked at her fingernails. "Well, I plan to hold onto my heart. There isn't a man alive who will ever own a piece of it."

Michael and Demi threw a large extended family party the day after Thanksgiving. Usually a day to unwind with leftovers and watch holiday movies, this year Demi decided she wanted to be surrounded by the entire gang. And so, the 'Honey Hill Girls' were reunited for the first time since their vacation in Aegina over the summer.

Newly engaged couple, Mindy and Matt, brought Mindy's parents, Harold and Edna Bloom, along, and Donna brought RJ and her own parents. Amy, Ezra and Adam drove down from their Westchester home and everyone was happy to see they were able to make it.

It was an unseasonably warm day for late November. The sun forced its way through the fiery ombré-colored leaves that clung to the old oak trees on the perimeter of the lawn. The slight chill in the air though was a reminder that colder days were just around the corner.

The teens, engaged in friendly bickering, chose sides for their annual football game, while the adults hovered over the outdoor fireplace, sipping cocktails and chatting away.

"Stella," Cia tugged at her sweatshirt, "I want to be on your team."

"Of course! I wouldn't want you on the other side. We'd lose for sure."

"So this is our secret weapon!" RJ picked her up and hefted her onto his shoulders.

"Not a secret pen, silly," Cia laughed, gripping the top of his head. "A lucky charm."

"Yeah, RJ," Stella razzed him, "don't you know the difference?" Stella possessed none of the self-consciousness or lack of confidence around RJ and Adam that she felt around other boys. It was all ease and familiarity. If she could only relax like that at school, especially around Joey, maybe then he'd think she was worth paying attention to, she thought.

After a while, Stella and Evvie left the game to help their mothers lay the food onto the table.

"Stella," Demi said, "Go back outside and see if your dad has the *souvlaki* ready for you to bring in."

Soula, Demi's mother, turned to Sophia and handed her a large, tin-foil-covered Pyrex tray. "Ana, put this on the table for me."

Sophia glanced at Demi, concerned. This was the third time that weekend she had called Sophia by her mother's name.

"Mom, this is Sophia," Demi said, gently taking her mother's hands.

A look of puzzlement came over Soula's face before it was replaced with annoyance. "I know who she is. What's wrong with you, Demi?"

"Demi is just being her silly self," Sophia said. She took the tray from her mother-in-law. "I'll take this now."

"Mom? Is Yiayiá okay?" Stella asked.

"I hope so." Demi sighed. "Go get the *souvlaki*. Let's not worry until we have to."

Stella went out to the grill to see what meats were ready to bring in. There she found her father and Uncle Dean rotating skewers. In a low whisper so her pappou and Alex wouldn't hear, she told them what had occurred in the kitchen.

"You said it was the third time?" Dean asked Stella. "Sophia never mentioned anything to me."

"I think she and Mom are downplaying it until they know for sure whether there's something to worry about. Sometimes Mom calls me the wrong name," Stella grinned, hoping to ease the anxiety she saw building in her uncle. "She'll look at me and call me Paul or Kristos, and then she shakes her head and corrects herself."

Dean handed her a platter. "You take this one and I'll take the other."

"Maybe I shouldn't have said anything," Stella conceded.

"No, I'm glad you did." There was a look of concern on Dean's face that had not been there minutes ago and Stella regretted telling him.

As they walked into the kitchen, Dean waved over Sophia and Demi. "What's this I hear about Mom?"

"I don't want to make too much of it," Demi said. "She called Sophia, Ana. Not for the first time, either. Once could be an honest mistake, but three times?" Demi's eyes widened and she opened her hands, palms up. "I don't know. I hate to make more of it than it is."

"I'm sorry, Mom. I shouldn't have said anything," Stella said, still holding the platter of grilled meats she had brought in from outside.

"You're concerned. It's fine," Sophia told her, taking the platter from her hands. "Go out with your cousins and don't give it another thought today."

"We'll just have to pay closer attention and see whether it gets worse. If it does, we'll have to talk to Dad," Dean suggested.

Stella frowned and began to walk away. "Hey! Come here." Dean put his arm around his niece. "It's all good. We might be overreacting. Go have fun, okay?"

Stella hugged him quickly and went to hang out with the rest of the teens. She had a great time with them as she always did, but concern for her yiayiá kept creeping into the forefront of her mind.

~Souvlaki~

4 pounds of lamb (I cube the meat from a leg of lamb, but other cuts are fine as well), pork tenderloin, chicken, or beef (for beef use chuck beef cubes or filet mignon).
Peppers & onions, cut equal in size to the meat cuts (optional)

Marinade
1 cup extra virgin olive oil
4 cloves garlic, crushed
2 tablespoons dried oregano, or 3 tablespoons fresh oregano
1 tablespoon dried basil or ¼ cup shredded fresh basil
1 teaspoon dried dill or 2 tablespoons fresh dill
Zest and juice of 3 lemons
¼ cup Dijon mustard
½ teaspoon black pepper
½ teaspoon paprika

* Please note—all herb measurements are estimated and up to personal taste. If you like the flavor of one over another, add more or less, or delete altogether.

Cut meat in 1½-inch cubes and marinate overnight. I often marinate the lamb or beef for two days, but the chicken and pork should not be marinated for more than one day. I choose to cut the cubes into smaller sized chunks. Since I am alternating vegetables and meat on the same skewer I don't want the veggies to burn and for the meat to not be cooked through. If you wish to cut larger cubes of meat, I suggest making separate veggie skewers. I generally only use onions and peppers, but mushrooms and cherry tomatoes are a nice addition as well. Do not marinate the veggies until the last 20 minutes. Grill and enjoy!

* For extra moistness and flavor, make a little extra marinade and reserve. When the souvlaki comes off the grill, baste with the reserve. Serve with tzatziki sauce.

~Tzatziki sauce~

2 cups Greek yogurt*
4 tablespoons white wine vinegar
3 tablespoons olive oil
3 large cloves garlic, crushed
2 tablespoons fresh dill or 1 tablespoon dried dill
½ teaspoon paprika
1 teaspoon sugar
Salt and pepper to taste
2-3 large cucumbers

*Greek yogurt is thicker than other yogurts. If you use any other yogurt, you must strain it from the liquid before making the sauce.

** **Prep** - Peel and core the cucumbers from the seeds and finely grate. Press through a mesh strainer to expel the liquid. The cucumber will make the sauce loose and runny if you skip this step.

Mix all the ingredients together with a whisk. Chill before serving. Serve with souvlaki. Tzatziki also makes a refreshing dip. Prepare a day ahead to allow for the flavors to intensify.

Chapter 11

Stella

Late fall 2005

The Monday after Thanksgiving weekend, Stella walked into her biology class ready to tackle the dissection of the crayfish lying on the lab table. The worm they'd cut up the week before didn't bother her so she didn't think this would be too horrible, even though watching a lobster dropped into a vat of boiling water for a diner's culinary delight made her cringe.

Maybe she could take notes and observations, she thought, while Danielle and Joey did the mutilating. Stella shivered, scrunching her face in disgust as she thought that, at some point this year, they would be assigned a frog to dissect. *Not me. I'll be absent that day.*

The bell rang and students scurried into the room before they could be counted tardy to class. With his arm around her shoulder and hers around his waist, Joey and Danielle were the last to enter.

"Hey—" Stella looked up to greet them but was stunned into silence. The excitement in her voice dropped off. She stood as stiff as the crayfish on the slab before her, knees as weak and rubbery as the day-old Jell-O served in the school cafeteria, her heart plummeting as quickly as a faulty elevator.

Clueless to her distress, Joey asked her how the rest of her weekend had gone. Danielle, an exaggerated grin plastered across her face, said little.

Joey clapped his hands together. "Who wants to do what?"

"I'll write the notes down," Stella replied meekly.

"I'm not touching that thing." Danielle said in a cutesy, baby voice.

"Okay, I'll be the surgeon." Joey rolled up his sleeves and slipped on the clear goggles. "What do you think? As hot-looking as my Wayfarers?"

Danielle giggled, brushing up against him and, at that moment, Stella thought she might lose her breakfast. How she managed to make it through the forty-minute period she had no idea. But somehow the time passed, and when the bell rang Stella was the first one to gather her things and bolt out the door as if her life depended on it.

"Where have you been?" Danielle asked Stella, but she offered no reply.

Stella had purposely hidden in the far corner of the crowded lunchroom, putting as much distance as possible between herself and the table where she and Danielle normally sat.

"Why are you sitting all the way over here?" Danielle took a seat in the unoccupied chair. "What's wrong?" she pushed when Stella didn't offer an answer.

What could Stella say? *You stole the boy I like? Best friends don't go after the same boys?* But Danielle didn't really steal Joey. He was never hers. Still, she was hurt by the betrayal.

Stella shook her head. "It's nothing. Why didn't you tell me about you and Joey?" Stella asked in a quiet voice.

"Because I haven't seen you all weekend," Danielle said, shrugging. "You were all tied up with your family. What's the big deal?"

Looking down at her plate, Stella drenched a fry in a pool of ketchup, swirling it around and around morosely. "No big deal."

"Wait a minute! Are you upset about Joey and me? You're not still hung up on him … are you? I mean, that was months ago. I've been through half a dozen guys since you even mentioned him."

Stella wanted to say, 'Well, I'm not you. I don't go through dozens of guys.' Instead she just shrugged. "No, I just wish you had told me. That's all."

"Well, I'll tell you now," Danielle said, leaning in closer to Stella. "After we left the vineyard on Wednesday night, Joey was going to take me straight home, but instead we ended up at the town beach parking lot talking and then he went for it. We made out and before I knew it we were in the back seat of his car and—"

"Stop! I've heard enough. I get it," Stella abruptly got up from her seat, gathered her books and dumped the contents of her lunch tray in the garbage.

"I don't think you do," Danielle stated. She cast Stella a pitying glare. "Maybe, if you weren't such a prude, you'd have a boyfriend too."

Stella walked out, not responding to her friend's cutting words. It was bad enough that she knew Joey would never give her a second look. He could have any girl he wanted. Why would he want boring, plain-looking Stella? But what really hurt was that she had thought Danielle was her friend. Now she realized she'd never been a true friend at all. Friends encouraged and complimented. They didn't make you feel small and walk all over you. Right then Stella decided she would be Danielle's doormat no longer.

"Paul," Stella knocked on her brother's door. "Are you going to Tommy's party tonight? If you are, can you give me a ride?"

"I can give you a ride, but I'm not sure I'm staying."

"Why not? Everyone will be there! You really need to get out more," Stella said.

"I get out just fine. Loud, out of control parties are not my idea of fun."

It was the middle of December and the kids at school were eager for the holiday break. Many would be away either visiting out-of-town relatives or escaping the dropping temperatures to warmer climates for the week. A good party was long overdue and who best to have one but the classmate with the most lenient parents—parents who would most likely not be home at all.

By the time Paul and Stella pulled up in front of Tommy's home, dozens of cars were parked along the street, teens drifted from the front lawn to the back, and every light in the house was lit.

"Be careful," Paul warned. "Don't drink anything you didn't pour yourself, and call me when you want to come home."

"You sound like Mom," Stella complained, rolling her eyes. "Are you sure you don't want to come in for a little while? I bet a lot of your friends are here."

"I should, just to keep an eye on you."

"I don't need a babysitter." Stella unbuckled her seatbelt, opened the door and slid out of her seat. Turning, she frowned at her brother. "Sometimes I wonder if you're eighteen or forty-two."

"Never mind the wise cracks. Call me."

Stella nodded, shut the car door, ran up the walkway and entered the house.

There had to be over fifty teens in the house alone, not including the ones huddled by an open fire pit in the backyard. Stella made her way through the maze of bodies looking out for anyone she knew. Some she recognized as upperclassmen, others she had been barely acquainted with, but eventually she found a group of her friends, one of which lunged forward to hug her and spilled beer on Stella's jeans.

"I'm sorry. I'm so excited you came," the girl said, shouting over the blasting music.

"It's okay, Dawn. It was only a few drops."

"Let's get you something to drink," Dawn said.

"Oh, I'm fine."

"Here you go." Tommy came up behind Stella. "A cold one from the cooler for you." He kissed her on the cheek. "Glad you could make it."

"Thanks." Stella took the proffered beer and popped the pull-tab open.

They danced and talked. Stella went for a second beer before suggesting they go outside by the fire pit for a while to see if anyone else they knew was out there. It was too cold and some guy offered Stella weed, which she refused, so they went back inside.

"I'm surprised Danielle isn't here," Stella said. Surprised but relieved, she wanted to add. She'd had enough of watching Danielle hang all over Joey in science class. Stella didn't need or want to see them now.

Dawn lifted her brows. "Oh, she's here," she said, stretching out her words. Pointing toward the staircase that led to the bedrooms, Dawn's critical expression told Stella all she needed to know.

"Ugh! Can't they do that somewhere else?" Stella's face revealed her disgust but she also feared it did a poor job at covering her hurt. "I'm getting another beer."

She pushed her way through the crowd and into the kitchen. Bending down to open the lid to the cooler resting against the wall, she clunked heads with a guy reaching in at the same time. "Ouch! Sorry."

"My bad. Hey, Stella," the guy said, checking her out. "You're looking pretty hot tonight. Where have you been hiding?"

"I've been around, Jake," Stella giggled.

Jake handed her a beer. "Here." Snaking his arm around her waist, he pulled her close to him. "What do you say we go out by the fire?'

"Sure."

"I'll grab a blanket, come on," he said taking her by the hand.

Outside, seated on a bench, a comfortable distance from the rest of the crowd, Jake wrapped the blanket around the two of them and they finished their beers. He crushed his can and threw it to the ground and then, taking hers, he did the same. Jake looked at Stella through darkened eyes. He licked his lips and cradled the back of her head with his hand. He wasn't gentle, she thought. His forcefulness could have been interpreted as passion, but it didn't feel like that to her. He kissed her, pressing his lips to hers and forcing her mouth open to invade her mouth with his tongue. Stella willed herself to relax. Isn't this what she wanted? Attention from a good-looking guy? For someone to want her?

Jake skimmed his fingers along her neck and continued inching his way down to the edges of her cropped sweater. Stroking the exposed flesh of her belly, he glided his hand upward until he reached her breasts, cupping one in his hand.

"No!" Stella exclaimed, pushing his hand away.

"Okay," Jake smirked. "Want another beer? It will loosen you up."

Stella placed a hand on his chest. "I don't need to be loosened up."

Lifting her onto his lap until she was straddling him, he ran tiny kisses along her neck, before traveling down to her modest cleavage and leaving his lips a little too long between the hollow of her breasts.

"Stop it, Jake. I'm not going to do anything more than kiss you."

He threw his head back in frustration and raked a hand through his hair.

A muscular arm dragged Stella off Jake's lap, startling her. She snapped her head around. "Joey?"

Joey glared at Jake. "Dude! The girl said no." He turned to Stella. "You're coming with me." Taking her hand in his, Joey walked briskly to the gate, outpacing Stella as she tripped along behind him.

"What the hell, Joey?"

"I'm taking you home."

"What?" she said angrily, wrenching her hand from his. "Who made you the boss of me?"

"You've had too much to drink and you don't belong near a guy like that."

"Oh, yeah? And who do I belong with?"

He opened the door to his car and gently pushed her in. "Not him."

"Why don't you worry about your own girlfriend and leave me alone."

Joey got into the driver's seat and hugged the steering wheel. "Someone else is taking care of her." He turned his head in Stella's direction and she could see by his rapid breathing and the angry look on his face that something was terribly wrong.

Joey banged his head against the steering wheel. "I've been replaced. Apparently, I can't compete with a senior."

"So, that wasn't you she was with upstairs?"

A humorless laugh rumbled from his chest. He shook his head.

"I'm sorry."

Joey shook it off. "Don't be. It wouldn't have lasted anyway. She's not a keeper. It would have ended soon enough."

Stella frowned. "I don't understand. If you knew it would end, why did you bother?" Stella asked.

"Because I'm not looking for a keeper. If I was, I would have asked you out."

Stella tried to control the gasp of surprise that was begging to escape. She hoped he didn't see the shock in her eyes or the flush heating her skin.

"Hey, I hope that didn't come out the wrong way. It's just that a guy can tell, you know?"

"No, I don't."

He turned to face her, resting his back against the car door and looking directly at her. "Danielle is Danielle. She's got a reputation. She's a flirt and she'll act on it. But with her, after a while, the relationship, if you want to call it that, has an expiration date."

"Does she know that?"

"She's your friend. How many guys has she gone through?" Joey cocked his head. "Who's she with right now? Not me."

"I suppose you're right. Not a good girlfriend for you. And certainly not a good friend at all." She muttered the last part under her breath.

"Now you—you're a good one, which is why I pulled you away from Jake. You're too good for that."

"So, he's not looking for a keeper either?" Stella asked.

Joey chuckled. "No, definitely not. He just wants to get laid."

"And that's all you want too?" She tried not to sound naive.

"Shit, Stella. Why are we talking about this?"

"You started it!"

He scrubbed his palms over his face. "I guess I did. But I was just trying to save you from doing something stupid."

"Well, it's very noble of you to save me from the 'big, bad wolf,'" Stella said sardonically, "and at the same time, I'm completely insulted that you'd never touch me because I'm a 'keeper,' whatever that means." Stella gestured 'keeper' with air quotes, shooting Joey a look of indignation.

"That's not what I said or what I meant."

"Then what did you mean?" Stella said, raising her voice.

"You're a nice girl. Okay?"

She was aware she'd backed him into a corner but she didn't care.

"If I was looking for a girlfriend, I'd want a girl like you. But I don't. I'm not going to be that guy in the yearbook labeled 'class couple' with a girl he's been with his entire four years of high school. Life is too short. High school and college are for exploration, not for getting tied down to limited experiences."

"Wow! So, the 'nice girl,'" Stella air quoted again, "loses out because no one will date her."

"No!" Joey said in utter frustration. "She dates the yearbook guy."

"What if she doesn't want the yearbook guy? What if she wants 'I need my freedom guy'?"

"He knows that things can only go so far with 'keeper girl' and he needs someone with whom he can take things further, so he vows not to ruin her and they stay friends." Joey reaches for a strand of Stella's hair.

An awkward silence hung in the air as they stared at one another. Stella was the first to avert her eyes from his.

"Of course, this is just a hypothetical case," he said turning the ignition key.

"Yup, hypothetical. Just like our science lab experiments," Stella said under her breath.

Chapter 12

Evvie

December 2005

"Hurry down or we'll be late for church," Sophia called to Evvie from the bottom of the staircase.

"I'm coming," Evvie snapped at her mother as she descended.

"Oh, Evvie, really. Can't you find something more festive to wear? It's Christmas."

"I know what day it is. This is what I want to wear. I think I'm old enough to pick my own outfits."

"You look like Morticia Addams."

Dean put a hand on his wife's shoulder. "Pick your battles," he suggested quietly.

"Who is Morticia Addams?" Evvie asked snidely.

"A TV character from a show I watched and she looked just like you. Black hair, black clothing, black jewelry and ..." Sophia swirled a finger in her daughter's direction. "... all that makeup. All black all the time. You're a pretty girl. Wear some color."

Evvie rolled her eyes, retrieved her black coat from the closet and walked out the front door.

In church, Evvie was seated on the end of the pew closest to the center aisle. Directly across from her, on the other side of the church, sat a boy about Evvie's age. Halfway through the liturgy they made eye contact and he waved, mouthing, 'Hi.' Evvie looked around, confused, and then leaned into Kristos. "Do you know that guy? I don't and he just waved at us. He keeps looking our way."

Kristos leaned forward to get a glimpse of the person Evvie was speaking of. "Nope. I don't know him."

The boy with the shaggy, bleach-blond hair, black clothing and black leather ties around his wrists caught her eye once again and waved. Evvie scowled at him and then swiftly shifted her focus elsewhere.

After the service had ended, the priest made a few announcements.

"It's good to see all of our college students back home for Christmas," he said. "I thought it would be nice to have a mixer for you while you're still here. So, for all of you who are now too old for G.O.Y.A. I've arranged a gathering with a few of our other Greek churches in the area for Tuesday, December 27th at seven o'clock. I hope to see all of you there."

As they filed out of the pews, Sophia caught Evvie's arm. "You should go. It sounds like fun. I'm sure your brother and Kristos would go with you."

"Why? So I can meet a nice, Greek boy? Not on your life!"

"Are you sure she isn't my biological daughter?" Dean joked.

"What do you mean by that?" Evvie asked.

"Your stepfather over here fought tooth and nail not to go out with any Greek girls." Sophia looked at her husband with mock annoyance. Or what Evvie thought was mock annoyance. "And what is your objection to Greek boys?" Sophia asked.

"Yes, Evvie, tell us, please. I'm a Greek boy," Kristos needled her. "And I might cry all the way home," he said, wiping away his nonexistent tears.

"Shut up." Evvie punched him in the arm. "It's not Greek boys, it's all boys. I don't need them or want them."

"When the right one comes along, you'll feel differently," Sophia said, placing her arm around her daughter.

"And I bet you'd *love* the right one to be a Greek one," Evvie mumbled.

"Would that be so horrible?"

"That all depends. Dad wasn't Greek and he turned out just fine."

Sophia kissed her daughter on the forehead and held her tightly. "Yes, he did. And I know you still miss him terribly."

A few days after Christmas, Evvie and Nicky left for Athens. They were between semesters until the end of January and wanted to spend some time with their great-grandmother, Yiayiá Sophia. At eighty-nine years old, she was still spry and completely capable of caring for herself, but she had outlived her husband and both of her children and, although she had Sophia, the twins and Cia, there was an underlying sadness about her that never abated.

It was Evvie who had convinced her brother to take the trip with her, and his tender and compassionate soul agreed without argument. Evvie, who seemed to those who didn't know her to be impenetrable and maybe a little bit heartless, would do anything for the people she loved. She needed the comforting arms of Yiayiá Sophia and, in turn, her great-grandmother needed to be surrounded by family.

The taxi pulled up in front of a well-maintained apartment building in one of the more elegant neighborhoods of the city. Evvie and Nicky had left the damp, cold weather in New York only to find the same dismal conditions in Athens. Dull clouds, the color of wet concrete, promised rain. They retrieved their bags from the trunk and ran up the front steps leading to the pale yellow double doors.

Before they could knock, the door swung open. "*Evanthia mou! Nikólaos mou!*" Yiayiá Sophia exclaimed. Grabbing hold of Evvie's face, she kissed each of her cheeks before doing the same to Nicky. "*Engonia mou! Ela mesa*," she said, motioning for her great-grandchildren to enter the house.

The twins rolled their suitcases down the hall to the rooms they usually stayed in when they visited. Many years ago, Yiayiá Sophia lived in a grand home in the affluent neighborhood in Kifisia. But once her husband, Spyro, had suddenly died, the house seemed too big and painfully lonely for her. She had outlived not only her husband but also both of her daughters and the space, sacred as it was to her, held too many memories that emphasized her loss.

With her granddaughter, Sophia, and her family in mind, Yiayiá Sophia moved into a one-story, two-bedroom apartment, large enough for her family to visit.

"We'll be right there," Evvie answered her great-grandmother when she called the twins to come to the kitchen table for a meal. She was so hungry and couldn't wait to see what she'd prepared for them.

Scents of lemon, garlic and oregano lured Evvie and Nicky to the kitchen. Three place settings atop an embroidered tablecloth held piping hot baked chicken breasts, roasted lemon potatoes and fresh peas seasoned with cinnamon. Steam rose from the warm, crusty bread in the middle of the table accompanied by the tangy scent of thick wedges of lemon.

Evvie couldn't pick her fork up fast enough. She cut a chunk of chicken off the bone, drenched it in the natural gravy enhanced by the lemon and herbs, and popped it in her mouth. She smiled approvingly. "This is exactly the way Yiayiá used to make this for us."

"Mom makes it too," Nicky reminded his sister.

"I know. But hers doesn't taste quite like this one. This makes me remember cooking with Yiayiá so clearly."

"Who do you think taught your yiayiá?" their great-grandmother said.

Evvie looked up at her, the old woman's eyes warring to hold back tears. Yet, there was a contradictory fusion of delight and sadness reflected in them, all expressed in one fleeting second. "I miss her," Evvie said quietly, the words catching in her throat.

Yiayiá Sophia placed her hand over Evvie's. "I know. I do too. I think of her every day. She was my blessing for sixty-eight years."

"We only had her for twelve," Nicky said, looking directly into his sister's eyes.

He had pulled the thought from her mind and said the words before they could fall from her lips. But that is how it often went with the two of them—her brother—her twin.

Yiayiá Sophia palmed each of their cheeks. "It wasn't enough time. Can we ever have enough time with the ones we love? My Ana was my greatest joy and losing her was my cruelest sorrow." She dabbed the corners of her eyes with the napkin she lifted from her lap. "Tell me, would you trade one day with her just so you wouldn't have to feel that pain?"

Both Evvie and Nicky shook their heads.

"Every moment is precious. A gift from God. Every memory a treasure. My heart is filled with gratitude and that keeps the grief from swallowing me."

"I wish I could be like you, Yiayiá," Evvie murmured, rising from her chair to hug the wise, elderly woman she loved so dearly. "But I'm ..."

"Afraid?" Yiayiá finished her sentence.

"Life is uncertain and ... disappointing." Evvie confessed.

"And to think, Evvie was once the outgoing, positive twin," Nicky joked.

"Life is what you want it to be. What you choose for yourself." Yiayiá rose from her seat to clear the plates.

"I'll do that," Evvie said.

"*Katse,*" Yiayiá insisted, placing her hand on her shoulder and pushing her firmly back into the chair. "*Evanthia mou,* do you know what I see right now?" She didn't wait for her answer. "Your yiayiá, my beautiful Anastacia, my daughter. She's here, in you and in Nikos. You have her hair, her eyes and her beautiful skin. Nikos, you have her smile and you have my Spyro's eyes. Make no mistake," she advised, shaking her finger at them. "We lose no one. They're bound in our souls and our bodies."

"I wish we had a chance to know Pappou Spyro," Nicky told her.

"Nothing was more important to him than his family," she said. "He was a good man." She motioned for the twins to wait, scurried out of the room and shuffled back in with a picture frame. Setting the photo down in front of them, she pointed to the image captured within. "Now tell me I'm wrong. Tell me they are not alive within you."

The old black and white photo had the year 1947 etched into the corner. The family portrait told no lies, and it was unmistakable that Evvie and Nicky were related to this family.

"Is that Yiayiá?" Nicky asked. He took a closer look. "How old was she?"

"Sixteen," Yiayiá Sophia answered. Her eyes sparkled and Evvie could tell her pro-yiayiá's mind had traveled to another time and place.

"I've seen plenty of photos of Mom at that age and they look so much alike." Evvie said, amazed at the resemblance."

"Ev!" Nicky exclaimed. "What about you? "You look so much like her too."

"I do, but … is that you, Yiayiá?" Evvie asked, pointing.

"It is."

"Wow! I think I look more like you."

"Our threads are all pulled from the same cloth, *koukla.*"

"I like that." Evvie smiled.

"There are other things that bind us. Not just our features. Who we are inside," Yiayiá said, gently tapping her chest, "the things we enjoy and those that make our soul sing." A shadow dulled her eyes before she continued. "Even our character, good or bad, might come from the ones before us," she sighed. Snapping herself out of whatever thought she was pondering, Yiayiá clapped her hands together. "Enough talk for tonight. You must be tired. Go! Get ready for bed."

But Evvie looked at her great-grandmother, curious. She wondered where her mind had drifted. The remnants of the past seemed to have come back to haunt her, if only for a moment, but the anguish on her face, even in its subtlety, could not be missed.

Chapter 13

Evvie

January 2006

Sunlight streamed in through the kitchen window, deceptively emitting a sense of warmth beyond the confines of the cozy Athenian apartment. Evvie sat quietly, her mind drifting as she snapped off the ends of string beans. Yiayiá Sophia seemed deep in her own thoughts, and together they worked in tandem as if beating out a rhythm—pick up a string bean, snap one end and then the other, throw it in the bowl; pick up, snap, snap, throw; repeat.

Nicky had left on some mysterious mission. He wouldn't say where he was going, only that he would be gone for four or five days. It wasn't like him to keep secrets from her, but he'd promised to tell her all there was to know when he found what he was looking for.

Evvie glanced at the old woman before her. As long as she remembered her, she looked the same—cloaked in black, gray hair pulled back in a low-sitting bun and barely a line on her face but for the creases around her eyes.

It never occurred to Evvie that she was young once. Funny how easy it was to forget that the elderly earned the privilege of their years. It surprised her how much she looked like her great-grandmother when she had pulled out the old photo. But more than the resemblance, she recognized something deeper—conflict—of what was, as opposed to what should have been or, in Evvie's case, who she wanted to become.

"Yiayiá, what did you mean the other day when you said that our traits and character comes from the ones before us?"

"Talents and interests can be inherited, not just the shape of your face or the color of your hair."

"I suppose," Evvie said. "Like, if someone is a musical prodigy, his son might be one too?"

"Possibly. Or if the mother is a gifted dancer, her daughter might be also." She tapped Evvie on the nose.

"Or," Evvie emphasized, "it could be that the gifted dancer simply taught her daughter everything she knew and talent wasn't really a factor at all. Just a learned skill."

"You're too bright to believe that." Wrapping the discarded string bean ends into a dishtowel, Yiayiá Sophia emptied them into the trash-can. Turning, she looked at Evvie as if to contemplate something. "Did you know that my Anastacia wanted to be a dancer?"

"My Yiayiá?" Evvie asked.

"My Spyro would not let her take lessons."

"Why?"

"He said good girls didn't dance."

Evvie looked incredulous. "Ballet? What could possibly be improper?"

Yiayiá Sophia covered her mouth to stifle a laugh at the memory. "Sypro took me to the ballet for our anniversary one year. I loved every minute of it, but when the male dancer lifted the ballerina in the air he leaned in to me and swore he would never let his daughters dance."

"But, why?"

"Well, it was bad enough that he touched her waist and legs, but when he lifted her high in the air, holding her with his hand between her legs—" She slapped her hand on either side of her head. "That did it for him!"

Evvie held her stomach, laughing. "Poor Yiayiá. She didn't stand a chance."

"No! And there was no changing his mind when it was set. But she made sure that her Sophia had the opportunity to experience what she was never allowed to."

"So, you think Yiayiá had the talent and passed it down to my mom?"

"I know she had the talent. I would catch her in her room dancing when she thought no one was looking." Yiayiá Sophia laid her hands over her heart. "She had a grace about her and there was always a dreamy, faraway look in her eyes as if the music carried her to magical, enchanting places."

Evvie took a deep breath and nervously nibbled the inside of her lip. "What did you mean when you said bad traits could be inherited too? What were you talking about?"

The brightness left her great-grandmother's eyes. "I was thinking out loud, I suppose. It's nothing we need to stir up." She took the bowl of string beans from the table and set it by the stove.

"But something is troubling you. I can tell."

"Hand me a head of garlic." Yiayiá Sophia turned the stove on and poured a generous amount of olive oil into a large pot.

"I'll slice the garlic," Evvie said, coming up alongside her.

They worked silently but for the sound of the knife smacking the wooden board as cloves of garlic were cut into slivers.

Yiayiá Sophia added the garlic to the pot, stirring it into the hot oil. Chunks of beef sat on the counter ready to be added. Sighing, she placed the meat into the pot, browning it on each side. Unconsciously, she stirred and sighed, stirred and sighed.

Evvie watched her with concern. She took the wooden spoon from her great-grandmother's hand and continued to brown the meat.

"Do you believe that meanness can be passed on from generation to generation?" the old woman asked.

"Meanness? Like being nasty? I don't think so."

"Worse than mean." She motioned for Evvie to continue browning the meat and took a seat at the table. "I'm afraid to say it. Wicked."

"Like evil?"

A distressing sigh rumbled from her chest. "What if it's my fault that my daughter was the way she was?"

"Who? Irini?" Evvie looked at her in utter astonishment. Why on earth was she carrying such a burden? Evvie lowered the flame and knelt to her pro-Yiayiá's side. "What would ever make you think that? You're not to blame for her bad behavior."

"It is possible though, that I could have passed on a bad trait to her."

"You, who I believe has the wisdom of the universe, are questioning yourself? At your age? You're the one who always holds the answers to *my* questions."

"Ah, but *koukla*, there is always something more to learn. Mistakes to correct. When we stop questioning, we stop growing."

"Yiayiá, even if you did pass on selfish and malicious qualities in your DNA to Irini, it's not something you had the power to control or choose. What if I took it out on Mom that I was born with brown eyes instead of gray ones like Nicky has?"

"Brown eyes have no effect on what kind of person you are."

"I'm just trying to make a point," Evvie said. "But I don't understand. This particular trait couldn't have come from you."

"Not from me directly. A cousin. Daphne. A terrible girl. *Polí kakós.*"

"So, she was related to you and you think that her bad blood was in Irini." Evvie pondered this information for a moment. Latching onto her great-grandmother's hands, she asked, "Do you think I have this bad blood?"

Yiayiá Sophia cupped Evvie's cheek in her hand. "What would make you think such a thing?"

"I'm not the nicest person. I give Mom a hard time. Often on purpose. I'm not the warmest person and I'm not very loveable. I've come to realize that. I push people away. Isn't that what Irini did?"

"*Agapi mou*, do not compare yourself to Irini. You've lost so much in your young life. Your sadness comes from grief." She took Evvie's chin in her hand. "Look at me. Maybe the problem isn't that you don't love, but it's that you love too much. Distance is your way to protect yourself. That is very different compared to going out of your way to hurt others the way Irini and Daphne did."

"Do you still see her?"

"Daphne? No. She passed away, but even then, I hadn't seen her in many years. We lived on a vineyard together in Kefalonia. That was long ago, before my parents left the island for good."

"Vineyard? You lived on a vineyard?" Evvie had never heard this before.

"As I told you some interests and talents are handed down. This is what I meant. The grapes are in your blood too. My father and uncle had a vineyard and, like you, I lived on the same land as my cousins."

"Will you tell me about it, Yiayiá? Everything. About the vineyard and your cousins?"

Wearily, she agreed. "After dinner. It's a long story and I haven't spoken of it in many years."

Chapter 14

Kefalonia, Greece – April 1928

Sophia Georgatos

Sophia Georgatos stood on her tippy-toes, grasping the rail of the small, weathered ferryboat shuttling from Lixouri to Argostoli as it did several times a day. Anticipation grew as the vessel approached the shoreline and the throngs of people walking about the pier came into view.

April was not typically warm on Kefalonia, but the seventy-degree Fahrenheit temperature was higher than average for that time of year. Wisps of clouds that looked as if they'd been painted by an artist's hand were too sparse to block the sun from shining down upon the crystal blue waters of Argostoli Gulf.

Last year, Sophia's mamá had not allowed her to take the twenty-minute trip alone, and as much as her parents looked forward to attending the traditional celebration, they couldn't always afford the time away from their responsibilities on the family vineyard. In addition, the preparations for the upcoming Easter holiday added extra work for her mother.

Her mother had agreed that, at twelve years old, Sophia was now mature enough to go on her own, as long as she was accompanied by her cousin, Daphne, two years her senior, and Elias Maryiatos, the family's closest friends' son and the boy Sophia had been promised to from birth.

"If you lean any farther forward you'll be swimming with the fish," Daphne remarked. She kept an eye on the two siblings she was asked to take with her. The three left behind were too young to be out of their mother's sight. Eight-year-old Marina preferred her cousin, Sophia, to her own sister, and seven-year-old Ari yanked his hand from his sister's to stand by Elias.

"I'm just so happy!" Sophia threw her arms in the air and spun around. As she turned, her long, thick pigtail braids whipped around and she giggled.

"I'd be happy too if I had no one to be responsible for," Daphne said sourly.

The glow that had brightened Sophia's face was replaced by a shadow of sorrow. "You don't know how lucky you are." She held Marina in front of her, wrapping her arms around the precious child. "They aren't a responsibility. They're a gift."

Daphne rolled her eyes. "Easy for you to say. You don't care for them night and day."

"That's enough, Daphne," Elias admonished her. "You're being insensitive."

Daphne stomped away, leaving the children with Sophia and Elias.

"How do you live with her?" he asked.

"You know we don't live in the same home, just on the same property."

"It's almost the same thing. That vineyard wouldn't be large enough for both me and her," Elias frowned.

Sophia shrugged off her friend's complaint. Her attention was focused on the docking boat and she couldn't wait to disembark so they could rush to the town square. She was attired in one of her finest dresses. She'd worn the pale yellow, floral frock that morning to church. All week she'd attended Holy Week services in dark colors and modest clothing. But today was Holy Saturday and the solemn, spiritual atmosphere of the past several days was over, replaced by the anticipation of the resurrection of Christ. This was her favorite holiday of the year—every ritual and tradition. Each moment, from catching the rose petals the priest showered on the congregation on Holy Saturday morning to the midnight candlelit *Anastasi* service under the stars, and everything in between, caused Sophia to be giddy with excitement.

"Daphne!" Sophia called to her. "Hurry. There's no time to waste."

Elias kept pace with Sophia who briskly walked to a near sprint once her feet touched land, the children skipping alongside them and Daphne dragging behind.

The town square was brimming with onlookers. Women in traditional folk dress carried wicker baskets filled with thin, beeswax candles decorated with ribbon and flowers.

"*Efharisto*," Sophia said as one of the costumed women approached them, handing each of them a taper. She admired the beauty of the young woman, her head covered by a white cotton scarf to match the sleeves and apron of her dress. The sky blue skirt was a sharp contrast to the brilliance of the yellow, orange and red bodice, but all together it looked magnificent and, by the way the woman carried herself, was proudly worn.

"*Kali Anastasi*," the beautiful woman said, wishing the youngsters a good resurrection.

"*Episis*," each one of them said in unison.

Shopkeepers stood at their entranceways, priests dressed in colorful vestments blessed the crowd, musicians stood waiting in the middle of the square and people hung over their balconies anticipating the ringing of church bells. Dozens and dozens of clay pots lined the alleyways.

As the hour drew closer, the crowd thickened, and an electricity of excitement hung in the air as the buzz of jovial chatter and laughter could be heard amongst families and acquaintances. The music in the square came to a stop and the crowds froze in place waiting for the moment they had traveled to this place for.

"Look!" Elias pointed to the bell tower above the church. "There they are!"

The first clay pot was to be thrown from the roof of the church as the bell rang. The men held them high above their heads as a roar came from the crowd. Rhythmic claps and thunderous cheers followed as the large earthenware hit the ground, smashing into fragments and shards. No one moved, heedfully avoiding the falling pots and urns being tossed from the balconies above. When the last piece of terra-cotta had fallen, red banners were hung from balconies, the musicians began to play and the costumed ladies joined hands to dance a tradi-tional Kefalonian circle dance.

"I have a little money," Elias said. "I'll buy a bag of *mandoles* for us to share."

"Yes, yes!" Ari jumped up and down. "I want *mandoles*!"

They walked to the other side of the square, kicking away sharp remnants of the clay pots as they made their way to the bakery. Elias asked the woman behind the counter for an order of *mandoles*. The almond confection, candy-coated with sugar, was dyed in a mouth-wa-tering shade of deep red.

After he'd paid the woman, Elias doled out a handful of the treat to each of them as they made their way back to watch the dancers. Others had joined in and more and more spectators had now become part of a growing spiral chain.

Sophia's eyes lit up. "Let's join in!" she shouted to Daphne and Elias.

"And who will watch these two?" Daphne asked, waving a dismis-sive hand in her siblings' direction as if she was swatting an annoying fly buzzing around her.

"I will," Elias offered, taking the children by the hand. "Go," he said to Sophia, grinning. "Have fun."

Cutting between two dancers, Sophia momentarily broke the

chain so that she and Daphne could join in. For Sophia, there was a sense of deep connection to the people around her in the tradition of this dance, these meaningful age-old customs and a culture that had come long before her, one that would last long after she was gone.

Beaming, her feet joyfully moved in the repetitious sequence, her lips mouthing the words to the song. Sophia knew what was important in her world—people, family, kindness, love, and joy. It saddened her that Daphne didn't seem to value what Sophia deemed most vital, but she prayed for her and hoped that someday she would.

"We should go," Sophia told Daphne finally, out of breath. "Our mothers will need our help." Sophia broke from the circle, urging her older cousin to follow.

"Thank you, Elias," Sophia said, taking Marina by the hand. "We should take the boat back now. My mamá will be expecting me."

"Did you have a nice time in Argostoli?" Sophia's mother asked, handing her daughter a stack of dishes. Three rectangular tables had been joined together to form one long one covered with a linen tablecloth cross-stitched by Sophia's yiayiá.

"Yes, mamá. I enjoyed it very much and Marina and Ari were so happy they were allowed to come with us."

Her mother stopped what she was doing and rested her hand on her hip. "And Daphne? How was she with them?"

There was no need for Sophia to answer. She could tell by the way her mother asked the question that she already knew the answer. "The usual. She couldn't be bothered with them. Maybe that's the way it is with brothers and sisters though." Sophia shrugged it off. "Anyway, I'm more than happy to amuse Marina. She's a sweet girl, and Ari never left Elias for a second."

"He's a good boy, that Elias. He'll make a good husband for you." She pointed her finger in Sophia's direction. "Good family. Good match."

Sophia drew her eyes down to stare at the place settings, fiddling with the silverware. "Mamá? What if I don't want a good match or any match?"

"What are you saying? Don't you like Elias?"

"I do. I love him. I've known him my whole life. But I think of him more like a brother. Not someone I'll marry someday."

Her mother came to her daughter's side and took her hand. "*Moro mou*, you're still a child. You'll feel differently when the time comes. You'll see."

"But how do you know that?" Sophia asked with a hint of desperation. "What if I don't feel differently? Shouldn't I be able to choose who I'll spend my life with?"

"Come, sit down with me," her mother tugged her toward the sofa. Seated facing each other, her mother sighed. "Elias' mother is my best friend."

Sophia nodded. "I know that."

Her mother playfully pulled at her braids. "I know you do. We've always dreamed of being part of the same family. Your father and Elias' father were also good friends before both of you were born. They always talked about the possibility of going into business together. If they combined their two small vineyards, they could expand and be more profitable."

"But what does this have to do with me?" Sophia asked.

"Well, when Elias was born, his father came up with the idea that if we had a girl someday, then we should have them marry. This way we would not only be family, but the vineyard would be a family-owned business and not merely a partnership between friends."

"What's the difference? If they're such good friends, why would it matter?"

"This is why you are too young to understand these things," her mother said. "It may not matter now, but it will later when the property and business is handed down. Don't you see? It would stay in both our families that way."

"But you're forgetting something, Mamá."

"And what is that, *koukla*?"

"Where does that leave Theios Savvas and Theia Olga?"

"Ah, yes. That has been a sore subject for years. When Daphne was born your aunt and uncle said she should be the one promised to Elias since she was the first-born girl. But that wasn't the agreement, or what we'd hoped for. They would still retain one third of the vineyard. Your father would never cut his brother out."

"I don't want to be sold for a business deal," Sophia said in a barely audible whisper, but her mother heard her and lifted her daughter's chin with her fingers.

"I am not selling you," she said sternly. "I am insuring your future."

"A future I don't want," Sophia said with uncharacteristic defiance.

"You're too young to know what you want," her mother said, shaking her finger. "What is it you think you want?"

"I want to grow up and fall in love in my own time and with someone of my own choosing." Sophia stood up, clenching her fists with determination. "Do you remember in *Les Misérables* when Cosette fell in love with Marius?"

"Stories! What does that have to do with anything?"

"That's what I want. To fall in love on my own, even if there seems to be no hope in a grim world racked with war and parents who force a future on me; I want to find the one person meant for me."

"Is that what you think? The world is grim and I'm forcing a life on you?" Her mother crossed her hands at her throat. The creases in the corners of her eyes became more pronounced, announcing her distress. "What happened to my sweet, happy child?"

"I meant them. Cosette and Marius. They lived in grim circumstances, but they found love even through all the destruction around them. I'm just saying that I want that also."

"But you said I am forcing you."

"Aren't you, though? Jean Valjean did the same thing in a way. He tried to keep Cosette away from the one she loved. He was thinking of his loneliness. His intentions were good and he gave her everything except what she wanted most in the world. But in the end, he saw it was wrong, and if he truly loved his daughter he had to let her find her own happiness." Sophia grabbed onto her mother's shoulders. "Don't you see, Mamá, I want you to do that. Let me find my own happiness."

"You know I love you," her mother said, folding her into her arms. "I only want what's best for you."

Sophia buried her face in the comfort of her mother's warm embrace. "I know," she said, trying to hold back her own tears.

The stars sparkled brightly against the cloudless, ebony sky. A springtime chill in the air along with a light breeze carried heaven's ambrosial scent from the priest's golden censer.

Only moments before the church had been dark, lit by a single flame flickering at the end of a tall candle, adorned with a white and red satin bow. The holy light was a symbol of rebirth, joy and the hope of eternal life. Emerging from behind the altar doors, the priest held his candle reverently, chanting a proclamation for all to rejoice and repeat the hymn together many times over.

"Come ye and receive light from the unwaining light, and glorify Christ, who arose from the dead."

And the light was spread from one person to another. From parent to child; husband to wife; friends to cousins; neighbors to visitors, until every candle was lit and the church was glowing in firelight.

Slowly and carefully the congregation filed out surrounding the priest and the chanters. Anticipation hung in the air until the crowd heard the words they waited for. *Christos Anesti!* Christ has risen! The crowd sang the traditional hymn along with the clergy as they held their candles, raising them high in exultation.

"Christ is risen from the dead, trampling down death by death, and to those in the tombs, granting life."

Bells chimed furiously, the sounds simultaneously ringing out from churches throughout the island. The heavens above erupted in celebration. Colorful bursts of red and gold showers of light exploded. In every corner of the sky glorious displays of illumination added to the magnificence and joyous atmosphere of this most holy night of the year.

After Sophia and her family arrived home, the women went immediately into the kitchen to set the food on the long table they'd prepared earlier. Sophia's mother and Dora, Elias's mother, ladled *mayritsa* into bowls and handed them to Sophia and Daphne. Elias entertained Ari, Marina and their two-year-old brother while Olga took her youngest child to a quiet space to breastfeed him.

The men had already pulled a bottle of *tsipouro* from the icebox and exclaimed toasts to one another while pouring shot after shot of the strong liquor.

When everyone had finally gathered around the table, hungry after a long fast period and the late hour, Sophia's father, Lambros, raised his wineglass. "To our families. To a long, prosperous life. May we have many years together with our families joined as one. *Stin ygeia mas!*"

Her father's toast sat like lead on Sophia's chest. The expectation for their families to become one in order for their vineyards to merge was resting on her, and her future happiness. Suddenly, the excitement of the day's events had dulled. Sophia picked at the food that, only hours before, she was salivating to devour. Elbowing Elias, whom she'd been sitting next to during the meal, she whispered in his ear and they both got up and left the room.

Pacing, Sophia wrung her hands together.

"What?" Elias questioned. "What's wrong with you?"

"I—" she opened her mouth to speak but stopped herself. She and Elias had never spoken about this and she didn't know whether or not he felt the same as she did. "Do you want to marry me?"

"Isn't it customary for the man to do the asking?" Elias chuckled. "And I think it's a little soon. After all, you're only twelve."

"That's not what I mean," she said, frustrated. "Do you *want* to marry me?"

"Sophia, why do you look so distressed?" He bracketed his hand on her shoulders. "Our parents bound us together. Someday we'll wed."

"But you're not answering my question." She laid her hand on his. "We've never talked about it and I think we should."

"I honestly haven't given it much thought. It's what I've always known and accepted." He took her hand in his. "You're young still. There's no need to think about this yet."

Releasing herself from him, she turned away. "How can you just accept a future mapped out for you with no thought of what you might want?"

"I don't understand. We've been good friends for as long as I can remember." He brushed the palm of his hand across his stubbled jaw. Hesitantly, he asked, "Do you have an objection to me as a husband?"

She had hurt him. It was written all over his face. Sophia didn't believe that he actually wanted to marry her, but nonetheless, she could see her ambivalence stung and she felt awful.

She threw her arms around him, burying her face in his chest. "Oh, Elias, you'd make a wonderful husband. I know you will some-day. But don't you want to choose your own wife, fall in love and make that decision for yourself? That's what I want and you should too."

"And when you've arrived at the age to fall in love, you don't think it could be with me?" Elias asked.

"You're my friend and like a brother to me. That's how I think of you. That's how I love you." Sophia broke from his hold. "Why are you so willing to accept a fate you didn't ask for?" She'd been certain that he would understand and feel the same. She'd hoped they could go to their parents together to change their minds.

"Maybe because I could do a lot worse. You're sweet and beautiful and we get along. I could have been stuck with someone awful."

"Then what would you have done?"

"I don't know, Sophia. I really don't know," Elias conceded. "I never had to think about it because all along I knew it was you."

"But if it wasn't me and it was someone you didn't like at all, you'd consider going through your whole life miserable just to make your parents happy?" Sophia asked, accentuating her disapproval.

"My parents were matched that way," Elias said, stating his case, "and they came to love each other."

"*Came* to love each other," she repeated, muttering under her breath.

"Sophia, it's late and we're all tired. The sun will be up in a couple of hours. We can continue this conversation in a few years when the time comes."

Sophia sighed. "Sure," she relented. "We'll talk about it then." Walking past him, she pecked him on the cheek before crossing to the doorway.

Chapter 15

Kefalonia, Greece 1928

Daphne & Sophia

Daphne stood with her ear pressed close to the ajared door, eavesdropping on Elias and Sophia's conversation. She instinctively knew that she would find out something important—something she could use for her own benefit. She'd bet her father's last *drachma* on it, and now, with what she'd overheard, she wished she had. Her mouth fell open in disbelief before a sly smile reaching up as far as her mischievous eyes crossed her face.

If Sophia refused to marry Elias, then the door was open for her instead. It was a stupid agreement anyway—one that her aunt and uncle made with Elias' parents before she and Sophia were even born. Daphne was the older child between the girls and she should have been promised to Elias, not Sophia.

So what if it was a pact between best friends. The vineyard belonged as much to her own parents as it did to Sophia's. But her cousin was the one on whom fortune always fell, what with Sophia being the prettier of the two and Daphne resented her for it. Sophia's long, nearly black tresses were straight and manageable, while hers were mousy brown and at times a bit unruly. Daphne's eyes were as black as coal. So dark the pupil was indistinguishable from the iris, whereas Sophia's eyes were the warm color of melting chocolate, rimmed by long, feathery lashes.

But Daphne had some attributes of her own that she was proud of. She was much taller than her younger cousin and it wasn't likely that Sophia would ever catch up to her. At fourteen, Daphne had the beautifully, curvy figure of a grown woman and she had hoped that Elias would notice, but unfortunately, he showed no signs of interest in her.

Listening in on conversations was a favorite hobby of Daphne's and she'd overhead her parents argue often when it came to the inevitable marriage between Sophia and Elias.

"They will cut us out of the business eventually," her mamá would say. "You'll see."

"He's my brother. He wouldn't do that to me. Once our vineyards are combined we will own a third of a much larger establishment," her babá said. "Equally."

"You're a fool. They will own two-thirds when those kids marry."

Oh, yes, Daphne knew her mother would be very interested in what she had learned tonight, and she scoured the house until she found her in a quiet bedroom changing her baby brother's diaper.

"Mamá," Daphne called out as she burst into the room.

"Shhh," her mother said, pressing a finger to her lips. "He's falling asleep."

"But I have something important to tell you." Daphne's eyes went wide with enthusiasm.

"Can't it wait until tomorrow?" her mother asked harshly, not bothering to glance her way.

"Well," Daphne drawled out, "if you don't want to know that Sophia won't marry Elias, then sure, it can wait," she said, starting for the door.

Her mother's head snapped up. "Wait!"

Daphne narrowed her eyes and with a nefarious grin, she pivoted to face her mother.

"Tell me what you know," Olga, Daphne's mother, said anxiously, patting the bed for her daughter to sit beside her.

"I was walking down the hallway and I just happened to overhear Sophia telling Elias that she doesn't want to be forced to marry him."

She looked at her daughter suspiciously. "You just happened to overhear?" She raised a doubtful eyebrow. "Why would she feel that way? They seem to be very close, even with their wide age difference."

Daphne waved a dismissive hand. "Something about Elias being like a brother to her and Sophia wanting to make her own decisions when it comes to love."

"Bah! It won't matter. The decision has been made. Your Uncle Lambros will make sure of it."

But Daphne could see that her mother was giving the matter some thought. "What is it, Mamá?" she asked as her mother tapped a finger to her chin.

"If Sophia's objections could be brought out in the open, then we can jump in and offer for you to agree to the arrangement yourself."

"And how am I supposed to do that?" Daphne asked.

"You're a smart girl. You'll figure it out."

Sophia followed the aroma of lamb roasting on a spit in the courtyard. Her father, uncle and Elias' father hovered around the fire, each with a cigarette in one hand and a shot glass in the other. Something had them rolling around with laughter, her uncle having trouble catching his breath from his state of hysteria.

"Mamá wants to know when the lamb will be ready," Sophia interrupted.

"Tell her about an hour or so," her father said before turning his attention back to the other men.

Sophia waved to Elias from a distance before heading back into the house. Marina and Ari were tugging at him and, always the good sport, he entertained the younger children while their mother was tending to the babies.

Inside, Sophia found her mother pulling out aromatic trays of *spanakopita*, *moussaka*, and a codfish pie made with phyllo and flavored with dill, chives and marjoram. "Bábá said the lamb should be ready in an hour." Sophia leaned down to breathe in the mouth-watering scent emanating from the rising vapors swirling above the baking pans.

"Everything is done. We can rest for a while then." Her mother called out for Olga and Dora. "Go get Daphne," she instructed Sophia. "We have time to give our thanks and say a prayer."

When Sophia entered her mother's bedroom, Daphne dragged along behind her, and together they joined their mothers and Sophia's aunt by the *iconastasis*. The glass door to the case holding the vast collection of family icons was open and Elias' mother, Dora, had one in her hand.

"Where did you get such a treasure, Khloe?" Dora asked Sophia's mother.

Daphne perked up. "Treasure? Let me see." She elbowed her way in front of Sophia. "Oh," she shrugged. "It's just an icon."

"Daphne!" Olga scolded. "Have some respect. This is a holy item and a valuable one."

"The value doesn't matter. It's the sentiment that's important to me," Khloe said. "This icon has been in my family for generations. And it's always passed down to the eldest girl." She took the icon from Dora, stepping next to Sophia. "This will be yours someday and, God willing, you'll have a daughter to pass it down to also."

Sophia took the icon from her mother and gingerly ran her hands over it. It was far more precious than she could ever imagine. The once colorful image of *Panayia*—the Virgin Mary—holding the Christ child, was now dulled, but the radiance of the metals and jewels that embellished their halos and garments were breathtaking. Sterling silver made up a good portion of the postcard-sized icon. Medallions of gold bordered the edges imprinted with small images of apostles. The spiky crowns that extended from the golden halos of the holy mother and child were adorned with tiny jewels—diamonds and blue sapphires for the Virgin—rubies and diamonds for the Christ child.

What made the icon truly precious was the connection this blessed piece of art had to Khloe's ancestors. "See," her mother said, turning it over in Sophia's hand, "the name of each person who had once possessed it is etched into the wood."

"Why don't we have something like that?" Daphne complained. She sounded like a jealous, petulant child and everyone stared at her mildly disgusted.

But Khloe rallied and answered her politely. "A long time ago there was an iconographer in our family. My great-grandfather. He made beautiful icons for many churches and one day a man sought him out to work on a chapel he wanted to build on his property. The man was quite wealthy and he'd commissioned many projects from him over the years. Each sacred image was unique. Some were created using tiny mosaic tiles, many were oil paintings and others comprised of precious metals."

Sophia was fascinated by what her mother was saying, but Daphne made it obvious by her facial expression and posture that she was bored.

"The man's daughter had become very ill and he prayed for her to be healed. He asked my great-grandfather to create a most glorious icon of *Panayia* to venerate and pray to."

"Why did it have to be so elaborate though?" Sophia asked. "Any icon blessed by the priest would have been just as good."

Her mother placed the priceless icon back in the *iconastasis*. "He wanted to show he would spare no cost to save her life and that he was willing to spend his money to honor Christ's mother. After all, no one knew better than she what it was like to watch your child die a painful death. He prayed and prayed to the Holy Mother, asking her son to intercede and save his child."

"And what happened to the child?" Olga asked. "Was she spared?"

"Yes," Khloe said solemnly. "She was spared."

"That still doesn't explain why you have the icon now," Daphne said. "Did the iconographer steal it?"

"*Vre, morí*, Daphne!" Olga scolded her daughter.

"Of course not!" Khloe continued, slightly shocked at her comment. "After the man's daughter recovered and had remained healthy for many years, he was so grateful that he gave the icon to my great-grandfather."

"Why? What if he needed it again?" Daphne sneered.

"It's a sacred icon, not a magical object," Sophia said reprovingly.

"I'd like to believe the man understood that his faith had healed his daughter and God had answered his prayers simply for that reason. When he gave the icon to my great-grandfather, he told him he was returning a great gift and hoped that it would bring health and happiness to his family."

"What a generous man," Dora said.

"Yes, he was. But he had what he wanted the most in the world. His daughter," Khloe added. "My dear ancestor promised to give it to his daughter in honor of the girl that was saved from death. After that, it became a tradition to pass it on to the oldest daughter in the family."

"That's quite a history for such an object," Olga said.

"It's over one hundred and twenty years old," Khloe said, crossing herself rapidly three times in reverence. She lifted a worn photo resting on the table under the *iconastasis*. "It didn't save my Raphael," she said as tears welled in her eyes. "I suppose my faith was not strong enough to heal my child." She kissed the paper image of her six-year-old son, and placed it back where it had rested.

"Don't say that, Mamá." Sophia flung herself into her mother's arms. "I wish that I had half your devotion."

Khloe hugged her daughter tightly and kissed the top of her head. "Two years without my Raphael." Raw pain ripped through her chest as she said the words. Sophia recognized the sound of her mother's lament.

"Today is a happy day, Mamá, and Raphael is singing with the cherubim."

"Such a sweet, mature girl. You'll make a good wife for my Elias someday," Dora told her.

Sophia attempted a smile. "I'll go check on Babá and see if the lamb is ready." Uncomfortably, she turned for the door and headed outside.

At the dinner table, the men piled food onto their plates, refilled their wineglasses and spoke rapidly, shifting from one subject to another. The children jumped in and out of their seats, eating bites of food, running out to play and then coming back in when they wanted something more.

But for Sophia, something she couldn't put her finger on had changed from the time she'd left her mother's bedroom to when they had sat down for their *Pascha* meal. Self-consciousness traveled over her like invisible ants irritating her skin. The source of her sudden discomfort was a mystery to her.

With their heads bent together, Daphne and her mother whispered, throwing a glance Sophia's way every so often. Dora, Elias' mother, stared at her as if analyzing her, and her own mother sighed in between bites of food.

"Sophia," Dora finally addressed her, "may I ask you a question?"

The clanging of Daphne's silverware slipping through her fingers and onto the porcelain plate caught her attention before she answered.

"Of course," Sophia said nervously.

The woman leaned in and lowered her voice. "Do you—" She looked at the eager faces staring at her. Daphne and Olga waited with eyes wide in anticipation. "It's come to my attention that—"

"Maybe this can wait until you can speak to my daughter in private," Khloe said.

"What's going on? Is something wrong?" Sophia asked.

"No. At least I didn't think so. You and my Elias get along, no?"

"Sure, you know that. We've always been great friends. I like him very much."

"But not enough to want to marry him someday?"

Sophia's mouth opened. Her heart jumped in the way it did when something terribly wrong happened. "What makes you ask that?" She turned to her mother with hurt written on her face. "You told her?"

Khloe shook her head. "No."

"Did Elias speak to you?" Sophia asked softly.

"No, he did not, but in light of what I was told, I'm surprised he didn't come to me himself."

With a sick feeling brewing in her stomach, Sophia was afraid to ask her next question. "If not Mamá or Elias, then who?"

There was silence among the women until her mother could no longer contain her anger. "Daphne," Khloe said, a hint of disdain in the accusation. "Daphne told Dora when you left the room."

Daphne straightened her posture, stiffening defensively.

"Why?" Sophia asked, wounded.

"Why? Because you get everything and you don't deserve it!"

"*Skase,*" Olga said firmly but quietly to her daughter. "This is not the way to handle this."

Daphne ignored her. "Why should Elias be forced to marry an ungrateful child when he could have me? It's not fair. I'm closer to his age and the oldest girl in the family."

Sophia scraped back her chair and stood. "I am not ungrateful. And who are you to judge me?" Sophia raised her voice. Everyone was looking at her now. Even the men stopped what they were doing to stare at her. "Elias shouldn't be forced to marry me or anyone else. If he wants you and you want him then I will be very happy for the both of you."

"Whoa! Wait a minute. Why are you all talking about me like I'm not in the room?" Elias looked horrified. "I'll decide for myself."

"No!" Elias' father, Fotis declared. "The matter was decided many years ago and is not open for discussion."

Dora turned to Daphne. "This is not an insult to you. It was an arrangement made between us before either of you girls were born. Khloe is my closest friend and it was our way of uniting our families."

"And our vineyards," Fotis added.

"And a way to cut us out little by little," Olga scoffed.

"Olga!" Savvas, her husband scolded. He shot her a murderous look.

Lambros, Sophia's father, stood and shot his hand in the air. "*Stamata!* All of you. What is this nonsense? Arguing on this holy day." His tone was firm, if not reprimanding, yet he spoke with a gentle calmness to his voice. "There's no matter to discuss. When my Sophia reaches the age of sixteen, she and Elias will wed as planned. Shortly after we will combine our vineyards and our resources." He turned his focus to Olga, his eyes searing into hers. "No one will be cut out of the business. Each of our families will own one-third. This is how it will go without argument."

Sophia closed her eyes and hung her head. Her fate was sealed. The dream of discovery, falling in love and finding her own way to a future she dreamed of was dead. When she lifted her head and met her mother's gaze, she saw her own sadness reflected in them.

Locking eyes with her daughter, Khloe began to shake her head, slowly at first and then more animatedly. "No! No!"

"No, what?" Lambros bit out.

"No, we will not make these children hold to an agreement made for them long before they were born."

Olga's brows rose with interest and Daphne pressed her lips together, biting back her glee.

"Khloe," Dora pleaded, "you can't mean that. We've dreamt of this for years."

"It cannot be changed," Lambros affirmed. "It has long been decided." Bracing his hand on his friend's shoulder, he looked at Fotis apologetically. "My wife has lost her head. She speaks out of turn."

Khloe jumped to her feet. With a murderous glare, she pointed her finger in her husband's direction. "Don't you dare," she threatened. "Sophia is my daughter and I will decide what is best for her."

"She's *our* daughter," Lambros corrected, "and we made this agreement together in her best interest."

With her hands covering her face, Sophia silently wept into them. She had ruined their holiday and had caused her parents to argue. She alone was responsible for the wounded expression on Elias' face. But he was still the kindest soul, and quickly he gathered the little ones and bustled them off outside, away from the contentious situation. Cocking his head, he motioned for Sophia to follow but she refused.

Khloe sunk back down into her chair. Resting her head in her hands, she took a moment to compose herself and then looked around the table, sighing deeply. "I've already lost one child." She fisted her hands over her heart. "I could not save my Raphael, but I will not lose my Sophia too." Lambros opened his mouth to speak but she lifted her hand. "Living a life she doesn't want will be a slow death for her. Eventually, it will break her spirit and infest her sweet soul with bitterness." The look of determination on her face could not be disputed. "I will not allow it. My daughter will not be sold off like a piece of property. Not for wealth, or land or ... friendship." She turned to her friends. "I'm sorry, Fotis. Forgive me, Dora. Elias is a wonderful boy. Should they fall in love, they'll have my blessing. But they will no longer be bound to a promise we had no right to impose on them."

"What the caterpillar calls the end of the world, the master calls a butterfly."
—Richard Bach

Chapter 16

Sophia Georgatos

Kefalonia 1928

The weeks following Easter were fraught with tension and Sophia blamed herself for causing trouble amongst the families. Olga and Khloe traded insults and accusations, both defending their daughters' positions. The friendship between Dora and Khloe frayed a little more with each passing day, and Olga swooped in to befriend Dora in a way she never had before, hoping to forge an alliance with her on behalf of their children.

Spring was in full bloom and the wisps of gentle wind had lost the stinging bite that made Sophia shiver so easily. Clay pots overflowing with variegated flowers in fuchsia, magenta and cobalt lined the door leading to the back patio.

But the warmth and bright colors did nothing to lift Sophia's spirit. From the doorframe she observed her father. Seated in a wood and rattan chair, staring out over the expanse of his vineyards, Lambros manipulated the *komboloi* between his fingers reflexively repeating the same pattern over and over. The amber-colored worry beads were given to him by his father before his wedding day and Sophia had often seen him flick them back and forth, one bead at a time with his finger.

But tonight his grip on the strand of beads was tighter as he poured himself drink after drink. He seemed lost in thought.

"Babá," Sophia said, pulling him from his trance. She took a seat beside him. "I'm sorry I'm the cause of your distress. I've disappointed you and I didn't mean to."

Lambros shook his head. He set his worry beads on the table by his shot glass. With a humorless laugh he took his daughter's hand in his. "Maybe it's the adults who should be disappointed in themselves. You're not to blame."

"But I've caused everyone to argue."

Running his fingers over the *komboloi* tassel hanging off the edge of the table he shook his head. "No, you haven't. Fotis, Savvas and I are not fighting." He smoothed out his black mustache, puffing his chest out like a proud peacock and continued. "We look for solutions, not battles."

Sophia wondered what those solutions were and, once again, she caught her father staring out at the vines as though taking them in one last time.

"The marriage between your mother and I had been arranged. Did you know that?"

Sophia looked at him skeptically. "No. But, you and Mamá love each other so very much."

"We do, very much." He sighed. "We handled this situation all wrong with you and Elias. You were made aware of your match when you were too young. It put pressure on you that a child should not need to worry over. Your mother and I knew nothing of our own match. We didn't even meet until we were fifteen and, even then, we weren't told."

"What happened when you found out?" Sophia asked.

"As luck would have it, our feelings had grown to love before we were told that we had been bound to one another."

"So that made it easy for you."

"It should have, but I got so angry. I felt tricked. As though my parents had made me fall in love with someone whom they had chosen for me."

119

"But, Babá, they had no way of knowing. I don't see how you were tricked at all. It seems to me they let the two of you see how you felt about each other without their influence."

"You are very wise for your age, *koritsi mou*. I realized this later on, but not before I lashed out at everyone, hurting your mother's feelings in the process. It took me some time to realize our parents had given us a great gift—the chance to see where our hearts would take us. I'm afraid I didn't give you that same chance. So it's me who should be apologizing to you."

Sophia leaned into her father, wrapping her arms around his neck and kissing his cheek. "Babá," she asked, "what would have happened if you and Mamá hadn't fallen in love?"

"We still would have been expected to marry," he sighed. "You know, many strong marriages have begun this way. The love and respect comes eventually."

Sophia cast her eyes to the ground. Her mother was fighting for her but her father still expected her to go through with the arrangement.

"You and Elias are no longer bound by this agreement," he said, lifting her chin to meet his gaze. "Alternative plans have been made."

"Alternative, how?" she hesitated to ask.

"We will be leaving the island for Athens."

"Why?" Sophia shrieked. "For how long?"

"For good, most likely."

"What about the vineyard?" The heaviness in her heart was pressing against her lungs, the guilt weighing even heavier.

"Don't worry your pretty head. I'm not losing my piece of the vineyard. We've been talking for a long time about getting more exposure for our little vineyard. We will still go ahead with the plan to combine the Georgatos and Maryiatos land, and with more vines and more wine to sell, someone needs to find new ways and places to distribute."

"And Athens is where you want to do this?"

"It's a big city with many restaurants and hotels. I've been building contacts there for years. But all this is not for a child to worry about."

"But I do. If it wasn't for me, we would stay here."

"If it wasn't for Dora and Olga we could stay here. The whole business is upsetting your mother."

"Did Mamá agree to this?"

"Yes. It's what's best for all of us."

With a twinge of melancholy, Sophia smiled at the beauty before her—this corner of the world she had lived her entire life, where she played hide and seek with her cousins and Elias, between the rows and rows of vines, where she had harvested grapes alongside her father, where her home stood and she had cooked with her mother and told stories to alleviate the tedium of cleaning—suddenly she felt as though she'd lost an important part of herself that day, aware nothing would be the same once they left the island.

Chapter 17

Evvie

January 2006

"Oh, Yiayiá," Evvie said with sympathy. "You left everything you knew behind. Did you ever go back?"

"Yes, but not until many years had passed," she answered. "My father went back from time to time because we still owned a third of the vineyard, but my mother never returned. Elias' mother felt betrayed and Daphne's mother fed off the opportunity. Every day was torture until we left the island."

"But you got used to Athens and made it your home. You love it here, right?" Evvie asked.

"Yes," Yiayiá Sophia said wistfully. "I came to love it very much. And it wasn't long after that when I met a young man who also had to leave his island. You could say we saw something we understood in each other from the moment we met."

"Who was that, Yiayiá?"

She threw her hands in the air, palms up. "My Spyro, of course!"

"That's right. He was from Chios. That's why we have a home there too. I want to hear all about how you met Pappou Spyro and what happened when you finally went back to the vineyard. And was it before or after you met Pappou?"

Evvie jumped from her seat and poured herself and Yiayiá Sophia a glass of water. She wanted to know everything, and she handed the glass to her great-grandmother and planted herself beside her once more. "Oh my gosh! Can we go to the vineyard? I'm going to look it up on the computer. It still exists, right?"

"Siga, siga, pethi mou," Yiayiá Sophia smiled, telling her to take it easy. She was amused by Evvie's enthusiasm, but she couldn't keep up with her rapid-fire questions. "I will tell you everything in good time. But enough for today. And yes, the vineyard still exists and thrives."

Evvie squealed with delight. "Thanks, Yiayiá." She kissed the elderly woman on the cheek and began to walk away. Pivoting with the grace her ballet training afforded her, she asked, "One more thing. Can I see that icon you said was handed down in your family? It must be so beautiful."

Yiayiá Sophia closed her eyes, pressing her fingertips against her brow. "No. It was one more thing lost to me. We were never able to find it when we unpacked our belongings." She shook her head. "Mamá and I packed it together. I know it was in the box with the other icons. But we never found it."

"That's awful! It was priceless. It must have been worth a fortune."

"What made it precious was not how much money it could be sold for. That was immaterial. We would never have parted with it. My Anastacia should have inherited it so she could have passed it to your mother and then to you."

Evvie saw a shadow of sadness come over her great-grandmother. "Do you understand what that would have meant?" the old woman asked.

"I think I'm beginning to. Yes." Evvie wanted to cry as she recalled one of her last moments with her yiayiá before she passed away. She had carefully and thoughtfully given her most sentimental pieces of jewelry to the ones she loved the most in the world.

In a velvet box, in her bedroom drawer, Evvie cherished a pair of diamond earrings, tucked safely away for an important occasion. Her yiayiá's wish was clear and she would honor it. Someday, she would wear them to her wedding and know that the spirit of her grandmother was standing beside her.

Her own mother wore a ring that was handed down through the generations—a gift that transcended time and even human mortality. The disappearance of that ring would have been devastating, just as it must have been for her pro-yiayiá to discover the icon was missing. As Evvie showered later that evening and prepared for bed, her mind drifted to back to everything she had learned that day. She couldn't resist logging on to her computer, searching for any information she could find on the Georgatos / Maryiatos Vineyard and the elusive holy heirloom.

"Where have you been," Evvie asked Nicky as he slipped into his great-grandmother's home around midnight. He'd been gone for days and was very mysterious as to his whereabouts.

His backpack dropped off his shoulder in a loud thump. "Ikaria," he answered casually.

"What's there?" she asked as if it was the last place on earth anyone would think of going.

"It's not a colony for lepers," Nicky said sardonically. "As a matter of fact, people seem to live a very long life on that island."

"So what's there that had you so intrigued?" She could think of at least five other more interesting islands to explore for a few days— Santorini, Mykonos, Samos, Rhodes, Sifnos. Friends had told her that Ikaria was also beautiful, but she'd never heard of anyone vacationing there unless they were visiting relatives.

"Our roots." He began to climb the stairs and Evvie followed him curiously.

"We don't have family from there, Nicky."

"Yes, we do. Our grandfather. Our biological grandfather," he emphasized.

"Oh, no, no, no. I don't think you should go there, and certainly, absolutely, don't tell Mom about it."

"Don't you think we should at least find out if there's any family left from that side? Heritage and family has always been something Mom has valued. But now there's DNA in us that's off limits?"

"It's not like you to be so insensitive, Nicky." Bracing her hands on her brother's shoulders, Evvie playfully shook him. "That's usually my rep to uphold," she laughed.

"You don't fool me," Nicky said, hooking his arm around his sister.

"I never could, could I?" Evvie planted a tender kiss on his cheek. Her twin had always been the one person to know what was in her heart and mind, even with the absence of words. "So, what did you find out?"

"Not much really. Jimmy was an only child. His mother returned to the island after his father passed away, but we already knew that." He pulled a photograph from his knapsack. "I looked up the Pappas name. It's pretty common, but I narrowed it down to the village where Jimmy's mother lived and discovered that he had an uncle there." Nicky lifted his shoulders. "Long gone, but his kids still live on the family land."

Evvie examined the photo. "So this would be … Jimmy's first cousin?" She pointed to an elderly man posed between two boys a little older than they were.

"And those are his grandchildren. Jimmy had never been to Ikaria. They didn't know him but they knew of him. His mother complained that she rarely heard from her son and he'd never once come to visit her on the island."

"So, we're distantly related to these people?" Evvie examined the photo for physical similarities.

"The boys would be our grandfather's second cousins. I'm not sure how it works. Would that make them our second cousins once removed?" Nicky asked.

"I'd say completely remove them from your mind because Mom won't want to know about any of this."

"She made peace with it."

Evvie rolled her eyes. "Making peace with it doesn't mean she wants to jump in and embrace these strangers. It just means she's accepted it and has moved on." She handed the picture back to her brother. "I suggest you do the same. You had your little adventure, found a few long lost relatives and you can now sleep at night knowing they don't have some weird mutation that's going to shorten our lives. Put the picture away, Nicky. You've satisfied your curiosity."

"I suppose you're right." Nicky agreed.

"Let's spend our last few days with Yiayiá Sophia before heading back to school," Evvie suggested.

And that's exactly what they did. The weather had taken a dip in temperature and Yiayiá hated the cold. Evvie and Nicky stocked up on groceries, helping her cook and freeze enough food for a number of weeks while prodding her for more stories of her youth.

As Evvie listened, she became more and more obsessed with the idea of traveling to her great-grandmother's childhood home and seeing for herself the vineyard on which she had grown up.

"Maybe someday," Yiayiá promised her.

~Yiayiá's Lemon Chicken and Potatoes~

4 chicken breasts
3 pounds of medium sized potatoes, peeled and quartered
1½ cups chicken broth
2 tablespoons olive oil
2 tablespoons butter
5-6 cloves garlic, sliced
3 large lemons
3 tablespoons dried oregano
Salt & pepper to taste

Preheat oven to 350°

Place the chicken breasts in a roasting pan. Pour the chicken broth in the pan and arrange the potatoes around the chicken. Drizzle the olive oil over the chicken and potatoes and add a pat of butter on top of each breast. Squeeze the juice of two lemons over the chicken and potatoes, reserving the last one to be sliced and added with the rest of the ingredients. Sprinkle the garlic, salt, pepper and oregano evenly and place in the oven. Bake until the chicken is tender and the potatoes are crisp, about 1½ - 2 hours.

Chapter 18

Sophia

January 2006

When the twins arrived home from visiting Sophia's yiayiá they were eager to tell their mother everything they'd learned from her. Even with the chilly temperature, they'd had a wonderful time and were happy they could help their great-grandmother while there. Sophia worried about her. She had friends who checked in on her regularly but, essentially, she was alone and the only family she had lived on another continent.

Or so Sophia thought. Evvie nearly exploded with exhilaration when she mentioned the vineyard where Yiayiá Sophia had been born and raised. "How come you never told me?" Evvie asked.

"This is the first I hear of this, Ev." Sophia looked at her daughter with skepticism. "Are you sure you understood correctly? As far as I know, she's always lived in Athens."

"I'm completely certain. Yiayiá told me the whole story while Nicky was away."

Sophia turned to her son. The three of them were seated at the kitchen table, each with a mug of steaming hot cocoa piled high with whipped cream. Nicky rolled his eyes. Pressing his fingers to his forehead, he exhaled loudly. She shifted her eyes in her daughter's direction who, in turn, stared at her brother apologetically. Sophia wondered what they were keeping from her.

"Are you going to tell me where you went off to by yourself?" Sophia questioned.

"It was nothing," Nicky said. "I just went off to explore a little and take some photographs. It was really uneventful. Evvie's story is far more interesting."

"You didn't know Yiayiá had cousins in Kefalonia on a vineyard that her father owned with his brother?" Evvie asked.

"No. Come to think of it, the only family history I ever learned about was on my pappou's side," Sophia said. "Yiayiá was an only child so I assumed there wasn't much family to learn about. Odd though," she pondered. "My grandmother is usually so forthcoming."

Sophia thought about the fascinating tale Evvie had told her of her grandmother's youth on the vineyard as she folded the laundry. It was strange how pieces of her family history seemed to elude her like a drought and then suddenly rain down on her all at once in a deluge.

Climbing the stairs, she carried the basket of clean clothing up to her childrens' bedrooms. After placing Cia and Evvie's garments in their dressers, she headed to Nicky's room.

"Boys!" she exclaimed when she opened his top drawer. All the t-shirts, which had been neatly folded, were now strewn into rumpled balls. One by one she refolded them, but when she pulled the last from the draw, she noticed a batch of photos hidden underneath the messy pile.

There were pictures all over Nicky's room—wedged into his mirror frame, pinned onto the walls, and dozens and dozens in his desk drawers. Why these were tucked in here as though they were being hidden was a mystery to her. Sophia didn't recognize the people in the photographs, except for her son of course, who was also in several, smiling along with the others. She turned one of the images over for a clue and, there, her questions were answered. Ikaria was written in her son's handwriting. Below it several names were listed and in parentheses, 'Jimmy Pappas relatives,' was written.

Sophia stared at the names, deep in thought, until Stella and Cia drew her from her thoughts.

"We're home!" Stella shouted from the front door.

"I'm upstairs," Sophia answered.

Stella had been kind enough to pick up Cia from the bus stop. Her niece was always willing to lend a hand with Cia, but lately Stella had spent more time than usual with her little one. Sophia made a mental note to discuss that with Demi. She was concerned that Stella was hiding away, as if she was retreating. But from what? Sophia wondered.

"Hi, is there anything else you need help with?" Stella asked when she found her aunt in Nicky's room.

"No, sweetie. There's nothing to be done but I do have a question," Sophia said. "Aren't you interested in any after school activities? Clubs or sports? You seem to be spending a lot of time at home."

"I'm not much of a joiner," Stella shrugged, "and I like being home, especially when it's cold outside."

Sophia didn't completely believe her answer but she didn't want to press her. "One more thing." She lifted the stack of photos. "These were hidden at the bottom of Nicky's drawer. I saw them when I was putting away his clothes. By chance do you know anything about them?"

"No, Aunt Sophia," Stella said, examining the pictures. "I've never seen them."

Evvie and Nicky only had one week left before they headed back to their universities. They had both been out all day catching up with friends but when they arrived home that evening Sophia sat Nicky down and asked him about what she had discovered in his room earlier that day.

"So that's where you went? That was the exploration you were so cryptic over?" Sophia asked after Nicky confessed that he'd searched out his biological grandfather's family.

"I'm sorry, Mom. I was curious to see if we had any relatives from that side."

"I don't know what to say. I wish you had told me."

"Evvie suggested that I didn't. She said you wouldn't be happy."

Sophia furrowed her brow. "She's right. I really don't want to dredge it all up again." Sophia shook her head. There was so much she wanted to say but she wasn't sure how to express all of her conflicting emotions. "Nicky, I did the right thing in the end for Jimmy. I didn't let him die alone and I allowed him to have a few days with a daughter he had no previous relationship with. And yes, my heart went out to him even though he'd betrayed my mother. He was a dying man and, after all, I'm not heartless. But once I had fulfilled my obligation I never wanted to look back again."

"I never meant to hurt you," Nicky said sincerely.

"I know you didn't, and I don't blame you for your curiosity." Sophia smiled softly and patted his hand. "Did you ever wish you could rewrite history? I do. I wish that Jimmy never existed and that my father, Alex, was my biological father. I'd like to wipe that portion of my history away."

"Pappou says you have to go through the rough stuff to appreciate the good times."

"Yes, he's said that many times. Although he stated it a little more eloquently than you just did," Sophia laughed. You know, in the long run, it really doesn't matter that Jimmy helped to create me because he didn't raise me, Alex did, and I couldn't imagine my life without him."

"Me neither," Nicky agreed. "Look, Mom, I met them, I got it out of my system. It's highly unlikely that we'll cross paths again. They were very nice people and greeted me warmly but they seemed more like acquaintances than family to me and I'm pretty sure they felt the same."

"Okay, Nicky." Sophia hugged her son.

"You're not mad?"

"No, of course not." Sophia shook herself from her pensive

mood. "Now I want to press Evvie for more details about my yiayiá's childhood."

"Oh, you won't have to worry about that. It's all she talks about," he laughed.

Chapter 19

Stella

April 2006

For Stella, junior year, so far, hadn't turned out the way she'd hoped it would. And with only a little over two months left, it didn't look like anything would change.

Since the night of the party she'd attended that fall, her existence at school had been just that—an existence. She had not only severed her friendship with Danielle, once she saw the conniving backstabber for who she truly was, she'd also kept her distance from the entire group they'd both hung out with. No great loss, Stella thought. They were nothing but a pack of cloned witches in pretty clothing. They could stir up as many cauldrons of brew filled with negative drama that they desired, but she was done with them. It took entirely too much energy to stand up to their nastiness or to stand by and do nothing when they aimed it at someone else. Her yiayiá often told her it was far better to have one or two truly good friends than twenty you couldn't count on or trust, and she wished she had heeded that advice sooner.

Unfortunately, she still had to endure Danielle as a lab partner. The girl tried her damnedest to make Stella's life miserable by attempting to sabotage her end of a science experiment or 'accidently' spill liquid on her clothing. But Joey always came to Stella's rescue, stopping Danielle in her nasty little tracks before too much damage had been done.

But Joey was another problem. Stella had become uneasy and self-conscious around him. He viewed her as a child, someone he had to protect, but not as a girl worthy of his attention. The chat they'd shared after the party had cemented that in her mind. What Joey wanted was a free-spirited, fearless girl who was willing to do anything without expectations. Stella knew she was not that girl. She wished she could be, but it wasn't in her nature and she simply didn't know how to be that way.

After school, life wasn't any more exciting for her either. She worked for her parents, either assisting her mother, Demi, with an upcoming event, or helping out her father, Michael, on the vineyard. Unlike the rest of her overachieving family, she had no great passion or interests and she often felt as though she was sailing along, heading into a fog without a single clue as to where she'd end up.

When Stella arrived home from school the last day before spring break had begun, the aroma of baked goods made her smile. She knew exactly what was in the oven from the unmistakable scent wafting from the kitchen. *Koulourakia*. It wouldn't be Easter without them.

"Hi, Mom, I'm home." Stella dropped her bag and books by the front door, a habit her mother constantly scolded her for, and strolled into the kitchen. "Oh, Yiayiá, I didn't know you were here. I didn't see your car."

"Pappou dropped me off to help your mother with the baking. He and your father are running errands," Soula said.

"Can I help?" Stella asked. She swung her leg over a kitchen island stool. The large granite slab held half a dozen baking sheets of elaborately shaped cookies ready to go into the oven. Many were braided but others looked like swirly 'S' shapes resembling mini works of food art.

"Of, course you can." Yiayiá handed her a container of sesame seeds. "Sprinkle them onto each cookie and we'll put them in the oven." She slid her oven mitts on and pulled out three trays of cookies from the oven. Stella filled the racks with new trays and then picked off some raw dough from the large mound on the counter, popping it into her mouth.

"Demetra, let me show you how to roll the dough so it doesn't crumble."

"Stella, Yiayiá," she corrected her grandmother. "I'm Stella."

Soula smiled blankly as though she didn't hear her and continued to expertly form the *koulourakia*. "Where's Sophia today? You girls are usually stuck together like glue."

Stella didn't respond or bother to correct her again. Her yiayiá's mind was somewhere else—in another time and place—in the past. At first it was just a slip of a name, or a forgetful moment. She'd go to a cabinet to retrieve an item but stand in front of it with the door open for several minutes, not remembering what she needed. Lately, it had become more than that. Soula would have brief lapses, believing it was decades earlier.

"Hey!" A voice called out from the foyer. "Where is everyone? No one's at my house." Evvie walked into the kitchen.

"You're home!" Stella jumped from her seat and threw her arms around her cousin.

"Yup! For a week anyway. So, where is everyone?"

"Beats me! Yiayiá was the only one here when I got home," Stella said.

"See," Soula motioned to Evvie. "It's just like I said. Stuck like glue. Come give me a hand, Sophia. The three of us will finish quicker if we work together."

Evvie and Stella looked at one another with widened eyes. Stella shook her head, indicating that she shouldn't correct her.

Soula went on and on about how Dean and his father were arguing again and how much alike they both were in their stubbornness. "You try to talk to him Sophia. He listens to you most of all."

135

"He does?" Evvie asked. She was curious about what Soula had to say about her mother and stepfather as teens.

"That boy cares about you. I know he tries not to show it, but I can tell. I know these things." She opened the oven to check the batch that was just about done. Turning, she pointed a finger at Evvie. "You don't fool me either, *koukla*. It's written in your eyes. You love him."

"When will she be back in 2006?" Evvie asked Stella.

Stella shrugged. "It could be in five minutes or five hours from now."

"It's so sad," Evvie said. "She didn't seem this bad when I left for school in January."

"I know. But at least she always goes back to a time in her life that made her happy," Stella said. "Last week she was a fourteen-year-old working in her parents' flower shop in Athens."

"We're back!" Demi called out as she and Sophia entered through the mudroom door leading to the kitchen.

"You're home!" Sophia dropped the grocery bags and scooped her daughter into her arms.

"Yes, I'm here," Evvie laughed. "You act as though you haven't seen me in years."

"It feels like it. It's been months." Sophia pulled away from her daughter just far enough to examine her. "You look good. I like the softer makeup. All that heavy black liner hides your beautiful eyes."

"Well, that didn't take long," Evvie said dryly.

"I'm not criticizing. On the contrary. You look happy. Relaxed. And very pretty."

"Thanks. Yes, things at school are going well," Evvie said.

"Who are you?" Soula asked Sophia. "And why are you in my kitchen?"

"It's me, Sophia." She pressed a gentle palm to her mother-in-laws cheek. "I'm all grown up now. And Demi is too."

"Mom, do you want to rest for a while?" Demi asked.

Soula looked at them with sudden recognition. "It happened again, didn't it?" The color drained from her face, revealing her fear.

"It's okay, Mom," Demi said in an attempt to reassure her.

"It is now. But what happens when I don't ever remember again?" Tears welled, glazing Soula's eyes before falling down her cheeks.

"We'll do the best we can to make sure that doesn't happen," Demi said. "You've done enough today. I'll make you a cup of tea and you can watch TV."

The next day, Evvie and Stella went to church. It was the day before the Orthodox Palm Sunday and a group of mostly teens and young adults had volunteered to form palm reeds into the shape of crosses for the priest to hand out the next morning. They had been doing this since they were twelve or so and looked forward to it each year along with the many other Easter week rituals.

Their hands moved expertly, twisting and bending the palms until they were perfectly formed, all the while chatting and catching up with friends. The long work table was covered in cross-shaped palms and, every once in a while, a lady from the Philoptochos, the women's group, would scoop them up, filling a large wicker basket.

"That weird looking boy keeps staring at you," Stella whispered to Evvie.

"Where?"

"At the far end of the table. Do you know him?"

"Nope," Evvie answered.

Stella giggled. "He takes the Greek thing a little far, don't you think?"

"I'd say so. He looks like a Hellenic smurf." Evvie covered her mouth and nose to stifle a snort. "A smurf with hieroglyphics," she added.

Evvie glanced over to him and quickly looked away when their eyes met. He didn't fit in with the rest of the young people here, sporting a blue mohawk that looked as stiff as the spikes on a porcupine, black jeans, Doc Martens, and a t-shirt that read, 'Born in America with Greek parts.' He also had quite a bit of ink on his arms. He was totally out of place at this little church on the East End of Long Island.

Evvie and Stella soon forgot about the strange boy, each picking up another reed and continuing to work.

"Excuse me," a voice from behind them interrupted.

Turning, Evvie was face to face with Mohawk Boy.

He stuck out his hand to shake hers. "I'm Zak. I've been trying to introduce myself to you for a while."

"To me?" Evvie pointed to herself with a surprised expression.

"I'm going to the restroom. I'll be right back," Stella said.

"Oh, no you don't." Evvie shoved her back in her seat.

What a coward, Stella thought. She just wanted to give the guy a chance. Who knows, he could turn out to be really nice. But she should have known better. Evvie never gave any guy the time of day.

"Yes, you." His lip curled in amusement. "I tried to get your attention at Christmas." Zak looked at Evvie, waiting for some form of recollection. "No? I was in the pew across from you? I waved."

Stella was glad she hadn't left. This was getting interesting. She leaned in to see her cousin's narrowed eyes assessing Zak.

"That was you?" Evvie asked. "You looked so different."

"Yeah, well, I like to change things up sometimes."

"That's an understatement."

"We go to the same school," Zak said, changing the subject.

"What school?"

"Do you go to more than one?"

Stella snorted a laugh. "I think he means Cornell."

"Really? I've never seen you there," Evvie said firmly.

"But I've seen you. I even tried to approach you once but you were otherwise occupied and didn't notice me."

"You're kind of hard to miss."

"Well, sometimes we don't see beyond what we want to," Zak said.

"Wow." Stella hung on his every word. "I don't know what you meant by that, but it sounds profound."

"Just one of life's little lessons," he said to Stella. "Sometimes I forget it myself."

"Still don't know what you're talking about but it sounds deep. I'm Stella, by the way, Evvie's cousin."

"Nice to meet you, Stella." He turned toward Evvie. "And I assume you're Evvie?"

"Yup. Evvie from Cornell."

"Well, I hope I see you around at school, Evvie from Cornell. Maybe coffee sometime?"

"Sure, maybe if our paths cross."

Zak walked away and took his seat at the other end of the table.

"Aw, he was nice," Stella said. "Did you see his eyes? I've never seen eyes that color of blue before. Do you think they're real or contact lenses?"

"No one has eyes that color. He looks possessed."

"He seems to really like you," Stella told Evvie excitedly. Why don't you give him a chance?"

"Give me a break!" Evvie scowled. "Now that one over there," Evvie nodded in the direction of a boy around Stella's age, "he's been checking you out all night, and he's adorable."

"No, he hasn't."

"Yes, he has. Why don't you go over and say hello?"

"I could never do that," Stella said. "Besides, it's been brought to my attention that you either need to put out or wait until a guy is ready to settle down, which can take decades. Too much work and heartache."

"Where on earth did you hear that? That's so not true."

"Isn't it? It kind of explains what happened with you and René and it's basically why Joey won't date me."

"You don't know that."

"Yes, I do. He told me so."

"Asshole. Why are they all such assholes?"

"I don't know," Stella sighed. "There's got to be some good ones out there."

"You're still in high school. It might take a while for the boys you meet to grow up. There's no rush, you know, Stella."

"I know." A wicked smile crossed her face. "But hurry up, Evvie. You're getting old. Before you know it, you'll be twenty-one. You have no time to waste!"

~Koulourakia~

9 cups flour
3 tablespoons baking powder
Juice and zest from 1 large orange
1 dozen large eggs
4 cups sugar
1 pound unsalted butter, softened
1 additional egg (for the glaze)
1 teaspoon water
Sesame seeds

Pre-heat oven to 350°

In a bowl, mix together the flour and baking powder. Set aside. In a separate bowl, mix together eggs, sugar, orange juice and zest. In a large bowl, cream the butter. Add the egg mixture to the butter, blending well. Mix in the flour. Form into a dough that can be worked to form shapes without sticking to your hands. If necessary, add more flour until the desired consistency is achieved. Form each cookie into small braid-like twists, circles, and S shapes. Lightly beat an egg with 1 teaspoon of water. Brush the egg mixture onto each cookie and sprinkle sesame seeds over the top. Bake for about 20 minutes. Yields approximately 120 cookies.

Chapter 20

Stella

April 2006

Yup. It's that time of year and all anyone thinks of is prom. Who will ask them? What dress will they wear? And what will be the big weekend plans afterward. Of course, Stella was only a junior, and although they had their own prom, she didn't know what the big fuss was about for a dance held in the school gym.

Still ... it would be nice to go, but if she had to watch one more promposal on the school grounds she ... she didn't know what she'd do—laugh, cry, or lose her lunch.

Turning the dial to the combination on her hallway locker, she stopped midway when a girl who occupied a locker a few feet from hers squealed. Turning, Stella groaned inwardly. A flood of rose petals poured from the girl's locker, leaving a puddle of red at her feet.

A boy holding a single rose sauntered over to her, handing her the proffered flower. "Will you accept this rose and be my date for the prom?" he asked smoothly, a charming smile revealing dazzling white teeth.

Seriously? Stella thought. Does this guy think he's on an episode of *The Bachelor*? She slammed her locker shut and was about to walk away when an arm leaned against her locker, blocking her route.

"Hey!"

"Hey, yourself, Gary," Stella said, surprised he had approached her. He was one of the popular boys and had never paid her any mind before.

"Well, that was something," he chuckled, flicking his head in the direction of the 'prom' couple. "I'm not into all that flashy shit. I like to get straight to the point. How about we go the junior prom together?"

Before she could answer, a body pushed his way between them. "She can't. She's going with me," Joey said. "Nice try, man, but back off."

Gary threw his arms up in surrender and without another word to Stella he stalked off.

"What the hell, Joey?" Stella shoved him, glaring at him with fury.

"I had a good reason for doing that." He grabbed her wrists before she could storm away.

"And what could that possibly be?"

Joey sighed deeply. Stella narrowed her eyes at him. There was something he wasn't telling her. He motioned for her to follow him into an empty classroom where they could talk privately.

"Gary only asked you because he's under the impression—*the wrong impression*—that if he takes you to the prom he'll get something out of the deal."

"Like what?" Stella asked. It took her a minute but Joey kept his eyes fixed on hers with a humorless expression. "No! Why? Where would he get an idea like that?"

"Before I tell you, promise me you won't do anything crazy."

"When do I ever do anything crazy?" Stella asked.

"True, but you might flip out on this one," Joey warned. "Danielle."

"What about her?"

"She's telling some of the guys that you're planning to have sex on prom night, and that it's been something you've talked about for a long time."

"That little bitch. How did I ever believe she was my friend?" She looked up at him in horror. "You know that's not true, right?"

"You know I'd never believe that or anything that comes out of her mouth."

"But that's what you want too. You told me so yourself." Stella wiped away a tear that was beginning to drip down her cheek. "Go. Take a girl who will do what you want. You don't need to be saddled with me." She turned the knob on the classroom door. "Thanks for the warning. I'll handle it from here."

"Wait! Stella. Listen to me. I really do want to go with you. We can help each other out. Danielle did this for revenge. She thinks you came between her and me and that's why we broke up."

"Oh? The fact that she cheated on you is my fault?" Stella threw her head back in disbelief, laughing humorlessly. "What did I have to do with that?"

"She wants me back and blames my reluctance on your hold on me."

"I have a hold on you?" Stella asked, incredulous at the thought.

"She knows I respect you and our friendship," Joey said. "She's jealous. You would be doing me a big favor. Danielle would know she had no fucking chance that I'd take her back, and all the other guys would back off if they found out you already had a date."

"But you could have your pick of any girl in this school."

"But I don't want to go with just any girl. I want to go with someone I can have fun with and talk to. I want to go with you."

"Okay." Stella stepped into Joey's space and gave his cheek a quick peck. "You're a good guy, Joey Ardis." And she meant it. He may not feel about her they way she had hoped, but he'd proven to be a good friend and that meant a lot to her.

Stella walked away with a smile on her face, but anger was seething just below the surface.

At the end of the day, Stella walked out the school doors searching out her bus when suddenly she was startled by a firm tap on her shoulder.

Turning, Stella glared icily at Danielle. "If I were you, I'd walk away now."

"Pfff! Like your threats scare me." Danielle laughed. "Word travels fast. Joey is taking *you* to prom?"

"Not that it's your business, but, yes." Stella fisted her hands on her hips. Her raised eyebrow warned Danielle not to mess with her. "Your evil, pathetic plan didn't work." Stella turned, heading toward the bus, but then she pivoted back around to face Danielle. "Stay away from me. Don't even breathe my name. If you spread one more rumor about me, I promise, you will be sorry. I was a good friend to you. But now that I know who you really are, your loss is my fortune."

Chapter 21

Evvie

April 2006

May was only a few days away, but there was still an unwelcome chill in the air. Students sported jeans and sweatshirts around the Cornell campus, even during the middle of the day when the sun should have been at its warmest. But that was springtime in the northeast, Evvie thought. Soon she'd be home working on the vineyard in the sweltering heat and loving every second of it.

But first she had to get through finals and pack up her belongings. And of course, there was Slope Day. She and a group of her friends had volunteered to work the annual campus event.

"Hey! Hey! Wait up," Evvie heard a voice call to her as she walked across campus grounds.

A blur of black and bright blue was heading toward her. "Hi! I've been hoping to run into you. Where have you been hiding?"

"Not hiding, just busy." Evvie took a good look at Zak. He had the same ridiculous hair he'd worn when she had first met him during Easter break. The black jacket was almost identical to the one she wore and his Greek flag t-shirt was switched out for a Linkin Park 'Numb' t-shirt with some morose lyrics quoted across his chest.

"Do you want to grab a bite to eat?" Zak asked.

"No, thanks. Not hungry."

"Coffee then. I believe you agreed to if our paths ever crossed."

A tiny groan rumbled from her throat. "Okay, but it has to be quick. I really need to study for finals."

Together they walked in near silence until they reached the campus café. Evvie had no time for this and she couldn't imagine what this strange boy wanted with her.

"What would you like?" Zak asked as they approached the counter.

"French vanilla. Light and sweet," Evvie said. "Thank you."

Zak ordered a black coffee with one sugar for himself and then spotted an empty table at the far end of the café.

"You know," he started, "last year I noticed you on campus pretty often. Most of the time you'd be walking in the direction I was coming from."

"I don't remember seeing you." Evvie's eyes gazed up at his prickly blue hair. "And you're kind of hard to miss."

"Last year my hair was black." He ran his fingers over the top of his stiff mane. "And it wasn't in this style."

"Oh."

He looked at her sheepishly. "I change it up a lot."

"When I tried to get your attention in church at Christmas I had just dyed it blond. What a surprise when I saw you in my hometown—in my own church! Who would have thought?"

"I recall. I had no idea who you were. I asked my cousin, Kristos if he knew you."

"Nope. I'd been hoping for a chance to speak to you for a long time. There was something about you from the moment I saw you. I guess it was that Greek connection."

"The Greek connection," Evvie said dryly. "That's what drew you to me?"

"Not at first, since I didn't know. But it makes sense, right?"

"Not really," Evvie shrugged. "There has to be something more in common with someone for a connection to exist other than just being Greek."

"We have the same jacket," he teased her. "Come on. Lighten up and give me a chance. I'm just trying to get to know you. Something tells me we might have more in common than you think."

Relenting, Evvie asked, "What would you like to know?"

"Let's start with your major."

"Oenology. That's the study of—"

"Winemaking," Zak cut her off. "I know."

Evvie was curiously surprised. She usually had to explain. "What about you?"

"Computer science and game design with a minor in fine arts."

"Impressive."

"Not really. It's what I love to do."

"Now that, I understand," Evvie said. And for the first time since she had agreed to coffee, she made eye contact with him for more than a fleeting glance.

"Next question," Zak continued. "What's your favorite Greek food?"

Evvie leaned back in her chair and covered her face with her hands. "Back to that? Let's make a pact. No Greek related questions for the rest of this afternoon."

"What *can* we talk about?" he asked.

"Anything but that. Are you going to Slope Day?" Evvie asked. "I'm volunteering at the SlopeFest."

"I don't know. I wasn't planning on it. Did you see the talent this year?" Zak pulled a face. "Not my taste in music."

"Not everyone likes that stuff." Evvie pointed to his Linkin Park t-shirt.

"You have something against great rock bands?"

"Great is an overstatement," Evvie argued. "Why those words?" she asked, pulling his jacket open to read what it said.

"That's *my* off-limits subject." He sipped his coffee, hiding his face behind the oversized mug. "What's your job at SlopeFest?"

"I'm going to be at the Gatorade ring toss booth for about an hour or so and then I'm switching to the henna station." Evvie shot her head up. "Hey! I have an idea. You must be a good artist, right? We could use face painting volunteers."

"Uh, I don't know," he said with hesitation.

"Please? You'll be right next to my henna station. If you agree I'll even let you ask me all the Greek related questions you want."

"Great! It's a date," Zak grinned.

"More like, it's a deal," Evvie corrected him.

When Evvie returned to her dorm, she kicked off her shoes and threw herself onto her bed. She sure hoped 'Greek Boy' didn't get the wrong idea. Part of her job was to recruit volunteers for Slope Day. Somehow, she ended up giving him the idea they would spend the day together. He was nice enough, friendly and, although he seemed open, there was something mysterious about him. She'd be lying to herself if she didn't admit she wanted to know what was underneath the layers, but not curious enough to get too involved. One thing was for sure, he was certainly persistent.

"Whoo hoo! You win!" Evvie said to a moppy-haired co-ed in a Slope Day t-shirt that read, 'It's downhill from here.' He had successfully landed three rings around the Gatorade bottles that were symmetrically organized and evenly spaced for the game Evvie was manning.

Ho Plaza was buzzing with energy as college students stuffed their faces with nachos and chips, cotton candy and sno-cones. Friends cheered each other on, competing in various games and pranks as they celebrated the end of the semester, even though finals still loomed over their heads.

Evvie handed the winner his prize before his friends pulled him to the next game station.

"I hope my prize will be better than that one."

Evvie looked up to see Zak standing in front of her.

"If you land all three rings over a bottle, then you can choose from those prizes." Evvie pointed to the rack behind her.

"Six rings and you go to the concert with me." Zak wagered.

"You said you hated the music."

"I'll suffer for the cause." His eyes raked her from head to toe.

Evvie, like the rest of the volunteers, wore an orange t-shirt with the letters 'SOS' written on it. With her cutoff jean shorts and her tee knotted at the waist, it didn't escape Evvie that Zak was checking her out.

"Nine rings," she said, confident there was no way his aim was that keen.

Zak's lips quivered, attempting to hold back a cocky grin as he took the handful of rings from her.

"Oh, and here's your volunteer shirt." Evvie bent down to retrieve from a bin a shirt identical to the one she had on. She tossed it to him.

"No, no, no. I'm not wearing that."

"Yeah, you are." She crossed her arms over her chest. "T-shirt, face painting and nine rings. That's my final offer."

Grunting, he pulled his own t-shirt over his head and slipped on the one she gave him. "I look like an idiot."

"Thank you," Evvie said, giving his shoulder a punch. "Then I must look like one too."

He was worried about looking like an idiot? With that peacock hair and those possessed, fake blue eyes? And the tattoos! She had noticed the ones on his arms before, but when he pulled his shirt off, well, she was completely at a loss for words. His body was scrawled with Hellenic-inspired ink. This boy gave Greek pride a whole new meaning.

For someone who was surrounded by male cousins and a brother of her own, Evvie should know better than to challenge men in any sort of competition. Zak's aim was impeccable, so she admirably submitted to her defeat and was stuck with weird Greek Boy for the rest of the day. She finished her shift at the ring toss and had a quick break before working the henna booth. Suggesting they get something to eat when Evvie's stomach began to rumble, she led him to the food stands.

"How about a beer," Zak asked.

"I hate beer. I'm more of a wine drinker."

"Of course you are. Shocking!" he mocked her.

"Why don't you stand in that ridiculously long beer line while I get the nachos," Evvie offered.

Zak reached into his pocket and handed Evvie money, but she waved it off.

"No, I got it, thanks."

"So, what's with the tattoos, if you don't mind me asking?"

They settled on an empty spot on the lawn and stretched out.

Zak laughed. "Not all of them are real. I drew most of them on myself for Greek Independence Day on a whim and, like the hairstyle, I decided to keep them."

"But if they're not real, how did you manage to get them to last from March?" Evvie asked. "And how did you draw so expertly on yourself?"

"I drew the designs and created stencils. I reapply them when they begin to wear off."

"So, which ones are real?" Evvie tugged at the neck of his t-shirt, exposing the Greek key design that framed his collarbone and extended to the top of his shoulders where the head of a Greek warrior sat on each side. "This one?"

"Nope. That's a stencil."

"Wow! Amazing. Can I see the one on your back? I only got a glimpse."

Zak turned his back to her, lifting his shirt and craning his neck around. Evvie ran her hand over the image and she felt him shiver as their skin made contact. She lifted her eyes slowly to meet his.

"If this isn't permanent then you need to paint this onto a canvas," she told him.

The nineteenth century soldier stood proudly, his uniform battered and ragged from battle. In one hand he held an icon of the *Theotokos* – the mother of God. In his other hand he waved the Greek flag above his head in triumph. 'Freedom or death,' written in Greek completed the message.

"Thanks, I never thought about it."

"I mean it. You're very talented, Zak. Hey! Maybe you should create a Greek coloring book for children."

"Now you're mocking me."

"Maybe a little." She rolled down his shirt. "But not about how talented you are. I meant that."

"Thanks." Zak scooped a glob of gooey, orange cheese onto a tortilla chip and handed it to Evvie. A tiny dollop lingered on the corner of her mouth after she greedily ate it. He wiped it away with his finger and her eyes flew up to his and held them. The gesture seemed a little intimate to her. Zak must have sensed her uneasiness and quickly broke eye contact, dropping his hand from her face.

"Messy but delicious," Zak said casually before taking a pull from his beer.

"What about the one over your chest?" Evvie asked, reverting back to his ink. "I only saw it for a second when you changed your shirt, but it caught my eye."

Zak didn't say a word. His face was unreadable, but he lifted the shirt for Evvie to take a closer look.

On the left side of his chest, over Zak's heart, a beautiful angel stood. A boy knelt at her feet, his head hung low, as she enveloped him in her loving arms.

Of all the ink he'd drawn, this one was truly a masterpiece. Evvie instinctively knew without asking that this image was, in his heart as well as his body, indelible.

The halo above the angel's head was comprised of the Greek word *Elpida*—hope. But, oddly, this image didn't seem hopeful at all. It was ethereal, hauntingly beautiful, but also sad. Very, very sad. And what she saw was despair rather than hope in the little she could see of the boy's face.

"This one is real," Zak whispered.

Evvie didn't press for answers. The pained expression on his face and the tone in his voice told her enough. They really didn't know each other and they weren't acquainted enough for her to pry.

Zak flipped open his phone to look at the hour. "I think it's face painting time." Tenting his fingers, he wiggled them in mischief. "I think I'll take you for my first victim."

"Hmm. Okay, Hellas. But only if I approve of what you'll turn me into."

"What did you call me?"

"Hellas! Unless you'd like Greek Boy better." She raised her eyebrows in challenge.

"You'll pay for that. I'll find a way."

Thirty minutes later, unbeknownst to Evvie, her face was made up like the ancient Greek monster, Medusa. Green, venomous snakes framed her hideous, mustard-colored face and the red lining around her eyes made her look even more repulsive.

Zak handed her a mirror and asked her how she liked his artwork.

"You couldn't make me a dainty butterfly? I'm going to scare small children."

"No worries!" Zak laughed. "There isn't a child around for miles."

Evvie applied henna to dozens of hands for the next two hours, rocking her Medusa makeup. Meanwhile Zak's table was busy with requests once they saw what he was capable of.

His intensity and focus as he drew was mesmerizing and Evvie couldn't help but stare in fascination. From Sonic the Hedgehog and Spongebob Squarepants to skulls and pretty fairies, each facial creation was beyond her expectations or imagination, as though magic flowed from the tips of his fingers. The Cornell mascot bear blew Evvie's mind—the fur, the dimension and the round, deep-set eyes. How did he do it?

"I think that's about it for me," Zak said. "How about we head over to the concert?"

"What?" Evvie blinked in surprise. "And subject yourself to *that* music?" she asked sardonically.

"I'm trying to be open minded." Zak said.

"*Páme, Hellás,*" Evvie said.

"And the girl does speak Greek!" Zak pumped his fist in the air.

Evvie laughed. "It was one word," she said. "Not a big deal."

Zak couldn't take his eyes off the girl standing beside him at the concert. Evvie admitted rap music was not something she normally enjoyed either, but the crowd really got into it and it became contagious.

Evvie had wiped the Medusa artwork off her face before they left for the concert and, as much as he'd admired his handy work, he much preferred to see her in her natural state. She was a hard girl to read, but from the moment he'd laid eyes on her, he had felt a connection that was deeper than simple attraction. There was something that bonded them, something neither of them were aware of yet, but he relished in the thought of discovery. If only Evvie wasn't full of mixed signals. A wall seemed to be between them, Zak thought. But oh, he sighed, in those tiny moments when her defenses were down, he could almost taste the possibilities.

"He's really good!" Evvie shouted in Zak's ear.

He nodded in agreement. "Better than I expected him to be, considering it's not my choice of music and all." But then Ben Folds began to play a song that had the crowd going wild and Zak connected with the lyrics. Not because of the enthusiasm or the roar surrounding him. Not because it was the artist's biggest hit, but because like the man singing his soul to the masses, he felt like 'The Luckiest.' Lucky to have met this girl who, from the first moment he saw her, he knew in his bones was the one meant for him.

Staring at Evvie's profile as her attention was fixed on the stage, Zak only had eyes for her. Rather than the deadpan expression she usually displayed around him, she was smiling and uninhibitedly singing along with the music.

Turning, she faced him. "What?" she asked.

"Nothing," he said with a slanted grin. "I just like seeing you let loose and having some fun. Shit!" Zak yelled. A body from behind slammed into him, propelling him forward and crashing into Evvie. The beer he was holding spilled down the front of her shirt. Grabbing her by the waist, Zak pulled her close to him, keeping her from bumping into the person next to her.

"I'm sorry. I didn't mean to drench you in beer."

"It's only a little. I'm fine," Evvie said.

Zak kept his arm around her. He could feel his heart quicken as he held her. Gently, he lifted her chin, urging her to make eye contact with him, but just when their eyes connected she swiftly looked away.

"I think we should go. It's getting too crowded," she said.

"Sure. I'll walk you back to your dorm."

Evvie spent the next few days holed up in her room cramming for finals. She needed fresh air and sun, and since it had finally decided to warm up and make an appearance after a few days of clouds and drizzle, Evvie followed suit and crawled out from the piles of notes sprawled across her bed.

The top of the hill at Libe Slope was a favorite spot amongst students to gather or quietly take in the view on their own. Evvie abandoned her books, pulled her iPod from her bag and flung a quilted blanket over her shoulder.

The heat from the sun warming Evvie's body was a welcome change from the stale air in her room, and she savored the feel of it on her skin as she relaxed back onto the quilt. Few people were on the hill and, right now, she was grateful for the solitude and the songs on her playlist.

"Hey! What are you listening to?" Zak plopped himself beside her, startling her from her reverie.

With a groan, she paused her iPod and pulled out her earbuds. "What are you doing here? Are you stalking me?"

"Snarky Evvie is back," Zak teased.

"Snarky? Who says that?"

"Would you rather I said bitchy?"

"I'd rather you get off my blanket and let me lie here alone the way I was hoping to." Evvie laid back down, reinserted her earbuds and closed her eyes. She protested when Zak pulled one from her ear and inserted it into his own, laying down beside her.

"I'll be quiet, I promise," he said. "Lifehouse?"

"Yes. 'You and me.'"

"I like the lyrics."

"Shh! You said you'd be quiet," Evvie complained.

"I will." Zak turned on his side and propped himself up on his elbow. "Evvie, when we get back home for the summer would you hang out with me?"

Evvie, losing her patience with the constant interruptions from the peace she'd hoped for, yanked the earphone from the jack. "I'm not sure I'll be around much. I have a lot going on this summer." She wished that Stella were a few years older so she could take him off her hands. She seemed to be fascinated by Zak, and Evvie was sure that

Stella would be more than happy to spend her time with him.

Before he could say another word or make another attempt to see her again, she pushed the jack back into the iPod, searched for a song and handed him one of the earbuds. "Here. I think this is more your taste."

"Black Sabbath?" He looked at her in amusement. "You have Black Sabbath on your playlist?"

"Let's just say my parents exposed me to all kinds of music. This one is from the rebel years. When pissing off a father was the goal." She was speaking of her stepfather, Dean, who, at that time, would do anything to incite his father's ire. "I was told there was a lot of yelling to 'turn down the noise,' or 'don't bring those devil records into my house,'" Evvie said, imitating Stavros' accent.

"I've been known to do that a time or two," Zak said, raising an eyebrow. "Piss off my father."

"What did he say about that?" Evvie asked, pointing to his unconventional hairstyle.

Zak cleared his throat and in his best imitation of his father's thick, Greek accent, he mimicked, "'Why would you want to show yourself like a half bald, blue porcupine?'" He threw his hands up as his father would and they both laughed. "Then he would start to mutter in Greek and walk away. But if that wasn't enough, you should have seen my mom when she saw my first tattoo."

"Why? What did she say?"

"It was more like what she did," Zak said. "She started to cry. I didn't know if it was because of what I had tattooed on myself or because she was upset with me. I soon found out when she began making the sign of the cross and recited a prayer over me. 'Branding your body is against the laws of the church,' she scolded me."

"And I thought I had it bad when my mother got on my case for wearing too much black makeup and nail polish." Evvie checked the time on her phone. "Relaxation time is over. I really have to get back and hit the books. I've got a huge final tomorrow."

She rose and gathered her belongings. Zak picked up the blanket, folded it and draped it over his arm. "Sorry I cut into your quiet time," he said as they walked across campus.

"It's fine. Your stories kept my mind off the million things I still have to do."

When they reached her building, she took the blanket from him and wished him a good summer. She could see the disappointment in his eyes and the slight slump in his shoulders. Evvie really didn't have time for this right now.

Later that evening, after hours of studying for her Organic Chemistry final, Evvie's growling stomach signaled for her to leave the 'abyss' she'd crawled into and venture out to find something to eat. She flipped open her phone when it rang and saw on the display that it was her mother.

"Hi, Mom."

"You sound tired."

"I am. I've been studying non-stop."

"Take a break. Are you eating?"

Evvie shook her head. What was it with Greek mothers and food? "I'm heading over to get something to eat now."

"Good. Do you need me to come up there and help you pack up?" Sophia asked.

"Nope. What little I'm keeping up here is going into storage. It's all arranged."

"We're planning a party for the weekend after you get home to welcome all of you kids back."

"Sounds great. It will be good to see everyone."

"Also, the church is having another gathering for the college students. You should go," Sophia suggested. "You never know who you might meet, she said in an upbeat sing-song voice.

Evvie rolled her eyes.

"Now before you make a face at me—"

"I'm not, Mom," Evvie lied. "But there's no need for me to hunt down a Greek at a meet-and-greet. I've already met one here and I'll be bringing him to the party."

"Really! How come you didn't tell me about him? Who is he? How long have you been dating?"

"It's new, Mom. Not much to tell. His name is Zak."

Chapter 22

Stella

May 2006

Stella stood in front of her full-length mirror surrounded by her mother, Yiayiá, Sophia, and Evvie, all of whom were making a huge fuss over her. The two-piece, jewel toned gown she'd chosen reflected the Arabian Nights prom theme and was stunning against Stella's naturally Mediterranean-kissed complexion.

She had no need for a necklace since the sleeveless, one-shouldered, tangerine top cut across her collarbone, but her hair, professionally coiffed, secured the intricate curls and braids with delicate jeweled pins.

A tease of belly showed between the elegantly exotic top and the full-length magenta skirt. Slits high enough on the sides to showcase her matching tangerine stiletto sandals snaked up her legs as if they were asps being charmed from their baskets.

"You look beautiful," Soula said, tears rimming her eyes. "I remember your mother's prom like it was yesterday." She reached over to squeeze Demi's hand. "And now, here we are. The years fly by too quickly."

"I'm so happy you're here, Yiayiá." Stella wrapped her arms around her grandmother, kissing her cheek.

"Where else would I be?"

But Stella didn't answer. She'd been granted a precious gift, and at any moment, her yiayiá might be gone—in some other place and time when Stella hadn't yet existed.

"He's a very nice, young man, your date," Sophia said. "I'm sure you'll have a wonderful time."

A ringing noise interrupted them.

"That's the doorbell!" Demi jumped up. "I'll get it." Demi left the room, followed by her mother and Sophia.

"Now that we're alone," Evvie said, cocking an eyebrow. "Don't let that little bitch get to you if she tries to do anything to upset you. Just ignore her. She's not worth it."

"Thanks. I'll try. It's just hard for me because I get intimidated. Especially since I know Joey isn't interested in me." Disappointment was written all over her face. "He's only taking me as a friend. Danielle will see right through that."

"I wouldn't be so sure about Joey's feelings. And what do you care about what Danielle thinks? Stop dwelling on a girl unworthy of your friendship and just have some fun."

Stella nodded and hugged her cousin in appreciation. Arm in arm, the girls headed downstairs.

When Stella and Joey walked into the high school gym, they felt as though they had been being transported into an enchanting fairytale. The prom committee, along with the art department, had performed magic. The school's cinder block walls were transformed with paint and jewels into an elaborate Moroccan backdrop. Golden minarets, white marble cupolas and large archways with detailed arabesques lent authenticity to the Arabian themed architecture. Many of the walls were textured with mosaics the students had made from broken china, and a faux, Persian carpet runway led to the large entryway.

Strands of jewels hung from layers and layers of tulle, hiding the industrial bareness of the ceiling. In lieu of balloons, glittering palm trees lined the dance floor and lantern centerpieces illuminated the tables.

"I should call you 'Jasmine' tonight," Joey joked. "You fit in perfectly here."

"That was the idea," Stella said. "But this is beyond anything I ever expected!"

"Only equal to how incredible you look tonight."

Stella was beginning to believe he might mean it. She'd seen the look on his face when she came down the staircase. When he whispered in her ear how beautiful she looked, a tingle ran through her entire being.

"Dance?" Joey asked.

"Love to!"

They moved to 'Hips Don't Lie,' until the DJ mixed in their prom song, 'A Whole New World.'

Stella began to walk off the dance floor, assuming Joey wouldn't slow dance with her, but he clasped onto her wrist before she could get away.

"Where are you going?"

"I just thought—I didn't think you'd want to—" But before she could finish her sentence, he pulled her into his arms for a slow dance.

With her four-inch heels, she was close to his height, but she avoided eye contact, preferring to keep her head turned away from him. Other couples were kissing as they swayed to the music, but Joey kept his hands chastely on her waist, and Stella kept her lips from getting close to his.

"Aren't the two of you sickeningly adorable," Danielle sneered as she came up beside them.

Stella stiffened and Joey must have felt her shrink into him because he kept a firm grip on her.

"We'll take the adorable and we'll leave the sick to you," Joey said undeterred. He took Stella's hand and escorted her off the dance floor.

They walked to the courtyard. That, too, was decorated ornately.

Three brightly colored tents with plush cushions needed only a sultan and a harem to complete the décor.

"Stay here. I'm going to make us a plate of food," Joey said.

A few minutes later, he came back with two plates piled with an assortment of appetizers and hot food. They chatted while feasting and Stella felt more at ease than she had all night.

"All I need is a bunch of grapes to feed you, Master," she joked.

"I think I know of a place where we can get all the grapes we want."

"Don't I know it!" Stella laughed. "Here. Right now, you'll have to settle for this olive instead." Again, she felt that same tingle as her fingers touched his lips. Vulnerable, caramel eyes met stormy, blue ones and held each other entranced. The seconds felt like an eternity. Stella wanted to look away but this time she couldn't. Slowly, Joey leaned in, and Stella's heart pounded so loudly that she was sure he could hear each beat.

When his lips made contact with hers, Stella thought she might pass out. Everything in front of her went black. She saw nothing, heard nothing, and the only sensation her body was aware of was the feel of him and what his lips on hers did to her. She had dreamed of this kiss and when the contact broke she wanted to protest.

"You make it difficult for me to resist you," Joey said, threading her fingers through his.

"So why do you?" She looked down at their interlocked hands.

"Because it's the right thing to do. And I always want to do right by you."

"You don't think I'm old enough to decide that for myself?"

"I do. But you deserve someone better than me with more than what I have to offer you." He cocked his head toward the gym. "Ready to go back inside?"

Later, when it was time to go home, Stella and Joey walked back to the car. Before he could turn the ignition, Stella stopped him.

"Joey, I've been thinking about what you said before and I don't know why you'd say such a thing about yourself. You're kind and sweet and not at all like some of the other guys at school. Anyone would be lucky to have you."

"You're wrong. I'm no different than anyone else."

"I get it, Joey. Loud and clear. You don't like me the way I hoped you would, or think of me like the other girls you date." Stella's emotions ran between embarrassment, hurt and anger. "I appreciate you taking me tonight but you don't need to treat me like a child."

"You have it all wrong, Stella. I care for you too much." He leaned back on the headrest, looking up through the sunroof. "It's all about timing. You know?"

"No! I don't."

"We've gone over this before." Joey kept his eyes fixed on the view from his window. "You'll only end up hurt."

"And you think this doesn't hurt?" she asked.

"Listen, if we met, let's say, five years out of college, it would be a different story. And, I hope, when that day comes, we meet up again and, who knows?"

"So ten years from now you'll consider going out with me?" Stella rubbed her forehead, trying to make sense of his crazy logic.

"I won't only consider it. I'll pray you're available and jump on it. But for now, as much as I'd like to, I won't do anything that would hurt or disrespect you."

"But you don't mind hurting and disrespecting other girls?" Stella said flatly.

Joey huffed out a breath. "No," he bit out. "What I do with other like-minded girls is understood between them and me that it is purely physical." He started up the engine and began to drive. The silence was deafening, if not unbearable.

When they arrived at Stella's home, Joey reached for his car door to get out and come around to open hers but Stella stopped him.

"No need," she said, as she opened the door herself.

Before she got out, she turned to him and placed a hand on his arm. "You really are a sweet guy, Joey. Don't let anyone tell you otherwise. Thank you for a really nice time."

Stella didn't look back as she strode up the walkway to her front door. She didn't dare. Joey might have seen the glistening of the tears on her face reflecting from the porch lights.

*"We delight in the beauty of the butterfly, but rarely admit the changes
it has gone through to achieve that beauty."*

—Maya Angelou

Chapter 23

Evvie

June 2006

Evvie and Stella had been given a 'To Do' list by their mothers on the day of the party. They inflated colorful pool tubes, set baskets of beach towels down near each side of the diving board, and strung lights along the porch overhang.

The boys had gone down to the vineyard storage room and come back with a portable dance floor to assemble. And Cia wandered from person to person asking what she could do to help.

"Nothing until you wash those sticky hands," Evvie told her.

The child was working a Blow Pop down to the stick and had managed to get the blue raspberry coloring all over her face and hands.

"Then can I help?" Cia asked.

"Absolutely. Mom has a few things she wants Stella and me to pick up. You can come with us if you'd like to," Evvie said, pointing to the house. "Now go. We're leaving in five minutes."

"Do you want me to come in and help you?" Stella asked.

"Nope!" Cia answered cheerfully. "I can do it myself. I'm seven now!"

The vineyard had closed to the public by six o'clock that evening and, although there was a wedding at the Carriage House, Demi had assigned her assistant and a competent crew to handle the event.

Guests of all ages seemed to pour in by the dozen. The Greek weather gods had sprinkled fortune over Long Island, granting a warm, sunny day to make the festivities perfect. Children swam in the heated, inground pool, men hovered around the outdoor bar, and the teens were playing volleyball or bopping about on the dance floor.

"Where's your guy from school?" Dean asked, smirking. "Your mom has been waiting to meet him."

"He's not *my guy*," Evvie corrected her stepfather. "But he'll be here soon."

"I need to re-fill the ice buckets," Dean said, grabbing them off the bar.

"I can do it." Evvie took the buckets from him and headed inside the house. She filled them with fresh ice and was about to head back outside when the doorbell rang. With all the noise and commotion in the back, she assumed any newcomers would have the sense to head directly there.

"Hey," Evvie said when she opened the door to find Zak standing on the front porch with a tray of pastries his mother had baked.

"Hey! Thanks for inviting me." Awkwardly, he hugged her, almost dropping the platter.

"I got it," Evvie said.

"My mom made them."

"I'll give them to my—oh! Here she comes. Mom!" Evvie waved her over. "Mom, I'd like you to meet Zak. He's the Greek boy I met at school."

"Zak, it's nice to meet you," Sophia said. Her mother had the smile you wear when smiling for the camera a little too long.

Evvie tried to conceal the smirk on her face as she watched her mother take in Zak's appearance.

"Why don't you kids go out and enjoy the party."

"Thank you," Zak said, politely. "It's nice to meet you, Mrs. Papadakis."

"You too, Zak."

No one else seemed put off by Zak's appearance. He immediately clicked with Nicky, Kristos and Paul. The four of them teamed up with RJ and Adam for a volleyball match against a group of girls, and after that they hit the dance floor.

When the DJ switched from Sean Paul's 'Temperature' to 'Zorba the Greek' the insanity began. When the music shifted from one traditional Greek song to another, the competition became fierce to outdo one another. Ultimately, it became a battle of jumps and kicks between Kristos, Zak and another boy they knew from youth group.

Stavros went wild with excitement, joining his grandson and the others on the dance floor. With a white napkin in hand, he took the lead, swinging it high above his head in rhythm with the song.

"That's enough showing off," Michael teased the boys. "Let the old men have a crack at it," he said, as he, Dean and Alex joined his father-in-law. At least a half dozen other men jumped in, bracing each other arm to shoulder, each taking a turn leading with the white linen.

Evvie and Stella cleared some tables off and took the empty plates into the house.

"I wish you had seen my mother's face when I introduced her to Zak," Evvie said, placing the dishes in the sink. "I don't think he's exactly the kind of Greek boy she had in mind for me."

"You didn't invite him here just to make a point to Aunt Sophia, did you. He's a really nice guy, Evvie," Stella said.

"I'm not saying he's not," Evvie defended. "Let's just say, I don't think my mom will be on my back anymore."

Stella's eyes grew wide and Evvie turned to see what they were trained on. Evvie froze when she saw Zak emerge from the hallway.

"Is it true?" Zak moved in closer to her.

"Is what true?"

"Don't play with me, Evvie."

Stella pointed to the door. "I think they need me outside." She was gone in an instant.

"Is it true that you only asked me here because you thought your mother wouldn't approve of me?"

Evvie didn't know what to say. She nervously picked at her nail polish.

"I guess I have my answer," Zak bit out. He drew in a deep breath and closed his eyes. When he opened them, his stare could have frosted a pot of boiling water. "I liked you, but you never gave me a chance. Even through your sarcasm and your unapproachable attitude, I saw something in you I connected with. Something I felt was special."

"I—" Evvie was cut off when Zak held his hand up for her to stop.

"The one thing I didn't think you were was cruel. But I was wrong. You are. Cruel. I would never use anyone the way you just used me."

Evvie shook her head slowly. She felt awful and the lump in her throat was almost as constricting as the tightness in her chest.

"Please thank your parents for me." He turned and walked toward the hall leading to the front door.

Evvie ran up to her room. She wanted to be alone and wished the party was over. What had she done? She felt like the worst person in the world. Again. Why did she do these things? Somehow, she needed to make this up to Zak, but she had no idea how.

Chapter 24

Evvie

September 2006

The Campus at Cornell University was in full swing. Students were already knee deep in assignments and Evvie was excited for her junior year. Finally, all her prerequisites were out of the way and she would be taking the classes she'd longed to take.

She'd stayed home for the summer, working with her Uncle Michael, even when almost everyone else in the family headed to Greece for a month. After a year of badgering him to produce their own sparkling wine in the authentic *méthode champenoise*, Michael finally relented, partially anyway, and allowed her to plant the grape-vines needed to make the traditional blend. The Angelidis Vineyard already grew Chardonnay and Pinot Noir varieties, but they had never planted the Pinot Meunier to complete the trio of grapes used to make champagne.

Still, her uncle had not yet committed to investing the money for the equipment required to produce, bottle and age the sparkling wine, which called for different conditions than the still wine they currently produced. Evvie had been doling out her plan in morsels, hoping he would agree bit by bit if she didn't hit him with it all at one time. But she really pushed the limits when she told him everything she had in mind, and she only hoped she hadn't blown the whole idea out of the water.

"You want to do what?!" Michael asked, when Evvie said she wanted to mimic the conditions of the natural chalk caves she'd seen in Épernay. "And how on earth are we going to do that here?"

"I'm not sure yet. I think I might make that my school research project," she told him. "If we could build our own chalk cave in one of the cellars, or at least create the same conditions temperature and humidity-wise, then it would make all the difference in the quality of the final product."

"I'm not making any promises. I'll take a look at your research and look into the costs."

"Thank you, thank you, thank you!" She leapt toward him, giving him an enthusiastic hug.

Michael laughed. "That's not a yes," he warned.

"But it's as good as one," Evvie said, as she continued tending to the vines. "You'll see!"

Evvie had returned to school with a vengeance, ready to soak in and absorb everything she could. She would drive her professors insane with questions if that is what it took to discover everything she wanted to know.

What she didn't want were any kind of distractions. But she had them all the same. She harbored guilt over what had happened with Zak at her home. She had tried to call him a number of times, but the calls went straight to voicemail. Her texts also went unanswered. Evvie was nervous of running into him on campus, but she wanted the chance to apologize. The conversation she had with her pro-yiayiá kept playing over in her head.

Do you think I have Irini's bad blood running through me? I'm not the nicest person.

Her great-grandmother assured her it wasn't true, but she kept doing things to prove her wrong.

Maybe the problem is that you love too much.

Love hurts, Evvie thought. She'd do anything for her family. That she knew without hesitation, but the price she'd paid each time she lost someone important to her was too painful to bear.

"You need to get your butt off the chair and your eyes away from the computer before you go blind," Evvie's roommate, Dana, said, dragging her from her seat. "We're going out. There's a big party tonight and you're going with me."

Evvie opened her mouth to protest, but Dana waved her pointed finger at Evvie. "I'm not giving you a choice."

Evvie groaned. "I guess I could use a break."

She changed into a pair of black skinny jeans, a gray, form-fitting sweater with bell sleeves and over-the-knee, black leather boots. Her skin still retained the sun-kissed tan from working in the vineyard all summer, and the only makeup she wore was a dark, berry lip stain and a coat of mascara.

Dana and Evvie were greeted at the door by ear-splitting music and red Solo cups filled with beer. "Hey, Kevin! Do you know my roommate, Evvie?"

"No, I don't think we've ever met." Kevin pointed to an archway that led to another room. "Go through there. Jessie, Ryan and Dylan are in the back playing beer pong.

They pushed their way through the crowd, stopping to say hello to other friends and partygoers along the way until they made it to a table surrounded by observers watching a competitive game played with party cups, beer and ping-pong balls.

"I'm out," one of the boys said. "Someone take my place."

"Hey, Ryan!" Dana shouted over the music, motioning him over.

"Dana! Where have you been hiding? I've barely seen you since we've gotten back."

"I know! My classes are killing me and we're only in the first couple of weeks." Dana planted her hands on Evvie's shoulders, turning her attention away from the drunken pong players. "This is my roommate, Evvie."

Before he could respond, Dylan, another one of Dana's friends, jumped between them, sloshing beer onto Evvie's boots. "Dana, girl! Let's get you a drink."

"Why don't I just drink a little of yours? It looks like you've had more than enough already."

Ryan walked away and came back a moment later with a pile of napkins. "There's an empty seat over there," Ryan said, pointing by a large window. "Sit down and I'll dry the beer off before it ruins the leather."

Evvie looked at this boy kneeling before her cleaning her boots. It was a sweet thing to do considering he didn't know her at all. He was sort of cute in his own way. Not the type she would normally have been attracted to, but there was something endearing about him.

"You really didn't have to do that," Evvie said. "It was very nice of you."

"It was the least I could do," Ryan said, flicking his platinum hair off his forehead when he looked up at her. "After all, it was my drunken buddy who spilled it on you."

"I think they're fine now. Thanks."

"Can I get you a drink?" he asked.

"Maybe a Coke?"

"Not much of a drinker?"

Evvie laughed. "Oh, I drink enough. I live on a vineyard and I'm studying oenology—winemaking," she clarified before he had a chance to ask.

"That's an actual major?" He seemed astounded.

"Yes." She laughed at the expression on his face.

"So, let me understand this. You make and taste wine in class?"

"Before you think about switching your major, the answer is no. The classes are more scientifically based."

"Bummer." He handed her a Coke from inside a cooler.

"I love what I do. What about you?" she asked, as they stepped outside. "The fresh air feels great. What are you studying?"

"Computer science—IT, software engineering. You know all that geek stuff that keeps me inside."

"Geek, huh? You don't look like much of a geek to me."

Yeah, he was fair, Evvie observed, looking him over, but he was solidly built and she was sure he worked out when he wasn't glued to his computer.

"And what exactly does a geek look like?" Ryan asked her, pressing a hand against the wall Evvie rested her back against.

"Oh, you know," she started, her mouth curving into an impish grin. "Braces, bad haircut, broken eyeglasses taped at the bridge."

He narrowed his glacier blue eyes, the delight at her banter evident as he flattened both palms against the wall around her petite body. "You have it all wrong. Don't you know that computer nerds are cool? We're taking over the world. Who do you think will be buying your overpriced wine?"

"Overpriced!" Evvie feigned insult.

"So, what does a stereotypical winemaker look like? Do you get in a big tub with bare feet and stomp grapes?"

Evvie playfully slapped his chest. *Holy pectorals! The guy is made of iron.* "I can promise you, my feet aren't purple. Anyway, I don't think that's been done since the Middle Ages."

"Well, then they must be tan and glowing like the rest of what I see."

"Maybe," Evvie shrugged. "I spend a lot of time outside."

"You know what we are?" Ryan didn't wait for her to answer.

"Direct opposites who compliment each other. We're a pair of salt and pepper shakers."

"You're very funny, Ryan, The Computer Geek."

"And you're very beautiful, Evvie, The Wine Girl." He lowered his head and gently kissed her.

She pulled her lips from his, studying his face before she slid her hands around his neck to kiss him back.

Slipping into a comfortable routine with Ryan had been seamless. There were no games or pretenses. He was simple, easy and always said what was on his mind. He'd been oddly accurate in his initial analogous assessment of the two of them. They were like salt and pepper. He brought light to her darkness. He was fun. Ryan didn't elicit deep thoughts and, slowly, Evvie stopped dwelling on all that could possibly go wrong. She never bared her soul to him, spilling all her fears or the details of what had bred such troublesome worries. With Ryan there was none of that heart-stopping romance that so many girls craved that usually ended up in disappointment and heartache. He was more than a friend but less than a soulmate and the only expectation between them was to enjoy the time they spent together.

As she and Ryan walked across campus one cold and windy November afternoon, Evvie ran into Zak walking toward the student center. She might not have recognized him if she hadn't knocked directly into him. When Evvie looked up to excuse herself, she froze. She'd been hoping to run into him all semester to offer the apology she owed him. There was a high possibility she'd passed him many times before, but with the blue mohawk replaced by jet black hair tied into a ponytail, she wouldn't have given him a second glance.

"Zak," Evvie smiled nervously. But Zak looked through her as if she didn't exist, offering no reply.

"Zak, please," she pleaded.

His stare could have frozen molten lava, until a girl bounced over to him, waving. Zak waved back, grinning, and when the girl made her way to him, he hung his arm around her shoulder and walked away, completely disregarding Evvie's presence.

"What was with that nut job? How do you know him?" Ryan asked disdainfully.

"He's not a nut job. Zak is a really good guy."

"Whatever," Ryan said dismissively. "Come on, let's get something to eat."

Evvie couldn't get Zak's cold stare and his obvious hatred for her out of her mind. It gnawed at her, the guilt of hurting him seeping through any fiber of goodness that was left in her. But she suspected there wasn't much good left because, although knowing Zak had moved on and found someone to make him happy should bring her relief, something about seeing him with that girl bothered her.

Chapter 25

Michael

May 2008

Memorial Day weekend, the beginning of the height of the summer season on the East End, had not yet arrived but the Angelidis Vineyard was alight with activity. Michael had commissioned a remodel of the space he used for his tasting room and retail store. The rustic style didn't match the elegance of the Carriage House and, although it had its own unique charm, a modern touch with an open, airy design would draw a more upscale crowd.

In part, his decision was driven by Evvie's push to produce a fine sparkling wine influenced by the method used in the Champagne region of France. With none of his three children showing interest in a career on the vineyard, Michael was not only happy to teach Evvie everything he could, he was also relieved that someone in the family wanted to carry on what he had built. Yet, if he was perfectly honest, he harbored some ambivalence over investing the money needed for the additional equipment.

"But Uncle Michael, you'll make the money back in no time," Evvie had said, pleading her case. "Think about it. How much champagne are you buying from your suppliers for weddings and events for the Carriage House? All that profit could be yours and you'd cut out the middle man."

She did make a point, he thought, and it would be prestigious to serve his own label along with the wines he already offered.

Later that night, he discussed it over dinner with Demi and bam! She was off and running with ideas as only Demi could do. She immediately texted Sophia and Dean and told them to get their butts over to their house ASAP.

"Hold on!" Michael stopped his wife. "How did creating a new sparkling wine and investing a shitload of money in new equipment, not to mention converting the cellar to a fermentation and aging cave, morph into a complete renovation of the tasting room?"

"Seriously, Michael. You're going to serve bubbly in a barn?" She looked at Sophia. "Am I right?"

"I'm staying out of this one. It's my daughter who got this all started," Sophia said.

"A modern update equal to the style of the Carriage House isn't a bad idea," Dean agreed. "We can use the same architect. It would give the property a nice cohesive look."

"If you're going to do it," Sophia said, "then I think you should have a large patio with outdoor seating overlooking the vineyards."

"Yes! Definitely." Demi scrunched her nose. "That giant tent doesn't cut it. It's cheesy."

"Suddenly there is nothing you like about the place?" Michael asked. They had done well over the years and they gained larger crowds each year.

Demi moved from her seat and onto Michael's lap. "I love it," she said, lacing her arms around his neck. "But we can do better and I can't wait to decorate and throw a big grand re-opening party."

Michael stood behind the new sleek, clear sea glass, mosaic bar, leaning on the white, marble countertop observing the reaction as patrons entered the newly remodeled building. The minimalistic, open design could have come off as cold and bare, but the opposite was true. Modern bubble chandeliers similar to the ones in the Carriage house hung from the fourteen-foot ceiling. The space was completely white but for a large wall mural of Angels surrounded by blue chrysanthemums. French doors led to a wide open patio with bistro tables, long rectangular tables for larger groups and several semi-circular outdoor couches, each wrapped around a fire pit.

In one year, he and Evvie would debut their very first sparkling wine. Michael thought about his own children. He'd expected Kristos to take over the family business one day. Instead, it was the management of the Carriage House that peaked his interest and now he was working side by side with his Uncle Dean. Paul surprised everyone by announcing that he wanted to go to the seminary and was now studying theology at a school in Massachusetts. This made Michael's mother ecstatic. And when Paul shared the news with his yiayiá, she kissed every part of his face after making the sign of the cross over him repeatedly and reciting a prayer of thanks.

Demi's reaction was not quite so jubilant. "It's not an easy life. Are you sure this is what you want?" she asked him.

"Very sure, Mom," he'd assured her. "I've thought about this for a long time."

And then there was Stella. God love the girl. Who knew what she'd end up doing. Michael chuckled thinking about her. There wasn't a sweeter girl alive, but she had absolutely no direction in life. Or, he corrected his thought, her direction changed as often as the seasons. After high school graduation, she was set on staying home, attending a local college and majoring in education. It took one semester for Stella to realize that it wasn't for her.

"I'd never get through all those requirements," she told her parents. "The classes are boring and there's like a million tests to pass before I can teach in a classroom."

The same school offered a culinary program. She loved to bake with her yiayiá, and decided she might like to be a pastry chef for the Carriage House, she told her parents. But halfway through the semester, her love affair with the culinary arts was over. "It's not fun to bake when you have to. I'd rather do it when I feel like it and there's no pressure," she said.

Michael could only imagine what she'd come up with next. For now, while the semester was over, his fickle daughter was waiting tables at the tasting room as well as assisting Evvie with the wine tours. He watched his daughter as she bounced from one table to the next. Stella was very friendly and personable with the customers. He didn't believe in the hippie dippy aura nonsense, but if he did, he was sure the colors around his daughter would be blue or gold for her kindness and ability to love. Or white, he thought. Stella was a pure and trusting soul.

Chapter 26

Stella

May 2008

Stella, with an open wine bottle in hand, made her way in between the outdoor seating to a table of four. Her white uniform could have been mistaken for a tennis dress but for the blue embroidered Angelidis logo framing the scoop neckline.

"This is Demetra, one of our Cabernet Sauvignons. It's been aged in oak barrels. You'll taste the spicy notes of cinnamon and cloves." Stella poured two ounces into each wine glass.

"I like this one," a nicely dressed middle-aged woman commented. "It's not quite as dry as most Cabs."

It pleased Stella when patrons appreciated her father's creations. He was passionate about his work and she hoped that one day she'd discover that magical, mysterious and elusive zeal that would drive her and make her feel as though she had something to contribute to the universe.

Stella liked this group of people. They were polite and were clearly relaxed and enjoying themselves. "Well, I'll give you a bit of trivia." She pointed to the label on the bottle. "My dad named this wine after my mom. That's her name, Demetra, but no one except my grandparents call her that. Most people call her Demi."

"So this is your father's vineyard?" one of the women asked. "What a treat to have the owner serving our wine today."

"Oh, I'm not the owner, just the daughter," Stella said modestly, eyeing another group walking in behind the hostess. "If you'll excuse me. I'll be back soon with your next wine."

She set down the bottle on an outdoor cart and headed to the table of newcomers. "Hi!" she said, smiling. "Back so soon? I think I waited on your table last weekend."

"You have a good memory. With all the people you see each week I'm surprised you remembered." The sandy-haired Liam Hemsworth look-a-like flashed her a magnetic smile. "I must have made quite an impression on you."

His equally handsome friends stared at Stella, but it was his sapphire eyes raking her that made her self-conscious.

"I do my best to remember all our repeat customers," she responded. *OMG! Embarrassing! I'm so lame.*

"All three of us will do the four-flight tasting ... and the charcuterie platter." He handed the menu back to her. "What's your name?"

"Stella."

"Nice to formally meet you, Stella. I'm Cain."

"Like in the bible? Cain who killed his brother?"

His eyes clouded over for a split second before the smile returned to his face. "He was also protected from death." He winked at her. "I like to focus on the positive."

"I'm sorry. I don't know why that came out of my mouth. It was a stupid thing to say." Mortified, she clutched the menu to her chest. "I'll go get your first tasting."

Blowing out a deep breath, Stella scurried as fast as she could from the patio and hid inside by the bar.

"Hey, what's up?" Susie, another server, asked. "You look like you lost your best friend."

"I just made a complete idiot of myself with the guys at table five. I think I really insulted one of them."

"You?" Susie's forehead creased examining Stella. "I highly doubt that."

"You'll have to take my word for it. Would you do me a big favor and take over that table for me?"

"Sure, if you really want me to."

"Thanks."

Stella was finishing up with the two couples she had been serving before when Cain and his friends walked in. They were on the last tasting of the flight they'd ordered.

"This one is our newest wine, created by my cousin Evvie, the newest oenologist in the family. It's a viognier, fermented in stainless steel. You'll notice hints of peach and citrus."

From the corner of her eye, she could tell that Cain was looking in her direction and asking Susie questions. She quickly excused herself after pouring the wine and rushed inside. Pushing through the double doors to the front entrance, she couldn't get away fast enough. She wasn't sure why the exchange had rattled her so. Naturally, she didn't want to insult a customer, but there was something more and she couldn't put her finger on it.

She sat on the front steps of the landing thinking about him. Cain made her both nervous and enthralled. He was compelling and confident and she was, as usual, her awkward self. He was a man. An eye-burning, too-hot-to-stare-at hunk of a man. And she was just a nothing-special, barely average girl.

"Stella?"

Turning, she saw Cain standing by the doorway, his hands planted on his hips. She didn't say anything. She just lowered her eyes to the ground.

"Why did you pawn off our table to another server?" he asked, coming to sit beside her.

"I was afraid I offended you and thought it was for the best."

He threw his head back in laughter. "You'd have to do more than that to offend me. I heard that and more growing up. I was called

'Candy Cain.' Or they'd say, 'Cain you fetch me a bowl of grits.'"

Stella couldn't help but giggle.

"But the best was, 'I'll Cain your ass!'"

"That's awful."

"That's what boys do."

"Don't I know it?" Stella agreed. "I have two older brothers."

"How old are you, Stella?"

"Nineteen. What about you?"

"How old am I?" He hesitated before answering. "Twenty-six." He looked at her as though waiting for a reaction. "I'd like to come back tomorrow with some other friends. I'm going to request one of your tables."

"Why?"

He slanted his head to one side as if to examine her. "Because I like you and I'd like to see you again. Unless our age difference is a problem for you."

"Pfff! I'm Greek. What's a few years? Half of my relatives are married to people with a ten year difference." Her voice trailed off as she closed her eyes. She wanted to slink away. "Not that I'm suggesting that we would get ..."

Cain's eyes sparkled with amusement. Taking her hand in his, he said, "It's good to know that age won't come between us."

Feeling the heat from the blush across her cheek, Stella drew her hand from his and stood quickly. "I need to get back."

"Of course. I'll see you tomorrow then?"

"I don't think so," she said. "I won't be working on the patio. I'm scheduled to give tours tomorrow."

"Another time," Cain said before Stella walked away.

The next day, Stella had just finished her last tour for the day. After taking her guests through the vineyards, she showed them to the various rooms where grapes were pressed and fermented and the wine, bottled. The dark, dry cellar was the last stop before making their way to a small room used for private tastings.

Stella was gathering up the empty bottles and dirty wineglasses when Evvie came in.

"Stella, there's a last minute add-on tour. I would do it myself but I have to take off early today."

"No problem. I can stay."

"Thanks. One person booked a party of eight. Hopefully it's not an obnoxious group of drunken bachelorettes."

"I doubt it," Stella said. "They wouldn't be interested in learning how the wine was made. They'd just head straight for the bar to make fools of themselves."

Stella waited at the designated tour meeting spot by the vineyards just beyond the crowded outdoor seating area. Today she wore the vineyard's logo t-shirt with a dove gray, slim-cut pair of ankle length slacks and comfortable, wedged-heeled sandals.

"Hello."

Stella, who had been preoccupied by two unruly children running close to the rosebushes planted at the end of a row of vines, turned around. Looking as ridiculously gorgeous as he had the day before, Cain stood in front of her and she slid her Rayban sunglasses off her face, pushing them up on top of her head to see if it was really him.

"I see you decided to come back today after all," Stella smiled.

"I don't recall saying I wouldn't."

Even with the sun shining directly on his face, his eyes lost none of their deep blue intensity. He looked like he'd just stepped off the pages of a luxury magazine, advertising a yacht or an Aston Martin.

"I'd love to chat but I'm waiting for my group to arrive for their tour."

"And I believe your group has arrived." Cain pointed to himself and mouthed, 'me.'

"I don't understand," Stella looked genuinely confused. She looked around to see if others were approaching. "This tour was set for a group of eight. Where are your friends?"

"It's just me today. I purchased all eight spots."

"But why?"

Cain flashed her a brilliant smile and chuckled. "To have your full attention. You're very unassuming, Stella. You have no idea how beautiful you are, do you?"

Stella looked down at her feet. Receiving compliments, especially from men, was not something she was accustomed to or knew how to take gracefully. Instead she continued briskly, "Are you ready to begin?"

Extending his arm toward the perfectly lined rows of grapevines, Cain gestured for her to lead the way.

Nervously, she went through the process—irrigation control, pH balance and harvesting. "The buds are just beginning to break. You won't see any grapes until summer is in full swing."

"So tell me, is this what you plan to do with your life?"

Stella felt the heat of his stare sear through her as she rambled off facts. He'd barely looked at the lush, green vines. "No, I'm not interested in the family business. It's just a summer job." She adjusted her sunglasses, sliding them up the bridge of her nose. "Let's go to the production building," Stella said, stepping up her pace to walk ahead of him.

"So what is your interest?" he asked, striding up alongside her.

"Huh?"

"What *do* you want to do if not work here?"

Stella had no answer to his very personal question. She wanted to state that his question wasn't relevant to the tour and demand to know why he wanted to know in the first place. But of course, she didn't. Cain was smoldering hot and, in her fantasies, he was exactly what she dreamed of. But in reality, he was out of her league and made her nervous as hell.

"I haven't figured that out yet," she said softly, hoping to not come off sounding like a child. Stella caught an impish gleam in his eye, which quickly softened seconds later.

After Stella had gone through the entire production procedure, she led Cain to the private tasting room and opened the first bottle of wine.

"Don't be so formal. It's just the two of us and since I paid for eight people we can drink this whole bottle if we choose," Cain said, tilting his head seductively to one side.

"You do realize that I'm not legally old enough to drink."

"Somehow, living here, I suspect you drink plenty. Besides, I won't tell if you won't."

Stella popped the cork on a Chardonnay, pulled two glasses from an overhead rack and began to pour. "I had a friend who was obsessed with Dunkin Donuts when we were kids, especially the jelly filled munchkins." Stella sat down at a round table for two across from Cain. "She swore she would get a job with them when she was old enough and, when we were sixteen, she did."

"And?"

"And she got so sick of filling them, smelling them and, eventually, eating them." Stella laughed, getting lost in the image of her friend's face dramatically expressing how she never wanted to look at anything that even resembled a donut again. "My point is that I barely ever drink." She shrugged. "It wasn't a big taboo in my family to have a glass of wine, so none of us kids ever felt like we had to steal the vodka from our parents' liquor cabinet like the other kids in school did."

"Ha! I remember those days!" Cain laughed. "So I guess I can't get you drunk and have my way with you?" he joked.

Stella sipped her wine slowly, the glass forming a barrier between Cain and herself as she hid her face with it. She inspected him as he gulped half the glass in one shot. "Is that how you want to be with someone?"

"Of course not," he answered. Tightening his grip on the glass, he smiled. "I was making a joke. But I would like to take you out without having to convince you why we'd have fun together."

"I don't know anything about you." She stood and took another bottle of wine from the bar cart. "Do you like red wines? My cousin developed this one. It's a blend similar to what you might find in Loire Valley, even though that region is mostly known for white wine." She poured a glass for Cain, leaving hers empty. "It's a blend of Cabernet Franc and Pinot Noir, which grows very well here."

"You might know very little about me; however, I've discovered quite a bit about you."

"I don't see how."

"I know you ramble when you want to avoid a subject. And that you fiddle with your sunglasses when you get nervous."

Stella's already round-shaped eyes widened to thick, lash-brimmed orbs.

Cain stood, walking around the table to narrow the distance between them. "I also know that you stare down at your feet when I compliment you." He lifted her chin, forcing her to meet his gaze. "Your eyes are the color of melting caramel."

"I've never heard them described that way before," Stella stumbled on her words. "You like caramels?"

"I do now." He still had hold of her chin and with his other hand pulled her in by the waist. "What will it take?" he asked almost inaudibly. "I live in the city. My family is in commercial real estate. I make my own hours, which is why I can spend much of my time in the summer at our Southampton house. I didn't want in on the family business at nineteen either, until I saw the light and had a change of heart. I went to Ohio State University and I have a much older sister who lives in London with her husband and two daughters."

Stella pulled far enough away to extend her hand and shake his. "It's nice to meet you, Cain."

He held her slim hand in his, not allowing her to release herself from his grip. "It's nice to meet you, Stella. Now, unless you're a vegetarian there's a place I'd love to take you for dinner on Dune Road."

"Dockers?"

"You know it?" he asked.

"Sure. I've been there many times."

"Not when I've been there. I would have noticed you. Well?" he pouted, in a seductively teasing manner. "Is it a date?"

Hesitating, Stella sucked in a deep breath and nodded.

"Adding wings to caterpillars does not create butterflies. It creates awkward and dysfunctional caterpillars. Butterflies are created through transformation."

—Stephanie Marshall

Chapter 27

Stella

July 2008

In the two months since Stella began dating Cain, a subtle, but noticeable transformation had taken place in her appearance. Gone were her age appropriate Abercrombie miniskirts and crop tops, replaced by sheath dresses designed by Kate Spade and Lily Pulitzer. She wanted so much to fit into his world and to look like the other young women in his crowd. And Cain was more than happy to take her shopping, helping her to choose outfits and molding her to run comfortably in his circles.

That evening, his parents were throwing a fundraising cocktail party at their home in Southampton, and Stella had lamented for weeks on what to wear until a visit from one of her mother's oldest friends saved the day. Mindy Bloom was a highly regarded fashion designer who came out to their home as often as she could.

"I need help, Aunt Mindy," Stella pleaded almost desperately. "I don't know what to wear to this thing. It's at his parent's home, but it's a semi-formal affair. How much do I dress up? Too much and I'll look ridiculous. Too little and I'll look completely out of my element."

"Have faith in yourself," Mindy told her, squeezing her shoulders affectionately. "It looks like you have been doing just fine perfecting your style, although …" Mindy narrowed her eyes at Stella "… why are you wearing a dress with that label and not one of mine?"

"Oh, don't be mad. Cain took me shopping and he chose this dress."

"I was only teasing, sweetie. You wear what you want." Mindy tapped her finger to her lip, her playful expression turning serious. "Let's go up to your room and see what we have to work with."

Halfway up the stairs Mindy asked Stella how often Cain chose her outfits. "He picked out a whole new wardrobe for me! He has great taste."

"I'm sure he does, but don't lose your own sense of style, okay?"

"I don't really think I ever had one before."

Mindy rummaged through Stella's closet and made a face. "You should be dressing like a nineteen-year-old, not someone in her thirties." She pulled out an outfit from the far end of the closet. "Now this is my Stella," Mindy said holding up a white, spaghetti strap, cotton sundress.

"I can't wear that to the cocktail party."

"And I'm not suggesting you do. I just want you to keep in mind that you should make your own decisions. Now, I've been to enough of these affairs to know exactly what you should wear. Leave it up to me and I'll bring you one of my dresses."

"No way!" Stella flung her arms excitedly around her mother's friend.

Stella looked in the mirror after she strapped on the blush-colored, high-heeled sandals Mindy had brought along with a dress in the same hue. Her hair was styled in an elegant, but youthful, up-do, to show off the bronze glow of her shoulders and back as well as the detail of the neckline that criss-crossed in the front of the form-fitting bodice. The slight flare of the a-line was sophisticated, yet age appropriate.

Stella descended the staircase to find her mother, Aunt Sophia and Mindy sharing a bottle of wine in the kitchen. They were huddled together, whispering, but all conversation ceased when she approached.

"Well, what do you think?" Stella asked.

"You look stunning!" Sophia said.

"I'll tell you what I think," Mindy said. "You'll be walking in my next fashion show."

"Me? I don't think so. You're just being kind."

"No, she's not," Demi told her daughter. "If you don't believe her then I'm taking you for an eye exam tomorrow. Cain will go wild when he sees you!"

The doorbell rang and a squeal erupted from Stella. "He's here!"

"I'll get it," Mindy offered. "I want to meet this infamous Cain."

But somehow, to Stella's mortification, all three of them followed her to the foyer as Cain stepped through the door.

He smiled politely. "Mrs. Angelidis, Mrs. Papadakis, it's nice to see you again," he said, bowing ever so slightly.

Mindy raised an eyebrow and Stella wondered why she held the assessing expression she had on her face. "Aunt Mindy, this is Cain."

Mindy extended her hand to shake his. "So I gather. I'm glad to finally meet you."

"Me too. I wasn't aware that Stella had another aunt."

"Not by blood, but through lifelong friendship," Sophia explained. She wrapped her arms around her friend. "Family comes in many forms."

"True," Mindy said, looking pointedly at Cain. "And we look out for our own."

"Okay," Stella said, wondering what the hell was going on. "Before you guys start with one of your stories, we're going to shove off before we're late."

"Have a wonderful time," Demi said, waving goodbye.

When Cain and Stella pulled up to his parents' summer home, at first, a tall hedge fence blocked the house from view. But as they drove up the long driveway, Stella was stunned to find a mansion before her. She wasn't ignorant to the fact that Cain had a good amount of money, but she'd never expected this level of wealth.

They were greeted at the front door and offered champagne. Cain lifted two flutes off the tray, handing one to Stella and, as she looked around the elegant surroundings, she suddenly felt out of place. Guiding her with his free hand at the small of her back, he suggested they find his parents, but before they reached them, two perfectly polished, designer clad beauties Stella had met on only two other occasions stopped them.

"Cain, your mother is the queen of party throwing," Madison gushed. "Everyone who is anyone is here."

"We were just about to search out my mother. Have you seen her?"

"You run off," Ainsley said, latching on to Stella's arm. "We'll introduce Stella to the others."

"Oh, I think I'll stay with Cain." Stella hadn't yet said hello to his parents, who she'd only met once briefly at their country club, and she wanted to thank them for the invitation. In truth, she wasn't completely at ease with these women and couldn't shake her sense of awkwardness and inferiority around them.

"It's okay." Cain smiled, brushing his fingertips along her bare back. "I'll be back in a few minutes. I need a word with my father anyway."

As soon as Cain disappeared into the crowd, so did Stella's courage. Madison and Ainsley each looped their arms around hers. "You'll never guess who's here. Be prepared sweet Stella. You're about to step into a whole different world," Ainsley warned.

"But don't worry," Madison added. "We've got you. You'll be our little apprentice tonight."

Stella was sure she'd detected condescension in their tone, body language and attitude. They thought they had it all over her with their long blonde hair and Barbie bodies. The dresses they wore had to be worth thousands and Stella couldn't imagine what the jewels dangling from their ears cost. She struggled to appear composed and unfazed by what she thought was their attempt to ruffle her, but on the inside a tremble within was bubbling its way to the surface.

"I'm not worried. I'm with Cain." Madison flinched ever so slightly at her words and Stella was pretty certain she detected a hint of jealousy in her.

"So, whose dress are you wearing tonight?" Ainsley asked.

"Mine. Why would you think I would be wearing someone's dress?"

"Oh, you are such a novice," Madison chortled. She fingered the string of pearls lying just below her collarbone. "Which designer are you wearing?"

Stella raised her eyebrows. "Oh. I thought that question was only asked on the red carpet." She was holding her own with these bitches, she thought. At least for now. "Mindy Bloom. It's an original."

"An original? Did Cain buy it for you?"

"No, Mindy had it made just for me. She's one of my mother's closest friends." Stella satisfied herself with the look of surprise on the two of their faces and hoped that would shut them up for now. "You never did tell me who was here that I had to see."

"So many people! Christie Brinkley, for one," Madison said.

"Really! Then I'll have to make sure to say hello," Stella told them. "I've met her a couple of times through my Aunt Mindy."

"Aunt Mindy?" Ainsley asked, puzzled.

"My mom and Mindy have been friends since they were like five years old. She's family." *Two points for me*, Stella thought. Flashing her best fake smile back in their face, Stella wondered how old women had to be before they stopped competing with and bullying each other.

Cain came up behind Stella and wrapped his arms around her waist, grazing the scruff on his jaw along her cheek. "Miss me?"

"You have no idea," Stella remarked.

The next day, after the vineyard had closed to the public, Michael and Demi threw an informal pool party and BBQ. The entire clan was there and then some, except for Evvie, who had left to spend a few weeks in Greece with her great-grandmother before returning to help with the harvest.

Cain had met most of the family on several occasions and was greeted with enthusiastic approval. It was clear he was attentive and caring toward Stella and always treated her with respect. And he was very sweet to Soula, even when her moments of clarity slipped in and out.

At seven in the evening the sun had not yet dipped into the horizon, leaving the sticky heat to linger. Relief came from the refreshing pool water and Stella, along with cousins and friends, sat on the steps of the pool.

"How about a game of chicken?" Kristos suggested.

"Can I play? Can I play, too?" Cia asked.

"Sure, squirt. But you have to find a partner," Kristos told her. "I already have Maggie, sorry."

"Come on, jump on my shoulders," Adam offered.

Cia clapped her hands before lifting them to climb onto Adam.

"Partners?" RJ asked Stella.

"Partners," she said, hopping onto his back.

After each team was formed, the entertaining chaos ensued. Laughter while wrestling made it nearly impossible to gain the strength for victory, but eventually bodies began to drop like swatted flies, hitting the water in loud kerplunks.

Stella conducted herself like the nineteen-year-old that she was, scantily dressed in a tiny, lime green bikini and hanging onto RJ for dear life. She snapped her head around when the disapproving sound of Cain's voice, calling out her name, caught her attention. Dismounting herself from RJ's shoulders, Stella hopped out of the pool to greet him but was met with a cold stare.

"What's wrong?" she asked when she tried to reach up to kiss him.

"Whose head were your thighs wrapped around?"

"What? Cain, don't be like that. That's RJ. He's like a cousin to me. I've known him my whole life."

Stella saw the fury leave him, replaced by a different heat. He bent down and grazed her ear with his lips. "No one should be where I haven't been yet." He took her chin, lifting it to look at her eye to eye. "We need to remedy that soon."

Stella made no reply, but with the sudden flip in her stomach, she feared that as much as making love was something she wanted to experience with him, it also scared her. She excused herself to dry off and change her clothing. When she rejoined the gathering, Cain was seated by her Yiayiá Soula, and the two of them seemed to be in the middle of deep conversation.

"Stella *mou, éla ethó. Na kathisei mazi mas*," Soula said.

"I'm coming, Yiayiá. But remember, Cain doesn't speak Greek. Okay?"

Soula put her hand over his. "Such a nice boy."

"I care about your granddaughter very much," Cain said, taking Stella's hand.

Stavros strode over holding a massive platter of grilled baby lamb chops. "Anyone?" he asked. He bent down and planted a gentle kiss on his wife's cheek. "Are you having a good day?"

"A very good day," Soula answered, cupping her palm to his cheek.

The gesture was so sweet Stella wanted to weep, and she worried that there may not be as many good days remaining as she would like.

A warm wind brushed over Stella's bikini clad body as she laid face up on the bow of the sleek sailboat Cain was steering back into the harbor. She'd been on the luxurious Dufour 40 E with him on several occasions, but this was the first time they were alone. Usually, a group of his friends would join them, all of which knew much more than she did about sailing.

But it was just as well. It was nice to have Cain to herself. His friends were nice enough, but they were a completely different crowd than she was used to. It was a bit intimidating; in very much the same way Cain had been when she'd first met him. But he proved to be a gentleman who doted on her and treated her like she was precious to him. Still, she sometimes felt like a child in the presence of his friends. The other girls were sophisticated and polished, and they had the ability to hold their own on a number of subjects that, for the most part, eluded her. Stella's mind wandered when finance and economics were the topic. And when the political debates began, she was clearly a fish out of water.

But today, Cain was all hers, and she smiled up at him as he steered the boat into the slip. She jumped up to help him, grabbed the rope secured to the dock and fastened it to the boat cleat.

"Look who's becoming a pro at sailing," Cain said impressed.

Stella had never done this before today, but she'd watched his friends closely and it hadn't look difficult. Shielding her eyes from the sun, she put a hand to her forehead and looked up at the sky. Only small wisps of clouds marked the bright blue sky. It was too beautiful to call it a day and she wondered why they had come back so early.

"Is there somewhere you need to be?" Stella asked.

"No. I'm right where I want to be." Cain came over to her and circled her waist with his arms. Pressing her body to his, he kissed her. "Let's hang out in the cabin for a while."

"Okay. But it's such a gorgeous day." Stella shook her head. "Don't you want to stay outdoors?"

"Later." He took her hand and led her through the cabin door. But they didn't stop at the plush indoor sectional or slide into the kitchenette seats for a glass of wine. Cain kissed her senseless, backing her into the bedroom.

"Cain?"

"Shhh," he said softly. "I've been waiting all day for you."

"But Cain," Stella started. She wasn't sure of what to say. Was she even ready for this? Stella didn't know.

"I need to make love to you, Stella." He kissed her neck, shoulders, and worked his way to her breasts, stripping her of the bikini top she had on. "I'm going to have you—to claim you."

Stella was racked with anxiety and confusion. Panic constricted her chest, her sensibilities telling her to pull away, while the throbbing down below wanted more of what Cain was doing.

He picked her up, laid her quivering body on the bed and shed himself of his own swim trunks. "Relax sweet girl." He crushed his mouth to hers, invading her with his tongue, and his hands explored every inch of her soft, sun-kissed skin.

The waves of pleasure building inside her were unexplainable and she wasn't sure if the whirling was in her mind or from the gentle rocking of the boat. He wasn't gentle with her the way she presumed he would be since he was aware this was her first time with a man. Instead, it was as though a savage need for her had been unleashed. Stella didn't mind his strong, possessive hold on her. She rather liked it. It made her feel wanted and needed. But then, without warning, and with one sudden thrust, he entered her and she cried out from the sudden shock of pain.

Cain didn't seem to notice Stella's discomfort and he continued to drive himself in and out of her until her body finally adjusted to him. In her mind, she wanted to please him but her body screamed, 'hurts, stop, hurts,' until the sting had subsided and she was able to breathe again.

"So good—all mine," he grunted, looking down at her, his eyes glazed over with lust and something else Stella couldn't put her finger on. He rolled off her and onto his back. Turning to face her, he tenderly stroked her cheek with his thumb. "I'm sorry. I got carried away. The first time can be painful and I should have been gentler."

Stella had a lump in her throat. She hadn't responded, but simply looked down at him with a vacillatory smile. She wanted to tell him that it had been good. That it's what she had waited for and dreamed it would be. But she couldn't. And the only thing on her mind was to where Cain's mind had disappeared. He'd become almost feral and animalistic. For most of the act, she'd felt like an observer rather than a participant. Cain, she reminded herself, was six years older than she was and had far more experience. She had none. What he'd expected from her, she didn't know and, the bigger question was, how much was she willing to do? It wasn't that she was naive. Her friends were very open and forthcoming about what should have been private activities, but she'd sat quietly and listened as they had over-shared, to her embarrassment.

"Stay put." Cain got out of bed, padding out of the room. Stella watched him as all his hot nakedness disappeared. A few minutes later, he returned with two stemless wineglasses in hand. Stella covered her bare breasts with the bed sheet and accepted the wine.

"Don't do that," Cain said firmly. His expression held a softness that his tone did not.

Stella shook her head, puzzled.

"Don't ever cover yourself in my presence." He pulled the sheet from her. "Lie down." Dipping his fingers into his glass, he splattered droplets of red wine onto her breasts. The erotic sensation startled Stella and she moaned when he bent down to suck the red liquid from her. He took her glass, set it on the bedside table and continued to drop beads of wine down her body, licking and stroking until Stella's body tensed under him. She groaned out his name several times, running her hands through his hair as his tongue fed on skin and spirits.

In those moments, all of Stella's insecurities disappeared. She was loved and accepted, just as she was, and that's all she'd ever wanted. She snuggled into him, her back to his front, and began to drift off.

"I want to talk to you about something, sweets," Cain said.

She leaned her head back, remaining nestled around him, waiting to hear what he had to say.

"I love you," he said.

With that declaration, Stella turned to face him. She hadn't expected to hear those words so soon.

"When you're not with me," Cain continued, "I think about you and I wonder what you're doing and who you're with."

Stella let out a quiet laugh. "That's easy. You can usually find me working at the vineyard or spending time with one of my dozens of relatives." She gave him a peck on the lips. "I'm a pretty open book, not a girl of mystery."

"You're a woman," he frowned. "Stop referring to yourself as a girl. It ... distresses me."

"Why?"

Cain brushed the stray hairs off her face. "That's what I wanted to talk to you about. I haven't been completely honest with you."

The constriction in Stella's chest returned. She jolted upright, eyes wide with apprehension. Shivering as she sucked in air, her mind ran off a thousand awful acts of deceit.

"Oh, God! Oh, God! Please don't tell me you have another girlfriend." Her eyes bulged "Or worse. Please don't say you're married. Cain! Are you married?"

"No! No, it's nothing like that. Nothing that deceptive." He ran his fingers through his already mussed hair. "When we first met, I asked you how old you were and I was fine with your age. But when you asked me my age I was worried you wouldn't feel the same, so I told you I was twenty-six."

"And you're not twenty-six?"

He shook his head slowly as she re-assessed him.

"Why did you lie to me?" She wasn't sure she wanted the answer for fear of what she'd learn.

"I was afraid you'd never agree to go out with me and, from the moment I saw you, I knew I had to have you. Why do you think I kept coming back to the winery?"

"How old are you?"

He didn't answer right away. Stella could see the tightening in his jaw before he admitted, "Thirty-two."

Stella officially lost her stomach. That's it. Gone, right along with the eyes that popped from their sockets and rolled away. Maybe her tongue had left her body too, because she was suddenly at a loss for words. She took a minute to mentally calm herself to bring her heart rate down and then find her courage.

"That's a thirteen year difference Cain. A six year lie." She shook her head. How could she look at him the same? He was a grown man. A real grown-up kind of man. Not one on the verge of manhood but one who was already there.

"I'm just still a teenager. And not a particularly mature and worldly one."

He reached for her and opened his mouth to argue but she inched away from him.

"No wonder I could never live up to the standards of your friends. I'm just a child compared to them."

"Stop it!" he said, grabbing her by the arms. "You're making more of this than you need to. You told me your grandparents have eleven years between them. How is that different?"

"That was another time and place. It wasn't unusual back then. This is different."

"A half an hour ago you gave me the most intimate part of yourself and I know that wasn't something you took lightly. I'm still the same man."

"The man who lied to me."

"The man who loves you and was desperate to have you."

Stella covered her face with her hands but Cain pried them away and kissed her fingertips. "Nothing has changed," he pleaded. "We're still the same two people. You don't love me?"

She hadn't yet told him that she did and she wasn't sure she should. With a heavy sigh she said, "I do. I love you."

"Don't make that sound like a death sentence." His reply held more hurt than humor.

"I need to adjust my brain, that's all." She began to climb out of bed.

"Where are you going?"

"It's been a long day, Cain. I should get going."

"Are we … okay?"

Stella nodded. "Sure. I just need a little time alone."

The car ride home was quiet. Cain held onto Stella's hand the entire time, occasionally bringing it to his lips for a kiss as he drove her home. She wanted to speak to Evvie and was calculating the time difference for Athens in her head. It would have to wait until tomorrow she supposed.

Chapter 28

Evvie

July 2008

When Evvie had made the decision to spend three weeks in Athens with her great-grandmother, Ryan was less than pleased. They had spent every day of the last two years together, but now, since they'd both graduated from college in May, they didn't see each other as often as he would have liked. His position as a junior software architect with Microsoft kept him in the upstate town of White Plains all week. Each Friday evening, after work, he'd take the two-and-a-half-hour drive to spend the weekend with Evvie. It wasn't an ideal scenario, but they both had careers that were important to them and, unfortunately, the distance was not geographically conducive to the harmony of a serious relationship.

Stealing time alone was also a challenge with Evvie's huge family constantly hovering. She adored her cousins and her ever-present extended family. There was always someone to hang out with or to give a helping hand when you needed one. They all liked Ryan and he was accepted as one of their own, but Evvie wanted to hit them with a brick sometimes. And that's what it would have taken for them to get the hint that, just once in a while, Ryan and she would like to be alone.

And then there was Mom and Dean, who made him sleep in a room on the opposite side of the house. Ugh! Parents!

She'd already purchased her plane ticket when she had finally gotten Ryan alone to speak to him about it. It was the last weekend in May and Evvie led Ryan to the furthest corner of their property. It was after midnight and the warm air from the day had held, the temperature only dropping fractionally. Evvie rolled out the blanket she'd carried from the house and the two of them laid down, face up to admire the golden quarter moon and the stars that bled through the darkness.

"Did you bring me out here to make out?" Ryan said playfully, rolling his body on top of hers to pin her beneath him.

"Hmmm, that too," she said. "But I thought maybe we'd meditate and stargaze for a couple of hours first," she teased.

"Yeah, right!" He rolled his eyes in over exaggerated disbelief. "You've never meditated a day in your life."

"Ryan." She circled her fingers around his wrists to stop him from inching up her thighs. "Ryan, I want to talk to you about something."

He raised his head from where it was buried in the hollow of her neck, bearing the expression of a worried man when he heard the serious tone in her voice. "Ev, what's on your mind?" he asked tentatively.

"It's nothing bad." But Evvie had been on edge all day wondering how he would take the news. It really was no big deal though; she had tried to convince herself. Ryan was very understanding and he rarely questioned her. "I'm leaving for Greece next week." She worried her jaw, waiting for his response.

"With your family?" Ryan asked, knowing they usually went for an extended time each summer.

"No. My parents are going in August, but only for ten days. I'm going alone … for three weeks."

"Three weeks?" Ryan looked completely crestfallen.

"Don't look at me that way." She pushed a lock of pale, white-blond hair affectionately from his forehead. "Hear me out. My great-grandmother is ninety-two years old. I'm not sure how much more time I'll be blessed to have with her." Evvie laughed under her breath. "Although we all believe that she'll outlive every one of us! But seriously, I want to see her and hear the rest of a story she started to tell me a couple of years ago. I couldn't get it all out of her, but I'm hoping she'll tell me the rest."

"What kind of a story."

"A true one. About her life as a young girl."

"And this is so important that you need to leave for three weeks?"

Evvie nodded. A momentary sadness took hold of her. Her daughter was my yiayiá, my grandmother. She would tell me fascinating stories of her childhood and family in Greece. And my pappou did too. He still does. It's history, Ryan. Family history from personal experience. Some of it's so awful I want to cry, and other parts make me so happy to know I come from these people. I want to know everything. I need to know."

Ryan took her hands in his, brushing a finger along the silver infinity ring he'd given her for Christmas last year.

"She lived on a vineyard when she was young before her parents moved them to Athens."

Ryan drew his eyes up to meet hers. "Really? That's interesting. The Angelidis Winery doesn't belong to your side of the family though, right?"

She shook her head. "Nope. I'm technically not even related. The vineyard belongs to my Uncle Michael, who is married to my Aunt Demi, my stepfather, Dean's sister."

"It's going to take me a few minutes to process that," he joked.

"Anyway … I want to convince my pro-yiayiá, that means great-grandmother in Greek, to take me to see the vineyard. It's still in operation by relatives from her side of the family, but she hasn't been back there in … forever."

"I'll miss you." He brushed his lips across hers. "But it seems important to you, so I understand."

"I'll miss you too," Evvie responded, looping her hands around his neck.

"I need just one promise from you."

"What's that?" Evvie asked.

"Make that two." Ryan shot up his index finger. "One. Keep your eyes off the Greek men."

Evvie laughed heartily. "That won't be hard. I'm surrounded by them. I think I've had my fill."

"Two. When you come back we need to have a serious discussion about our future together."

"I think those are two promises that I can keep," Evvie agreed.

Evvie thought of Ryan as the plane was about to touch down. She was going to miss him very much, but she couldn't wait to see her grandmother and discover everything she'd been wondering about since she'd last visited her. Once she returned home, she and Ryan would plan their life together.

Chapter 29

Evvie

July 2008

Evvie spent three days with Yiayiá Sophia before she began to pepper her with questions. Before that, she was about to erupt from within, attempting to contain her enthusiastic energy and thirst for information.

But regardless of whether or not Evvie learned any new morsel of family history, she was glad she'd made the visit. Her self-sufficient pro-yiayiá was not quite the spitfire she had been when she'd last seen her. She tired more easily and Evvie noticed the apartment wasn't as spic-and-span as it normally was. So Evvie scrubbed the floors and organized the closets. She dusted the furniture and cleaned the bathroom. Together they went to the market and cooked dinner and afterward they sat out on the balcony, enjoying the warm night air.

"Are you ready to tell me the rest of your story, Yiayiá?" Evvie asked eagerly.

"*Ne, Koukla*. I will tell you all of it."

"So, you moved to Athens but never went back, right?"

"I didn't say, never. I said, not for many years."

"Before or after you met pappou?"

"After. Long after."

"How did you meet pappou?"

"I was just about to get to that," Yiayiá Sophia said, tapping the tip of Evvie's nose. "You know why my Spyro had to leave his island, *ne*?"

"Yes. He and his brother left Chios because the island was still under the Ottoman occupation. My yiayiá told me."

Darkness shadowed Yiayiá Sophia's eyes at the mention of her daughter, her precious Anastacia. Nearly ten years later, the loss was still immeasurable to both of them. "His brother, Tasso made his way to the United States and built a new life there. My Spyro found his way to Athens, worked several jobs and saved every spare drachma. Now, remember I told you my father had taken a sales role for the vineyard?"

"I remember," Evvie said.

"Spyro was working as a bartender at a taverna. My father had approached the owner to carry Georgatos wines. Well, after a while, Spyro went to work for my father part time to earn extra money. Eventually, he saved enough money to open his own taverna with a little help from my father. Later, as he began to see a profit, he and my babá invested in a retail wine store."

"So you knew Pappou Spyro through your father's business?"

The corners of her lips turned up at the memory. "Yes. He was the most handsome man I'd ever seen. My babá would invite him for dinner and I wouldn't dare to look at him. I'd sneak a glance here and there when I thought he wasn't looking my way."

"That's sweet," Evvie said.

"How do you kids put it? I had the heats for him."

Evvie covered her mouth, stifling a chuckle. "The hots. You had the hots for him."

"Yes, that too. But he was so much older than I was. I never thought he'd look my way. But I was wrong. He'd spoken to my babá and had declared, 'I'm going to marry Sophia one day and I'd like your blessing.' My babá agreed without any understanding of what he meant when he said, 'one day.'"

"I don't understand."

"Spyro came to find me. I'll never forget that day as long as I live." A dreamy look came over her pro-yiayiá's face. "He wasn't looking for my father. It was me he sought out! He asked me if I'd like to go for a walk with him." She held her cheeks in her hands. "I was so nervous. I had no idea what he wanted or where we were headed, but when we stopped in front of a church I looked at him bewildered. 'Sophia,' he said. 'I brought you here because I was hoping that you would agree to become my wife.'"

"Oh-my-God! Had you ever even had a conversation with him?"

"No. I was surprised, but not unhappy about it. He wanted to wed right then, at that very moment. He asked me if I could learn to love him and I confessed that I already did." She slapped a hand over her mouth and laughed. "What did I know? I was only fourteen."

"Fourteen! How old was he?"

"Twenty-four."

Evvie gave her a horrified look.

"It was a different time, *agapi*."

"Maybe, but at fourteen I was … I don't know what I was thinking. But it was far from getting married, unless it was to Jonathan Taylor Thomas."

"He was your boyfriend?"

"No, Yiayiá. An actor," Evvie giggled. "So, what happened?"

"We got married that day and then it took me about ten minutes to be with child."

"This gets better and better. When I get back home, I think Ryan might want to talk about getting married. I'm not sure I'm ready for that and I'm twenty-two."

"If he's the right boy then the time will not matter. My Spyro and I adored each other." She motioned for Evvie to come closer and laid her hand over her great-granddaughter's heart. "This is what counts. Listen to it. Follow it and it will never let you down."

That night as Evvie drifted off to sleep, visions of the past played before her like an old-time movie reel. It all seemed so romantic—the era, the island vineyard and the impetuous elopement. Her great-grandmother had experienced a full and interesting life before she was even out of her teens, and Evvie hadn't yet scratched the surface on everything there was to know about her.

She wondered if she would have fascinating tales to share one day or had the luster faded from life in this modern era where she had everything yet nothing at all in comparison to the simple richness of the past. She envied the radiance that had illuminated her dear Yiayiá Anastacia. It was the same gleam that lit up her pro-yiayiá's face when she spoke of her Spyro. But Evvie knew that wouldn't be her destiny. Her heart was bound, protected under lock and key, and she only gave as much love as she allowed herself to.

Evvie was startled awake in the middle of the night. She'd had a dream. No, maybe not a dream. It seemed more real than that. She'd heard her voice, smelled her scent, and felt the warmth of her body. It wasn't the first time Evvie had experienced this, but it had been quite some time since her yiayiá visited while she slept.

Anastacia, looking younger than Evvie remembered, knelt down before her, running her fingers over the diamonds adorning her earlobes. She had given them to Evvie during the last days of her life and vowed to be with her spiritually when Evvie wore them at her own wedding, yet in her dream it was Ana wearing them. "You have so much love inside of you," she said. "One day, you'll wear them for the man you give your whole heart to." Anastacia extended her hand. "He's waiting for you."

In the darkness, Evvie went for the iPhone charging on the nightstand. She repeated the words that woke her. *He's waiting for you.* 'Missing you,' she tapped out to Ryan in a text message. His response was immediate. 'Missing you more.'

Chapter 30

Sophia Georgatos Fotopoulos

1946

N
ervous flutters churned inside Sophia's stomach as the land she hadn't planted her feet on in almost two decades came into view. Spyro held her at the waist while their two adolescent daughters stood by the ferryboat rail beside them. The ride from Athens to Patras was a long one, and it was refreshing when they were finally able to exit the car and stretch their legs.

Sophia was lost in her own thoughts and those reflections overwhelmed her. She wasn't sure what to expect when she returned to the vineyard after so many years. The people that lived there had been her world—her life, and because of her, her parents had been forced to make an unfair and impossible choice. But as she glanced at her family, she had no doubt she'd done right to speak up on her own behalf.

Still, she hated to be the cause of a splintered family and the reason a longtime friendship was destroyed. Her father had remained neutral where the business was concerned and was able to keep his share of the vineyard and Sophia was grateful for that.

But now, with his unexpected death, and Spyro taking over his role, it was time for Sophia to go back home to claim what was rightfully hers.

Spyro had a natural mind for business, and he had not only expanded Sophia's father's business interests by opening a chain of wine stores, but he also distributed their wine to every fine restaurant and hotel in Greece and the bordering countries.

Sophia's mamá, who had decided not to return to Kefalonia with them, remained behind, and had chosen to relinquish her interests in the vineyard directly to Sophia and Spyro when her husband passed away.

Her tears could not be contained when Sophia stepped onto her island.

"What can I do for you Mamá?" Anastacia asked, taking her mother by the hand.

"Nothing, Ana *mou*. I haven't been here in many years. That's all."

Irini made a sour face and rolled her eyes. She'd complained for the entire journey and had asked over and over again to stay back with her grandmother.

Forty minutes later, they arrived at Sophia's childhood home. Spyro had wanted to update it, but the only time the house was occupied was during Spyro's occasional visits to confer with Savvas and Fotis regarding the vineyard so they hadn't bothered. Besides, Sophia insisted she wanted the house to remain exactly the way she remembered it.

And it was. Every painting on the walls, every stick of furniture, even the potted plants on the steps flourished as they always had, and she wondered how they survived the neglect. Her heart tugged when she stopped outside her childhood bedroom. It was small, the furniture was sparse and marred from generations of use, but it was hers and she missed it.

"What's so great about this place?" Irini criticized. "Everything is old and run down. Our home is so much grander."

"Perfection is in the mind of a child's eye," Sophia told her daughter. "We've gone through some arduous years during the war, and I thank God every day that it's finally over. But one day, when you think of those days, it's the good times you'll recall."

Irini shrugged. "Maybe. We had what we needed. The rest didn't affect me."

Sophia sighed heavily. She hoped that, as Irini moved toward adulthood, her sense of empathy would blossom.

Spyro, carrying valises in both hands, stepped through the front door, behind him followed Elias, Daphne and their sixteen-year-old son, Petros.

"Look who I found. And they are very anxious to see you," Spyro said.

Sophia had told her husband what had happened all those years before, and of the expectation the families had for Elias and herself. But she'd also confided that she missed his friendship and that its loss was one of her biggest regrets. Her husband was being polite. She had no doubt her old friend wanted to reconnect, but her cousin Daphne? She wasn't so sure about her.

Elias and Sophia both kept their feet planted firmly were they stood; Elias' dreamy expression holding Sophia's teary gaze. "It's good to have you home, my friend," he said and she briskly walked to him, embracing the boy who had been lost to her for too many years.

Daphne cocked her head to one side, twisting her face in an expression of annoyance. Crossing her arms in front of her, she looked at Sophia with disdain.

"Daphne, it's good to see you as well," Sophia said. "These are my daughters." She motioned for them to come near and introduced them.

Petros invited the girls to join him in the courtyard while the adults were left to reacquaint themselves.

"You're welcome to stay at our home if you like," Elias offered and Daphne shot him a look of irritation. "This house hasn't had any renovations or repairs since you left."

"I rather like it though. I'd like to stay here, but thank you for the kind offer."

"You were always a girl who wanted very little," Daphne snickered.

"But now I lavish my Sophia with her every desire," Spyro said, speaking directly to Daphne. Lovingly, he stroked his wife's hand.

Sophia adored her husband and he knew her well. He wouldn't allow Daphne or anyone else to cut her down or make her feel inferior.

"Tonight you'll dine at our home and any talk of business can be left for the morning," Elias insisted.

When they entered the home that belonged to Elias and Daphne, Sophia felt the style and décor was more a reflection of Daphne than her husband. Although the rooms were filled with possessions that must have drained Elias' pockets, the house seemed cold and empty and it didn't emanate the warmth that Elias had exuded when they were children.

Soon after they'd arrived, the rest of the family came barreling into the house, anxious to see Sophia and meet her daughters. Elias' parents greeted her warmly and told her they were sorry her mother could not make the journey.

"She's still mourning my babá," Sophia told them. "And the memory of her life here with him is too painful."

"We understand," Dora said, nodding. "We miss him terribly."

Sophia wasn't sure of the reception she'd receive from her Uncle Savvas and Aunt Olga, but her aunt hugged her tightly, telling her how much she had missed her. And Uncle Savvas held her face in his hand, repeating, *glyko mou koritsaki*—my sweet girl—with a huge grin on his face.

For three days the reunion continued and Sophia was overjoyed when little Marina, all grown and married now, came to visit from a neighboring town. Meanwhile Anastacia found herself spending time more with the adults than she did with Irini and Petros, who seemed to disappear often.

On their last evening, Sophia took a stroll through the vineyards alone. The gentle breeze carried the lingering scent of wildflowers and she closed her eyes breathing in the long denied fragrance that was so familiar. The sun was just beginning to dip below the horizon and the reflection from the range of hues blanketing the sky cast a pink glow over the green grapes.

She was so lost in thought and memories that Sophia didn't hear the footsteps behind her.

"I long for the days when you and I walked along these paths," Elias said, rousing her from contemplation.

Turning, Sophia responded. "Those were good times ... the simple days of childhood."

"I've missed you," he said, lifting her hand to his lips.

"And I, you. You were my dearest friend."

There was nothing but innocence in the exchange, simply a sweet gesture between friends separated for too long. But as Daphne marched up to confront them, her accusing eyes conveyed she had witnessed something much more.

"Leave my husband alone, Sophia," she shouted.

"Daphne! We were just reminiscing." Sophia was stunned by Daphne's outrage.

"Go home. Back where you belong." Daphne inched closer to her and pointed a finger at her face. "You always wanted what wasn't yours to have."

"Daphne! *Skase!*" Elias scolded.

"How can you say that? It's simply not true," Sophia was on the verge of tears. "I left and you married Elias. It's what you always wanted."

"I got his name but you stole his heart."

"Daphne!" Elias grabbed her arm but she jolted free of him.

"No! She didn't want to marry you, but she didn't want me to have you either. And now, here you are together after all these years," she said, barking accusations to her husband. "Like mother, like daughter," Daphne spat.

"What is that supposed to mean?" Sophia asked.

"You taught your daughter well. I caught Irini with my Petros. She seduced my boy just as you are trying to seduce my husband."

Fire seared through her, crackling to the surface. She could have whipped Daphne with the flames that she felt burning from her eyes.

"Say what you want about me, Daphne. God knows you have been nothing but malicious to me my entire life." Now it was Sophia who inched closer, threatening her with her searing glare. "But don't you ever, ever speak ill of my children! My daughter is only thirteen years old. Your son is sixteen. If anyone has done the seducing I would suspect it was him."

Turning, Sophia addressed Elias. "My apologies for how this evening turned out." She lifted her chin toward Daphne. "I won't be disrupting your lives any longer." Sophia kissed Elias on both cheeks. "I'll say good-bye now. We'll be leaving in the morning."

"Sophia," Elias said, softly.

They looked at one another with regret. "It was so good to see you, Elias."

"It meant the world to me," he said as Sophia walked away. "It was everything."

Chapter 31

Evvie

July 2008

Evvie listened to Yiayiá Sophia's story with rapt attention. "And you've never been back since?"

"No, I haven't. What started out so pleasant, turned ugly. You can understand why I never speak of it."

Evvie nodded. "Yes, but that was such a long time ago. Over sixty years!"

"It wasn't worth it. Spyro would go for business when he needed to but he made it clear that he wouldn't even stand in the same room as Daphne."

"Yiayiá, did Irini and Petros have sex?"

The old woman laughed. "That's what you wonder the most from everything I've told you?"

"Well, I'm curious, but I understand if you don't want to tell me."

Her sigh rang from remorseful regret. "Yes, I believe so, and it was a behavior that became a pattern with Irini." She sipped the water Evvie had poured for her earlier and stared over the balcony down to the passersby below. "Somehow I failed with her."

"No, Yiayiá." Evvie squatted down beside her great-grandmother's chair. "It's just who she was. My yiayiá was your daughter also and there was no one more loving than she was."

"All gone now." Yiayiá Sophia seemed to drift off, lost in her own grief. "My Spyro and my Anastacia left me too soon … Irini too."

Evvie now feared that asking her to recall the past had been too painful. Her color looked pallid and Evvie became concerned when she felt the coolness of her fingertips. It was late and she suggested they go to bed. Suddenly, her pro-yiayiá seemed frailer than she had been the day before.

Once again, at the same hour as the night before, Evvie was roused from her sleep. A hand brushed along her cheek and down the length of her hair. 'Watch over her,' was whispered in her ear as though someone was standing over her. The floral scent her yiayiá had always worn lingered in the air. Evvie shivered, certain her grandmother had made another visitation. "I will. I promise," she murmured.

The next morning, she awoke to the sound of clamoring pots. Following the noise, Evvie padded into the kitchen. "What are you doing, Yiayiá?"

"What does it look like? I'm making you breakfast."

"I should be cooking for you. You weren't feeling well last night."

"*Ba! Eímai kalá!*"

"You weren't fine last night."

"This morning I feel strong." There was a sparkle in her eye. "Sit. I will tell you something, but don't think I'm a crazy old woman."

"Never."

She made the sign of the cross over her heart in rapid consecutive motions. "My Ana came to me last night. I felt her. She spoke to me."

"She came to me also." Evvie wasn't dreaming. If there was even a glimmer of doubt that Anastacia had come to her, it had vanished.

"What did she say to you?"

"It's all for her now." Yiayiá Sophia shrugged. "I don't know what she meant by that." She turned back to the stove and cracked a couple of eggs.

"I don't know either. Can I ask you something? I've never spoken to anyone about it but does everyone see … spirits in their dreams? I mean, it's happened to me before and Mom told me that it's happened to her several times in her life."

"I think when the love is strong, the soul finds a way to stay close and let us know they're watching over us. But for that you need faith, and not everyone believes." She shut the stove off and went to the refrigerator, retrieving a carafe of freshly squeezed orange juice.

"It helps me, a little anyway, to know I still have a piece of her and my dad with me."

"Here, an American breakfast for my *engoní*."

"Aw, you didn't have to do that."

She took a seat beside Evvie. "Once you asked me if we could visit the vineyard. How would you like to go to Kefalonia?"

Evvie, about to put a forkful of eggs in her mouth, froze. "You would go there? After what you told me?"

"Daphne is gone. She passed away five years ago. It was she that kept me from returning."

"What about Elias? Is he gone too?"

"No." She smiled thinking of her friend. "We keep in touch through letters." She lifted her hands. "I know, I know. Who writes a letter today when you can call or talk on the computer?"

"Or text," Evvie added.

She shook her head. "You kids! A letter is much more personal. Typing a few words on a phone is not."

"Anyway … the vineyard?"

"Yes, I'd like to see my island one last time and I know you want to see it, so I thought we would go together."

"Oh, Yiayiá!" Evvie jumped from her seat. She couldn't contain her excitement. "I was hoping we would go, but after what you told me I didn't think you'd want to."

Evvie made all the arrangements and four days later their plane touched down at Kefalonia Airport. A car rental was waiting for them and they drove up the winding mountains until they reached the vineyard where her great-grandmother had spent most of her youth.

She admired the landscape as they drove and commented on how different it looked from the other islands she'd been to. Kefalonia was lush with foliage—tall black pine and fir trees, wildflowers and orchids, and herbs whose fragrance was carried by the gentle breeze. The water was clear and pristine and Evvie stopped the car at the side of a cliff to appreciate the unique gradient shades of aqua flowing in gentle waves.

As they neared the vineyard, Sophia warned her great-granddaughter not to expect anything as grand as she'd seen in France. This was a simple island and the beauty was in the natural landscape and not in ornate man-made structures. But Kefalonia had changed. An earthquake in 1953 had destroyed many buildings. The old world charm was lost, replaced by structures that were new, holding their own beauty, if not history. Large homes appeared between peaks and valleys and, as the Kefalonians acquired more wealth, their satisfaction with minimalism must have disappeared.

"Are you nervous, Yiayiá?" Evvie asked as they pulled onto the gravel driveway.

"Not at all. True friendship is a bond that will not be broken. Time and distance can't change that."

When Evvie slammed the car door, it took only a moment for Elias and his son to swing open the front door to their home.

With his arms outstretched, Elias lumbered over to Sophia.

"He's been waiting all day for you," Petros said. "Welcome to our home."

"Can I believe my eyes?" Elias asked rhetorically. They kissed, first on one cheek and then the other as tears formed in their eyes.

"You must be Evvie," Petros said. "I hear you're a winemaker as well."

"Yes! I am and when I found out about this place I had to come and see it for myself."

Petros took Evvie's bags from her. "You must be hungry. We've prepared a meal. Let's go inside and afterward I'll show you the vineyard."

Introductions were made and Evvie tried to remember each of their names. Petros and his wife, Maria, had two children. Their son, Grigoris, was working in the fields but his wife, Anthoula, was setting the table. They seemed to be close to her own parents' age and she wondered if they had any children she could become acquainted with.

"Our daughter is in medical school," Anthoula told Evvie, but Grigoris has a brother who lives in the States and he has a boy who is here visiting."

"Where is my grandson?" Petros asked. "He's always running off."

"He mumbled something about the beach," Anthoula told him.

After their meal, they lingered around the table, reminiscing about old stories and looking through photos together.

"Too bad you never brought your granddaughter, Sophia, here," Elias said. "But it's good to see her daughter with us, and interested in the business."

"I don't think my mom knows this place exists," Evvie said. "Once I tell her about it, I bet she'd love to visit."

Sophia drew her eyes downward. "There were many years I didn't speak of it."

An uncomfortable silence filled the air. Petros broke the quiet. "This is your legacy too, Evvie. Your pro-yiayiá still owns one third of the vineyard."

Evvie looked at her with confusion but Sophia waved her off.

"After Spyro died, Sophia wanted to sell us her interest in the vineyard but Babá refused," Petros told Evvie.

"Because I wasn't contributing. You were doing all of the work," Sophia said, addressing Elias.

"And if it wasn't for Spyro, we would have lost everything during the war."

"What did he do?" Evvie asked.

"Before the war," Elias began, "Spyro expanded our distribution. He opened wine stores and a taverna, which was his own investment. Tensions were heating up all over the world and he didn't take any chances or trust anyone. He'd invested our profits wisely, and when the war broke out, he pulled the money from the banks and found ways to hide it."

"I was pretty young but once the Nazis began to come through, they took over everything. What was ours became theirs," Petros said.

"All our wine production was stolen. We could no longer distribute because they were loading our bottles by the truckload for themselves," Elias added.

"The situation in Athens was no better," Sophia said. "The wine stores closed, and what stock was left, the Germans took."

"When the war was finally over, it was the money Spyro hid that saved us. We would have been broke otherwise," Petros said.

"And for this reason, among many others, Sophia will always be entitled to her share of the profits," Elias said with conviction. "Now, are you ready for a tour of the land?"

"I've been ready since the second I got here," Evvie said enthusiastically.

Evvie and Yiayiá Sophia retired early that night. It had been a long, but enlightening day and she was exhausted. Tomorrow she'd explore the grapevines more closely on her own perhaps and meander the property, but now she needed a good night's sleep.

Chapter 32

Evvie

July 2008

E vvie awoke bright and early the next morning, zipped herself
into a pair of worn denim cutoff shorts, and pulled a white,
cropped t-shirt over her head. Forcing her feet into her black
Converse sneakers without bothering to untie the laces first, she looked
in the mirror and wound her hair in an elastic band.

She nearly skipped down the hallway of the sprawling ranch home,
and skipping was not generally something Evvie did. Well, not since
she was a small girl anyway. But she was nearly giddy with excitement.
This land, this vineyard, was a part of her family history. She wanted
to wander, row by row on her own, daydreaming how it must have
been when her pro-yiayiá was a young girl. It wasn't hard for her to
imagine it with all she had learned over the past several days.

When Evvie entered the kitchen, only Petros and Grigoris were
standing over the center island gulping down coffee and biting into
koulouri, small bread rounds covered in sesame seeds.

"*Kalimera*," Evvie said.

"*Kalimera*, Evanthia," they answered in unison.

"You're up early," Grigoris said.

"I'm used to waking up at this hour when I work on the vineyard back home. I was hoping to explore on my own this morning."

"Feel free to go anywhere you wish. But first you must eat." Petros handed her a *koulouri* on a plate. He slid a platter along the marble countertop. "*Graviera kai feta tyrí?*"

"Sure! Both. I never say no to cheese," Evvie said.

"We're heading out but why don't you go sit on the veranda. Relax, take your time," Petros suggested. You have all day to roam and it's such a pleasant view."

"My nephew sits out here every morning," Grigoris added.

Evvie nodded, poured herself a mug of coffee and then carried her breakfast outside. Taking a seat by a small table under a grape arbor, she admired a view that was so different than the one she enjoyed at her vineyard back home. Beyond the acres of grapevines, mountains stood proudly. From what she had seen so far, Kefalonia was a most unique island. The varied landforms alone in this one corner of the world made it so. Green forests and ample sandy beaches with crystal blue water were rare to find in such close proximity. And she hadn't yet seen half of what had been described to her. Wild horses ran free and magnificent caves drew tourists from around the globe to explore.

Evvie's thoughts were broken when a male voice called out to her.

"I was hoping we'd run into each other this morning," he said.

Evvie knew it must have been the grandson she'd yet to meet. Before she could turn to greet him, he stepped in front of her. When she looked up at him, they just stared at one another in shock. His expression must have been as stunned and confused as hers. Her jaw went slack and her eyes widened. If she had passed him on the street she wouldn't have recognized him. Once again, his look had changed. A mop of golden hair with brown tips was mussed in all the right places but the sides were much shorter in a buzz cut.

"What are *you* doing here?" Zak demanded harshly.

"Me? What about you?"

"I came to visit my grandparents."

"Your ... grandparents?" Confusion morphed into sudden under-standing. "Wait. Petros is your grandfather?"

He nodded, crossing his arms over his chest, widening his stance. "Well, you still haven't explained what you are doing here." He planted his feet firmly on the ground.

"I came to visit with my great-grandmother," Evvie answered. "She grew up on this vineyard."

"Is she Sophia? My Great-grandfather Elias' Sophia?"

"It seems so," Evvie said, as completely floored at this revelation as Zak appeared to be.

"So your great-grandmother and my great-grandfather both grew up on this vineyard and were best friends?"

"You can keep asking the question, but the answer will still be the same," Evvie told him.

"What are the fucking chances?"

"I don't know. It's beyond weird," she said. "Church, school ... here. It seems that fate keeps throwing us together." She thought she saw a moment of softness reflected in his face until his eyes went cold.

"I'll stay out of your way if you stay out of mine," Zak bit out.

Evvie took a deep intake of breath at his sharp tone and held it. He went for the door but she called to him and he halted, his head hang-ing low as he avoided eye contact.

"Zak, please don't go. Can I talk to you for just one second? Give me a chance to—"

"Apologize? No need. It's ancient history." He looked up at her and shrugged. "You're just not that important," he said before walking away.

Evvie closed her eyes and pressed her fingertips against her eyelids to prevent the flow of tears that were sure to fall. If it was at all possible to feel any worse than she had the day of her parents' BBQ, then she was sure this was it. All this time, she hadn't even so much as seen him from a distance around town or at their church, but she traveled five thousand miles from home and this is where she ran smack into him? The one person who reminded her of the most shameful moment of her life? And the worst part of it was that Zak was a nice guy who didn't deserve to be treated how she had treated him. What she did was never meant to hurt him, but after what he'd overheard her say to Stella, what else could he feel?

"There you are," Yiayiá Sophia said walking onto the patio while tying an apron around her waist.

Lost in her thoughts, Evvie wasn't sure how much time had passed. She looked up at her pro-yiayiá with red-rimmed eyes, and saw the immediate look of concern on her great-grandmother's face.

"*Pethi mou?*"

Evvie's words were caught in her throat and she shook her head. She feared that if she spoke the tears would fall, and she wasn't certain that once they did, they could be stopped. The old woman came up beside Evvie and brushed her hand over her hair.

"It's nothing. I'm just a little emotional today."

"Ah, I'm like that too at times." She cupped Evvie's chin in her hand. "Would you like to help me with something?"

"Sure. What is it?"

"Tomorrow is the feast day of the saint my Aunt Olga was named for. I'm going to make *kollyva* to bring to the church in the morning to pray for her soul. I thought that since next month will be ten years since my sweet Anastacia left this earth, you might want to make another one for her while we're together."

Those sweet words were what finally broke her. Evvie covered her face with her hands and, with shaking shoulders, her breaths became shallow and rapid. The tears that followed erupted from deeply suppressed emotion once hidden by dark moods or combative behavior.

"It never gets easier," she cried. "It still hurts so much."

"I know," her great-grandmother agreed. "Come, we will do this together for my Ana."

Evvie rose from her seat, nodding her agreement to help. She wasn't sure how the beautifully decorated, sugar covered wheat helped the souls in heaven but it was a tradition she was familiar with—a beautiful ancient tradition.

Together, they worked side by side, and as Sophia always did, she told Evvie stories from days gone past. She had boiled and dried the wheat the night before and was now instructing Evvie on what to add next. Thoroughly, she mixed in the cinnamon, raisins, pomegranate seeds and walnuts.

In equal measure, they poured the mixture onto two silver platters. Pressing the wheat with their hands, they formed a solid mound on each tray. "Now the fun part," Yiayiá Sophia declared. "We decorate."

She topped the wheat with a blanket of powdered sugar, packing it down and smoothing it. Evvie followed her technique until both platters looked like mounds of freshly fallen snow. Evvie found the container of candy dragees in the pantry closet. Yiayiá Sophia formed a cross down the middle of the *kollyva* with the decorative, silver confections. On either side of the religious symbol, initials of the deceased were drawn with smaller-sized dragees.

"For my Yiayiá," Evvie said, somberly, satisfied she'd done something important to remember her by. She removed her apron, cleaned off the counter and kissed her great-grandmother on the cheek. "Thank you for teaching me how to prepare it. Why don't you rest for a while?"

Evvie poured her a glass of water and escorted her to a lounge chair on the veranda.

"If you don't mind, I'm going to take a ride," Evvie said. "Don't hold dinner for me. I might be out for the whole day."

The next morning, Evvie walked into the kitchen dressed for church.

"There she is," Elias said. "Did you enjoy the island yesterday?"

"Very much. I took the ferry to Argostoli."

"You and my grandson keep missing each other. I'm sure he would have enjoyed your company at dinner last night," Maria said.

Evvie could feel her body tense at the mention of Zak.

"Ah, here he is," Elias said. "Zaharias, come meet Evanthia."

"Hello," Evvie said in a low voice, her eyes cast downward.

"Hi," he answered curtly.

"Are we all ready?" Petros asked.

Evvie and Sophia lifted the trays of *kollyva* from the counter.

"I'll take that," Petros insisted. "Zaharias, take the other tray from Evanthia and bring it to the car."

"You kids should ride together," Maria suggested.

"I'm going to drive Yiayiá in my car," Evvie said.

When the liturgy had ended, the priest came over to the table holding the *kollyva*. A golden cross had been placed between the two trays and on each end were glass vases filled with fragrant violas indigenous to the island. With his prayer book in one hand and a smoking censer in the other, the priest chanted his plea to God for the souls of the departed. Evvie managed to keep it together until the memorial hymn was sung. A short but guttural sob escaped from within her just as it had the first time it was sung on her Yiayiá's behalf. She couldn't fathom how, sometimes, it seemed as if a lifetime had passed since she'd last held her yiayiá, and at other times the pain of losing her was so fresh it was as though it had happened only days ago.

Sophia rubbed Evvie's back and held her close. As Evvie went to wipe her tears, she caught Zak bending around his pappou to look at her and their eyes met. She couldn't decipher what she saw in them before she looked away, but she sensed kindness emanating from within just as the day before until he'd quickly replaced his stare with stone-cold hardness.

When it was time to leave the church, Zak stepped alongside her. "I'm sorry ... about your yiayiá."

She smiled tentatively. "Thank you. It was a long time ago, but I still miss her terribly."

228

"I know." He shoved his hands in his pockets. "You want to go somewhere? It looks like you could use something to lighten the day."

"You don't have to do that. I'll be fine."

"I—no, really, it's okay. You're a guest in my pappou's house and it looks like we'll be together for the next several days."

"But you hate me," she said, fidgeting with the tissue she had cried her tears into.

Sighing, Zak rubbed his forehead. "I don't hate you," he said softly. "I never have. I liked you but, as much as I tried, you never let me in. And when I finally thought you did, you made a fool of me."

"It wasn't my proudest moment, but I never intended to hurt you." She dug her keys out of her bag. "Thanks for the offer but I can't go anywhere with you."

"Evvie, wait." He placed his hand on her arm. "You wanted to talk. Let's talk. First you should let me show you around the island and then we can talk later. What do you say?"

This boy wielded more emotions in the span of an hour than anyone she'd ever met, Evvie thought. He'd gone from mad to sympathetic, angry to kind, and now he simply looked at her with a hopefulness shining in his eyes.

"Okay, but only if you're sure you want to put up with me," she said, attempting to wash away the bleakness from her mood.

Evvie's grandmother rode back to the house with Petros and Maria. Evvie, at Zak's insistence, handed the keys to the rental car over to him.

"How would you like to go to Melissani Cave?"

"It's on my bucket list," she answered.

"Great! It's about an hour from here and the lines are long, so we'll stop at Agia Efimia for lunch."

They drove silently for a while until Evvie finally broke the silence. "Did you find a job yet?"

"I did," he shrugged, glancing at her before looking back at the road. "Junior visual designer. And I only got that because I was interning with the company as a game tester and they liked me."

"It sounds like a great job and a good start."

"I guess. I don't really get to design anything myself though, but I'm working on a game concept of my own that I want to market when it's fully developed."

"Ryan, my boyfriend, got a job with Microsoft as a junior software architect."

Zak grimaced, contradicting his enthusiastic endorsement of Microsoft as a solid company. "I'm on the art end of the business so I'm more of an Apple user."

"Ryan is itching to work for Google one day."

"Good luck to him with that! What about you? Working?"

"Where I always wanted to be. The vineyard. When I found out that Yiayiá Sophia grew up here, I bugged her until she agreed to bring me."

Zak pulled into a parking spot across from a dock lined with sailboats gently rocking in their slips. A row of gift shops, spice stores and cafés came into view as they walked down the street.

"Do you like seafood?"

Evvie nodded and they took a seat at an outdoor table under a canvas canopy. Zak ordered a platter with shrimp, crab and scallops to share, along with a *horiatiki* salad. Evvie had the waiter add an order of *skordalia* as a dip for the seafood. She was having a nice time and Zak seemed interested in her quest to produce a sparkling wine in the *méthode champenoise.*

"We've been cultivating the grapes, and last year my uncle invested in the production equipment. This year we'll try our first attempt using two out of the three traditional grapes. We only planted the Petit Meunier last year. We won't be able to get any fruit from those vines for another two or three years."

Evvie found herself either talking excessively, something she didn't normally do, or asking him a battery of questions about his own career in order to avoid any awkward silence. When a quiet moment finally hung between them, Evvie put down her fork purposely and looked up at him.

"Zak, I need to say something."

He dropped his fork and pushed back his chair. "You're not going to try to apologize again, are you?"

"I'd like to, yes. I owe you at least an explanation."

He made a face of displeasure but motioned with his hand for her to continue.

"I'll admit that I had no intention of dating you."

"Whoa! Good start. Just what a guy likes to hear."

"I already feel bad enough," she groaned. "But we were beginning to become somewhat friendly."

"Somewhat ... you have a way with words."

She huffed out a breath. "I'm trying to be honest. When I asked you to the party it was an impulsive decision."

"I think we were better off without your brand of apology."

"You don't understand. I had just gotten off the phone with my mother and she had suggested that I go to the church mixer they were holding for the college students who were returning home. She said I might meet a 'nice' young man there. Code for a nice Greek boy."

"I vaguely remember my mom mentioned that mixer to me. So?"

"Well, to be completely honest, I figured if I brought you home, a Greek boy, she'd finally get off my back. Face it, Zak, you weren't exactly what my parents had in mind, blue mohawk and all."

"It's still no excuse to play me the way you did."

"No, it wasn't, and I felt awful about it because I never meant to hurt you."

"You said that already."

"I'm sorry. I really am. The expression, 'don't judge a book by its cover,' really never made any sense to me until then. I judged you. By the way you dressed and wore your hair. I never bothered to crack the cover, to examine the pages. To go beyond skimming the surface. I was wrong because there is so much more to you than I bothered to discover."

Evvie felt a sense of relief flood through her at finally saying the words and telling him how utterly wrong she was. Zak, however, just stared at her, as if processing what she had just said.

"It makes me wonder how I might have been judged also," she said. "The black clothing, the overly made-up eyes. Who knows what people saw ... or thought they saw."

"What were they supposed to see?" he asked, reaching his hand across the table to take hers.

The contact of his caring gesture cracked a fraction of her armor.

"Just a sad girl, angry at the world and confessing to grief she couldn't let go of in the only way she'd allow herself."

"That's something I understand only too well," Zak said, his eyes penetrating hers.

And Evvie believed him. She had never said these words out loud, had barely admitted it to herself, but at times, she recognized in Zak what she'd seen in her own reflection.

After lunch they continued to Melissani Cave and found the area flooded with tourists. Hundreds of people stood in line waiting for the boat ride at the base of the cave.

"This isn't what I expected," Evvie said. Tour buses, mopeds and cars were everywhere. The line wrapped around the gift shop and spilled out onto the parking lot. "We'll be waiting for hours!" she exclaimed.

"We're not in a rush," Zak said, handing her the ticket he'd purchased for her. "It will be worth the wait," he smiled.

Evvie's phone beeped, signaling a text message had come through. She pulled her phone from her bag and looked at the display. *Ryan.* She opened the message to read it and Zak turned his back to her.

"Hey, I'm going to get an ice cream bar while we're waiting in line. Want one?" he asked.

"No, thanks. I'll be right here. This line isn't going anywhere."

He nodded, walking over to the snack shop.

This time zone difference sucks. I can't seem to catch you at a good time, Ryan wrote.

Evvie replied, telling him that the service wasn't great either. *I'm in line to get inside a cave.*

Ryan responded, *Have fun. Miss you.*

You too, Evvie replied.

"You're sure you don't want one?" Zak had already finished half of his.

She shook her head.

Slowly, they inched up to the front of the line. "Don't you wonder what this must have looked like in Elias and Sophia's time?" Evvie asked. She waved her hand around. "I'll bet there was none of this commotion."

"Hmmm, probably not," he agreed. "I wonder if they came down here? Maybe swam in the lake? Now that would be fun."

"Oh my God!" Evvie pulled out her phone and snapped a few pictures, hoping to capture the way the rays of the sun shone down into the water. The roof of the cave had collapsed centuries before and, with the lake below, it looked more like a giant well than a grotto. A rainbow spectrum of light beams reflecting off the cave walls and lake water cast an electric neon shade of blue that one would only dare to imagine in a mythical land.

"I told you it was worth the wait," Zak beamed, seeing how impressed she was.

When they finally got to the head of the line, they climbed into a rowboat with several strangers. Evvie held a wide smile during the entire ride, snapping pictures at every possible angle to capture the magnificence of this unique landform.

"Give me that," Zak said, taking her phone from her. "I'm sure you'd like one with yourself in the photo."

They had only spent ten minutes in the cave after standing in line for over an hour, but Evvie thought it was one of the most beautiful natural sites she'd ever seen. They got back into the car and Evvie assumed they were heading back home, but Zak had other plans.

"Let's go to the beach," he suggested.

"But I'm not dressed for the water."

"We won't be going into the water. Not today. We'll grab some dinner at this place nearby and then we'll sit and watch the sunset."

"Okay, if you really don't mind, that would be nice. But I don't want to monopolize all of your time."

Zak's eyes met Evvie's. It looked, to her, like he wanted to say something. But he seemed to shake the thought from his head and instead simply jammed the key into the ignition.

"It's fine. You're not."

After dinner, they walked from the taverna to Petani Beach. Zak led her past large sunbeds and bright orange umbrellas. "Where are we going?" Evvie asked.

"It's too crowded here. I have a favorite spot that's quiet and has the best view of the sunset."

He stopped at a small cove with large rock formations and high cliffs soaring into the sky above them. They sat on the pebbly sand looking out onto water, so crystal clear that Evvie could swear she saw the fish beneath the surface.

"Now we wait for the magic to begin." Zak hugged his knees to his chest.

Evvie was using her finger to draw circles in the sand. "Zak, is this like starting over?" She didn't dare look up at him. "Can we be friends?"

He hung his head between his bent knees. "It's all good. I'm not mad at you anymore, if that's what you're worried about."

But it did worry her. He'd been nothing but sweet and kind all day. He could have continued to ignore her, but when their eyes locked in the church that morning, he knew she was hurting and he had done everything in his power to alleviate the sorrow that gripped her. Still, guilt from her past transgression sat between them and she wondered if every time he saw or spoke to her, the memory of her callous behavior would be the first thing that came to his mind.

"Where did your mind go?" Zak asked.

"Just thinking."

"Me too. I was thinking you haven't called me *Hellas* even once today."

She covered her mouth with her fingertips. "I forgot about that. But then again, you ..." She swirled her pointer finger in the direction of his hair. "... aren't covered in blue anymore. Not even your eyes." She inspected them, coming almost nose-to-nose with him. "What color are they now?"

"Sea green. What color are yours?"

"Brown. Isn't it obvious? Should I give my brown a fancy name?"

"Let me inspect them and I'll let you know." He took her face in his hands and looked deeply into her eyes. "Yup, brown. Natural brown."

"It's late. I hope no one is worried about us," Evvie said a bit too quickly as he removed his hand from her cheek.

"I called my uncle and told him we'd be out until after dark."

The golden sphere of the sun descended slowly into the horizon, orange radiating over the expanse of the darkening sky. The water looked as though it had turned to flame. From the cool heat of the blue waters to the golden incandescence emanating from the sun itself, nature cast her grace upon the sea.

They remained silent, soaking in the beauty and occasionally glancing at one another if only to confirm their reactions were reciprocal. When the sky grew completely black, Zak offered his hand to help her up, but he didn't let go of hers as they slowly strode back to the car. This should have been awkward for Evvie, yet somehow it wasn't at all.

The rocky road was hard to negotiate in the dark and Zak was being nothing less than a gentleman. Nothing like the boy she expected him to be when she'd first met him at school, Zak had been sweeter than his hard appearance seemed. Now, he utterly surprised her with the unwarranted kindness he bestowed upon her.

They arrived home at nearly midnight, and Evvie kissed him on the cheek. "Thank you for brightening my day."

Chapter 33

Sophia Fotopoulos

July 2008

Sophia had gone to bed before Evvie and Zak arrived home the night before. She was anxious to hear how they had gotten along and how they'd spent their day. Thinking of the two of them exploring the island together, just as she and Elias had done in their youth, filled her with a source of pleasure. But sadness crept in, if only momentarily, when she thought of how many years had passed by and how, although she'd been blessed with longevity, there was never enough time.

Maria and Anthoula were at the kitchen table, each holding a mug of steaming coffee in their hands when Sophia entered. After offering her morning greetings, Sophia asked if she could use the kitchen.

"I thought the children would like some *tiganites* for breakfast," Sophia said.

"Make enough for all of us!" Anthoula said. "I haven't had them in ages."

"Yes," Zak joshed, overhearing his elders as he came down the hallway. "The 'children' would love some Greek style pancakes."

"I've got seventy years on you." Sophia waved a wooden spoon at him. "To me, you and Evanthia will always be children." She gathered the few ingredients needed and mixed them together in a glass bowl. When it was evenly blended, she covered it with plastic wrap and set it aside, allowing the yeast to bubble.

"*Kalimera*," Evvie said as she joined everyone hovering around the kitchen island. Petros and Grigoris had left the house earlier, but Elias came up behind Evvie and took his seat at the table.

While Sophia fried the *tiganites* in a skillet and warmed honey to pour over them, Evvie and Zak told her where they had gone the day before.

"How about today?" Zak asked, forking a pancake from the platter Sophia had placed in the center of the table. "Would you be interested in giving diving a try? There's a beach I know of where the cliffs aren't too high and the water is deep." The pancakes were small and it took him merely seconds to consume three of them. "Or if we go to Sami, we can go tubing or jet skiing at Antisamos beach."

"Can we do all of it?" Evvie asked with a hopeful grin.

Pointing his fork at her, he grinned, "I like the way you think."

After breakfast, Evvie and Zak took off. Maria and Anthoula headed to the market, leaving Sophia and Elias to sit peacefully on the veranda, enjoying each other's company.

"I've missed you, my friend," Elias told Sophia. "I missed you terribly after your family left and then once again after you'd visited all those years later, never to return again."

"Ah, Elias, what can I say? At least we kept in touch through our letters."

"I'm an old man. Older than you. I don't know how much time I have left."

Sophia wanted to argue on his behalf. She wanted to scold him for speaking that way and assure him he had many more years. If only that were true. But, it wasn't—for either of them. In her mind, she was still a young woman—her emotions, dreams and desires were still alive—but she hardly recognized the stranger in the mirror, and being here now made her painfully aware that an entire lifetime had passed her by.

"Why are you speaking this way? Are you ill?" Sophia asked.

"No," he laughed, and she couldn't help but notice the twinkle in his eyes. "I'm as healthy as a horse. Strong like a bull." He beat his chest to make his point. "But I have things to say to you and I don't know if I'll ever have the chance to again if I don't do it now."

"You know you can tell me anything."

He looked at her pensively. "When I look at you, all I see is the twelve-year-old girl with the bright attitude and the loving heart."

"You need new eyeglasses then," she teased him.

"I would have been happy with you, you know?" They were sitting beside each other and he placed his hand over hers. "It would have been a good life, and even at my adolescent age I knew that. Although our parents had arranged our match, I could have never done any better than to have had you as my wife."

"I was twelve and you were seventeen. I didn't know what I wanted at that age or what I would want later on. That wasn't a decision I was prepared to make at such a tender age and I didn't want it made for me." She sipped some water from her glass to moisten her drying throat. "You know I always loved you, my dear friend. I wanted what was good for both of us. You deserved to choose your bride."

"But if only I got to choose. Your aunt and uncle forced the issue. My father still wanted a merge between vineyards and Daphne wanted me."

"I'm aware," Sophia sighed. "But did you grow to love her?"

"No. And I didn't like her very much either, but she wasn't all that bad. I suppose that I could have done worse," he said with melancholy regret. "She loved me and, even though she must have sensed her feelings were not returned, she was good to me."

"She was always sweet on you, but you and I had forged a bond and she hated that."

They sat in quiet contemplation, both lost in their own thoughts.

"We had Petros and made a life together. It wasn't perfect but we had a mutual respect for each other. Well, that is until you came to visit with your girls," Elias said.

Daphne, Elias told her, lost her mind after Sophia's sudden departure from their home. She made horrible accusations, blaming Elias of adultery and claiming that the only reason Sophia came back was to steal him away from her. It was ridiculous of course and he'd told her so. She had come with her husband, a man he'd befriended, and Sophia was a childhood friend who he'd longed to see, but that was all. But there was no getting through to Daphne though. Her delusions had taken hold of her like an evil spirit, possessing ownership over her entire soul.

After that, the marriage had completely died. Between her jealousy and deplorable behavior to Sophia and her family, he could barely stand to look at her.

"I should have never come," Sophia said. "It wasn't my intention to interfere in your marriage."

"It wasn't your fault." He looked at her as if he wanted to say more. At ninety-seven he had remarkably few wrinkles on his face, save for a few lines in the corners of his eyes. As she examined his expression, the crinkles deepened and a crease formed on his brow. "There's more that you don't know."

"Please tell me. You look so burdened."

"I am. But not for the reasons you might suspect," he said. "When Daphne died five years ago, I never went through her belongings. It took me a year to finally decide to pack up her clothing to give to charity. In the middle of it all, I found something hidden in a hat box, wrapped in a scrap of material."

Sophia noticed Elias had unconsciously clenched his fists at his sides. "What was it that could have upset you so?"

"I'm going to show you, because it rightfully belongs to you and it's about time it was retuned." Elias rose from his seat and gestured for her to wait. Sophia watched as he left the veranda, his shoulders hunched a little more than they had been earlier. She couldn't imagine any possession she'd owned so many years ago or had lost that warranted Elias' distress.

When he returned a few minutes later, he held in his shaking hands a small object wrapped in what looked to be the remnants of an old, red tablecloth.

"All I can say is, I'm so terribly sorry," he said, handing it to her. "Had I known she had it all these years I would have returned it sooner."

Sophia gasped when she unraveled the worn cloth. "She hadn't laid her eyes on the object in over six decades. "My mother's icon!"

There it was before her in all its beauty—the silver and gold, the precious gems and the faces of the Virgin and Christ child, worn and faded, a testament of age and the many generations that must have prayed in front of the holy image.

Sophia looked up at Elias, bewildered. "We thought we'd lost it in the move. My mother was heartbroken. It had been in our family for so long and then it simply disappeared."

She held the precious heirloom against her heart, astonished to have it in her possession after all these years.

Sophia stretched her memory, recalling an encounter she'd had with Daphne. "My mother showed the icon to both of us and explained how it had been handed down to her and that, someday, I would be the next one to own it. Daphne threw a bit of a tantrum and asked Aunt Olga why she wouldn't be given one like it."

"That sounded like her," Elias said bitterly.

"She was always jealous, not just of me, but of anyone who had what she desired." Recollections of her childhood played back in Sophia's mind; the fragments of information and images flashing before her. "She was livid that I had been promised to you when she felt it should have been her."

"I can only assume she took it to get back at you. It was hidden all these years. It wasn't as if she displayed it." Elias cupped his hand on

Sophia's cheek. "I can't tell you how sorry I am about this. If I had only known ..."

"You have nothing to apologize for. You did nothing wrong and now you've returned it. Thanks to you, I'll be able to continue the tradition of passing it down through the generations." Sophia's eyes filled with tears. "For me, there is a heaviness in my heart that my Anastacia never had the opportunity to inherit it as she should have. Or at least see it." She wrapped the icon back in the weathered, old cloth. "But now my Sophia, Anastacia's daughter, will have it. Evanthia will take it to her."

~Tiganites~

1 packet dry yeast (¼ oz.)
2 cups lukewarm water
2 cups flour
½ teaspoon salt
1 tablespoon sugar
Vegetable or corn oil for frying
Golden raisins (optional)
Garnish – honey, crushed walnuts, cinnamon

In a large bowl whisk the water and yeast until the yeast dissolves. Add the flour, salt, and sugar, mixing thoroughly. Cover and set aside for 15 minutes. Add the raisins (optional).

Heat a skillet pan and pour enough oil to cover the bottom. Ladle in the batter to form pancakes, leaving enough room not to crowd them. Fry on each side until golden brown. Transfer to a platter lined with paper towels to absorb the oil. Remove from the paper towels onto another platter. Drizzle with honey and garnish with crushed walnuts and cinnamon.

Chapter 34

Zak

July 2008

Zak and Evvie came barreling through the door that evening, laughing jovially. They were bantering back and forth about everything from who dove the furthest off the cliffs to which one of them went flying off the high-speed tube first.

Zak could still feel the arms Evvie wound around his waist when she pressed her body against his while he'd steered the jet ski. Every cell in his body responded to her touch and he wanted so badly to hold her in his arms and kiss her.

Evvie had finally unleashed her true, unguarded self to him—a girl capable of letting loose and even allowing herself to share a few secret thoughts with him. This Evvie was the person he always knew was hidden behind her defensive attitude, and the fact that she was able to drop her guard with him was a huge step. In Zak's mind, it meant they had a deep connection, even if, at this point, she wasn't aware of it yet.

From the moment he'd met her, Zak had sensed an unexplainable link with Evvie, an unspoken and undiscovered bond. They were kindred spirits in many ways. Zak was as certain of this as he was of his own name. He recognized grief when it stared him in the face. And in

Evvie, he was able to identify the kind of pain that gripped the heart and stole any joy left in your soul. Now, discovering they were connected by the same strip of land, as well as through families with a shared history, Zak was convinced that he and Evvie were meant for each other.

Zak and Evvie followed the sound of music and chatter coming from the yard. They found Zak's family and Yiayiá Sophia on the veranda sipping after-dinner drinks. Maria greeted them and offered to heat up some food for them if they were hungry.

"I have something I want to show you, Evanthia *mou*," Sophia said. "Come inside with me."

"What is it, Yiayiá?" Evvie asked. "You seem very excited."

"I am!" She turned to Elias. "You come too. Zaharias, you may come also."

Zak and Evvie looked at each other, shrugging. They couldn't imagine what she could have gotten in the few hours they were away that she didn't have before. They followed her into the house and down the hallway until they reached the guest bedroom.

"Do you remember the stories I told you about my childhood?" Sophia asked her great-granddaughter.

"Sure! It's why I wanted to come here and see the vineyard."

"I told you about an icon that was passed down in my family. One that was crafted by my great-grandfather."

"Yes," Evvie said sympathetically. "You were sad because you lost it when you moved to Athens."

Sophia removed a cloth-wrapped item from the bed and handed it to Evvie. "Open it."

With curiosity, Evvie looked at Yiayiá Sophia's eager expression and carefully took the parcel from her. She unwound the material and stared at the icon in disbelief. "This is it? Your icon? But how?"

Elias placed his arm over Zak's shoulder and smiled at him.

"What's going on?" Zak asked Elias.

"It's been here all these years. For safekeeping, you could say," Sophia said.

"But you said you didn't know where it was."

"Your pro-yiayiá is too kind. Daphne, my wife, stole and hid it before the family left for Athens. I only found it recently," Elias explained.

"Elias, the boy," Sophia warned.

"What about me?" Zak asked. "What does this have to do with me?"

"Nothing," Elias answered. "Sophia is trying to spare your opinion of my late wife—your pro-yiayiá. But what she did was wrong and unforgiveable."

Zak could see Sophia was concerned for his feelings over this. He looked to Evvie for her reaction over what his great-grandmother had done, but she didn't seem to have one. Instead Evvie ran her fingers over the jewels framing the faded faces on the icon. Uneasiness hung in the air and the levity from earlier had all but been forgotten.

"*Katse, pethia.*" Sophia moved to make room on the bed for Evvie and Zak to sit on either side of her. Elias took a seat in an upholstered slipper chair against the wall opposite the bed.

"I want you to understand that we were all very young. I was only twelve and Daphne was fourteen. Looking back now, I see it all a little differently, maybe more clearly. I'd always thought my cousin, Daphne, was a mean girl. At least to me she was. And she wasn't much kinder to her siblings. But now I wonder if it was her circumstances that made her behave in the way she had."

"That's not an excuse for stealing what wasn't hers," Elias grumbled.

"We all do stupid things when we're young, Pappou," Zak said. "Don't be so hard on her."

"Elias, she had the responsibility of caring for her brothers and sisters. I didn't and she always resented that. It was a lot to expect of a young girl. And then there was you. As far back as I can remember, she had a crush on you, and that crush turned to love. She wanted you, but you were promised to me." She clasped her hands together. "Don't you see? In her mind, I had everything she wanted. With no control over the marriage agreement our parents had made, Daphne took what she could from me—something she knew was precious to my family."

"I made my share of regrettable moves when I was fourteen," Zak admitted.

"If she was remorseful then she should have returned it," Elias said. "And to think I was married to her all those years, never knowing what she'd done."

"Maybe she felt it was too late to give it back," Evvie said. "It's possible she couldn't figure out a way to undo the damage without making herself look bad."

"Well, I have it back now. And what matters is that it will stay in the family." Sophia crinkled her brow, narrowing her eyes as if in deep thought. "Zaharias, your pro-yiayiá was not a bad person. She was simply misunderstood. I see that now." She turned to Elias. "She loved you so much and her jealousy got the best of her. But even you admit she was a good wife to you." Sophia patted Elias' cheek. "Hold on to that."

Elias and Sophia exited the guest room, leaving Zak and Evvie to their thoughts.

"Are you okay?" Evvie asked tentatively.

Zak laughed humorlessly. "With what? The fact that my great-grandmother stole from yours?"

Evvie smoothed her hands over Zak's shoulders and a ripple of electricity traveled through him. His heart swelled just a little more for this girl who could have used this as yet another excuse to reject him. Instead, her touch soothed him, and the empathy in her expression told him she understood how he felt.

"They were just kids. It's ancient history and she has it back now, so it's all good." She took his hand and dragged him out through the bedroom door. "Come on, I'm starved."

"Ev? Are you up for doing something tomorrow?" he asked without his usual self-assurance.

"Oh, your uncle promised to take me around the vineyard again. I want to see what his typical day is like here."

"Can I tag along?"

"Sure," Evvie said hesitantly. "But I thought you told me you never had much interest in working the land."

"Not since I was a young boy. But I think I'd like to see what keeps your attention."

Chapter 35

Evvie

July 2008

The next morning, Evvie woke earlier than she had since she'd arrived. She was more than willing to give Petros and Grigoris a hand in the vineyard. On the front steps of the house, she was tying the laces on the work boots she had borrowed from Anthoula when Zak came through the door.

Turning, she looked up at him and smiled. "I didn't think you'd really wake up this early."

With an expression of mock surprise, Zak pointed to his chest. "Me? I've been known to get up early."

Evvie raised an eyebrow in disbelief.

"I'm awake now, but if you need further proof, let me take you to the beach at sunrise tomorrow. There's this perfect, isolated spot with the best view."

"Of course, there is. Have you scoured this entire island?"

Their vineyard was unique to any other she'd seen before. Manicured symmetrical rows of vines like the ones she worked on at her home vineyard did not exist here. Nor did the hillside vines of Épernay. Here the terrain was mountainous and rocky. Vines seemed to be planted haphazardly, as if they had grown wild. But the vines located closer to the house, on less hilly land, were planted in the organized fashion she was accustomed to.

Grigoris explained that the Robola grapes grew best down the sides of rocky mountains. Evvie bent down and picked up a handful of white, jagged stones. Beneath the layer of rocks was deep red earth.

"That's limestone," Petros said. "You went to the cave? It's made mostly of limestone. And the earth underneath has minerals that feed the roots."

"And these grapes grow best like this? What if you were to grow them by the vines near the house?" Evvie asked.

"They wouldn't survive," Grigoris answered. These grapes are indigenous to Kefalonia. No one else grows them or can grow them."

"How do you harvest? It must be a difficult task."

"The old way. By hand," Petros said. He patted his grandson on the back. "Zaharias has helped us with that a time or two." A sorrowful look passed between them and Evvie was puzzled by it.

For hours, they worked side by side, Evvie lending a hand where her expertise could assist, yet fascinated by all she learned. Zak, she was surprised, stuck it out for the entire day, and seemed to know what to do without much instruction.

Later, with sore muscles and covered in dirt, Evvie and Zak went back to the house. She peeled herself out of her clothing, rinsed off in the shower and then did something she hadn't done in a long while—soaked in a hot bath until she pruned like a raisin. The bath oil smelled of fragrant rosewater and she closed her eyes, inhaling the pleasant scent.

She would be sad to leave this place and she hoped it wouldn't be her last visit. The island was so different compared to any other she had explored, but the people who lived here—Zak's family and her pro-yiayiá's friends—were so kind and loving and she would miss them terribly.

Evvie let her hair air dry naturally while applying a hint of makeup. With her skin already bronzed, pink lip gloss and a touch of black mascara was all she needed to complete her look. The buttons on her white eyelet sundress ran from bodice to hem and she examined herself in the mirror while she fastened them.

Downstairs, everyone had gathered for dinner on the veranda and she apologized for her tardiness. She hoped they hadn't waited for her. Zak was flipping meat on the grill with his pappou and, when he turned to greet her, she noticed he was wearing large, black eyeglasses.

The frames were similar to the ones Buddy Holly wore in old photos, except Zak's were tinted slightly gray. She walked over to him, wiggled the frames on his face and asked, smiling mischievously, "What's this all about?"

"My contacts were irritating me. Probably from all the dirt that got in my eyes."

"Huh!" Evvie exclaimed. "You really are a chameleon, aren't you?"

Zak always managed to make a statement with his appearance. No matter what he wore, he never looked conventional. His blond hair, spiked with black tips and those heavy-framed glasses would have looked silly on anyone else, but somehow, he pulled it off. Zak asked Evvie to hold the platter while he transferred the grilled meats and vegetables onto it.

It was a hot, arid evening and everyone was enjoying it. Elias began to sing old songs from their youth. Sophia, appearing as though she had fallen back to another time, looked years younger as she sang along with him. Zak rose from his seat and left the room, only to come back with a bouzouki.

Sitting on a chair across from the elder crooners, he propped the instrument on his knee and began to play. He never ceased to amaze Evvie. He had talents she never knew of and some she had only become aware of recently. She felt she was only just beginning to discover the scope of his artistic creativity. On both occasions when they had spent time together, he had a sketchbook in his hand and, although he drew mostly comics and fantasy characters, his landscapes were breathtaking as well.

"Sing for us," Elias requested.

"What would you like to hear?" Zak asked.

"Surprise us," his yiayiá said.

He kept his head down, examining the strings as he thought of what to play. He glanced up for the briefest second to glimpse Evvie. "'*Esi, Mono Esi*,'" he decided.

"Anthoula clapped her hands together. "Such a beautiful choice."

Zak's elegance and command over the instrument proved equal to the one he had when his hand glided over his sketchpad.

He was good, Evvie thought. Really good. She watched him intently as he lost himself in the music, closing his eyes and singing the beautiful lyrics. Words of the future and forever fell from his lips as he sang of two lovers becoming one.

His eyes penetrated hers and her heart jumped. She wasn't sure what had perpetuated such a reaction. She tried to blame it on the lyrics, the moon and the brightly shining stars that graced this beautiful island. The scenery was enough to make anyone feel romantic.

Breaking her pensive mood and falling back to the joking sarcasm that covered her insecurities, she rose from her seat when he finished. "Of course you play bouzouki! No guitar for you, Hellas?"

"That's the first time you've called me that all week."

Evvie patted him on the shoulder. "I had to do it at least once and that," she pointed to the bouzouki, "warranted it." She covered her mouth to hide a yawn. "I'm beat. I'll see you in the morning."

"Don't oversleep or I'll drag you out of bed by your feet. We have a date with the sunrise."

"Goodnight. Oh, and Zak, I've never heard that song played better."

~Chickpea Spread~

1 large (29oz.) can chickpeas
2 cloves garlic, crushed
2 scallions, sliced thin
1 teaspoon paprika
⅛ teaspoon cayenne pepper (optional)
Juice and zest of 1 lemon
2 tablespoons red wine vinegar
5 - 6 fresh basil leaves, sliced in shreds (chiffonade)
¼ cup olive oil
2 teaspoons salt
1 teaspoon pepper
1 teaspoon sugar
1 teaspoon oregano

Mix all the ingredients in a large bowl. Mash the chickpeas just enough to break them up. Do not puree. The texture of this spread is not meant to be smooth. I use a pastry blender to break up the chick peas. The sharp edges give me the results I like. Serve with pita bread or add to a wrap for another layer of flavor.

"As with the butterfly, adversity is necessary to build character in people."

—Joseph B. Wirthlin

Chapter 36

Evvie

July 2008

Early the next morning, Evvie walked into the kitchen to find Zak, dressed in black and white board shorts, filling a straw picnic basket. A large cotton quilt was draped over a chair and his sketchpad was leaning against it.

Evvie, wearing a sheer, white cover-up over her black bikini, greeted him. "What's all that for?" she asked.

"Last night, after you went to bed, I put together some food to take with us today."

"That was thoughtful," Evvie said. "Let me help you with that." He handed her the soft drinks he pulled from the fridge and she placed them in the basket. Gathering up the quilt from the chair, she glanced at him. "Ready?" she asked.

Zak grabbed the basket and his sketchpad. "Now I am!"

Sitting side-by-side, Evvie and Zak looked out beyond the shoreline. When they'd arrived, the ebony sky accentuated the golden points of lights from the thousands of stars still glowing above. Slowly, before their eyes, as if by a supernatural power commissioned by Apollo Helios himself, the sun began to rise in a spectacle of color.

Leave it up to Zak, Evvie thought, to find the most secluded spot with the most glorious view imaginable to spend a picnic. He told her he'd spent the summers of his youth exploring the island and Evvie was beginning to believe most of it was spent here. He seemed to know every intricate nook and cranny of this hidden beach.

Ebony faded to the most breathtaking shade of royal blue. Evvie didn't think a sky of this color was possible in anything other than animated films, and as the majesty of the expanse before her transformed to violet, the water below rippled like a pool of pink lemonade.

When the sun made its appearance over the horizon, the orange orb cast a golden glow on land, sea and sky until the final metamorphosis for the day was complete.

Evvie sighed deeply in utter awe and appreciation of the ethereal experience. She could feel Zak smiling at her. Self-conscious, she turned to him. "What?" she drew out.

"Nothing. Your reactions make me happy, that's all."

"It's the most beautiful sunrise I've ever seen," she said, grinning happily. "Thank you for bringing me here."

The corners of his lips turned up before he drew his concentration back to his pad and began sketching again. Evvie was so mesmerized by the colorful sunrise that she hadn't noticed he'd been drawing the entire time.

"Can I see?" She assumed that he'd drawn the landscape and wondered if he captured what she thought could only be a fantasy until she saw it with her own eyes.

She wasn't sure what to make of his reluctance. Insecurity, perhaps, that she may not like his work? She didn't think that was likely based on the temporary tattoos he had drawn on his body a few years back. Almost shyly, a trait she wasn't accustomed to in him, Zak turned the pad around and her eyes went wide with surprise. He did indeed depict, in stunning detail, the colors of the horizon and the sun beginning to peak above the sea, but what Evvie didn't expect was an expressive portrait of herself, captivated by the breadth of beauty she'd witnessed.

She looked at him questioningly and he replied as if reading her mind. "You've never looked more beautiful," he told her, trying to hold her gaze but, instead, he looked away almost shyly the moment he'd said the words.

Evvie had her hair pulled off her face in a haphazard ponytail, not a stitch of makeup on her face. She was prepared for a day at the beach—not for a day out on the town. She hadn't given her appearance a second thought and she certainly didn't think she looked beautiful. But it wasn't the first time Zak had complimented her when her face was bare from cosmetics.

"I wish I could reciprocate and do justice to your devilishly good looks," she laughed, "but you'd only get stick figures out of me." Joking deflected the stirring she felt in her belly each time he looked at her.

"Devilishly good looks," he repeated, sitting up straighter, proud as a peacock. He wiggled his eyebrows. "I finally got a compliment out of you."

Evvie gave his arm a playful slap. "I've complimented you before."

"Like when?"

"Like now. I said your drawing was amazing." She squinted her eyes thoughtfully. "And your song last night—I complimented that. And I said you were a great tour guide the other day."

He twisted his face. "I don't know. That wasn't what I was looking for. But hot, now that's a start."

"I didn't say hot."

"Devil—hot. It's all the same," he said.

Zak opened the picnic basket, handed her a glass and uncorked a bottle of wine. Then he removed a ball of crusty bread and unwrapped a platter of cheese, olives, fresh vegetables and a chickpea spread.

Evvie couldn't remember the last time she'd felt so carefree and relaxed. After they finished off an entire bottle of wine, Zak took her by the hand, lifting her to her feet, and suggested they go for a swim.

After they splashed around in the water and playfully tried to drown each other, they returned to the beach blanket and let the warmth of the sun dry them off. After a few minutes, Evvie dozed off. When she awoke the sun was partially covered by a cloud that looked like a fluffy ball of cotton. The sky was clear blue with not a threat of rain. The only other visible cloud was looming high above them.

"When my brother and I were little we would make a game of picking shapes out from the clouds," Evvie said.

Zak looked up at the single, white, asymmetrical puff. "Did you both generally see the same thing?"

"Sometimes, but not usually."

"Interesting. I guess each person sees what he or she chooses to. You know what I see?" Zak asked. "A super hero or maybe an ancient warrior."

"Explain to me how you see that," she mocked.

He pointed upward. "Look, that's his head and his rippling muscles. And in back there," he said, swinging his finger around, "is his cape flying in the wind."

"No, that's not a cape! Those are grapevines. And what you call muscles, are a cluster of ripe grapes."

"Oh, that's just ridiculous. Is that all you ever see?"

"Look who's talking! Would that happen to be a Greek super hero, Hellas?"

"You're asking for it. If you keep calling me Hellas, I'm going to start calling you Greek Girl."

Evvie rolled onto her stomach and changed positions so she was face to face with Zak. Propping herself up on her elbows she told him pointedly, "You'd have to call me Half Greek Girl."

Mimicking her pose, he propped himself up, and was nearly nose-to-nose with her. He looked confused. "What are you talking about?"

"I'm a mudblood," she said, quoting the Harry Potter books. "I'm only half Greek."

"I don't understand. I know your mother is Greek and your last name is Papadakis, which couldn't be more of a Greek name."

"Evanthia Brewster Papadakis. Dean is my stepfather. He adopted my brother and me when we were sixteen."

"Oh, I didn't know." He opened his mouth and was about to say or ask something but he stopped himself. After a moment he said, "You know, technically, that wouldn't make you a mudblood. If you use the analogy properly, mudbloods are children that have neither parent possessing wizardly powers."

"You're such a dork."

"I know. But a lovable, sensitive one." Zak grew quiet for a few seconds. "Do you want to tell me what happened to him? Your dad, I mean."

Evvie rolled onto her back and pressed the heels of her hands over her eyes. Her chest expanded as she took in a deep breath.

Zak moved to her side and gently gripped her shoulders. "Evvie. I'm sorry. You don't have to say a word."

She shook her head. "No, it's okay. He was killed in a plane crash when I was ten years old."

"Ten? That horrible."

"It was," she sighed. "And what made it worse was that it was a highly publicized crash and there was no getting away from it. The reminders of what he might have gone through were constant." Evvie looked up at him with saddened eyes. "I still miss him terribly."

It wasn't in Evvie's nature to open up this way to anyone, save her brother and cousins. When Ryan had asked about her father, she'd glossed over it, and didn't go into detail. But there was something about Zak that unlocked a door, and once it was opened, it couldn't be slammed shut.

"Nicky was always by my mother's side, but me, I was Daddy's girl, and I didn't want to believe that I'd never see him again."

Zak, who had been gently stroking her arm, stopped to wipe a tear from her cheek.

"Then two years later, my yiayiá died, and that was more than I could take. She was everything to me. A second mother really. We were very close. To this day I feel her loss, but at the same time, I also feel her near me. It's just not enough though, you know? I want to hug her, talk to her and listen to her advice like I used to."

Zak didn't interrupt, but he looked into her eyes, nodding with sympathy. And in that instance, she knew he understood.

"Anyway, after nine-eleven happened, Dean insisted on adopting Nicky and me. I fought him tooth and nail and I resented him for that, and other reasons at the time, but he was only doing it to protect us. I realized that later. So many children had lost a parent that day."

"Losing two of the most important people in your life, especially at such a young age, sucks," Zak said.

Evvie burst out laughing. It was a welcome relief from spilling her sorrow. "Only you would say that. It's refreshing to hear something other than the cliché remarks people usually make, thinking it'll comfort you."

"Don't I know it?" he agreed. "'I'm so sorry for your loss, but she's out of her suffering,'" he mimicked in a high-pitched female voice. "'She's in heaven now.' And let's not forget, 'may her memory be eternal.' No shit! Like I'd ever forget her."

Now it was Zak who looked forlorn and Evvie's heart went out to him. "Zak?" She laid her hand over his heart where his tattooed angel wrapped her garments around a boy kneeling before her. "Would you tell me about her?"

Evvie kept her hand on his chest and Zak covered his hand over hers, gently clasping it. Their eyes met and Evvie shuddered. She'd felt as though her soul had passed through his and she could sense the depth and gravity of whatever it was he'd gone through.

Zak kept hold of her hand, even as he shifted to lie on his side. "Do you remember when I told you I suspected we had more in common than we both knew?" he asked.

"Not really. When did you say that?"

"Back at Cornell, when I was trying to get you to spend more than five minutes with me." He sucked in a deep breath. "At the time, I had no way in hell of knowing we had a common piece of land on this island. I'm still trying to wrap my brain around that. But I could tell by looking at you that, even when you were trying to cover it up, there was a sorrow within you that I recognized in myself, one that comes from a grave loss. A death." He took his free hand and grazed his fingers along her cheek. "Of course, I didn't know for certain until now." He closed his eyes as if to lessen the pain. "My sister died when we were sixteen."

"What do you mean by we?" Evvie asked, carefully, suspecting the answer, but praying for it not to be so.

He blinked his eyes open. "That's the other thing we share—you and I. I'm also a twin."

Evvie sat up, lowered her face into her hands and sobbed. The morning had started with beauty and promise, and now it was tainted with the stench of death. She hadn't learned the details, but that angel permanently marked on Zak's body was his twin. She was certain of that. His sister was as much an extension of him as Nicky was to her. If Nicky ever died, she'd lose the best part of herself, and that would be a grief she couldn't even begin to imagine.

Zak wrapped his arms around Evvie, rocking her and assuring her he'd be okay and so would she.

"What happened? Was it an accident?" she asked through her tears.

"No. She was ill and it's because of me that she died."

"What?" Evvie was stunned. "How could that possibly be?"

"She had a rare form of leukemia. The last six years of her life she was in and out of hospitals and treatment centers. The doctors felt her best shot was to have a bone marrow transplant. Obviously, we weren't identical twins, so when the doctors said I was a match, I was so happy to be the one to save her."

"That poor girl. Was she constantly ill?"

"She went in and out of remission. Just when she'd start to feel normal again, she'd get hit with another blow. I made her so many

promises, telling her all the things we'd do when the marrow transplant was done and she had beat this thing once and for all. But I let
her down and I'll never forgive myself."

"You didn't let her down. You went through, what I understand to
be, a very painful procedure in order to save her life."

"But I didn't!" he cried out. "I didn't," he repeated almost inaudibly. "Her body rejected my marrow. It poisoned her. She got something
called graft versus host disease. It's when the donor's cells attack the
body of the receiver."

Evvie's heart went out to Zak as she looked at his ravaged face.
"It's not your fault. You had no way of knowing, Zak. If you didn't try
and she died anyway, you would have spent your life wondering if you
could have done more." She took his face in her hands. "Look at me.
You did everything humanly possible to help your sister. I understand
your grief. If I lost my brother, I don't know how I would get over it.
But I know he'd want me to go on and not waste a day on this earth
feeling guilty for what was not in my control to change."

"Logically, I understand that, but emotionally I can't."

Evvie lowered her hands to rest on his shoulders. "That's a start, at
least. I never met your sister, but I know in my bones that she would
want you to be happy." She ran her fingers over the tattoo. She wondered
about the Greek word for hope written above the angel. "Why *Elpida*?
What were you hoping for?"

"That was her name."

"It's a beautiful name. I'd like to see a picture of her one day."

He pointed to the face of the angel.

"She looked like you. Zak, promise me, whatever happens, you'll
find a way to be happy. You deserve it. Do it for her. Do it for yourself."
She touched the little boy weeping at the feet of the angel. "This sweet
boy needs to forgive himself."

Without thinking, Evvie bent down and pressed her lips to Zak's
inked image. She felt him tremble under the warmth of her mouth
and she heard a soft groan rumble from his throat. Gently he lifted her

close to him until they were face to face. Time stood still as they stared at one another, and when he finally leaned in to kiss her, everything inside her unhinged. Shivers ran up and down Evvie's spine. Every cell in her body tingled and her stomach did back flips. Her heart raced so rapidly, it might fly away, and, against all reason, her normally level-headed mind was in a complete fog.

She and Zak shared the kind of grief that few their age had. The connection between them was pulling her in and, in that moment, his kisses felt right. Too right. Without breaking the kiss, he laid her down, hovering above her and threading his fingers through hers. Zak traced light kisses down her jaw, neck and collarbone, and Evvie moaned from the reaction her body was having from his touch. His fingers skimmed the outline of her breasts and Zak looked into her eyes, searching for confirmation.

"I'll stop if you want me to," he whispered.

"Don't want you to," she barely breathed.

Zak pressed the full weight of his body on hers. "Evvie," he murmured and ran the length of his nose along hers before claiming her mouth.

She was officially no longer in control of her senses. Her body and soul had taken over, and for once in her life, the next few hours had not been calculated or rationalized. She hadn't felt this much passion since René. But even with him she hadn't allowed herself the freedom to feel what she did at this moment. That had been more of a crush. This was raw and intoxicating. More than she dared to hope for and everything she feared.

With only a few scraps of material between them, it didn't take much effort to shed the bathing suits they wore. Soon, they were body to body. Skin to skin. Making love, making love, making love. And she knew this was the way sex was meant to be. Floating in tandem with the gentle waves hitting the rocks on the walls of the cliffs beside them. Harmoniously with his body, in rhythm with his strokes and thrusts as he worshipped every inch of her. Evvie's eyes glazed over as she reached her peak. The world went blank except for the explosion of virtual color running through her veins. Crying out his name was all it took for Zak to fall over the edge with her.

Zak pushed the hair off her face and rolled her on top of him to take his weight from her. "Hi," he said, as if trying to gage her reaction.

"Hi, yourself," she said. "I wish you'd take those things out so I could see your true eyes," she said softly.

"You see me," he said, his meaning far reaching.

"Zak, do you ever wonder what happened to the parts of ourselves that we lost?"

"What do you mean?"

"I mean who we were ... before. I used to be this little girl with so much enthusiasm for everything. I'd try anything, had dozens of friends and was so open to new experiences. I could be a little chatterbox at times and I was always laughing." She rested her chin on his chest. "What happened to that little girl? How did I get here? It was always Nicky who was the reserved one. Now I'm the one who's guarded all the time."

"I know." He kissed the inside of her palm. "I get it. I was never the same after Elpida died either. We all react in different ways. We grieve uniquely." He shrugged. "We grow up and our childhood, the good and bad of it, molds us."

"Sometimes I want that little girl to shine through my darkness, you know? I want her back, but I'm afraid she'll just get hurt again."

"I see her—that little girl—she can come out to play any time she wants," he said with a crooked smile.

"Want to skinny dip?" Evvie asked.

Zak's eyebrows practically lifted to his hairline. "Is this Evanthia speaking?"

"I've always wanted to do it and ... we have no clothing on now."

He dragged her to her feet. "You don't have to ask me twice."

In the water, Evvie wrapped her legs around Zak's waist. They kissed and floated. Kissed and floated. The sun was shining down on them and the heat of the day was upon them. The water was warm and inviting and Zak ran his hands up and down Evvie's body. For the second time, they lost themselves in each other while the water splashed up against them.

They had just about made it back to the beach blanket when they spotted a couple walking along the shoreline.

"Shit! Shit! Shit!" Evvie shrieked, lunging onto the blanket and rolling it around her body. "Get under here before they see you."

Laughing, he joined her under the rolled up cover, cocooning Evvie and himself inside while initiating another kiss.

"Stop. We have to get dressed. Who knows how many others will come by?"

"They're gone," Zak said, amused. "They didn't even notice us."

Evvie craned her neck to make sure the coast was clear. When she was certain it was safe, she unraveled herself from the cover and slipped on her bathing suit. "Crack open that other bottle of wine. I think I need it," she told him.

"I didn't know you rattled so easily," he teased.

"I'm not exactly into exhibitionism, Zak."

"Let's remember whose idea it was to skinny dip." He poured her half a glass. "And a damn brilliant idea it was," he said, leaning in for a long, lingering, feel it to your core, kiss.

Since it was Evvie's last day on the island, she didn't want to head for home after the beach. Instead, Zak drove around to areas of the island they hadn't explored together. She was completely at ease, having drunk almost three quarters of the second bottle of wine herself and, for once in her life, she wasn't thinking about what she'd be doing five years from now, or about the work that needed to be done when her vacation ended, or who was waiting for her at home. Until, that is, they finally pulled up to the gravel driveway at the vineyard home and Evvie's cell phone beeped, indicating a message had come through.

Ryan: *Hey! Can't wait to see you. Missing you.*

Evvie sobered from the euphoria of one of the most perfect days she'd ever experienced. The entire week had been like a dream, slowly building to this final day when she'd let herself go way too far. What had she done? She'd lost control, only to be seduced by a temporary, pretend existence—one with no responsibilities, commitments or the need to keep her guard up. And now she'd pay the price and she feared Zak would too.

"What's wrong?" Zak asked when they walked through the front door. The look on her face and her hunched shoulders gave her away.

"Nothing. A little too much sun and wine," she lied. "I'm going to bed. Thanks for a nice day."

Evvie began to walk down the hall to the guestroom but he took hold of her hand and stepped in to draw her close. "Let me get you something to make you feel better."

"I just need my bed," she said in a deadpan tone.

"Okay."

Zak seemed rightfully worried and maybe a little confused. So was she, but right now what she needed was some time alone to think.

"Goodnight. Feel better. If you need me, knock on my door." He tried to kiss her goodnight but she turned her cheek to him.

"Goodnight, Zak."

The next morning, when she didn't come out of her bedroom to have breakfast, Sophia went to check on her. She'd been crying and her eyes were red and swollen.

"*Ti eheis, pethi mou?*" Yiayiá Sophia asked, alarmed. She took Evvie by the chin and made her look at her.

"I'm not feeling well. Can we leave now instead of this afternoon?"

"Maybe we should stay until you're better. Maybe another day or two?" Yiayiá Sophia suggested.

"No!" Evvie exclaimed. "Please, I'm all packed. I really want to go."

"Yesterday you said you could stay here forever and today you can't wait to leave? Evanthia?"

"Please, Yiayiá, don't ask me questions."

"For now. But we will talk about this later." She shook her head and left the room.

Ten minutes later, Zak was knocking at her door, asking to come in, but she told him she wasn't dressed. After a while had passed, he knocked again.

"Let me in. I want to speak to you," Zak pleaded.

"Not now, Zak. I'm leaving in a few minutes anyway. I think it's best we say goodbye now."

"Goodbye? You make it sound like we'll never see each other. I'm coming home in a—"

"We won't. I'm sorry. I'm really sorry."

"Evvie open this fucking door and talk to me or I swear I'll kick it in."

Resigned, she opened the door. There would be no escaping the house without seeing him one last time. With a stone cold look on her face, she gestured for him to come in.

"What the hell? Did I do something wrong last night?"

"No, Zak. You did everything right. It was a perfect day. I was the one who did something wrong."

There was so much hurt in the sound of his voice that Evvie couldn't bear to look at him, aware she was the cause of his distress.

He scrubbed his face with his hands, trying to make sense of what she was saying. "I don't understand."

"I have a boyfriend, Zak! I was so absorbed in what we were doing all week, I'd barely thought of him. He texted me last night to tell me how much he missed me. And what was I doing?" Tears welled up in her eyes, blurring her vision. "I was having sex with you."

She covered her face with her hands and Zak grabbed her wrists, lowering them so he could look her in the eye. "We didn't have sex. We made love. Three times, if I recall."

"We had sex, and it's not like me to do something like that. I cheated on Ryan. Do you have any idea of how awful I feel? It's just not like me," Evvie cried.

"No, I don't believe it's like you to cheat on someone you care about. But what does that tell you? It meant it was more than just sex, Evvie. I know it and you know it too."

"Zak, this isn't reality. We've been living in a fantasy world. I'm committed to Ryan. I've been with him for two years. Two good years that I can't ignore when he's done nothing wrong and has been nothing but kind to me. He wants to have a serious talk about our future when I get back. You can't expect me to throw that away for a one-week fling. A lapse in judgment."

"A lapse in judgment." He laughed humorlessly. "I was a fling? Someone to occupy you from boredom?" Zak muttered under his breath. "Nothing but a fucking lapse in judgment?"

"You make it sound awful. It wasn't like that," Evvie cried.

"No. Then what was it like? Because obviously what I felt was happening between the two of us was very different from what you're expressing." His eyes drilled into hers acidly. "I'm waiting," he said when she offered no response.

"I don't know," she whispered.

"You don't? Well, I do. You're a coward. You're afraid to feel too much. Terrified of what's real and pure. So you'll settle for two good years instead of taking a chance on something amazing. Can you honestly tell me you didn't feel something different, something more for me than you do for him? Does he know you the way I do? Your mind, your soul? Does he even understand you?"

"It doesn't matter." Her voice came out wispy. "He's simple and uncomplicated. He doesn't ask the hard questions and I don't have to explore what's below the surface. I prefer it that way."

"I know more about your fears and desires from this week alone than I bet he knows in the two years you've been together. What does that tell you, Evvie?"

She turned her back on him and looked away. Evvie tried to harden herself to him but it wasn't working. His words were shredding her heart. His truths were ripping her soul from her body. She refused to face him. Refused to answer him.

Zak grunted loudly. "Somehow we always get here. Just when I think I've touched a part of you that no one else has, you hit me with a blow straight to the heart."

Evvie couldn't speak. She felt as though she was going to vomit. It was agonizing to hear Zak say what she knew was true and have her worst traits and flaws exposed. But the worst of it was to know that, once again, she had hurt him. "I'm so sorry."

He started for the door and placed his hand upon the knob. Turning, he looked back at her. "It's you I'm sorry for. Have a nice life," he said, slamming the door behind him.

Chapter 37

Stella

August 2008

It was late afternoon on a Sunday when Evvie arrived home from Athens, and Stella couldn't wait to finally speak to her. She had texted her several times and even called her, but then decided she'd rather have this conversation face to face.

Sophia, Evvie's mother, had been preparing a family dinner to welcome her home, but Stella was the first one to come dashing through the door and head directly up to Evvie's bedroom.

"Did you sleep on the plane?" Stella asked.

"Hello to you too!" Evvie said. "Yes, why?"

"Just making sure you're up to that discussion I wanted to have with you."

"Sure," Evvie said, patting the bed for her to sit beside her. "But I'll warn you that I'm probably the worst person to give you any advice since I have a knack for royally screwing things up."

Stella looked at her with interest. "It seems like you have a lot to tell me too."

"First, you. What's on your mind?"

"Well." Now that Stella had her attention, she wasn't sure where to start. "It's about Cain."

"I figured that."

"He confessed something to me and I'm not sure how I feel about it."

"Okay. Well, first you need to decide how you feel about what he confessed and then what you think about the fact he hadn't told you about it from the get-go."

"I guess I'm a little conflicted about both." Stella was fidgeting nervously in her seat.

"Stop!" Evvie said, grabbing hold of her knee. "Just spill it."

"When I met Cain, he told me he was twenty-six. But he's really ... thirty-two."

"Thirty-two?" Evvie repeated, dumbfounded. "That's a big gap at your age."

"But if you think about it, that's the same age difference as my yiayiá and pappou."

"Different times," Evvie shrugged. "And there was no deceit involved."

"He didn't want his age to be the factor in my opinion of him," Stella explained. "He was afraid I wouldn't have accepted a first date with him based solely on a few years."

"It sounds like you're buying it, or justifying what he did, anyway," Evvie said. "So ... how do you feel about him now?"

"He told me he loves me," Stella said emphatically, hoping to convince Evvie the relationship was worth fighting for.

"That's a little soon, don't you think?" Evvie asked. "Do you love him?"

"Have you taken a good look at him?" Stella asked with dreamy appreciation.

"That doesn't answer my question."

Stella was getting annoyed. She'd expected her cousin to be on her side. If Stella needed someone to talk to, Evvie always had her back. So why was she giving her the third degree today?

"Cain is very good to me. There isn't anything he wouldn't do for me, or ... I for him."

"And what exactly does that mean?" Evvie asked.

"It means we had sex," Stella blurted, challenging her older cousin.

"Do you love him?" Evvie asked, enunciating one word at a time.

"Why are you acting this way, Ev? I've been waiting to speak to you and all I'm getting is attitude."

"Did you want advice, or just someone to say 'yes' to whatever you said?"

"No," Stella whined. "I just thought you'd be more supportive."

"I am, Stella. But I'm also protective of you. I'm going to ask you again. Do you love Cain?"

"I told him that I did," Stella replied. "Ev, should I tell my mom and dad Cain's real age?"

"I'd leave it alone right now and see where this goes. I have a feeling it's not going to go over too well. And between your dad and Dean, he'd be lucky to come out alive."

"Awesome," Stella said with uncharacteristic sarcasm. She eyed Evvie. "So, are you going to tell me how you royally screwed up?"

"Ugh, you're going to love this one," Evvie said with dread. "Do you remember Zak?"

"Sure. How could I forget him?" Stella thought he was a sweet guy.

Evvie went on to tell Stella the entire story of how they ended up on the same vineyard.

"Of all the crazy coincidences!" Stella exclaimed. "He must have been as surprised to see you as you were to see him."

"He was," Evvie confirmed, "and he wasn't happy about it one bit. But Zak is a really nice guy and I finally got the chance to apologize to him."

"That's good. And I bet it was more fun to have someone your own age to hang out with," Stella said.

"It was the best," Evvie said softly, averting her eyes from her cousin.

Stella knew Evvie only too well. Well enough to know there was something she wasn't saying. "Evvie? Spill. What aren't you telling me?"

Evvie looked at Stella as though she were deciding what information to share. She closed her eyes, huffed out a breath and smacked her forehead with the palm of her hand. "Zak and I got close."

"How close?"

"Very. We did everything together." Evvie went on to tell Stella about the cliff diving and the sunsets, the trip to Melissani Cave and their walks on the beach, working on the vineyard and the evenings under the stars.

"That all sounds amazing," Stella said, narrowing her eyes. "But I feel like there's something more."

"There is," Evvie admitted. "But please, this doesn't leave this room. I'm not proud to say this, but I cheated on Ryan. I—I kissed Zak," she said in a hurry as her mother and Aunt Demi stepped into Evvie's bedroom.

Stella looked at Evvie suspiciously, and she was sure that her cousin amended her last words when she caught sight of their mothers.

"Are you girls catching up?" Sophia asked.

"Sounds like boy talk," Demi said. "The best kind."

"Did I hear you say that you kissed another boy in Greece?" Evvie's mother asked.

"The bigger question is," Demi said with a wicked grin, "if that's code for, 'had sex with him.'"

Sophia scolded her. "Demi! Come on."

"Oh, for God's sake, Sophia. Have you forgotten what it's like to be young with all those hormones bouncing around in your body like balls in a pinball machine?"

"You would know. All you ever talked about was sex."

"Ah, but I wasn't the one having it now, was I? But you and my brother couldn't keep your hands off of each other."

Stella and Evvie stared at each other with incredulity. Did her mother and aunt forget they were in the room? Stella wondered.

"You really don't know when to stop, do you, Demi?" Sophia looked totally pissed off, which was rare since Stella's mother and aunt never fought. "This isn't one of our bedroom floor tell-alls on Honey Hill Circle. These are our daughters."

Stella could only dream of what it was like for them back then, having four best friends to share all their secrets with. She had Evvie to confide in, and Nicky of course, but there were some things you just didn't divulge to your male cousin.

"Sweetheart," Sophia said, "if you got caught up in the moment after meeting someone else, don't beat yourself up over it. That's what dating is for. To find out who the right person is for you."

"There's no way in hell you would have kissed someone else back then," Demi said to Sophia. "Even when my idiot brother wouldn't admit how nuts he was about your mother, Evvie, she still wouldn't look at another boy."

"Must we rehash all of this?" Sophia said with irritated impatience.

"So you never once cheated on Dean when you were teenagers?" Evvie asked.

"Of course not. Why would I?"

"She wouldn't because he was 'the one' for her," Demi chimed in.

"Demi," Sophia growled in warning.

"It's okay, Mom, I know you and Dean had some secret thing going on long before you met Dad. But did you feel the same way about my father? Did you or would you have ever cheated on him?"

"I never did and I never would have. A commitment is just that." Sophia rested her palm on her daughter's cheek. "You need to decide what and who makes you happy, and once you do, stick to it and don't toy with these boys' emotions."

Evvie nodded and hugged her mother, but Stella could see that Sophia's advice weighed heavily on her cousin.

"We'll leave you girls alone to talk," Sophia said.

"Really? This was just getting interesting," Demi said.

"Let's go," Sophia ordered, dragging her by the arm. "Be the mom not the buddy."

Stella closed the door behind them. "That was a little off the wall. Especially since I know my Uncle Dean and your mom's past is not your favorite subject."

It's okay," Evvie shook her head. "I came to terms with that a long time ago. Mom loved Dad, just differently. It used to bother me that my father came in second place in my mother's heart. But she explained to me that he was the only one other than Dean she was ever interested in and, because of him, she took a second chance on love."

"Let's go back to the subject we were on before our mothers decided to go all teenager on us and join our convo," Stella said. "Finish telling me about Zak. Was it really just a kiss?"

"No," Evvie groaned out, covering her eyes with her hands.

Stella shrieked and pried Evvie's hands from her face. "Holy shit, Ev."

Evvie told her the rest of what had happened in Kefalonia. When she had finally finished, her shoulders slumped in defeat. "So, when my mom said, 'don't toy with their emotions,' the guilt flooded what little sense I have left in my brain. I really hurt Zak … again."

"You don't do anything without thinking it through or wanting to. I think you feel more for Zak than you're admitting to yourself."

"Can we get back to your dilemma with Cain?" Evvie requested. "I'm concerned for you. When someone isn't honest about one thing, there is usually more he is hiding."

Stella lifted a brow at her.

"Don't look at me that way. It's not the same thing. I'm not going to tell Ryan what happened because it would put a wedge between us for no good reason. I'm going to put it behind me and move on." She picked up the worn, stuffed unicorn she'd dragged around everywhere she went as a toddler, hugging it to her chest. "Let's set up a double date so I can get to know Cain a little better," Evvie suggested. "I need to figure out what the deal is with this guy."

Once again, Stella had changed her major and, naturally, that meant switching schools as well. Cain urged her, rather forcefully, to choose a New York City school so they might spend as much time together as possible. Her latest so-called passion, if she had one, was in fashion merchandising. She enrolled at The Fashion Institute of Technology to finish out her last two years of college, thinking it might lead to a position as an assistant buyer at one of her favorite clothing stores.

Instead of moving into the cramped dorms, Cain asked her to move into his luxury apartment, but Stella explained that it simply wasn't possible. There was no way on earth or in hell that her parents would allow it. Stella had come to learn that Cain could become quite moody when he didn't have his way and she often found herself compromising to appease him.

"Get the dorm if you must, but you'll be spending little time there," he informed her. "I prefer to know where you are at all times."

"Cain, that's not realistic," she told him. "I have school and you have to work."

"I can still keep tabs on you and I expect you in my bed at night, not in some sub-par cot in a building with drunk teenagers."

Stella complied. She loved spending time with him. He treated her well, took her to nice places and, she had to admit, his apartment was far more spacious and lavish than the small space she shared with the two girls she had only recently met.

Cain was a hard worker from what she could see, but when he was free, he expected her to be available to him. She thought he'd be more understanding when she had tests to study for or a group project to work on. But he didn't seem to take her studies seriously and that was beginning to bother her. Sure, it was flattering that he always wanted her by his side, but he left her little opportunity to make new friends her own age or to have freedom in the city beyond the boundaries he set for her.

Stella was a girl who liked being surrounded by family and she'd planned to go home most weekends. However, it seemed that less and less often she found herself in the company of those she loved most in the world. Cain usually had elaborate weekends planned for the two of them, keeping her occupied in the city and far away from the vineyard. Broadway shows, charity galas and celebrity chef dining events were far more interesting, Cain told her. He took Stella to whatever and wherever he could, and she was beginning to suspect it was nothing but a ploy to keep her in the city.

One weekend, in early November, when they had no solid plans, Stella packed a duffle bag and rode the Long Island Railroad home without telling Cain. When she was halfway there, she informed him via text message.

A war of words erupted in a series of text alerts and Stella defensively tapped out her replies. Cain didn't offer to come and be with her. No. Cain threatened to come and get her if she didn't turn around and come back 'home.'

But for once, Stella stood her ground. *I'll see you Sunday night*, she typed out. *I need some time with my family. Please understand.*

Stella was nervous when she walked through the front door to Cain's apartment. His calls and messages throughout the weekend never ceased. He wanted to know whom she was with and where she was every hour of the day. She loved him but, at the same time, he frightened her a little. He was too intense and possessive. The attention he continually bestowed upon her, which had originally flattered her, now worried Stella.

Cain sauntered over to the foyer just as Stella removed her jacket. Standing a good distance across from each other, they stared the other down, stone-faced, as if preparing for a duel.

"Don't you ever fucking leave me again without telling me," Cain said, his fists clenched at his side.

"I texted you."

"After you were already gone. Unacceptable."

"You're—" Stella was afraid to say what was on her mind. She squared her shoulders and tilted her chin upward to meet his gaze. "You're stifling me. I need to be able to make plans without your permission."

Cain alarmed Stella when he took two swift strides toward her and circled his fingers around her arms, squeezing them tightly and shaking her as if she were a rag doll.

"It's not about permission," he bit out. "You belong to me and I to you. We make our plans together."

He squeezed harder and Stella winced. "Let go! You're hurting me."

"Don't leave me again," he said, tightening his grip.

Stella feared Cain's words sounded more like a threat than a desperate plea. Either way, she was very disturbed by his behavior.

"I said take your hands off me!" She yanked herself free of him. "I'm going to my dorm."

"No."

Stella groaned, shooting him a disbelieving glare. "This has to stop. I can't live with you ordering me around. You need to calm down and I can't be near you right now with the way you're behaving." She put her hand out to halt him from touching her again. She picked up the jacket from the chair she'd laid it on and put it back on.

"When are you coming back?" Now, he did sound desperate to Stella's ears.

"I don't know." She turned the knob on the door. "I need some time to think," she said, without looking back.

Chapter 38

Stella

November 2008

Cain was relentless. He couldn't quite comprehend the meaning of 'I need space,' which Stella repeatedly told and texted him every time he contacted her. A week had gone by, and each day a dozen long stem roses appeared, waiting for her at the front desk of the dorm lobby. Tiffany & Co. had delivered a delicate gold chain in their signature turquoise box along with a handwritten note. Dangling from the end of the necklace was a heart and key. The note read, 'You have the key to my heart. I'll do anything to earn yours back.'

The fingerprint bruises on her arms had faded, but the blemish on her heart was still fresh. No one had ever loved her the way that he did and it physically hurt her to stay away from him. Stella knew she needed the chance to grow and discover what she wanted from life. But Cain was so much older than she was and he had it all figured out. It was impossible for her to keep up with him. No wonder he felt the need to guide her and protect her. It was her fault he grew frustrated and lost his patience. She wasn't sure why he bothered with her at all.

The cab ride to Cain's took longer than it should have, considering it was after eight in the evening and the traffic in the city was light. Neon signs and car lights whizzed by as the taxi drove steadily up Fifth Avenue, blurring Stella's vision. Her heart was racing, wondering how Cain would react when he saw her.

She greeted the doorman, smiling as she passed. Blowing out a breath and shaking her hands loose of lingering nerves, Stella pressed the elevator button for Cain's floor. When she reached his door, she didn't use her key, deciding it was best to ring the bell instead.

Cain's expression of delight and relief calmed Stella immediately. He took her in his arms, burying his face in the hollow of her neck. She pulled far enough away to look at him and take his face in her hands. "I'm sorry, she said. "I should have told you I was planning to go home."

Cain pulled her body to his, kicked the door closed, and bent down for a deep, heartfelt, toe-curling kiss. "I thought you'd never come back to me," he confessed, breaking the kiss. "I love you more than I could ever explain. I go a little crazy when you're not around." He kissed her again with the same intensity. "You're what keeps me sane and grounded."

"Cain, I love you too. I do. But I'm so much younger than you are and I have a lot to learn. And so much to figure out, all the stuff that you've already gone through and are over and done with. I don't want to hold you back, but I also need the freedom to learn for myself what it is that I want."

"You're not holding me back. And as long as what you want includes me then I'm okay with whatever you need to do."

As the weeks went by, Stella delved, with as much enthusiasm as she could muster, into her studies, but she didn't find it rewarding. By nature, she was kind and caring. Always willing to lend a helping hand and to focus on the positive attributes of a person's character rather than their flaws.

Cain's 'guidance,' insistence and possessiveness were overlooked as red flags by Stella. Instead, she saw these traits as a sign of his love for her and for her wellbeing. Cain had changed since they'd had the argument, Stella convinced herself. He held back on his forcefulness, allowing her to make her own decisions. In reality, Cain was simply cagier with his manipulations, and in the back of her mind, Stella sensed that. However, it was easier for her to live in the fantasy she'd written for herself, rather than to face the truth of who this man truly was.

Every so often Cain would slip up, and when he did, the vision of his fingers constricting her arms like a vise and bruising them came to mind. He was obsessively fastidious and often criticized her for not being tidy enough. He corrected her if her coat was not hung properly in the closet, or if her shoes were left by the front door. Heaven forbid she should leave a dish in the sink. But even with the frequent censure, Stella's mind twisted his condescending behavior into something positive. After all, he had her best interests at heart, she thought.

The evening before Thanksgiving, Stella and Cain had dinner with Cain's family before heading to the island for the weekend-long holiday celebration at the vineyard. Stella was looking forward to it as she did every year. It didn't matter how old she and her siblings, cousins and friends were, they still held onto their childhood traditions such as the cookie decorating, football games and hayrides. Not to mention a weekend of delicious food.

Cain was surprisingly accommodating when Stella said she wanted to spend the weekend at home. He was happy to accompany her, foregoing the day with his own family to spend it with hers. He was not too happy though, judging by the look on his face, when Demi showed him to the guestroom.

"You didn't actually think my parents would let us sleep in the same room?" Stella whispered when they carried their overnight bags upstairs.

"What do they think we're doing in the city? Just holding hands?" he asked a little too loudly.

"Shhh!" She clamped her hand over his mouth and giggled. "You'll just have to restrain yourself for a couple of days," she teased.

Cain was a man of many moods and faces. Charming Cain, the very same one that had captured Stella's attention the first day they'd met, woke up the next morning, ready to immerse himself in whatever this tightly knit family had planned. And once he did, the competitive side of him came out. From winning the 'most crepes consumed in one sitting' contest, to creating the most decorative autumn themed cookies, to making sure he was on the winning football team, Cain was determined to win. Stella laughed watching him and she relaxed as she witnessed an ease in his demeanor that she had not seen for a long time. He almost seemed like the twenty-six-year-old he'd pretended to be when they'd first met, and not the thirty-two-year-old with a tremendous amount of responsibility and impossibly high expectations.

Later that afternoon, when family and friends had arrived, Cain remained by Stella's side, assisting her in passing around trays of finger foods as they laughingly wove in and out of the cheek-pinching crowd. But when Adam and RJ arrived, lifting her off her feet in a gregarious bear hug, Cain's frivolity instantly disappeared. He glared at Stella's friends with cool civility and said, "That's enough of that," pulling her out of their hold.

"Cain! You've met Adam and RJ before. They're the sons of my mother's best friends. We grew up together as though we were blood relatives." Stella said, surprised by his reaction.

"However, you are not," he addressed the young men. "Stella's relatives, that is."

"We'll catch up with you later, Stella," Adam said, flicking his head, signaling RJ to follow him.

Stella caught the disapproving look they shot Cain and she was certain she heard RJ mutter 'asshole' under his breath as they walked away. She felt nothing less than mortified that he had behaved this way with her closest friends. So much for the relaxed Cain, she thought. She was tempted to say something to him, but with his sometimes volatile and jealous nature, she didn't want to take the chance of him erupting in front of everyone she loved.

Huddled together around the circular coffee table in the living room, her mother, Aunt Sophia, Mindy, Amy and Donna were laughing at some debacle that had happened at one of Mindy's photo shoots. She and Cain approached them with a platter of triangular-shaped *tiropita*. "It's nice to see you relaxing, Mom."

"Thanks to all the help you've given me today. And Evvie too," Demi said, smiling up at Stella.

"Where is my daughter?" Sophia asked. "I haven't seen her in the last hour."

"She's amusing the little ones. Actually, Cia has the whole thing under control, including her big sister!"

"And you're surprised? Donna asked.

Mindy turned her attention to Cain. "So tell me Cain, how are you enjoying your first Thanksgiving with our zany little group?" Stella knew Mindy well enough to know her tone was laced with false sweetness. For some reason, Mindy had an uncharacteristically blatant dislike for Cain.

"It's much different compared to the holidays I'm used to with my family," he said. "Livelier. But any time I spend with Stella is good enough for me." He pulled her in by the waist, drawing her closer.

Mindy eyed Cain suspiciously, flashing him an insincere smile. Matt, her husband, came up beside her, seating himself on the sofa armrest. "What's shaking ladies? Discussing my Godly good looks?"

"Sure!" Amy mocked. "That's all we ever talk about."

"We were just getting to know Cain a bit better." Mindy's tone held a touch of cynicism.

"If you'll excuse us, we have to pass the rest of this tray along," Cain said. Stella nearly tripped as he quickly strode away, gripping her hand.

"What the fuck is with that woman? She clearly has something against me."

"I don't know, Cain. It's not like her," Stella told him.

The rest of the afternoon went on without incident. Three long tables had been festively set for the meal, and after all the wishbones had been cracked, two cases of wine consumed and everyone stuffed as full as the turkey, the cleanup began. Paul got a video game marathon started in his bedroom, while several men hovered around the TV, watching football. Demi and Sophia went into the kitchen and, as always, so did about a half dozen other guests and family.

After Evvie and Stella set the tables for dessert, they went over to check on their grandparents.

"Can I get you anything, Yiayiá," Stella asked Soula.

"No *koukla*, just your company," Soula replied. So far, she was having a good day, and Stavros hadn't left her side. When the confusing moments took hold, Stavros was usually there to soothe her and when he wasn't other members of the family banned together to keep her from panicking when her mind sunk into a world muddled by time.

"Sit next to me *korítsia mou*." Soula patted the couch and the girls complied. They each pecked a kiss on her cheek and took her hand. "You girls, so young and beautiful." Soula's eyes began to take on a faraway look. "I remember when I was your age, so many years ago." She outstretched her hand to Stavros and he extended his to clasp it and kiss her fingertips.

"I fell in love with your pappou the very first time he stepped into my parents' flower shop," she said, grazing Stella's cheek with her free hand. "He was looking for work and my parents hired him. My heart soared knowing that I would see him every day." She turned to Evvie. "It was the same for your pappou. Even before Ana knew he existed, Alex had already fallen for her."

"How were you all so sure, without a doubt, that you were right for each other?" Evvie asked.

"You just know." Tears welled in the corners of Soula's eyes. "You feel it in here," she said, pressing her hand to her heart. "And if you have doubts, always look at the eyes." She leaned in, whispering, "Call his name. The first second your eyes meet will tell you everything you need to know."

The girls looked at each other, lifting their brows and shrugging.

"That first glimmer will tell you what's in his heart and what kind of man he is. It's that first vulnerable second before time allows him to cover his true self or intentions." Soula pointed a finger at the girls. "Trust me. Yiayiá knows. My Stavros tried to hide his love when we first met. But my mama taught me how to look for the signs. Once I took her advice and paid attention, I saw it. The love was there."

"What's got my Stella so mesmerized?" Cain sauntered over to them, lifting Stella to her feet.

"Yiayiá was telling us how she fell in love with Pappou."

Cain bent down to place a kiss on Soula's cheek. "I'd love to hear all about it," he said. As his eyes met hers, a look of horror shadowed her face.

"What are you doing here?" she scolded. "Go away, Jimmy, before Ana sees you."

Cain was confused. Evvie and Stella looked at each other, stunned. Stavros looked at Alex to find him gripping the arm on his chair as if he'd been hit with a blow to the heart. Any mention of how Ana's first husband treated her troubled him, even to this day, knowing what he'd put her through.

Stavros jumped from his seat and knelt down beside his wife. "This is Cain, Stella's boyfriend. Jimmy's not here." He took her face in his hands. "Look at me, Soula. It's okay. Everything is fine."

"We should leave her," Stella said. "She's agitated and confused."

"Don't go with him, Ana. He's no good!"

"I won't," Stella played along. "See? He's going." She motioned for

Cain to leave the room.

"We've had a full day. Maybe it's time we left," Stavros suggested.

"What if she went upstairs and rested?" Evvie asked.

"She slips in and out of the past," Alex told his granddaughter. "I think it's best that we get her home."

Evvie nodded and hugged Stella. "Go to Cain. He looked upset."

Stella found Cain on the front porch with an open bottle of whiskey in hand. He took a swig before he turned to look at her.

"Come inside," she told him. "It's cold out here."

"Who's Jimmy?"

Stella crossed her arms, rubbing them to keep warm. "What difference does it make? My grandmother drifted off into the past. It wasn't personal."

"Whoever he was, she hated him, and she confused me with him. That's personal."

"He wasn't a nice guy from what I've heard," she said reluctantly. "He was married to Ana, Evvie's grandmother, and he cheated on her and extorted money from their family."

"And this is who I was mistaken for?" Flinging the liquor bottle across the lawn, it hit a tree and shattered. "I think we should go."

Stella flinched.

"This is my home. I'm not going anywhere."

"Well, I sure as hell am not staying here after that," Cain said. "Between your grandmother going off on me and your mother's friend sending me death stares, it's apparent I'm not welcome here."

"That's not true. You're making too much of this." Stella turned to return inside the house. "Cool off and come back in."

"Don't fucking tell me how to feel. I'm getting my things and you're coming with me." Cain grabbed for her, pulling her by the hair before she reached the front door. Her head jerked, slamming into his chest and bouncing back. Taking hold of her wrists, he yanked her closer.

"Let go! You're hurting me!" The clasp of her gold bracelet beneath Cain's strong fingers cut into Stella's skin. Resisting, she tried to dislodge herself from him to no avail as she pleaded with him to let go of her stinging wrist.

Realization sunk in when Cain felt warm liquid drip between his fingers, and he immediately dropped his hands. "I'm sorry." Stella pulled away when he tried to take her hand and examine the injury. "Let me help you."

"You've done enough. Get your things and leave. Better yet, go now. I'll send them to you." Stella ran into the house before he could stop her.

As she locked the door behind her and made a run for the staircase, she bumped smack into RJ.

"Hey! Where are you running to?" Narrowing his eyes, RJ took notice of Stella's shaken state and her bloodstained fingers and arm. "What happened?"

From the corner of her eye she saw Mindy looking at her with concern, but she ignored her mother's friend, bringing her attention back to RJ.

"I cut myself on a loose nail on the porch railing," Stella lied.

"Let me help you clean it up," RJ offered.

Together, they climbed the staircase and entered the bathroom connected to Stella's bedroom. RJ found her first aid supplies, cleaned out the cut, and applied anti-bacterial ointment before affixing a band-aid to the affected area. Gently grazing his fingers over the darkened areas on her lower arms, RJ looked up at her curiously. Taking hold of her other hand, he slid the sleeve of her dress up to find similar gray-blue marks on that arm as well.

Softly, with no accusation in his voice, he asked, "What really happened, Stella?"

She squeezed her eyes shut, hoping to keep her betraying tears from falling, but they spilled through the slits of her lids against her will.

"Hey," RJ lifted her chin. "You can tell me anything. Anything and it will be just between the two of us if you want it to be."

"It's nothing, really."

"It must be something if you're crying." He ran his thumbs over the marks that had bloomed on her skin. "And this," he seethed, trying to hold back his anger, "is not *nothing*. Did Cain do this?"

"Why would you ask me that?"

"Well," RJ answered, "he's not here, and I found you crying. It doesn't take a genius to figure it out."

"It wasn't his fault. Sometimes he loses his patience with me. We just had a small argument, that's all. He didn't mean it."

RJ, after his brother had taken his own life, had begun a suicide hotline with his mother, Donna. He had completely changed careers, going back to school to earn a degree in social work. Stella could see his jaw tighten, but instead of the angry reaction she'd expected, he spoke to her calmly.

"Stella, there's no excuse for laying hands on a woman. I don't care what you said or did, there isn't a reason in the world to justify that behavior. Do you understand?"

"But—"

"There are no buts." He took her face in his hands, his eyes penetrating hers. "You are to be treasured. To be treated as an equal in a relationship. Not to be made to feel as though you're less, or for him to think he has the right to control your body and mind."

"He's very good to me, RJ. It was just a misunderstanding." She removed his hands from her cheeks. "Please don't say anything, okay? Please. I don't want my family to think less of Cain because of one little fight."

RJ let out a groan of exasperation. "Respect. He has to have it for you. More importantly, you must have it for yourself. Remember that."

Stella nodded. "I will." She kissed him on the cheek. "Thanks," she said, exiting the bathroom.

"One more thing," RJ stopped her. "If you ever need me, for anything, you call me. Anytime. Day or night."

"Do ye not comprehend that we are worms born to bring forth the angelic butterfly that flieth unto judgment without screen?"

—Dante Alighieri

Chapter 39

Mindy

November 2008

Mindy had recognized the distress in Stella when she re-entered the house. It was painfully easy to identify what was only too familiar to her, and if she was on point, as she thought she was, sweet Stella was in the manipulative hands of a sadistic, controlling bastard just as she had once been.

The few times Mindy had been in Cain's company, goose bumps prickled the back of her neck. His fake pleasantries didn't fool her. She could see right through his cocky and underlying sinister air. So all afternoon she had kept a close watch on him. She analyzed his body language and the possessive way he kept a tight hold on Stella. She sensed his jealousy boiling to the surface when any other young man who wasn't related to Stella took her attention from him. It didn't escape Mindy. No. Not one bit. Now, looking objectively, she was able to see what she wasn't able to when she was in Stella's shoes. Mindy was certain this little fucker was somehow either emotionally or physically abusive to her.

Mindy motioned for her husband, Matt, to come by her side. He'd been nursing a bottle of Samuel Adams Lager while speaking to Ezra, her friend, Amy's, husband. Still newlyweds, Matt snaked an arm around her waist and nuzzled the hollow of her neck.

"What's up?" he whispered in her ear. "Can't be away from me for a second?"

"That too," she placated him. "But I need your help with something else right now. Did you happen to catch what went on with Stella and Cain?"

"No. Should I have? Is Cain still here? I saw Stella sitting with Evvie and RJ."

"Exactly!"

"I'm not following."

"If Cain was still here he wouldn't let her out of his clutches, much less allow her to talk to RJ. Remember over the summer when I told you there was something about him I didn't trust?" Mindy didn't wait for Matt to answer. "My instincts were correct. I'm sure of it."

Mindy told her husband the little she'd witnessed and her suspicions that went along with it. She wasn't about to let what happened to her with Apollo be repeated with her friend's daughter.

Matt, who hosted a travel television series, had been a journalist for a national publication prior to landing the show. Many of his friends were investigative reporters with connections in law enforcement, and Mindy had every intention of tapping into those resources if necessary.

"I want you to find out everything you can about Cain Benningfield."

"I'll see what I can dig up, but don't be surprised if there isn't anything. You might just be a little overprotective where Stella is concerned."

"There's no end to the lengths I'd go for any one of those kids," she said, pointing to the whole lot of them attacking the dessert table.

"That's one of the many things I love about you." Matt gave Mindy a lingering kiss.

"Enough you two," Demi interrupted them. "I can rent you a room if you'd like."

"Mercenary."

"Yup that's me! Always looking to make money off my friends," Demi laughed. "Anyway, I'm breaking up this love fest for a reason. The congresswoman has requested your presence in my kitchen."

"Is that an official petition? Amy can be so demanding!" Mindy joked.

"Now that you're all here, I have something to tell you," Amy announced.

Good news. Please let it be good news, Mindy thought. With her distrust in Cain's motives toward Stella, she had enough adversity to possibly lay on her friends once she gathered some proof.

"Well, spit it out," Demi said. "Don't just sit there with that smile plastered on your face."

"Give her a chance," Donna said. "I could use some good news."

"You're running for president!" Sophia said eagerly.

"That's not good news," Demi flicked Sophia on the head. "Her life would never be the same."

"Ouch!" Sophia elbowed her back.

"Are you done behaving like we're still in grade school?" Amy asked. "Good!" she exclaimed when they apologized.

"So, what's the good news?" Mindy asked anxiously.

"I got a letter from Sam. He's getting married!"

"That's wonderful!" Sophia said excitedly. "When?"

"This coming summer," Amy replied. "Naturally, I picked up the phone immediately and called him. Sam said to make sure all of you free up your schedules to attend."

"We wouldn't miss it!" Demi said.

"Definitely!" Sophia agreed.

"I can't wait to tell Matt!" Mindy shrieked. "I'd like to send Sam's bride some wedding dress designs to choose from if she'd like."

"That's too generous of you." Amy hugged Mindy. Wow, she must really be over the moon, Mindy thought. Amy wasn't much of a hugger. She'd do anything to help, defend or encourage a friend, but she was never a touchy-feely type of person.

"Michael!" Demi called out as her husband came into the kitchen with a tray of empty wine glasses. "Pop the cork on a bottle of champagne. Amy's son, Sam, is getting married!"

"*Na Zisete!*" Michael said. "Or should I say, "*Mazel tov?*"

A Greek Sephardic Jewish family from Thessaloniki had adopted Sam after Amy gave birth to him while staying with Sophia's grandparents.

"Either in this case, but Sam taught me that the Sephardics say, '*Be-siman tov.*' It has the same meaning of congratulations."

Michael found the champagne while Demi pulled flutes from the cabinet.

"What's going on in here? What's the occasion?" Dean asked, coming up behind Sophia. Affectionately, he grazed his fingers along her neck and the tops of her shoulders.

"Grab a glass," Mindy told him. "Sam is getting married!"

"To Sam!" Dean raised his glass.

"The first one of our children to be married!" Donna mused. "I wonder who will be next?"

"Maybe Evvie?" Demi inquired. "She and Ryan have been together a long time."

"She's still young," Sophia said. "There's no rush."

"I think right now Evvie is more focused on winemaking than taking the next step in her relationship," Michael added.

Every set of eyes at the kitchen table stared at him in astonishment.

"What?" Michael answered their leers. "Evvie and I spend a good part of our day together. I know a thing or two about where her head is at."

"Hey, Ev!" Michael yelled across the room as she entered with an armful of empty platters. "Are you ready to get married?"

Demi slapped her husband. Sophia groaned. Amy and Donna shook their heads despairingly and Mindy covered her eyes in disbelief.

"Hell, no!" Evvie declared, giving her uncle and the rest of them a questioning look.

"I rest my case." Michael downed the rest of his drink. "With that solved, Dean and I will leave you ladies and watch football."

The women poured themselves another glass of bubbly. The more they drank, they giddier they became. Matt strode into the kitchen and watched them, amused by their banter.

"This is like déjà vu," he said, making his presence known. "If I didn't know any better, I'd think we were all back in high school."

"If we were," Demi slurred, a little tipsy, "you'd be pining over Sophia, and my brother would want to kick your ass!"

"And thank you for that, Demi," Mindy said sardonically.

Matt and Sophia simply laughed. They were both over that a long time ago and had remained friends.

"What do you say we hit the road?" Matt suggested. "I have an early start tomorrow."

On the way back to the city, after they dropped Mindy's mother home, Mindy went on and on about Cain. Matt promised to get right on it and make some phone calls. If it wasn't for Dean and his father rescuing Mindy from her abuser, she might have been killed. She would do the same for Stella before, she prayed, her involvement with Cain resulted in an immutable and disastrous fate.

Chapter 40

Stella

January 2009

A light snow fell, coating the city sidewalks and covering the mounds of unsightly, black snow that had not yet melted from the previous storm. With all the festive holiday lights and elaborate window displays removed, the delicate lace-like flakes made an otherwise dreary day lovely.

Walking from her last class of the day at the Fashion Institute of Technology to the restaurant where Stella would meet RJ took her around fifteen minutes of enduring the frigid temperature.

Ayza Wine & Chocolate Bar was only a few blocks from Penn Station, which was one of the reasons Stella had chosen it. She always considered the comfort and convenience for others before herself and she wanted RJ to be able to get back to the train quickly that evening. In the past few months, RJ came into the city more often, and when he did, he always called to meet with Stella, even if it was just for a quick cup of coffee.

But tonight, Cain was working late and Stella was free to dine with RJ. Less and less often, she had time to see her cousins and oldest friends. Most of her time was spent in the city, taking classes, studying and working a couple of days a week in an intern program arranged through the school. What little time was left was spent only with Cain, as he insisted on every one of her free moments.

They had their ups and downs, she and Cain, but she knew he loved her and, up until she'd met him, she'd never been the sole focus of any one man before. After the Thanksgiving disaster, he had sent flowers, letters of apology and undying love and a diamond encrusted infinity necklace. She took him back when he swore it wasn't his intention to hurt her and promised it would never happen again.

Until it did …

This time not with physical force, but with his constant manipulation and cutting words when he didn't get his way. "I know what's best for you," he'd say. "You're young yet. You need me to decide for you," he'd tell her, making her feel like a child he had to endure until she grew into a 'real' woman. "No one will ever love you the way I do. You belong to me," he'd said to cement the depth of his feelings for her.

Hadn't she waited for someone to love her for long enough? For someone to put her above everything else? Cain loved her and she loved him. Stella often feared their age difference would come between them and he'd become bored with her. And this was why she supposed he lost his temper at times. It was her fault and she would do what she could to keep him happy.

Telling Cain she was having dinner with her very sweet and handsome childhood friend was not the way to keep his temper at bay. Cain just didn't understand that it wasn't like that with RJ. She was like a little sister to him or a cousin at the very least. So Stella was happy when the opportunity presented itself for her to have dinner with her friend on an evening when Cain was working late.

A smile crossed Stella's face as she rounded the corner and spotted RJ standing by the front door of the trendy little restaurant.

"What are you doing out in the cold?" Stella said, falling into his open arms for a friendly bear hug.

"Waiting for you," he grinned. "I've already checked us in. Our table is ready." He pulled his North Face beanie off his head, brushed out the hat hair and stuffed the cap in his coat pocket.

Following the hostess through the narrow, dimly lit restaurant, they were seated at a table by the window. The intimate setting was ideal for a cozy date or for a group of friends hanging out at the bar, which ran the full length of the restaurant.

"What made you choose this place?" RJ asked.

"Don't you like it?" Stella asked concerned.

"No! It's great. I was just wondering what you like about it?"

"Well, the food is delicious and the desserts are even better. Just wait! You won't be able to decide. But mostly, I didn't want you to have to walk back too far to get to Penn tonight." *And it's far, far away from Cain's apartment*, she thought.

The waitress came over, introduced herself as Lauren and handed them a couple of menus. "I'll be back in a few minutes," she said, flashing RJ a brilliant smile.

"You may be the only one getting food tonight," Stella giggled. "She didn't even glance my way."

RJ waved her off.

"Come on! She's gorgeous. And she's interested."

"But I'm not," he said matter-of-factly, showing more interest in reading the menu.

"Are you seeing someone?" Stella asked.

"Since I saw you two weeks ago when you asked me the same question? No," he answered, sounding mildly annoyed. "What are you having?"

"Two appetizers, I think. It all looks so good." She bit her lip, trying to decide for sure. "The white truffle pizza and the goat cheese brûlée salad."

When Lauren returned, RJ ordered for Stella and then asked for a pulled pork Panini for himself. "And a beer for me, thanks."

"And you?" Lauren asked Stella. "A glass of wine?"

"Thanks, but I'm not twenty-one yet. I'm fine with water."

Stella had to stifle a laugh. If Lauren had smiled any wider, she'd be able to see if their server still retained any of her wisdom teeth.

"I'll need to see your identification," Lauren told RJ.

"Here," he said after reaching into his back pocket and pulling out his wallet.

"Thank you, Richard," she said, flirtatiously using his proper name. "I admire a brother who takes interest in his younger sister."

"This is not my sister."

Stella saw a wicked expression cross his face. The same one she'd seen many times over the years when RJ and her brothers pulled annoying pranks on her and Evvie.

"If you could put in our orders and leave us alone for a while I'd appreciate it," RJ requested. "I've been trying to find the right moment to ask my girlfriend to marry me." He reached across the table and took Stella's hand in his."

"Oh, Richard!" she said, exaggerating the name. "I didn't think you were ready to take that step." It took all her will to keep from laughing, especially when she glimpsed the disappointed look on Lauren's face.

Standing, RJ leaned over the table and, without warning, planted a kiss on Stella's lips. When he pulled away Lauren was gone and what was left in her place was an awkward moment of silence. "I'm sorry. I got a little carried away."

"It's fine," she said, brushing it off. "Mission accomplished. I wouldn't be surprised if someone new was assigned to our table!"

Stella's mind wandered throughout dinner. RJ had kissed her. It was all for play acting, but he'd kissed her all the same. It was a little weird. Like kissing a brother. But, not really like kissing a brother at all because the second his lips touched hers, adrenaline had pumped through her body and her heart had begun to race. But why? He had taken her by surprise and that could be the only answer. That, and the thought that if Cain had seen them he would have blown a fuse.

"Stella, are you still with me?" RJ asked. "You seem a million miles away."

"I'm fine. Just thinking about dessert."

He shook his head, amused. But then he took her hand in his again, rubbing the spot on her wrist he'd bandaged two months prior. "How are you, really? Is Cain treating you well?"

She pulled her hand from his. "Yes," she answered defensively. "Why do you ask me the same thing every time you see me?"

"Because I was there. I was the only one who saw you in the state you were in that night."

"It was a fight. An isolated incident. Couples have arguments and then they make up. It's that simple." Changing the subject, she smiled up at him and suggested they order dessert.

"How are we going to finish all of this?" he asked when their desserts arrived.

A trio of Jacques Torres dark chocolates dusted in gold powder was enticingly placed before them, along with two mugs of chocolate ganache hot cocoa and a twenty-layer brûléed crepe cake.

Stella had no doubt the two of them could finish every last bite. She had seen RJ scoff down three large pieces of her mother's baklava in one sitting.

When their evening had ended, RJ hailed a cab for her, but before saying goodnight he'd left her with one last thought. "If you ever need someone to talk to, or you need help of any kind, you have my number. Call me."

Stella sighed a deep breath. "You say that every time I see you. I'll keep it in mind."

Two days later, Mindy called Stella and asked her to join her for lunch the next day. Her mother's friend was vague about the reason she wanted to see her, but since Stella had begun classes at the Fashion Institute, Mindy constantly had career advice for her. Still not sure in what direction she wanted to take her life, Stella listened with little comment. Most of her friends at school would be envious if they knew of her connection to the famous creator of Bloom Designs. Many of them hoped to gain entry-level positions working for a designer when they graduated. Stella had the opportunity if she wanted it, but she wasn't sure she did.

Mindy greeted Stella with a kiss when her assistant announced her arrival. "Come into my office," she said. "I thought we'd have lunch privately without interruption."

A variety of salads, cold meats and bread were spread across a low, rectangular cabinet that ran the length of the window above it.

Stella filled her plate, chose a beverage from the personal-sized fridge and then took a seat across from Mindy seated at her desk.

"I know why you wanted to speak to me, Aunt Mindy."

"Do you?"

"Yes, and the truth is, I'm not sure if I like this area of study any more than the last two I've tried. I've been interning with the buyer a couple days a week at a boutique and ... eh. It's not as exciting as I thought it would be."

"At some point, you'll discover what truly interests you enough to stick with it. But Stella, you've changed your major three times. You must have lost some credits along the way."

Stella frowned. "You, mom and Aunt Sophia each had something you were good at since you were really young. Even Evvie knew she preferred grapes over Swan Lake. Me? I have no talent that stands out."

"The first thing you need to do is to stop comparing yourself to everyone around you. But ... as much as I would like to revisit this in the future, it's not why I asked you here today."

"Why did you then?"

"Do I need a reason?" Mindy asked.

Stella crinkled her brow. "Well, no, but there usually is. I know how busy you are."

"What I have to say is not easy," Mindy began. "And you might get very angry with me but I need you to hear me out."

"What is it?"

"It's about Cain."

"What about him?"

"Sweetie, he's not who you think he is."

Stella put her fork down. "I know exactly who he is. I know his family, where he works, and he tells me everything."

Mindy leaned in and folded her arms on her desk. "Did he tell you he just turned thirty-three?"

"Is that what this is about? His age!" Stella rose from her seat. Leaning her hands on the back of the chair she said, "I know, Aunt Mindy. I know. He told me after we were dating a couple of months."

"Do your parents know?"

"No."

"He's too old and too domineering for you."

"No, he's not. He's good to me."

"Sit down. We're not done," Mindy ordered.

"How did you find out?" Stella demanded.

"I had Matt investigate him." She lifted a hand to halt Stella from lashing out at her. "I saw you on Thanksgiving. You were clearly upset." She shook her head. "No, worse. You were nearly broken. Little by little he's going to chip away at your spirit until your heart, mind and soul are shattered. And maybe even your body."

"It was just an argument," Stella whispered unconvincingly.

"That's what I used to tell myself."

"What?" She didn't understand what Mindy was talking about.

Mindy got up from her chair, moving around the desk to guide Stella to her office sofa. "Sit."

Stella's stomach clenched. Something told her that whatever Mindy was about to say wasn't going to be pleasant.

"Do you remember a man named Apollo? I brought him to your home years ago."

"I think so."

"I thought we were so in love. We visited each other often and made plans for our future together. He was perfect in every way … or so I thought. But he had a dark side. It didn't take much for his temper to flare. He was jealous, possessive and he had a rage inside that he couldn't control."

Stella looked down at her clasped hands.

"The first time he hit me, I left him. But he swore it was a mistake and that it would never happen again. But it did. Over and over again. And for some reason, I convinced myself, or he did, that it was my fault. And I believed it." Tears formed in Mindy's eyes and she wiped them away before they had a chance to spill. "One night he beat me so badly, I thought he would kill me. I locked myself in the bathroom and called your Aunt Sophia. If it wasn't for your Uncle Dean and your grandfather, I'd probably be dead today."

"I don't know what to say. I'm so sorry you went through that, Aunt Mindy. I can't imagine how awful that must have been."

"You can't? Are you sure about that?" Mindy cupped Stella's cheek with her palm. "When I saw you run into the house with your hand bleeding and the despondent look on your face, I saw myself in you."

"It's not the same!" Stella argued.

"Oh, but it is. You just can't face it yet."

"The only thing you learned about him was that he's older than I told you he is," Stella said.

"Not quite. Apollo had done this before, but it was washed under the carpet because of the family's status in his town. Apparently, he was warned not to let it happen again. Don't you think Cain's family would stop at no lengths to protect his reputation?"

"What are you saying?"

"Cain has no police record. But Matt's contact dug a little further. He couldn't find an ex-girlfriend willing to talk, but the sister of a girl he was engaged to ten years ago told him all we needed to know."

"You mean a jealous girl who wants to badmouth Cain? And you believed her?"

"Do you want to know what she said," Mindy asked.

"Whatever," Stella replied, irritated.

"Her sister tried to break off the engagement more than once, but Cain managed to talk her out of it. She claimed he was too bossy and angered easily if something didn't go the way he wanted it to. The final time she broke up with him, she took the ring off her finger and placed it in the palm of his hand. Cain went wild. He tried to force the ring back on her finger, claiming he couldn't live without her. He had never hit her before, but the struggle became violent and Cain, without realizing it, broke her arm."

"That's a secondhand story from the sister of a girl who didn't want him anymore." Stella stood up. "I appreciate your concern, but what happened to you isn't going to happen to me. Cain loves me. And I don't know what the true story is with that other girl, but it was a long time ago." She retrieved her coat from Mindy's closet. "I have a class in forty-five minutes. I have to go."

"Please, just think about everything I've told you, and if you sense danger of any kind, call me."

She kissed Mindy on the cheek. "I will. But stop looking at me with that worried expression. Cain will prove you wrong. You'll see."

When Stella returned to Cain's apartment that evening, she didn't bring up what Mindy had told her about Apollo or Cain's ex-fiancée's accusations. Coming through the door, he called out to her. Stella was in the kitchen preparing dinner.

"I followed the aroma," he said, wrapping his arms around her waist. "What's all this?"

"I wanted to surprise you." Stella could see that he was in a good mood. No, a great mood. There was a brightness in his eyes she hadn't seen in a while and it seemed as if the burden of darkness had lifted from him.

"Can this hold for a while?" he asked. He didn't wait for her answer. He began to unfasten the buttons from the front of her cashmere sweater.

"I guess so," she moaned into his mouth as he kissed her.

Cain never asked in the bedroom. He took what he wanted and gave in return. But in giving, he demanded, though Stella never seemed to mind. She was his, he'd told her so repeatedly, and she loved that she belonged to him.

Chapter 41

Stella

May 2009

On the last day of final exams, Stella and a few of her classmates celebrated by heading over to Madison Square Park for a Shake Shack burger. The bitter cold had finally gone and the only wind whipping through Stella's hair was a pleasant, warm breeze. At Cain's request, a mane of golden highlighted hair that teased the curve of her back had replaced the bob that barely grazed her shoulders.

He would not be pleased with the ensemble she wore today, but she was still only twenty years old and, when she was amongst her peers, she wanted to fit in. Her chestnut suede Ugg boots, worn with her frayed, denim mini skirt wasn't up to Cain's style standards and, God knows, if he saw what she was about to order for lunch, he'd rip it from her hands before she could take her first bite.

"I'd like a large vanilla shake, cheese fries and a 'shroom burger, please."

Yep, Stella thought, Cain would lecture her for sure on the pitfalls of fried food and high calories. But he'd never find out so she was going to enjoy and savor each bite, she thought, as her teeth sunk into a fried mushroom, oozing with gooey cheese. Then she'd go back to Cain's apartment, change into a sexy, but tasteful, black dress and figure out how to tell him about some recent decisions she'd made. She almost lost her appetite thinking about it.

When they all had their orders in hand, the three girls sat at an unoccupied table under a large budding oak tree.

"Hey, Stella!" her friend, Natalie, said. "What's on you're mind? You're attacking that burger like you want to rip it to shreds."

"Oh!" Stella put down the fried mushroom burger wrapped in logo parchment paper and wiped at the corners of her mouth with a napkin. "Just thinking."

"About what? Killing someone?"

"Ha! Maybe not killing, but definitely disappointing and infuriating him."

"What is it about Mr. tall, blond and hot that makes you so nervous?" Angela asked.

"More like tall, blond and moody if you ask me," Natalie corrected.

"You don't like Cain?" Stella asked.

"How would I know?" Natalie responded. "The few rare times I've met him he couldn't get you away from us fast enough. And, to be honest, your whole personality changes in his presence."

"Of course it changes!" Angela said. "If I had someone like that interested in me, I'd be a puddle on the floor."

Stella dismissed Angela's comment. Her friend could never look beyond the surface. The nicest, yet most average-looking guy had been vying for her attention for months and she hadn't noticed or cared to notice him. If she'd only pay him mind, she wouldn't give the complicated 'Cains' of the world a second thought. And it made her begin to wonder why she did.

"Natalie, Cain is older and has high expectations," Stella said. "I'm simply trying to live up to them."

"You shouldn't have to if he loves you," Natalie replied. Angrily, she balled up her burger wrapper and threw it in the paper bag. "Open your eyes, Stella."

That evening, in six-inch stilettos, a formfitting, above-the-knee black dress, and deep red lipstick, Stella checked the boneless rib roast she'd prepared for Cain in the oven.

Open your eyes, Stella. She couldn't get her friend's words from her thoughts. Nervous, she shook her legs out one at a time and stretched her arms above her head. Attempting to rid the tension in her body, she expelled the deep breath she'd unconsciously been holding.

Stella jumped at the sound of the door to the apartment closing. With a racing heart she unsuccessfully tried to calm, she made her way out from the kitchen to greet him.

"What's all this?" Cain cocked his head to one side, smiling at her. He opened his arms and she went to him. "Special occasion?" Sliding his hands up and down the length of her lean thighs, he reached under the slit of her dress to cup her thong-clad bottom.

"I made dinner and ..." Stella paused. "I thought that you and I could enjoy some conversation while we eat." By the balcony window, she'd set a romantic, candlelit table. She loosened his tie and kissed him. "Come, sit down." Stella led him to one of the two chairs at the intimate table and Cain pulled her onto his lap.

He kissed her, trailing kisses from her mouth, down her neck and inching back up to her lobe. "You're my world," he breathed into her ear. "This is how I want to come home every night. With you waiting for me to make love to you."

"I want that too ... in time," she said, finding the courage to avoid her hesitation in telling him what she knew she had to.

Cain pulled her far enough away to read her eyes. His brow creased. "What does, 'in time,' mean?"

"Well ..." Stella tried to stand but Cain gripped her arms and pushed her back onto his lap. Stella sucked in a deep breath. "Promise me that you'll hear me out."

"I'm not promising anything until I hear what comes out of your mouth," he said sternly.

"Cain, I've been doing a lot of thinking and I don't think I'm cut out for fashion merchandising. I've decided not to enroll at F.I.T. again next year."

Relief washed over Cain's expression. He cupped her cheeks in his palm. "Is that all? I don't care. Go to school, don't go to school—you can do whatever you want. I want you to be happy."

"That's the thing ..." Stella bit her bottom lip. "I don't know what makes me happy, or at least what I want to do with the rest of my life."

"I make you happy, don't I? Or at least I thought I did."

"You do, Cain." She kissed him reassuringly. "You do everything for me and I love you for that, but I need to go home after the semester is over."

"No. You need to stay with me. You can transfer to another school in the city. Or stay here with me and get a job if that's what you want to do. This is your home now."

"No, it isn't." Stella braced her hands on his shoulders. "It might be someday, but for now I need to go back home to be with my family."

Jumping from his seat, she nearly fell to the floor from his lap. "Why the fuck would you leave me now?" he screamed.

"I'm not leaving you. I need to figure some things out and I won't spend another penny of my parents' money on tuition until I know what it is I want to do." Keeping a safe distance from him she tried to be reassuring. "We can still date. Nothing will change between us."

"Date!" he scoffed, lunging for her. "That's all it's been to you? Dating?"

"No, you know what I mean." Cain clamped his fingers so tightly around her wrists it was impossible to free herself of his grip. He had that wild look in his eyes. The crazed expression they took on when he was about to lose control. "Cain, stop!" She wouldn't allow herself to be intimidated. If she stood up to him, he might back down and come to his senses. She had to try or there would be no hope of a future for them. And she wanted there to be. She loved him.

"You promised you'd never hurt me again," she said through gritted teeth. "Let go of me or you'll never see me again." Stella's eyes seared like blinding lasers into Cain's icy blue ones.

Wordlessly, he stood there, utterly surprised at her steely conviction. Stella detected more than a hint of fear and disbelief revealed by the stunned expression on his face. He dropped his focus to the grip he had on her and released it as awareness struck him. Clasping his hands tightly on top of his head, he slowly inched away enough to put some distance between them. "I don't know what came over me," he said, not looking up at her.

For the first time, she had stood up to him and it had worked. Stella's courage emerged. Where it came from she didn't know, but now she was going to lay it all out for Cain—everything she had planned to tell him tonight.

"I am not enrolling in another school," she said firmly, enunciating every word. "I'm going home. I cannot tell my parents that we've been practically living together, which is why I can't stay with you now that the semester is over." He looked up at her and Stella thought she saw a glimmer of hope and understanding in his eyes. "Cain, sometimes I love the way you take control. You take care of me and do things for me that I'm not sure I could do on my own without you by my side." She rubbed her aching wrists, the purple fingerprints proving the rage that had begun to brew inside her boyfriend's complicated soul. "But I need to stand on my own and to be whole enough to feel as though I'm your partner, not your responsibility."

Cain's head shot up. "You're not! I just want what's best for you."

"And I need to figure out what that is. My family has been invited to a wedding in Greece this summer and I'm going with them. I'll be gone for at least a month. I'm going to spend some time there."

Stella saw the question in his eyes. From all the stories and memories of her summers in Greece that she'd shared with Cain, he knew that friends and boyfriends had accompanied the family on these trips.

"I won't be asking you to join me," Stella said softly. "It's not that I don't want you, I just need some time alone and time with my family."

"So you are leaving me," Cain said. He balled his fists at his side and Stella could see his wrath building once more, bubbling to the surface.

"No!" she tried to assure him once more. "I'm not. We can't be together every minute and this is one of those times. It has nothing to do with you. It's what I need."

Stella gasped when he suddenly stalked toward her, grasping hold of the back of her neck and crushing his lips to hers. "You need me," he said, stressing his point.

"I want you; I shouldn't need you." Stella spoke softly, trying to hide her alarm. She sensed the level of his anger building and the tension emanating from his body. And she also knew in her gut the moment when Cain snapped.

He squeezed her chin between his fingers, keeping his other hand braced around her throat. "Then leave!" he said, his voice laced with venom. "Go now!"

A storm of tears spilled from Stella's eyes. "Cain," she pleaded.

A furious growl bellowed from deep within him as he shoved her aside. Stella screamed when she lost her footing on her too-high heels and fell backward, the fall breaking as she hit a polished steel and glass coffee table. Pain seared through her as her crumpled body lay on the floor, shattered glass surrounding her. As she cried out in pain, every-thing went black in front of her and Stella feared she was about to pass out.

Cain, who had turned his back on her once he'd pushed her, spun around at the sound of crashing glass. "Stella!" he shouted, running over to her.

"Don't touch me," she grunted through the pain and stabbing feel-ing she felt shooting up her back and the stinging from the cuts on her arms caused by the slivers of glass that had rained on her.

"I need to get you off the floor. Away from this glass."

"I'm afraid to move. My back," she breathed out. "It hurts too much."

"I'll be careful." Glass crunched below Cain's feet as he bent down to lift her off the floor. Stella winced and flinched at his touch. He moved one arm under hers and the other under her legs, careful not to touch her back, and carried her into his bedroom. "I'm going to remove your dress. It's covered in glass."

As he did, Stella looked up at him. Concern shadowed his features and his shoulders hunched with remorse. She could see the regret written all over him, but this time he had gone too far.

"I'm so sorry. I didn't mean for this to happen."

She didn't think there were tears left to spill, yet they streamed out the outer edges of her eyes and dropped onto the duvet. She had no words of comfort for him and no fight left in her. Stella couldn't run or argue. The physical pain was too strong and the emotional upheaval was even worse. Lying on the bed like a torn rag doll and staring vacantly at the ceiling as Cain removed all of her clothing, she felt as though the world, her world, had just come to an end. She had nothing. She was nothing. At the very least, she had been very, very stupid.

Cain helped her shower and put her into comfortable clothing. Every step she took was laborious and every breath painful beyond belief. "I need to go to the hospital. Something is wrong. Really wrong."

"Your back is bruised. It'll feel sore for a while."

"It's more than that." Stella was nauseous and lightheaded. "Help me to the bathroom." She hated being at his mercy now but what choice did she have?

Cain held Stella's hair and tenderly rubbed her shoulders as she expelled all the contents from her stomach. "I may have hit my head too," she told him before she passed out in his arms.

Minutes later, she came to and found herself on his bed once again. Cain had his ear to the phone, explaining her symptoms and asking someone to hurry.

"I called for an ambulance, sweetheart," Cain said. Squatting by the bed, he gently brushed the hair from her face.

"Thank you," she said weakly. Shutting her eyes, Stella thought of the absurdness of the situation. She was actually thanking the man who had put her in this state. Ironic. Pathetically ironic.

Chapter 42

Stella

May 2009

It wasn't long before the 'Greek hotline' informed everyone that Stella had landed in the hospital. Stella asked the nurse assigned to her to call her parents and she could see the fear in Cain's eyes when she told him.

The story Cain had relayed to the triage staff was that Stella had tripped, lost her footing and crashed into the table before he could catch her. Stella hadn't disputed the lie. She was weak and in pain. Aside from that, she didn't have the emotional strength right now. Her heart ached. Her pride and self-esteem were shattered. She was a fool to think that any man would have the patience to love her. No boy ever had before. What would possess her to think a man of Cain's stature would?

Mindy and Matt were the first to come running through the hospital doors. Demi had called Mindy, comforted to know she could get to her daughter quickly. By the time they'd arrived, Stella had been admitted to a room, x-rays had been taken and a CT scan ordered.

"Sweetie!" Mindy ran to her bedside, ignoring Cain. "I came the minute your mother called." She kissed Stella's forehead and examined her. "Have the doctors said anything yet?"

"I have a cracked rib," Stella whispered. "A fever ... some blood when I pee." She looked beyond Mindy and Cain. "Hi, Matt." She looked between the two of them. "I wish mom hadn't bothered you."

Matt walked closer to the bed. Neither he nor Mindy had yet to acknowledge Cain, save a piercing glare.

"How's my Stella Dora?" Matt asked, using his pet name for her.

"Ready to climb Everest with you," she smiled weakly.

"Can you tell us what happened?" Mindy asked.

"She tripped," Cain said, 'and fell into the coffee—"

"I didn't ask you!" Mindy whirled around and shot him a vehement look of disdain. "I want to hear it from my niece."

Cain shot up. "She's not your niece," he barked back.

"She's everything to me and don't you forget it! Her mother asked me to be here."

"Watch how you speak to my wife, Cain," Matt threatened.

"The two of you are upsetting Stella," Cain accused. "I've got this."

Mindy poked a finger to his chest. "You have this? Do you? Or did you cause this?"

"Aunt Mindy," Stella tried to intervene.

"It's okay, sweetheart. I can handle them," Cain bit out.

"You can handle us?" Matt crossed his arms over his chest. "I'm going to ask you once, and only once, to leave quietly before you regret it."

Cain gave him a dismissive snort.

"Do you think I don't know?" Mindy growled. "I've seen the bruises on her and the wounded, confused look on her face only someone who's been there can recognize. So don't you dare spin your lies to me because I've heard them all."

Stella gasped as the tears began to fall. The movement from her sobs exacerbated the pain in her lower back and abdomen.

"I'm sorry, baby." Mindy wiped her tears. "What can I do for you?"

Stella shook her head.

"You're upsetting her with your accusations," Cain said. "She was fine before you got here."

"She was fine?" Matt said through gritted teeth. "Listen, you little, Goddamn son of a bitch. You're going to walk out that door and never return." Matt held his hand up to stop Cain's protest. "If you don't, I'll go to the police and tell them everything I know."

Cain pulled a cocky face. "You don't know shit, old man."

"Does the name Courtney Reed ring a bell?"

The color drained from Cain's face. "No."

"Are you sure? Because you look as white as the sheets on that bed." Matt rubbed his chin, feigning deep thought. "I believe you were engaged to the girl and she broke it off with you."

Stella watched Cain's response. Mindy had told her this and she hadn't believed her. At the time, she didn't want to believe her. But Stella could read the truth in his face, in the tightening of his jaw and the fear in his eyes he was trying to disguise with indifference.

"From what I've learned, you not only bruised her, but you also broke her arm." Matt shot Cain a pointed glare. "So, leave now and never contact Stella again, or if you do, I will personally make sure you're arrested and convicted of abuse."

Cain was rendered speechless. Frozen in place, he shook his head in disbelief and attempted to step closer to the bed. Matt blocked his path.

"Stella," Cain begged. "Don't let them do this to us."

She pulled herself up as best she could and glared at him. "Go Cain, just go."

After all the tests had been completed, the doctors told Stella she'd been lucky. With a little more force, the laceration her kidney had sustained could have been more severe and the threat of losing the organ imminent. But the nephrologist was able to treat her case in a conservative manner and with time and rest Stella would make a full recovery.

The nurses assigned to her floor named her room, 'Club Stella.' They'd never seen so many visitors in and out of one room—many of them carrying bags of mouthwatering food. Sophia bribed the entire nurses station with platters of Greek pastries to lighten up on the guest count rules, and they nodded in agreement with mouthfuls of baklava, as long as they promised to keep the voice level down.

Mindy had to console Demi after she blamed herself for not seeing what was going on with her own child. Matt and Dean had to nearly restrain Michael from seeking out Cain and beating the ever-living shit out of him. And her brothers and cousins hovered by her bed, amusing her with funny stories and making plans for when Stella recuperated.

RJ came too. Every single day. And it upset him that his fear had been realized and he hadn't done something to stop it. Checking in on her once in a while hadn't been enough and now he was going to make sure she was safe from here on in. He stayed with her after everyone had gone and held her hand until she fell asleep.

It was RJ who offered—no, insisted—he bring Stella home from the hospital. And by the time she left almost a week later, the bruises on her body had mostly subsided. Though the ones on her heart remained.

She and RJ were mostly silent for the ride home and Stella had so many things she wanted to say to him, but she didn't know where to begin. Fearing she'd come off as ungrateful, she couldn't form the right words, and every time she was about to open her mouth, she stopped herself. RJ, she knew, was the most caring guy she'd ever known. His brother, Anthony, had been even more so, but since his brother's death, RJ had become more sensitive to those in need of a little extra TLC.

Stella didn't want to become RJ's project or his burden. They had been friends for as long as she could remember and she didn't want to put that weight on him.

"Go home now," she told him, once she'd settled in at home. "I'm sure you have more exciting plans than babysitting me."

"Don't worry about my plans," RJ said. "You come first."

"But as you can see, I'm fine. I have a slew of people hovering over me." She latched onto his hands. "I can't thank you enough for every-thing. You're a great friend and I don't know what I'd do without you in my life." She cocked her head toward the door and released his hands. "Now go! I don't know how some lucky girl hasn't snatched you up by now."

He bent down and kissed her cheek. "I'd have to find one as sweet and as pretty as you."

Stella looked away, blushing. He was being too kind. She felt far from beautiful or desirable, especially after what had happened to her.

The next morning, Stella heard a rap on her bedroom door. Before she could answer, her mother, along with Sophia and Evvie, walked in. No one had pressed her for details in the hospital or when she'd come home the day before and she was grateful for not being bombarded with questions or handed lectures. But Stella had a feeling she wasn't going to escape the interrogation today.

"I brought you some breakfast," Demi said, setting down a white bed tray.

"I'm not sure I can eat all of this," Stella said. Tea, orange juice, and a large spinach and mushroom omelet were placed before her.

"Do your best," her mother replied.

"How are you feeling this morning?" Sophia asked.

"Much better now that I'm in my own bed."

"Are you ready to talk about it?" Evvie asked, sitting on the edge of the bed. "I know it's not easy, but the questions have been coming my way and I don't have any answers."

"I wish that Evvie had told us Cain was so much older than he said he was," Sophia said. "His initial lack of honesty should have been a warning sign."

"He had a reasonable explanation," Stella said, defending herself if not Cain.

"I thought I raised you in a way that let you know you could come

315

to me with anything. This all could have been avoided had you done that," Demi frowned.

"Mindy told us she'd had her suspicions and she's wracked with guilt that she didn't do something sooner," Sophia said.

"But she did! This isn't her fault." Stella reached for her mother's hand and clung to it. "I didn't want to believe her. I knew Cain; she didn't." Stella cast her eyes downward. "Or that's what I thought, anyway."

"He could have killed you," Demi choked out in a sob. "What would possess you to continue dating a man who hit you? You've seen firsthand what real love looks like in this home."

Stella hung her head. "I know, Mom, and that's what I wanted too. Cain loved and protected me when I didn't bring out his bad side."

"Stop blaming yourself," Evvie admonished her.

"Sweetheart, your father and I have been known to have some vocal arguments," Demi said, stifling a smile. "Have you ever seen him lay a hand on me? No. We talk it out and then we, um ..." She looked at Sophia "... make up."

Sophia pressed her lips together to suppress her smile. Stella and Evvie looked back and forth at their mothers. "Ew! Too much information, thank you," Evvie said, curling her lip in disgust.

Stella sat on the back porch of her home and stared out beyond the clear blue sky. Turning, her thoughts were interrupted by footsteps.

"Joey?" Stella was stunned to see her old classmate and the object of her teenage infatuation standing before her. He'd gone off to college in Ohio and the last time she'd seen him was the summer before he left when he was working for her father.

"Hey, Stella," he said, looking at her with careful interest. "Can I join you?"

"Sure." Stella motioned for him to take the seat beside her.

He flipped the chair around so it was directly across from her, pulling it close enough for their knees to touch. "I just saw your dad. I wanted to ask him if he needed any extra help for a couple of weeks while I'm home." Joey grinned. "He said he'd always have a job for me any time I wanted one. I always enjoyed my job at the vineyard."

"That's great, Joey," Stella smiled. "I'll be working there too this summer."

"I know." He sucked in a deep breath, expelling the air loudly. "Listen, I heard about what happened to you." Joey rubbed his palms nervously over his jeans.

"Oh God," Stella groaned, covering her face from embarrassment. "Is there anyone who doesn't know?"

"Don't worry about that. You weren't the one who did anything wrong. But ... I don't understand. Why would you settle for being treated that way? You're too damn trusting for your own good."

Stella saw the distress in Joey's face. A vein that ran from his jawline down his neck bulged.

"When I pulled that little bastard, Jake, off you at that party years ago, I thought you understood that wasn't the way a girl like you should be treated." He raked his hand through his hair. "You could have anyone. Anyone! And you let this guy lay a hand on you."

"I appreciate your concern but it's not as black and white as you make it seem." He shot her an incredulous glare and she pointed her finger at him. "I've been listening to everyone's lectures and advice for days. Don't you think I already feel like the biggest idiot for not seeing Cain for what he was?" She dropped her hand into her lap and looked down in shame. "I haven't seen you in almost three years. You were a good friend to me but ..." she looked up at him. "You say that I could have anyone? No, I couldn't. You didn't want me. Not in the way I wanted you back then." She huffed out a humorless laugh. "It seemed I was always rejected by the ones I wanted."

Joey's arms hung limply between his open legs, his eyes staring down at his feet. He lifted his head and leaned back, scrubbing his face with his palms. Stella watched his obvious discomfort and wished she had kept her mouth shut. What on earth possessed her to bring that up now?

"Stella," he said softly, taking her hands in his, "I never rejected you. You have no idea how much I care for you."

Stella scrunched her forehead in confusion.

"I rejected me, for you. I wasn't good enough for you."

"Why would you say such a thing? You were the most sought after boy in our school."

"Like property. A prize. And I took the bait. Girls were throwing themselves at me."

"I liked you for who you were," Stella said. "Not that the looks weren't a bonus," she joked.

"And that's what separated you from the others. But I wasn't ready for the kind of relationship you deserved and I'd be damned if I would have taken advantage of you."

"You're a good guy, Joey Ardis. You always were."

He leaned over and kissed her on the cheek. "And you're still that same, sweet girl. Don't let what happened to you ruin that beautiful spirit." He stood. "I have to get going. Your dad doesn't waste time. He put me on tonight's shift."

Stella stood and walked down the porch steps with him. "Hey! You said you're only working a couple of weeks? Why?"

"I'm doing a study abroad in London for the remainder of the summer."

"Wow! In what?"

"Architectural Engineering."

"I'm majorly impressed. Especially since I haven't figured out what I want to do with my life yet."

"You'll figure it out. Sometimes the answers find their way to you when you least expect it."

When Stella broke the news to her parents that she wouldn't be returning to school, instead of being upset with her, they were relieved. After what she'd been through, they thought the city was the last place she should be, and they were happy to keep her close by, where they could keep an eye on her.

A restraining order had been filed against Cain and he was not allowed on any of the vineyard premises, private or public. Stella was, for the time being, content to work at the tasting room and to stay close to home. Her renewed friendship with Joey put her in good spirits, and although she was sad to see him go, she was happy for the course his life was taking.

Evvie was around constantly for moral support. Her brother, Paul, scattered icons and other religious items in her room for spiritual protection. Kristos, her older brother, was determined that no man would date his sister ever again without his approval first. Nicky texted Stella every day, but he had won an internship on Matt's travel program and was currently on location with him on the Galapagos Islands.

Adam was sweet, checking in on her from Washington DC and he told her he was looking forward to spending time with her in Greece when they attended his half brother's wedding.

But it was RJ who doted on her the most. After all, he had seen the whole mess played out, and she understood his concern. He was trained to comfort and heal the minds of those who had been hurt either emotionally or physically. Losing a most beloved brother, she imagined, would mature a person and change their perspective on human kindness and sensitivity. Donna had done her job well in raising two spectacular young men. But now, as a result of personal tragedy, RJ had become more than any mother could hope for, and Stella recognized that. Now looking at it from the outside, the differences in character and temperament between Cain and RJ were vast, and she shook her head wondering at how she hadn't see it sooner.

"If nothing ever changed, there would be no such thing as butterflies."

—Wendy Mass

Chapter 43

Evvie

July 2009

E vvie hadn't been to the home that was left to her yiayiá in Chios for many years. As she looked around, she remembered playing with her cousins and brother in the yard when they were small children while the adults sipped on cool beverages with neighbors they'd connected with during their stay.

The bougainvillea vines had spilled over planters, trellises and stair railings, attracting brightly colored butterflies, which Evvie and Stella spent a good amount of their energy chasing.

Evvie stepped into the yard, and a warm breeze brushed lightly over her face. She closed her eyes and breathed in the air. Her memory of Anastacia was only too real, as she let her senses take over. *"Koúkles mou, afíste tin petaloútha móni tis,"* she would say in a gentle voice. They were forever trying to capture the butterflies and Evvie's yiayiá would continuously explain why they should be left to live the life they waited for, freely. A tear escaped from the corner of her eye and rolled down her cheek.

"Hey," Ryan said, joining her outside. "Why are you out here alone?"

She turned and looked at him pensively. "Thinking about simpler days."

He put an arm around her. Her relationship with him had been carefree. At school, their days had revolved around their studies and the social life they had with the crowd they hung with. She rarely spoke of the darker aspects of her life that weighed her down, but the one thing she had shared with him was how much she loved her grandmother. And at this moment the pain was almost as raw as it was ten years ago.

Now, she and Ryan had been thrust into the real world. College was over. They both had careers and lifelong plans to decide. This was the first time she'd asked him to join her family in Greece. Everyone was here. Everyone. And Ryan got along with all of her family and friends. But she never completely let him into the secrets of her heart, those private, locked up memories, both painful and beautiful, that made her who she was.

There was only one to whom she had bared her soul—one who understood her like no other—the very one that haunted her dreams and shamed her conscience.

"Come inside with everyone," Ryan said. "Try to focus on the future. We can't change the past."

He really didn't get it, Evvie thought. "The past leads us to our future. You've never been to Europe, Ryan, but you'll soon learn how important the lessons of the past are and what we can learn from them."

"Is that my granddaughter speaking philosophically?" Alex teased, stepping onto the patio steps.

"Yes, Pappou. You taught me well." She turned to Ryan. "Give me a minute with my grandfather."

Ryan nodded and disappeared inside through the French doors.

Alex strode over to Evvie. She wrapped her arms around his waist, clasping her hands together behind him and resting her head on his chest.

Alex ran his hands down the strands of her hair. "I know, *engoní mou*," he sighed. His voice held so much sadness as he continued. "I miss her too. So much that my heart feels it's been sliced open and shredded."

"I can feel her all around me. I think that's what makes it worse. I want to reach out and touch her and wrap myself in her arms one more time."

"Me too, *agapi*, me too."

They'd spent several days in Chios before traveling to Thessaloniki for Sam's wedding. Mindy, understandably after what had happened to her years ago in Chios, flew directly to Thessaloniki with Amy and her family.

During her stay on the island, Evvie took Ryan from place to place by moped. She wanted him to see Greece as she saw it—as it was for the natives. They went to Mavro Volia, a famed beach with a volcanic history. It's large, black pebbles and crystal clear water left Ryan speechless. She showed him the mastiha farms, shopped at open markets, and rode through Pyrgi so he could see the buildings decorated with geometrical designs.

Sometimes they'd drive off alone. Other times, the entire gang of young adults would go out together, hitting one taverna after another, eating, drinking and dancing the night away.

Paul spent much of his day exploring ancient churches, and he managed to drag his sister and brother along from time to time. But Stella was anxious to meet up with Evvie at one of the many beaches and ditched her brother the moment she could get away.

Evvie took notice that RJ had stuck close to Stella's side. He had become so protective of her since she'd landed in the hospital at the hands of Cain. She suspected that RJ harbored some regret over missing the signs of his brother's deep depression and the emotional torture that he had endured from their father and some of Anthony's peers. It wasn't his fault and neither was what happened to Stella, and hovering over her wouldn't change a thing.

The night before they left for Thessaloniki, Evvie had a difficult time falling asleep. "What's wrong, Evvie?" Stella asked sleepily. They were sharing the double bed in one of the smaller bedrooms. Stella had fallen asleep, but Evvie's tossing had awoken her.

"I don't know. Maybe coming here has stirred up too many memories. I can't help missing her." Evvie didn't need to clarify of whom she was speaking.

Stella simply stroked her cousin's hair. "Try to drift off thinking of her. The memories are your way of holding onto her. Those can never be taken from you."

Finally, Evvie drifted off; precious images and sacred moments playing in her subconscious state.

Evvie and Stella giggled, running circles in the yard, chasing a butterfly. "So pwetty," three-year-old Stella cooed. "Catch it!"

The beautiful creature paid the girls no mind. Flitting from flower to flower, its azure colored markings were a stunning contrast to the cerise shade of delicate petals that hung over the veranda.

Evvie, three years her senior, was able to corner the regal winged insect. Before she could touch and unintentionally harm it, Evvie's yiayiá, dressed in a pale yellow sundress, gracefully glided over to the girls.

"Koúkles mou, afíste tin petaloútha móni tis," Anastacia said softly.

"We just want to hold it," Evvie said. Stella bobbed her head up and down in agreement.

She took the girls by the hand. "Look at the butterfly, but don't disturb it. She's happy and has finally found the life she is meant to have." Anastacia kneeled to meet the girls' height. "Do you know how butterflies are created? No? Well, I'll tell you. This gorgeous, colorful butterfly was once a kábia—a caterpillar."

Evvie scrunched her nose. "Why? I don't like them."

"Like you and Stella, it needed to grow and learn how to become a petaloútha. It inched along, eating many leaves, growing slowly until it was time to rest. The caterpillar didn't know what was about to happen, but something was changing. It wanted to understand but the answers hadn't come yet. And again, it changed the way it looked, but it wasn't free yet. It had to wait until it was ready to soar through the air. Now the butterfly is grown and has figured out its life's purpose. And you need to respect that, okay, girls?"

They nodded. Evvie wasn't sure that Stella completely understood, but she had questions. She always had questions. "Yiayiá?"

"Yes, koukla mou?"

"Stella and me are growing bigger. Are we finding our purpose?"

"That's a big question for a seven-year-old girl. You will someday. Right now, all you need to think about is today. When you get older, you'll discover what makes you want to soar happily like the petaloútha."

"Look!" Stella pointed with glee. "Two."

"Ah! Now she's complete. She's found her mate. But remember girls, the butterfly must know herself before she can find the one to fly with."

Evvie opened her eyes, confused and a bit disoriented. It took her a few seconds to recall that she was in bed, in Chios, and with her cousin lying next to her. The dream seemed too real. Not like a dream at all. She had thought of her yiayiá and the butterflies earlier that day when she had stepped out onto the patio. She wondered if that's what prompted the dream. Or had her grandmother paid her a visit, as she had on other occasions?

Evvie climbed out of bed and peeked through the window blinds. Dawn was breaking. A golden glow was fading the sable night sky. Evvie turned when she heard the rustling of bed sheets.

"You still can't sleep?" Stella asked in a groggy voice.

"No, I slept. I was startled awake by a dream." It was still fresh in her mind and she relayed the details to Stella before she forgot them.

"I have a vague recollection of that," Stella said. "I remember both of our yiayiás telling us to stop chasing the *petalouthes* more than once."

"Maybe she's trying to tell us something," Evvie said. "Maybe she wants us to find our way just like the *petaloúthes* we used to chase."

"Maybe, but I think the butterflies are way ahead of us," Stella said. "I don't know about you, but I'm not even sure where to begin."

Chapter 44

Evvie & Stella

July 2009

Evvie and Stella joined their mothers for evening cocktails at the hotel's outdoor lounge. They had arrived in Thessaloniki earlier that afternoon, settled into their rooms, and dined with their entire spirited clan.

But the ladies wanted time to themselves—just their core group—the 'Honey Hill Girls' and the two blossoming young women who were an extension of what they once were.

Outside, they positioned their chairs around a low standing circular table. It was a comfortable night, dry and warm, a slight breeze gently drifting by. Chios had been near oppressive with its heat and level of humidity and now, this city, situated in northern Greece, was a welcome change.

"Aunt Amy," Stella addressed her mother's lifelong friend, I don't think I've ever seen you smile this much!"

"She's positively glowing!" Mindy agreed, taking Stella's hand. "How's my girl?" she whispered, leaning close her.

Stella nodded her assurance before bringing her attention back to Amy.

"Tell us what you've been doing since you got here," Stella asked.

"Well, of course I met Naomi, Sam's fiancée. She's such a lovely girl and they seem very happy together. It's been interesting, though." Amy grinned. "Let's just say, things are done a little differently around here than what I'm used to."

"In what way?" Evvie asked.

"I'm not sure if everyone still does all of this, but Sam wanted the wedding to honor his ancestors and the traditions of those who came before him. Many of whom had their lives stolen from them."

"I can understand that," Sophia said, "and I think it's very sweet."

"What kind of traditions?" Donna asked.

"Last night, Naomi's parents brought her dowry to Sam's home. Everything, including her china and linens, was all recorded in the *ketubah* by a third party."

"What is that?" Stella asked.

"It's a marriage contract," Amy answered. "But get this! The contract doesn't get officially signed until after the wedding night when it's been proven that the bride's ..." Amy cleared her throat. "... virtue was in tact."

Red wine sprayed from Demi's mouth as she began to roar with laughter.

"Is someone going to inspect the sheets for blood?" Mindy joked.

"Don't laugh," Sophia told her. "That's exactly what they do, or used to do. My yiayiá told me about this, years ago. You can ask her yourself in the morning. It's a Greek thing."

"Are you saying this isn't just a Sephardic custom?"

"No," Sophia answered. "It's an old-fashioned tradition and it's still done today throughout many of the islands and villages."

"And what if ..." Evvie wasn't sure how to pose the question, but her aunt took care of that problem.

"She already popped her cherry, rode the bull, had been deflowered, had her door unlocked?" Demi said, finishing Evvie's sentence.

"We get the picture, Demi," Amy scolded.

"I could go on and on." Demi downed the last sip of wine in her glass.

"Spare us," Sophia said. "I've been told," Sophia continued, with all seriousness, "that if the girl isn't a virgin, the bride's mother kills a rooster the night before the wedding. She gives the blood from the animal to her daughter to smear on the sheets."

"That's the most disgusting thing I've ever heard," Evvie said.

"To loopholes!" Mindy cheered, raising her glass.

"Well, guess what, girls?" Amy said. "We're all invited to help make up the bride's nuptial bed tomorrow, and after that, to join the *mikveh* celebration.

The next morning, after breakfast, the younger set went for a walk along the waterfront. As they approached the White Tower, a famed landmark and symbol of the city, Evvie and Stella told the boys what they'd be doing later that afternoon.

Several jokes were thrown around, some of them on the crude side, and Evvie elbowed Ryan and Stella, telling them to stop making fun.

"All joking aside, it's kind of sweet really," Stella said.

"We should find out if Naomi's parents serve rooster the night before the wedding," Ryan grinned. "I'll bet my life savings they are!"

"Why do I bother? You have no regard for tradition at all, do you?" Evvie chastised.

"Sure I do. I eat corned beef and cabbage every Saint Patrick's Day." By the impish expression on his face, Evvie knew he was teasingly challenging her. "You are aware that they don't actually eat that in Ireland?"

"Still a tradition," he argued.

"Do the two of you always go at each other like that?" RJ asked.

"They really don't," Stella answered for them. "Everyone should have such a steady, calm relationship."

Something about Stella's comment niggled at the back of Evvie's mind. Calm and steady. Is that what she wanted? She supposed she did. After all, it's the choice she'd made. And after what Stella had been through, calm would be a refreshing change for her as well.

At Paul's request, they headed to St. Demetrios, the cathedral where Evvie and Nicky's late relative served for most of his priesthood. They had only met Father Vasili a few times when they were small, but he was a man who wasn't easily forgotten.

For Nicky, his fascination was in the history of Thessaloniki, and he snapped photos of every significant landmark and site. His portfolio had grown exponentially since he began his internship with Matt and he hoped to now focus on the more political side of his photojournalism.

"This was nice," Evvie sighed. "But we need to get back."

"What are you guys going to do today?" Stella asked.

Kristos, smartass that he was at times, draped his arms over Ryan's and RJ's shoulders. "Head to the beach. Check out the women. Hit the bars later and pick up a few maybe," he said, wiggling his eyebrows.

Ryan grinned.

"You think that's funny?" Evvie smacked him in the head.

"Are you sure they're calm and steady?" RJ asked. "It doesn't seem that way to me."

Stella shrugged. "Maybe something's in the water."

When the women had all convened to prepare the bridal bed, it was agreed upon that Evvie, Stella and Naomi's younger sister would put the sheets and comforter on. Traditionally, it was unmarried girls who made up the bed and the three of them were the only unmarried women in attendance.

Once the bed was made, it was time to adorn it. Together, all the women joined in scattering rose petals, rice, sugared almonds and gold coins across the bed. The finishing touch was the baby. Naomi's cousin placed her male child in the middle of the bed. This was done for good luck in the hopes that the young couple would bear a son the following year.

"It's complete!" Naomi's mother exclaimed with joy. She held her daughter's face between her hands. "May you soon bear a grandson for me to spoil!"

Evvie pinched Stella's arm. "They mean business. They want her knocked up the minute the ceremony is over."

Stella clamped her hand over her mouth, but a squeal of laughter escaped.

Demi shot her daughter a death stare and quietly inched her way over to them. "What's wrong with you girls?" she whispered. "This is a beautiful moment for the bride."

Sophia joined them. "You don't see this every day. You girls need to appreciate a custom that's been done for centuries. It takes only one generation to abandon meaningful traditions like this one."

Everyone's attention went to the doorway of the room. There, Sam stood, waiting to enter and offer his approval. Evvie placed her hand over her heart as she saw the look in Sam's eyes when he saw his bride standing by the nuptial bed. He made his way over to Naomi, took her hands in his and kissed her. "I love you very, very much," he said.

"And I love you," she answered, lifting her hand to run it through his golden mop of curls.

Evvie was stricken by the show of love and the passion she saw between them as they stared at one another. "You're right, Mom. It's a very sweet tradition," Evvie agreed.

The house was brimming with guests, eating and drinking, but it wasn't long before Revekka, Sam's mother, announced that it was time for the women to leave for the *mikveh*.

"We're all going?" Mindy asked Amy, looking confused.

"Yes, it's a Sephardic tradition that all the women in the community attend with the bride," Amy told her.

"Okay. Let's go then." She looped her arm around Amy's. "Come on girls!" Mindy said, motioning for Stella and Evvie to follow.

Naomi immersed herself in the water three times after a prayer was said over her. Afterward, a celebration broke out and food and desserts were served in an adjoining room. The women gathered around Naomi as she was seated in a chair. It was their tradition to adorn the bride with henna. A beautiful design was dyed into her fingertips and nails as some of her relatives sang the traditional folk song, 'El Villano Vil.' The ritual was now complete, and Naomi was ready to stand before the Rabbi and join herself to Samuouél.

The following afternoon, a large crowd of family and friends entered the Monastirioton Synagogue. Amy looked at her husband, Ezra, and her friends as she was honored the privilege to walk her son down the aisle alongside Revekka and David, the couple who'd raised her child.

"Where's the chuppah?" Evvie asked Mindy.

"Amy told me it's not their tradition. Instead, they wrap themselves in a prayer shawl," she explained. "Isn't it nice that Sam asked Adam to be his best man?"

Evvie smiled in agreement.

Revekka and David presented Sam with a *tallit*, draping the shawl around his shoulders. Soon after, Naomi, escorted by her own parents, floated down the aisle to meet her groom. Facing their guests, the couple radiated joy. When the rabbi instructed them, they placed the *tallit* over their heads as a symbol of the new home the couple would dwell in together.

Sugared almonds in clusters of five, wrapped in tulle, were handed to the guests as they exited the synagogue. "Health, happiness, children, prosperity and longevity," Stella said as she popped one of the almonds in her mouth. "That's what Sam told me each almond represents."

"What more could anyone ask for from life?" RJ said. He offered her his bent arm and escorted her down the steps.

The reception was held at the hotel where most of the out of town guests had been staying. Sam and Naomi chose an outdoor setting, and the weather had cooperated nicely. Like every other Greek wedding Evvie and Stella had attended, the food was abundant, the dance floor crowded and the liquor flowing! Young and old, a good time was had by all and when it was over, sunrise was only a few hours away.

"Let's go to the beach and stay until the sun comes up," Evvie suggested. "I'm too wired to go to bed."

An hour later, the entire group had changed out of their dress clothes and was facing the shoreline waiting for dawn to break. Ryan was sitting behind Evvie, straddling her between his legs, his chin resting on her shoulder.

Wrapping his arms around her, Ryan whispered in her ear. "I think we should talk about our next step," he said nervously. "With the wedding today and all … and seeing how happy Sam and Naomi looked, it seems like a good time."

Evvie twisted her head to look at him. "Weddings have that affect on people," she said.

"Well, we've been going out for a long time and … obviously, we love each other."

Evvie didn't comment but Ryan waited for her confirmation so she nodded.

"Since we've been out of school, things haven't been the same. You're all the way out on Long Island and I'm working in the city. I think it's time we were in one place." He turned her around on his lap.

"I think we should move in together."

"Move in together? Seriously?" Evvie looked at him like he was out of his mind.

"Yes, seriously. I feel like we barely see each other."

"Ryan, do you know my family at all? That's not going to fly."

"They'll get over it. You're an adult," Ryan said.

"You really don't get it," she said, sliding off his lap.

"What? That you need to get permission from your family to breathe? Ev, this is your life. Our life."

"And what about my life, Ryan? My life and career are on the vineyard. It's what I've worked for. Unless you're planning to move out by me and commute to work."

"That would be impossible. There are other jobs in the wine industry you could get in the city. It would only be for a while. I have my eye on a position at Google. That's where I want to end up."

"In California? First of all, a job with Google is not easy to come by and second, how does that help us?"

"You could work in Napa," Ryan said as if it were no big deal.

Evvie wasn't even going to address that. After all, a career at Google was a long shot and one that was far off, if it ever happened at all. And when did she ever give him the impression she wanted to work in Napa. Sure, it would be a dream come true for any vintner, except for her. She loved her family's vineyard and it's where she always felt she belonged.

"I think we should take a step back and deal with the here and now," Evvie said. "I need you to respect my career the way I do yours. It's important to me. If we're going to stay together then we have to work it out so we can both do what we've worked so hard for."

"I don't know how that's possible," Ryan sighed, running his hands through his platinum hair.

"Well, we can both compromise. Eventually, we can look into living somewhere in between the city and Jamesport. But it can't happen if we're not married."

Ryan's eyebrows rose. "I'm not quite ready for that yet. Hell, Ev, we're only twenty-three."

"That's fine. I'm not asking you to marry me, but I can't move in with you. You need to understand. I've done a lot of things to upset my mother in the past and she would not be happy about this at all."

Meanwhile, on another blanket, Adam, RJ, Stella and Kristos were munching on the snacks they had brought and poking fun at one another.

"Take a walk with me," RJ said, leaning into Stella.

She looked up at him and smiled. "Sure." RJ extended his hand to her, helping her up. She brushed the sand off the back of her shorts and stepped in line with him.

They walked silently by the edge of the shoreline for a few minutes. The farther they walked, the more peaceful the atmosphere became. Stella always felt a sense of serenity in RJ's company. He made her feel protected and cared for, but it was more than that. She simply enjoyed being with him. She always had.

"I wanted to propose something to you, Stella," RJ began. "Something that I think would be good for you and help me out as well."

Stella halted and faced RJ, staring quizzically at him. "You know I would do anything for you," she told him. "You've done more for me than I could ever repay, but how could I possibly help you out?"

"You could work at the hotline with Mom and me."

"To do what? Paperwork? Filing?" Stella wasn't trained for much, even after three years of college.

RJ shoved his hands in his pockets. "No, to answer calls."

Stella's eyes grew wide.

He pulled his hands from his pockets and raised them, stopping her from rejecting the suggestion. "Before you say no, we would send you for training." He placed his hands on her shoulders and drew her in closer. "Look, Stella. You've been through a lot this year. The hotline isn't only for teens in jeopardy of committing suicide, it's for anything that's troubling them—abuse, rape, homelessness, depression. Anything. Since you know first hand what it's like to go through something traumatic and come out of it unscathed, you'd be an obvious candidate for a position."

Stella looked away. "I wouldn't say unscathed."

"You're right, I'm sorry. It left a lasting mark, but you've made great progress and you were able to move on with your life."

"I had you to help me get through it, and a supportive family, but ... moving on, I don't know. I feel a little stuck."

"That's why this will be good for you. It'll give you something to do while you figure things out." He motioned for her to sit. "This is important work. Think of how many people you could help. Even if you only get through to one person—if you manage to help only one person from a disastrous fate, it would be rewarding."

Stella dug her toes into the sand and considered what RJ had said. "You might be right. I'm not doing much now other than helping out in my dad's tasting room."

"I know I'm right. You're the sweetest and most caring person I've ever known. I suspect you'll be a natural at this."

"Okay, I'll give it a try. When do I start?"

RJ grinned victoriously. "Right away. As soon as we get home."

Chapter 45

Evvie

May 2010

Ryan was due to come in on the afternoon train in twenty minutes and Evvie was knee deep in mud. It had rained buckets the night before, and the young, barely budding vines were drowning in water. The buds could be subject to mildew or worse; the winds might have severed them from their delicate, spindly branches.

"You should go," her Uncle Michael said. "I can handle this."

"Look at me," Evvie waved a hand down the length of her grimy self. "I can't go like this and I'd never clean up in time." She pulled her iPhone from the back pocket of her cargo pants. "I'll text Stella. Is she home?"

"Don't bother. She's at the outreach center," Michael said. "She left pretty early this morning."

"She's been putting in a lot of hours."

"Full time since school let out for the semester." He grinned. "I think this major might actually stick."

Evvie laughed. "One can only hope!" She tapped in another message. Her brother was home and probably still in bed, she guessed, from the hour he'd come in last night. "Yes! He's the best. I can always count on Nicky. He said he's dressed and leaving now."

"It's three o'clock," Michael said dryly. "I should hope he'd be dressed by now."

"He's been working hard," Evvie said. "It's good to see him take it easy for once."

"It doesn't look like we lost too many buds. Hopefully the sun will come out soon and dry this up," Michael said. "Let's clean up, and then we can head over to start labeling. Are you excited to release your new sparkling wine?"

"Our wine. I am! This one is the closest we've come to producing anything near to what I'd sampled in Épernay."

An hour later, Ryan found Evvie and her uncle manning the labeling equipment. After shaking hands with Michael and planting a quick peck on Evvie's lips, he picked up one of the bottles. "So this is it?" he asked.

"This is it!" she squealed, clapping her hands together.

"What makes this one different than last years?" Ryan asked.

"It's the first time we've been able to use all three varieties of grapes traditionally used in French Champagne. We only began growing Petit Meunier when I begged my uncle," she said, tapping a quick kiss on Michael's cheek, "to let me make sparkling wine in the *méthode champenoise.*"

"Why don't you kids get out of here," Michael said. "I've got this covered."

"There's still work to be done. Ryan can wait for me at the house."

"Go! I'm insisting." Michael grabbed Evvie by the shoulders and turned her toward the door. "The two of you don't get to spend enough time together."

"We can go hang out at your house for a while," Ryan said as they waved goodbye to Michael. "And then, put on something nice. I'm taking you out to dinner."

"Okay. Dinner? Where? Will a nice pair of jeans do?"

"Not tonight. I asked your mom for a recommendation for a good restaurant. We are going to …" He struggled to remember the name. "… Something Hawkins."

"Jedediah Hawkins Inn?" Evvie asked with an expression that held bewilderment.

"Yeah, that's the one."

"Why do you want to go someplace that dressy? Wouldn't you prefer—"

"Nope, not tonight. I haven't seen you in almost two weeks." He threw his arm around her shoulder. "And I wouldn't mind seeing you in a pair of high heels."

Three hours later, Evvie and Ryan were seated at a small table for two, tucked into a cozy corner. The Jedediah Hawkins Inn was once an old Victorian home, now transformed into a restaurant run by one of Long Island's top culinary masters. The integrity of the historic structure was not compromised and it still looked as though one was stepping into a private residence.

Evvie had dazzled Ryan. It wasn't often he saw her dressed this way. In college, she was always in jeans and warm sweaters, and even now, she usually dressed very casually. So Evvie couldn't help but smirk when she saw the expression on his face as she exited her bedroom.

The messy bun she had secured with a hair tie was gone, replaced by dark, flowing beach waves. She'd slipped on the heels he'd asked for, black ones, with spikes so thin they could double as assault weapons. But her dress, a little, body hugging BCBG design in midnight blue, might just kill him first.

Ryan reached across the table, taking her hand in his. He leaned in and was about to speak when their waiter came to clear the dinner plates.

"I'll be back in a moment to take your dessert order," he said, handing them a list of the night's selections.

"You were about to tell me something?" Evvie asked.

"Let's order first and then we can talk."

Evvie didn't have a chance to ask him what he wanted to talk about when their server swiftly returned. Once they placed their orders, she was anxious to hear what was on his mind. He'd been acting a little weird all day. One minute he was affectionate and the next, jumpy. His behavior was a bit baffling and so unlike the even-tempered guy she was used to.

"Remember in Greece when I asked you to move in with me?"

"Yes," she stretched out.

"I still want that. To live with you."

"Ryan, we've been over this."

"I know. Let me finish, okay?" He now had both of her hands between hers. "Being apart all these months and seeing you once or twice a week isn't working for me."

Evvie sucked in a nervous breath. *He's going to break up with me,* she thought. She pulled her hands from his grasp. "I understand. I suppose eventually this was bound to happen. Hopefully, we can part as friends," Evvie said softly.

"Part?" Ryan was stunned. "That's not what I'm trying to do here."

Evvie stared up at him. With her hands planted in her lap, she fidgeted with her napkin.

"Evvie, I do want you to live with me. But I made a mistake that day. I should have asked you to marry me. I'm asking now." Ryan drew out a black velvet box from his suit jacket and opened it.

A small gasp escaped Evvie's lips and her eyes went wide. "I wasn't expecting that!"

With a lopsided grin he said, "I can see that."

She reached for the box to take a closer look at the oval diamond set in platinum. "It's beautiful."

"Well? Will you spend your life with me?" Ryan asked.

"Of course," Evvie said. Standing, she rushed to his side. Ryan rose from his chair and they kissed. He took the ring from the box and slipped it on her finger.

"It's official!" he exclaimed.

"Tell us everything!" Demi shrieked. "And I mean everything. Don't leave out one detail." For the fifth time since they'd sat down at the breakfast table, Demi had taken Evvie's hand to examine her ring.

Sophia handed Stella and Evvie a cup of tea, smiling at her daughter.

She and Ryan had gotten in late the night before. Once the initial excitement subsided, they had much to discuss. Evvie didn't like the idea of living off the vineyard, but she couldn't expect him to commute into the city from so far away. It would all get ironed out once they came to a workable compromise. It was the same for her mother when she'd married her stepfather, and she asked her mother now how she had felt about it at the time.

"It was a big decision, selling the dance studio and moving out here. But Dino was really invested in making the Carriage House a success and the commute was difficult for him."

"But you sacrificed everything you'd worked for? That doesn't seem fair."

Sophia handed her younger daughter, Cia, now a precocious eleven-year-old, a mug of steaming chai tea. "I didn't sacrifice a thing," she told her older daughter, pulling up a chair beside her. "When you love someone, the decisions you make to build a life together come easily and without internal conflict. Now, I'm not saying you should give up your hopes and dreams. If you're truly compatible, those dreams will align."

"I know. We have to iron out the details. But it's hard for me to imagine myself living anywhere but here."

"You could always go with Plan B," Cia told her sister.

"Oh? And what plan is that?" Evvie asked.

"Grow old and gray on this vineyard with your wine bottles and a couple dozen cats." Cia laughed into her mug.

"Funny," Evvie snapped.

"Are you sure she's not my daughter?" Demi laughed.

Sophia arched an eyebrow. "Sometimes I wonder."

"You know," Demi said, "when two people bring their lives together, it takes getting used to. You and Ryan each have your own set of career goals and it may take some creativity and flexibility to make both of you happy."

"Your aunt is right," Sophia said. "For now, enjoy this time. You should be walking on air. You're starting your life with the young man you love. Enjoy it."

"You're right." Evvie rose from her chair. "I'm going to see if my sleepy boyfr—I mean fiancé—has woken up yet so we can simply enjoy our first day engaged together."

Chapter 46

Zak

June 2010

It had been nearly two years since Zak had last laid eyes on Evvie. Two years since he'd challenged the tenacious glint in her eye. Two long years since his lips last touched hers or he had felt his body pressed against her while their hearts beat in harmonious unity. Two years since she'd broken his heart.

When he'd first seen her all those years ago walking across the college campus, he'd taken notice. There was something about her, an unexplainable force that drew him to her. Weeks later, when she showed up at the same church function, he was sure the fates had been on his side. Or was it someone else?

The tears he'd woken up with convinced him his sister had come to him.

"Elpida," Zak had called to her in his sleep, his arms outstretched.

"Live your life for both of us," his twin sister pleaded. "Don't spend your days in sadness."

"I'm so sorry I failed you," Zak apologized. "I don't know who or what I am without you."

"Alive. You're alive. And you never failed me."

He knelt at her feet and she wrapped all her goodness and light around him. "One like me will come to you. Be patient."

"What does that mean? Like you? No one can replace you."

"Patience, my sweet brother. Like me, but meant for you."

Zak awoke in a start when the apparition of Elpida faded away.

Later, when he'd discovered that Evvie had a twin brother, he replayed his sister's words over and over in his mind. *One like me will come to you. Like me, but meant for you.* The message was cryptic at the time. But one look into those pools of caramel eyes that were so much like his and he saw the reflection of his own soul staring back at him.

But Evvie wasn't prey to his charms. Indifference and a snarky mouth replaced the flicker of honesty from her first telling glance. But Zak recognized pain when he came face to face with it, and he knew there was so much more to this girl than he knew.

He had practically stooped to a stalker's level when he'd finally made a friend of her, and the pull between them grew when she laughed at his stories, shared a beer with him or they listened to a favorite song together using only a set of earbuds between them. He'd finally made progress with her, or so he thought, until he discovered that she'd used him for the sole purpose of getting her mother off her back. He wasn't sure which hurt more, the fact that she thought his appearance was so laughable it would frighten her parents, or that she never had any genuine feelings for him whatsoever.

The next time he saw her, she was arm in arm with that blond guy, and as much as he didn't want it to matter, it did.

Then, as if the Greek Gods above didn't hate him enough, Evvie ended up not only on the same Greek island, but at the same house where he'd been staying. And in some fucked up coincidence, her family was connected to his. When he saw her seated in a patio chair on his grandparents' veranda that first day, he thought the earth would swallow him whole.

But Zak was defenseless to the electricity that sparked between them, and slowly they had regained the friendship they'd previously only just begun to share. The beauty of those days held his most precious of memories, yet equally, they caused him the greatest pain. He knew what they had together was real and very rare. Each and every cell in his body responded to her in a way it never had with anyone before, and he wasn't imagining that she'd felt the same. He saw it when their eyes locked, as body and soul united as one. He felt it in her touch and in the sound of her voice every time she moaned out his name. He was hers, and she, his. He was certain of it, even as she chose to deny it.

Days passed, and then weeks and months. Zak waited for Evvie to find him, call or text. At some point she had to yearn for what was missing from her life. What was missing was him, and the love that only he could give her. But with each month that passed, Zak's hopes slowly shattered and, eventually, he came to realize it was never meant to be.

Until one day when his mother mentioned Evvie's mother's name. Zak's mother, Glika, and Sophia had volunteered for the same committee at the church's annual festival and had become friendly. Sophia had invited his parents to a party at their home. A twenty-fourth birthday party for her twins, and she told Glika to extend the invitation to their son, should he happen to be in town.

"Sophia has a lovely family, Zak," his mother said. "You should join us. There'll be plenty of young people your age there."

"I'll think about it, Mom. I'll have a look at my calendar and let you know."

His mother had no idea that he'd already been to the Papadakis home, or that he was more than acquainted with Evvie. He had never shared with his parents the connection their family had with them through Evvie's great-grandmother and he wasn't sure what Evvie had told her mother either.

Zak had spent the last few years building his career. He'd landed a job as a junior video game designer with Activision in Albany, NY. But after a year, he realized upstate was not where he wanted to plant roots and he found a position with an independent gaming company in New York City. After work each evening, he spent hours in his small studio apartment, hunched over his drafting table, sketching out panel-style illustrations for a graphic novel he hoped to publish.

In the two years since he'd last seen the girl who nearly broke what was left of his spirit, he'd grown up, and he wondered if maybe Evvie had too. She had always been clear about her goals and aspirations. He wondered if the timing between them had always been off, and now that a few years had passed, perhaps they had matured, perhaps she'd be more open to a relationship with him.

Zak felt the thrumping in his chest and the beat of his heart at every pulse point. Walking through the backyard gates behind his parents, he second-guessed his decision to come here. He blew out a nervous breath as Mrs. Papadakis spotted them and headed over to greet them.

"Evvie!" Sophia called out when her daughter walked by. "Come meet my friends."

If his heart wasn't beating hard enough, it was now about to leap up and summersault out his throat. When Glika made his introduction, Zak wouldn't have been at all surprised if she didn't recognize him at first glance. He would have laughed at the absurdity of how he looked back then too if he wasn't so uptight at the moment.

"Evvie, I want you to meet my friends, Glika and Demos Maryiatos ..." Sophia said.

Evvie looked up at them when she heard their last name.

"... and their son, Zak."

His parents parted, allowing him to step forward and come face to face with Evvie for the first time in two years.

Chapter 47

Evvie

June 2010

Evvie's breath caught as she stifled her reaction. Completely speechless, she stood frozen in place by the heavy weight of his stare. They were the most beautiful brown eyes on one of the most handsome faces she'd ever seen. *Brown*, she thought. She had never seen the true color of his eyes. This wasn't the same rebellious boy who'd sported a blue mohawk, or even the one she'd gotten to know at his grandparents' vineyard. Slacks and a collared shirt that bordered on preppy had replaced his signature grim-messaged graphic tees. The Zak before her was a man. And even without the short, trimmed beard that was barely more than a manicured, sexy stubble, he would have been the most beautiful man she'd ever set her eyes on.

Evvie's heart hammered in her chest. With a shaky voice, she found the resolve to speak. "Mom, Zak and I are acquainted."

Zak mumbled a curse and cleared his throat. His parents looked at him curiously.

"You met Zak a few years ago. I brought him to one of our summer parties."

Sophia took a closer look at him, trying to recall when she might have met this boy.

"I looked a little different back then." He ran his hand over meticulously styled hair that had an intentionally tousled look. "Think blue," he said, with an apologetic grin.

"That was you?" Sophia clamped her hands over her mouth.

"It was one of my son's many stages," Demos said. "He's finally decided to stop trying to give his old man a stroke."

Sophia smiled warmly. "Come with me," she said to Zak's parents, "and I'll introduce you around." She turned to Zak. "I'll leave you in Evvie's hands."

"It's nice to see you again, Zak." Evvie had an urge to touch his arm, but she thought the better of it. "So," she forced a smile, "I finally get to see the real Zak."

He stepped in closer to her, leaving only a few inches between them. He palmed her cheek and her breathing hitched at the sudden contact.

"You've always seen the real me." He took her hand and held it over his heart. "I'm in here. My hair style and the color of my eyes are inconsequential."

Evvie didn't pull her hand from his grasp or her gaze from his penetrating eyes. Every nerve ending in her body felt like a livewire sizzling in a puddle of water. She was about to say something but she wasn't sure what. Her mind had vanished and her stomach had done a backflip. Evvie was just about to figure it out when her stepfather got her attention.

"Ev," Dean called.

She jerked her hand from Zak's when he approached.

"Come on, it's time."

"Oh, Dad, could we not do this today?"

"What are you talking about? Your uncle is already pouring the champagne." Dean placed his hand over Evvie's shoulder and led her to the large stone patio.

Sophia and Nicky joined them with Cia trailing behind. Michael handed each of them a flute of champagne.

"As you all know, it's Nicky and Evvie's twenty-fourth birthday. I'm still trying to wrap my brain around that. It feels like yesterday I was frantically driving their mother to the hospital to give birth to them." He draped his arms over their shoulders. "I'm a lucky man to have been a part of their lives from the start. Today, I get to share in another important milestone." He gestured for Ryan to join them. "Evvie and Ryan have decided to get married. They're engaged!"

Evvie's eyes met Zak's and held them for only a brief moment before she pulled her focus from him. His despondently incredulous expression nearly made her cry out his name. Ryan pulled her into an embrace and kissed her. Then, in front of all their guests, he slid the ring she'd decided not to wear until the announcement was made onto her slim finger.

From the corner of her eye, she saw Zak weave his way through the crowd, heading for the gate. Reflexively, she wanted to stop him and explain. But what could she say? That she didn't expect him to be here? What difference would that make? Evvie hadn't seen Zak in two years, and the last time she did, she'd made it clear she was going home to Ryan. Why did Zak always make her feel like her soul was being ripped from her? And how did she always, unwillingly, time and time again, manage to wound this boy?

For the remainder of the party Evvie plastered on a fake smile. She didn't recall a single word of congratulations or the never-ending unsolicited marital advice bestowed upon her. Music blared and guests danced. Laughter could be heard throughout the yard. Evvie felt as though she was witnessing her life as if from the outside. Her stomach was tied in knots and her head was starting to throb. This day couldn't end fast enough for her.

Even after the sun had set, the party continued. Evvie needed a break from it all, just a little breather from the joviality and all the smiling faces. She made her way through the gates and down the driveway. A string of cars were parked on the gravel pathway that led from their home to the vineyard's public space. Evvie leaned back on a white Lexus, hoping she wouldn't trip someone's alarm. *That was all she needed*, she thought. *To bring more attention to herself.*

"Evvie," Zak said, emerging from the shadows.

For a split second, she was startled, until she saw him standing before her. "You left before I could speak to you," she said softly, not meeting his gaze.

Zak shoved his hands in his pockets. "I couldn't stay and watch," he said, kicking the gravel with the toe of his shoe. "But I couldn't stay away either. I drove around, fighting with myself on what to do."

"And you came back." She looked up at him.

"I had to. You need to hear me out. After you do, if you choose to walk away, I'll never come near you again."

"Zak—"

"Just give me that, okay?"

Her nod was nearly imperceptible, but even in the dark, with only moonlight illuminating their faces, she wordlessly gave him the permission to say what he needed.

"Don't marry him," Zak pleaded, as he ambled closer to her. "Choose me."

"Zak," Evvie softly moaned a cry.

He took her face in his hands, resting his forehead to hers. She could feel his breath tickling her neck. The scent of him was so close to her it played with her mind. Chills skated up and down her spine, as she remembered how she had felt the last time he'd touched her—the last time she'd had her body pressed to his.

"Choose me because my soul has chosen you, and I can't accept for one second that you don't feel what I do."

Tears escaped Evvie's eyes, rolling down her cheeks.

"Can he fill your heart the way I can? Every crevice?" His voice went thick with emotion. "Because you fill mine. You always have. I see you. I know you. You're my beginning and my end. My alpha and my omega."

"Why are you doing this to me?" Evvie asked. "It was all so uncomplicated before you showed up."

"If you love him, it shouldn't be complicated. He's safe? Isn't that what you told me when you walked out of my life?"

He broke contact with her and the loss of the warmth of his skin felt like a stab to her stomach. Evvie wrapped her arms around her waist.

"What is it you want safety from? A depth of feeling that comes around once in a lifetime?" He kept his eyes trained on hers. "Do you have any idea how hard it is for me to come here knowing I might have to walk away from you? It's splitting me in two."

"Then why did you come?" she cried. "What did you expect from me?"

"I don't know, Evvie. Maybe a girl who'd become a woman after a good amount of introspection? Or a woman who, after some soul searching, could be honest with herself." He looked up to the sky and shouted his frustration to the heavens. "I wouldn't have forgiven myself if I didn't make one last try. But I guess I have my answer."

"Zak, I'm engaged to someone else. Even back then, I told you he wanted a future with me."

"I so get that now," he said bitterly. "Go back to him, Evvie, and your happy little celebration. If a life of mediocrity is all you aspire for when all that glimmers in the stars are at your fingertips ..." He shrugged. "... then go for it."

Pointing his key fob in the direction of his car, he began to walk down the gravel path.

"Zak, I don't want to leave things this way."

He swung around and suddenly, without warning, was swiftly in front of her. "Neither do I." He drew her in by the waist, leaving their lips within kissing distance. "Is this better?" His lips barely made contact, but Evvie felt a shockwave rush through her entire body. Zak didn't move in to claim her mouth, but stood close enough for a challenge. His breathing was heavy, only to be outdone by the air panting from her lungs. Lightheaded, she felt limp in his arms, knowing the kiss she couldn't resist was coming. His release was sudden and Evvie whimpered at the loss.

"The next time you find yourself that close to me will be when you search me out, or never at all."

Evvie watched him enter his car and, without another word, he drove away. Running toward the house, she slipped in through the side door and ran to her bedroom. The party would have to continue without her.

Chapter 48

Stella

June 2010

The party that not only celebrated her cousin's birthdays, but also announced Evvie's engagement was beginning to wind down. The boys had decided to turn up the temperature on the pool heater and go for a late night swim.

"I'm in," Stella said. "I'll go find Evvie and get her to join us."

But Evvie was nowhere to be found and, finally, Stella knocked on her bedroom door, wondering why she wasn't with the rest of them outside.

"Ev? Are you in there?"

The muffled reply came from within. "I have a headache."

But when Stella stepped into the room, it dawned on her that Evvie wasn't simply suffering a headache. She knew her cousin and something was terribly wrong. Seating herself on the edge of the bed, she stroked Evvie's hair. "What's going on? Today was a happy day for you."

Evvie's shoulders were quaking and her head was buried face down into her pillow. Stella nudged her to turn around and face her and when she complied, her eyes were tearstained and swollen.

"Hey, hey, talk to me," Stella said softly.

It took a few minutes for Evvie to speak. It looked to Stella like she was battling whether or not to share. "You know you can trust me."

"Did you see Zak today?" Evvie asked, whimpering.

"Zak?" Why would I see him?"

"Because he was at the party with his parents." Evvie pulled a tissue from the box on her nightstand and dabbed at her eyes. "It seems his mother and my mother are friends."

"No kidding?" Stella frowned. "But Zak is unmistakable. He would have stood out. How did I miss him?"

"Did you happen to see a tall guy with short, brown hair, a little spiked on top, with a bit of facial hair?"

"Yes! OMG that guy was hot, but he disappeared before I could introduce myself."

Evvie cocked her head, raising an eyebrow.

"No! No way. That was Zak? Well, I always did think he was cute. Blue hair and all." She inspected her cousin's swollen eyes. "Does he still have feelings for you? After all this time?"

Evvie nodded, wiping away her tears.

"Is that why you're upset? What did he say to you?"

Evvie told Stella most of what happened. Stella kept shaking her head and slapping her face in disbelief. "Ev, the one thing you haven't explained to me is why you're up here crying. Do you—"

"Don't ask what I think you're going to ask. I just feel awful. I keep hurting him without meaning to. That's all it is."

Stella was unconvinced, but Evvie and Ryan made a good solid couple and she had no reason to believe otherwise. Besides, she was certainly no expert in relationships. The only one she'd ever had almost got her killed.

"Everyone is going for a night time swim. You don't want to give it a go?"

"No, tell Ryan to have fun for the both of us. He knows I'm not feeling well."

"Okay." She took Evvie's iPhone from her night table and laid it on the bed. "Text me if you need me for anything."

A little while later, Stella made her way down to the pool in a bright orange bikini. RJ was about to dive off the board when he noticed her edging her way over to the Roman steps. Losing his footing, he tripped and belly-flopped so hard that water splashed up onto both sides of the pool.

"What took you so long?" RJ asked, swimming over to her.

"I was checking in on Evvie. She's not feeling well."

RJ pulled himself up onto the coping and sat down next to Stella. "That's too bad. Is she okay?"

"I think so," Stella replied, rising to leave.

RJ grabbed her hand. "Where are you going?"

"To get you a towel. A wet body gets chilly in the night air." She retrieved a towel from a nearby bin and wrapped it around him.

"Thanks." RJ looked at her appreciatively. He tucked a few stray strands of hair behind her ears and smiled. "You really are a natural born nurturer. Do you realize that?"

"I care about the people I love. It's easy to do that."

"You're wrong. You care about everyone." He took her hand, threading their fingers together. "I've listened to the calls you've taken from troubled teens. And I've sat in on the group sessions you've participated in to help other women in abusive situations. You handle them all with a sensitivity that takes a special person, one with patience and kindness and a love for humanity."

Stella shyly averted her eyes from his. Taking compliments was not something she was good at but she was learning to. "You think so?"

He lifted her chin with his forefinger. "I know so."

"Can I ask you something then?"

"Anything," RJ answered.

She bit her lower lip, something she only did when she was unsure of herself. It was a habit she was trying to break. "Do you think I'd make a good mental health counselor?"

"I do. Is that what you want to do?"

"Yes, after all the school transfers and changes in my major, I finally know what I want to do. This past semester was the most invested I've ever been at school."

RJ's grin widened. "See, I knew you'd find your niche."

"Yes, I think I have. And I want to help people. Like you and your mom do. And it's all thanks to you."

"No, you just had to realize who you are and where your talents lie." He looked up and noticed they were alone. "It looks like everyone has left. We got so wrapped up talking, you never got into the pool."

Stella shrugged. "I was only going in because all of you wanted to."

"It's not too late." He slid his body back into the water. "Come on." He grabbed her by the waist and hoisted her in.

"Ahhh!" she screamed. "You gave me no warning."

"It's more fun that way," he teased.

They splashed each other like children, raced the length of the pool and judged each other's diving technique. RJ climbed onto the diving board and extended his hand to her with a mischievous grin.

"What are you doing?" she asked suspiciously.

"Let's jump in together and see if we can stay latched."

"Facing each other? That's crazy," she told him. "We'll bump heads and I'll break a tooth or something." This was the kind of thing they did when they were small and, even then they got in trouble for it.

He turned her around to face away from him. "My front to your back. We'll cannonball. One, two, three!"

Down into the bottom of the pool they sank. When their bodies popped up to the surface they were still entwined and they began to laugh. RJ turned her around to face him, keeping her in his embrace. He treaded over to the edge of the pool, never taking his eyes off her. Lowering his mouth to meet hers, he kissed her. It was gentle and sweet, yet Stella could feel how heartfelt it was in every brush over her lips and stroke of his tongue as it waltzed with hers.

RJ broke the kiss, breathing her name. "Stella." Tenderly, he ran his nose down the length of hers until his mouth found hers again. This time the kiss held more passion and need. The sweet waltz had turned into a fiery tango. "You have no idea how long I've wanted to do that," RJ said.

"You're the first person I've kissed since …" Stella didn't want to say his name.

RJ brushed his lips across hers. "I want to be the only one to kiss you."

"I didn't know you felt this way about me. We've known each other forever and you're protective of me like my brothers and Nicky are."

"Protective, yes, but not like your brothers. I want you in my life, but if you're not ready or don't feel the same way, I'll understand."

"I might not be ready if it were someone else," Stella said, brushing the wet strands of hair off his forehead, "but I trust you with my life and what I feel when I'm around you is like nothing I've ever felt for anyone else."

RJ buried his face in her neck and sighed. "I was afraid you were about to say that you trust me like a friend."

"I think that kiss confirmed for both of us that just friends might be off the table."

"Not might be, *is* off the table," RJ said, claiming her mouth once again. "You're shivering. Much as I hate to, we have to get out of the water." He picked up the towel from the edge of the pool and wrapped it around her. Hand in hand they walked toward the house.

Two days later, at the Anthony Callaghan Memorial Outreach Center, Donna called Stella into her office.

"So, RJ told me you've enrolled in classes for the fall semester and declared your major."

"Yes, I did. It's not another whim this time," Stella said. "I promise."

Donna smiled affectionately. "That's not why I'm bringing it up, and I hope that you don't mind RJ shared this with me."

"No, not at all."

"Good. Stella, I've known you since you were born and I've watched you through all your phases and growing pains, but in these last months, what I've seen in you is a young woman who's come into her own. You shine here, and it's clear that you've found your calling."

"Thank you, Aunt Donna. Your opinion means so much to me. Working here, helping others who are going through a crisis, it's been rewarding, and I hope to be able to do it on a professional level like you and RJ. I want to be able to make a real impact here."

"But you already do," Donna assured her. "By sharing your experiences and drawing from that, it helps others. By simply lending an ear and showing you care, other young people can relate to you, and more importantly, they trust you." Donna leaned forward, extending her hand to grasp Stella's. "It will take schooling and a tremendous amount of commitment on your part, but I believe you have it in you to see it through."

Stella beamed. "Thank you. I needed to hear that even though I'm more sure of this than I've been of anything ever before." She began to lift herself from her chair.

"Wait a minute. I wanted to ask you about something else." Donna leaned back in her chair. She seemed to be collecting her thoughts. "I hope I'm not overstepping but ... RJ also mentioned that your friendship might be shifting in a different direction."

A flush of heat traveled up Stella's face. "And ... you don't approve?"

Donna's head rocked back with surprise. "Why wouldn't I approve? I simply didn't want to make you uncomfortable by bringing it up." Standing, she walked around her desk and lifted Stella to her feet, embracing her. "I love you like my own daughter, you know that. I've watched the two of you over the last few months, and you may not have seen what was developing between the two of you, but I did."

"You did? I'm not sure I realized it myself. Spending time with RJ or Adam or … Anthony," Stella said his name with sadness, "was as natural to me as being with my brothers or cousins, until …"

Donna's eyes sparkled. "Ah, yes! Until." She released her hold on Stella and leaned back against the desk. "I brought this up, not to be nosy, or to prod you on how you feel about my son, but to let you know that I don't want you to feel you have to pretend that nothing has changed between the two of you. We all work together and I want everything out in the open."

"Okay. And I promise none of this will interfere with the work," Stella said.

"I have no concern that it will. Stella, my beautiful, sweet boy died in part because he had to hide who he was—afraid of being bullied, afraid of his father, tortured for wanting to be himself." She lifted the framed photo of her late son and held it to her breast. "I only have one son left on this earth, and I won't allow him to hide how he feels about anything. Not his very conflicted emotions for his father, or his grief for his brother, which he still struggles with at times. And he certainly shouldn't hide the one thing that brightens his day. You."

Stella dabbed a finger in the corner of each eye, attempting to keep the tears at bay. If it was at all possible for happy tears to flow in concert with sad ones, her tear ducts had accomplished its unlikely mission. Donna's continuing grief nearly broke Stella's heart, if the sudden awareness that RJ harbored so much internal conflict hadn't done so already. But the idea that she thought that Stella could brighten RJ's day and possibly make her son happy had Stella's tears sliding down her cheeks in a confused mix of emotions.

"So, my sweet girl, if you care about my son, and you want to let the world know, you can scream it to the heavens for all I care. I just want him to be happy and loved."

"Oh my God! I do. Aunt Donna, I do love him," Stella said, surprising even herself. "I love him. He just doesn't know it yet."

Chapter 49

Evvie

March 2011

"I would bring this in maybe three-quarters of an inch," Mindy said to one of her most experienced seamstresses. "What do you think, Darota?"

Evvie, standing on a box-shaped platform in front of a three-way mirror, was being pulled, prodded and pinned into the wedding dress Mindy had designed for her.

"I think if she eats a bite of wedding cake the seams will split," the tiny but commanding woman said dryly with an unmistakable Polish accent.

"She's right, Aunt Mindy. I can't breathe as it is."

"Okay, okay. You win." Mindy lifted her hands, palms up in surrender. "I just want you to look perfect on your big day!"

Sophia, Demi and Stella were seated on the adjacent couch admiring the beading on the gown and the flattering form-fitting cut of the dress.

Mindy arched an eyebrow at Stella. "Perhaps I'll be crafting one of these for you soon."

Stella blushed and waved her off. "Evvie," she asked, changing the subject, "is Ryan joining us for lunch?"

"No, not this time. He had to fly out to California for a meeting. He'll be back tomorrow."

"I bet you'll be happy when you're finally married and can see him every day," Stella said. "Working with RJ, that's never an issue for us. At the very least we have lunch together."

"The two of you have common interests, so that works for you," Evvie said. "Ryan and I have completely different career paths." She shrugged out of the dress when Darota unfastened the row of buttons that ran down the back. "For me, seeing him at the end of the day is enough."

Sophia furrowed her brow.

"What?" Evvie complained. "Something to look forward to, right?"

"Michael and I have the best of both worlds. Separate businesses, but on the same spot of land," Demi said.

"But somehow you still manage to argue about the most ridiculous things," Mindy retorted.

Pretending to conceal her comment from everyone but Mindy, Demi shielded the sides of her mouth with her hands. "Only because the make up sex is worth it."

"Mom!" Stella shrieked, covering her ears. "I need to scrub that image from my brain."

Sophia shook her head. "She never did have a filter."

"Let's go," Stella demanded. "I need food. Lots of it. Fatty, fried, high calorie food and enough dessert for a sugar coma so I can forget about you and Dad having sex."

Stella wasn't bluffing when she threatened a sugar overload. Mindy had chosen a little brasserie only a few blocks from her office that had an extensive dessert menu. After consuming a flourless chocolate cake, she ate two pistachio ice-cream-filled profiteroles and a third of her mother's crème brûlée.

"A girl after my own heart," Mindy laughed. Stella was now dipping her fork into Evvie's Nutella crepe.

"Why?" Demi asked sardonically. "Because she's a food thief like you?"

"What can I say?" Mindy clinked forks with Stella and they giggled. "We're kindred spirits."

"Ev, I forgot to tell you, the wedding invitations arrived yesterday," Demi said. "I looked them over and they came out just as we ordered."

"That's great. One more item to tick off the list," Evvie said. "Not that I've had too much to do thanks to you, Aunt Demi."

"Sophia, do you think your yiayiá will be able to make it?"

"Sadly, no. We decided it would be too stressful for her to travel overseas at her age. She's ninety-five now."

"Is she ill?" Mindy asked, lifting her teacup to her lips.

"No, she's amazingly healthy. It's just not the best idea," Sophia said.

"I considered having the wedding in Greece for that reason. I really wanted her to attend," Evvie said regretfully.

"And?" Mindy asked. "I think that would have been a great solution."

"Ryan was adamantly against it. He has a large family and they're spread all over. He said it's going to be hard enough to get them to Long Island."

"The guest list is now up to over three hundred people," Demi said.

Evvie pressed her lips together in annoyance.

"Ev," Sophia said, catching her daughter's expression of disapproval. "Between our family and his, it's inevitable."

"I guess. I was hoping for something a little more intimate." Changing the subject, she asked, "Stella, are you up for a girl's night tonight, maybe?"

"I can't. I'm sorry, Ev. RJ and I are meeting some friends he hasn't seen in a while."

"No worries," Evvie said. "I've been meaning to spend a little time with pappou. I think I'll see if he's free tonight and pay him a visit."

It wasn't too often that Evvie ventured to her pappou's home. Since her yiayiá had passed away over ten years ago, this house, once bustling with energy, good food and laughter, had dimmed to a melancholy quiet.

Alex hadn't changed a thing in his Ana's home. Not a single piece of furniture, or the dinnerware in the cupboards. But without the affectionate woman who'd brought the place to life, it was merely a structure that held bittersweet memories.

Evvie was seated at the kitchen table while Alex filled two bowls of beef and vegetable soup.

"There's nothing like a bowl of *vrasto* on a cold day," Alex said, setting it down in front of her.

"Nothing better!" Evvie agreed as she breathed in the aromatic steam wafting from the bowl. "When I was sick, yiayiá would make me a whole pot of this soup and bring it to our house." She took a lemon wedge from the center of the table and generously squeezed it into the broth.

Alex, aware of his granddaughter's tastes, handed her a slice of crusty Italian bread, which she ripped to pieces and dropped into the soup.

"Your yiayiá used to do the same thing," he said. With his chin resting on a fisted hand, he watched Evvie as she devoured her food. "Both you and your mother look so much like her," he said wistfully.

Evvie could see the tears in her grandfather's eyes. She set her spoon down and gently stroked his hand. "I miss her too. So very much."

"You would think that I'd be used to being without her after all these years." Alex tightened his grip on Evvie's hand. "But the opposite is true. There are days the loss is unbearable. I want to feel her in my arms again and hear her beautiful voice one more time."

This was exactly why Evvie stayed guarded. She loved Ryan, but giving her heart away to the point where it would destroy her one day was not an option. It had already been torn to shreds too many times and she wasn't sure she could survive another death.

"How did you know, pappou?"

"Know what, *koukla*?"

"Know that yiayiá was the one for you? How were you so sure?"

"I was taken with her from the moment I saw her," he said, closing his eyes as if to visualize her at that time. "But it was so much more than that. It was as if I could hear my soul sing—crying out with joy. She was all I thought about and my heart ached when I was any distance away from her. Her light overshadowed the dark in my past. To me, she was simply ... everything."

"Those are the most beautiful sentiments I've ever heard spoken," Evvie whispered, tearing up.

"Evanthia *mou*, are you having doubts?"

"No, it's not that," she answered. *Or was it?* she wondered. "I don't think everyone is blessed with what you and yiayiá had. Others simply aren't capable of loving to that degree." Evvie cleared the bowls from the table and placed them in the dishwasher.

"Leave those," Alex ordered. He gestured for her to return to her seat. "Don't underestimate your capacity for love. It's in there." He pointed to her heart. "I see how you are with all of us. Don't let fear decide your future. We are all going to die one day. And it's damn scary thinking I could lose any one of you without a moment's warning. But it's worth it. For every sweet memory I have of all of you, for every moment shared, it's worth the anguish I'd bear if I lost you. And that's what I want you to remember of me when I'm gone. Our many talks, the precious times we spent together when you were small, and everything in between."

"I don't know if I'm as strong as you are, pappou."

Alex used his thumbs to wipe away her tears. "Yes, you are. Don't forget, you have my mother's name, and she was one fierce lady."

Evvie half laughed, half cried. "Yes, she was."

"Open your heart and let your soul give itself to whom it's meant for. But give it freely and honestly."

After over an hour-long drive home, Evvie had gone over Alex's advice in her mind more times than she could count. She'd lived her life surrounded by couples who were crazy in love with each other—her grandparents, Aunt Demi and Uncle Michael, and now even Stella and RJ. *God, that boy would slay a dragon for her,* she chuckled.

Then of course there was her mother and Dean, whose relationship was so different than the one her mother had shared with her own father. With her father, a peck on the lips, dinner conversations and weekends spent with her and her brother was pretty much as intimate as her parents had been. It all seemed perfectly normal to Evvie until after her father had passed and her mother and Dean had married. She witnessed a passion between them that had never existed with her father.

Evvie wondered which type of marriage she was fated for and, if her suspicions were correct, would it be enough?

Chapter 50

Evvie

May 2011

Evvie opened the door to Ryan's apartment. "I'm here!" Evvie called out.

Meeting her halfway across the room, he lifted her off the floor and kissed her.

"Wow! You're in a good mood," she said, noticing his wide grin.

"I am! I have plenty to be happy about." He raised his forefinger. "One. It's exactly one month from today that I get to marry my girl."

Evvie smiled.

"Two. I just got the job of my dreams!"

"You did? I didn't know you had applied for another job. Why didn't you tell me?"

"It was a long shot. I didn't want to mention it unless I got it."

"So, is it a higher position? More money? Where is it? Tell me everything!"

"Yes, a little higher. Yes, more money, but I'd take it for the same salary. It's with Google."

"Google? Since when do they have offices in New York?"

"They don't. They're in Northern California. You know that." He looked at her as though she were dense.

The smile fell from her face. "Tell me you're working from home like so many tech people do these days."

"Ev, sit down." He took her by the hand and led her to the couch. "All I've talked about for years is that someday I wanted to be working for Google. I saw an opportunity that was a good fit for me and I went for it."

"I guess I never thought you were really that serious about it … not enough to want to move." Evvie covered her face with her hands and rubbed her forehead. "Ryan, we put the first and last month's rent on an apartment. We're getting married in a month. Aside from that, you didn't discuss this with me. What about the vineyard?"

"It's all worked out. They know I'm getting married and need time to relocate. I don't begin until July. We have plenty of time to iron out the details. I'm sure we can get out of the lease."

"Not without losing all that money," Evvie stated. "And what do I do about my obligations?"

"Your uncle will understand."

"That's not the point!" she jumped from her seat, her fists balled at her side. "I don't want to move to California and you accepted this job without talking it over with me. When did you interview with them? You never bothered to mention that to me either."

"Last month when I went to California on business it was really for an interview," Ryan admitted. "I didn't think there was a point in saying anything unless I got an offer."

"You've been back and forth a couple of times!"

"I know. It took three rounds of interviews to get the job." He raked a hand through his hair. "I thought you'd be happy for me."

"Really, Ryan? Maybe I could have been if I'd had some warning. You throw this at me suddenly, turning my whole world upside down, and you expect me to be happy?" She took a sofa pillow from behind her, clutching onto it for comfort. "Look, I am happy for you if this is what you want. But you have to understand that I'm not happy for me at this moment."

Ryan had a forlorn expression on his face. "Do you think at some point you might be?"

Without looking at him, she lifted her shoulders. "I don't know." Dragging her bag off the coffee table, she stood.

"What are you doing?" he asked.

"Leaving. I can't stay here. I need time to think."

"About us?" Ryan asked.

"About what to make of everything you just threw at me." She walked toward the door and turned to look at Ryan. His body sagged with defeat and Evvie's heart went out to him. "Give me a couple of days and we'll talk it over, okay?"

Ryan nodded and Evvie fled.

"What are you doing here?" Dean asked Evvie. She was sitting on the front porch settee nursing a glass of Cabernet. "I thought you went to see Ryan in the city."

"I did," she snickered dryly. "And that lasted less than an hour." She drained her glass in one gulp.

Dean's eyebrows shot up. "Want to talk about it?" He took a seat beside her.

"Ryan got a job with Google."

"And that's a bad thing?"

"The job is in California." Evvie looked for his reaction.

"Oh. Wow."

"Speechless, Dad? So was I since I didn't even know he had applied for a job three thousand miles away."

"I can't say that was a smart move on his part. He should have discussed it with you."

"He talked about Google for years and I guess, in his eyes, he'd made it clear that was his end goal." Evvie poured more wine from the bottle. "Maybe I wasn't paying enough attention. I don't know. I never took it seriously."

"Only you can decide what to do. If you love him, you'll want to let him see his dream through. And if he loves you, he'll consider how this will affect your overall happiness. Sometimes it comes down to compromise and a bit of sacrifice. Your mom did it for me when she moved out here. I know it was a big step for her to move from the home where you and Nicky were raised and give up the studio she had worked so hard to make a success."

Evvie thought about what Dean said. Was she willing to give up everything she had worked for and move far away from the people she loved most in the world? Did her love extend that deeply for Ryan?

"You're wrong, you know," Evvie said after a few minutes of silence.

"About what?" Dean asked.

"About you and Mom. She told me that when you love someone with everything inside you, anything you do for them is done with your heart and there's no sacrifice involved. She said her life had moved in a different direction and the changes she made were good for both of you. She had not a single regret."

"Hey," Dean tweaked Evvie's chin. "Thanks for that. And you know, if she had wanted to keep the studio, I would have moved heaven and earth to make it happen."

"I know. The thing is, I don't know that I feel that way about Ryan. How could I move heaven and earth for him when I'm not even willing to move to another state for him."

"It sounds like you've made some big decisions."

"No," she sighed. "I haven't. I have a mental pro and con list in my head right now that's driving me crazy."

"I'm going to make it easier for you. It's simple really," Dean said. "Forget Google and the move right now. You've agreed to marry him so you must love him. But the question is, how much? Imagine your life without him. Do you see yourself completely crushed? Like the life is being drained from your heart? Or, after a period of relationship grief, do you move on with your life and never look back?" Dean stood and bent to kiss her forehead. "The man for you is the one you can't live without. The very thought of it is terrifying. Is Ryan that man? Give that some thought and you'll have your answer."

Evvie tenderly grasped Dean's hand before he walked away. "Thanks," she managed to croak out. The lump in her throat rendered her speechless, but her stepfather's words had given her clarity.

It took two days of solid contemplation for Evvie to come to terms with her entire situation. Once she looked into her heart and was painfully honest with herself, she was certain Ryan's relocation was not the real issue. She simply didn't love him enough to make a life with him away from everything and everyone she loved. She wasn't consumed by him—just merely comfortable with him. They had stepped in time together, following the expected road that young couples walked as they grew to adulthood. They dated in college and practically lived together, built their careers, saved money and now were about to take the trip to the altar. Except for her one and only indiscretion, she was predictable and boring.

She'd thought about this the day before, as she sat by a window seat in Starbucks, sipping a grandé vanilla latte and picking apart a blueberry scone. She watched as patrons came and went, placing their orders and then rushing away as they sipped their coffee. It was the women that piqued her interest. Many were in their mid-to-late-forties, and most were wearing the same deadpan expression. It was as if their days held no excitement for them any longer. Many had gained a few pounds, she surmised, and had long ago stopped bothering to lift their spirits with a dab of makeup or a pretty outfit. Their day was likely spent doing laundry, cooking and engaging in dull evening conversation with a man they'd become bored with years ago. Somehow, by observing them, she feared that's how her life might turn out.

But then, a fashionably dressed couple, walking hand in hand, entered. They had to be around sixty years old and they mesmerized Evvie. The man released his hold from the woman long enough to pay for their order, but immediately after, his hand found its way to caress the small of her back. He led her to a table, pulling her chair out for her, and whispered something. The woman's eyes seemed to dance as she gazed up at him.

This little exchange made her wish for more than she could have with Ryan, yet wasn't this exactly what she'd been terrified of? A love so great it could one day break her? She thought about what her pappou had said. 'Don't let fear decide your future. For every sweet memory I have of all of you, for every moment shared, it's worth the anguish I'd bear if I lost you.' And the advice her stepfather had for her. 'The man for you is the one you can't live without.' Evvie knew what she had to do.

Nervously, she sat on Ryan's couch waiting for him to bring her the iced tea he'd offered her. Taking a sip, she was silently grateful for the coolness sliding down her dry throat.

"I've been doing a lot of thinking and I want you to take the job, Ryan."

Evvie saw his demeanor shift and a grin cross his face. *This was not going to be easy*, she thought. "This is your dream and I don't want to come between you and your aspirations. You deserve it. But Ryan, I won't be going to California with you."

Ryan did a double take. "What? I ... don't understand. How are we going to make this work?"

Evvie groaned out a sigh. She put her hands together as if in prayer and closed her eyes. Steeling herself, she looked up at him. "We're not. Ryan, I love you. I do. Just not enough to marry you. Not enough to change my whole life for you."

He looked at her, crestfallen and devastated, shaking his head.

"I'm sorry," she choked out.

"You're sorry? We're less than a month away from our wedding date and you're sorry?" He leaned back against the sofa and rubbed his hands over his face.

"Yes, I am. This is my fault. I shouldn't have let it go this far. We've been together for so long that we plodded along step by step and we took the conventional route."

Ryan pulled his hands from his face. His usually fair skin was now reddened with anger. "What the fuck, Evvie? Isn't that how it goes? You date, fall in love and then ask the girl to marry you. How else should it be done?"

"All I'm saying is that we took each other for granted. We fell into a comfortable rut and it shouldn't be that way."

"Life isn't a chick flick," he lashed out. "It's not romance and hot sex twenty-four/seven. In the real world we work at relationships and solve problems like where we're going to live and how to deal with the kids when they're sick."

"I get that," she agreed. "But there should be a spark. No, at this point in our lives there should be a flame hot enough to burn down a forest." She slid closer to him and grasped his hands. "Ryan, I've thought a lot about this over the last couple of days and I'm not doing this to be selfish. I'm doing this for you too. I truly care about you and if you're honest with yourself, you'll admit that you're with me more out of habit than passion. Tell me that I consume your every thought, that whatever you do or wherever you are I'm always on your mind, that when you're out with your friends, it's me you'd rather be with than playing darts with them. Can you honestly tell me that's true?"

Ryan held Evvie's gaze for what seemed like an eternity. She could tell he was taking stock in what she'd said. When he averted his eyes, he let out a shaky breath. "No, I can't admit that's true. But I know we're good together."

Evvie slid the engagement ring from her finger. "I know," she said somberly, taking his hand and placing the ring in his palm. "But that's not good enough." She kissed him on the cheek and rose from the sofa. Retrieving her bag from the coffee table, she hung the strap over her shoulder.

"Goodbye, Ryan. I think California will be good for you. I'm so happy you got the job you've dreamed of."

It wasn't until Evvie left Ryan's building that she shed her tears. She'd unselfishly done what was best for him and, what she knew in her heart, what was right for herself. But she had spent five years with him and now she would probably never lay eyes on him again. He'd been an important part of her life and she would have liked to keep in touch with Ryan, but Evvie held no illusion that it was even a possibility.

Chapter 51

Stella

July 2011

For Stella, it had been a long day at the outreach center and, as much as she found the work rewarding, it could also be draining. At Donna's request, she'd sat in on a session that included a half dozen teens, all of whom had been prey to some form of abuse. Stella had been older than this group when Cain took out his frustrations on her body, but most of these kids had been beaten since they were too young to defend themselves or cry out for help. She couldn't imagine how their tiny bodies had endured it or how sick their tormentors had to have been to inflict pain on such innocence.

One boy had been hospitalized after enduring several kicks by his mother's boyfriend. Several of his bones had been broken. In addition, the child required an emergency surgery due to the internal bleeding he'd sustained from the force of the blows to his body. Afterward, the child landed in foster care until his mother had severed all contact with her lover and had gone through extensive parental counseling. He was reunited with his mother and placed back in her home, only for history to repeat itself.

Each story was more tragic than the next. All Stella could do was share her experience and assure these youngsters that there was a better day coming for them, to show them a way to heal from their emotional wounds. Stella was a living example of that, thanks to her wonderfully supportive family, the counseling she'd received and her ever-blossoming relationship with RJ. Through his love and confidence in her, Stella had unearthed a strength she hadn't known existed within her. The feeling of inferiority and low self-esteem had disappeared and, when it had, it was as though she had seen the stars in heaven glimmering in her direction.

RJ was accurate when he called her a nurturer. But there was one thing that she no longer was—a pushover. Not anymore. That was one trait that was in the past, and God help the person who challenged it. Stella doled out sympathy when it was called for but when tough love was the answer, she spooned it out like an essential dose of medicine. And let a man—any man—try to lay a hand on her without her approval. She'd Krav Maga his ass into the next county. Stella had spent the past year taking self-defense classes and was close to convincing Donna to incorporate them into the services they offered. (Fingers crossed!) Her instructor had even offered to volunteer his services one day a week.

It was seven o'clock in the evening and the sun had not yet set. How Stella savored these hot summer days. Even after a full day at work, a few extra hours of daylight before darkness fell seemed like a sweet indulgence. Stella sprawled out on a raft that could easily fit two and peacefully floated in the pool. Her mind drifted to Evvie and she wondered what she was doing. Work had consumed her since she'd called off her wedding and what spare time she had afforded herself was spent mostly alone.

It broke Stella's heart, seeing her cousin day after day somber and dolefully plodding along as if she had nothing left to look forward to. And it wasn't because of Ryan. Stella was certain of that. Evvie had been definite and unwavering in her decision once she'd resolved to end it with him. Stella suspected Evvie had taken this time for reflection and introspection.

Stella flipped over onto her back. The sun was just beginning to dip, but its warmth still soothed and relaxed her. It was ironic how, when she was going through her worst times, Evvie had been in what she thought was a content and loving relationship. Now the opposite was true. While Evvie mourned a future that wasn't to be, Stella had found the happiness she never thought possible. Not only in her work but also with RJ.

Goosebumps pebbled over her skin as she thought of RJ's kisses the night before, trailing down from her earlobe to the hollow of her neck, causing her to shudder involuntarily. His touch was gentle yet had held determination when he had hooked his thumbs under the spaghetti straps of her sundress to caress her bare shoulders before skimming further to explore her breasts. At first touch, her response was immediate and needy and she'd pressed her body against his, begging for more. This was starlight and ocean waves sweeping her away. Spring blossoms and warm air delivering her weightless. The fusion of his body with hers was nothing less than divine, created from all that was perfect in this imperfect world. Stella reveled in her delicious thoughts until a splash of water cooled her off.

Stella popped up to see who had jumped into the pool. "Hey, Ev," she said with curiosity. "Join me?" she patted the oversized raft.

Evvie swam over and hoisted herself onto the float.

"You think you're ready to join the living again?" Stella asked.

Evvie twisted up the corners of her mouth and shrugged.

"Ev," Stella said, resting her hand on Evvie's knee. "Why don't you just call him?"

Evvie frowned. "Who?"

Tilting her head to one side, Stella shot her a look that said clearly, 'don't play that game with me.'

"You know who. You know as well as I do that you're not moping around wondering if you made a mistake calling off your wedding. This," Stella waved a finger at the frown Evvie wore, "is about Zak."

Evvie met her stare but remained deadpan.

"Don't give me that blank expression, Evvie," Stella scolded. "Let's finally get this out in the open. Look, I tried not to make too much of what you told me happened in Greece between the two of you. You chose to stay with Ryan and I didn't question it, even though I felt there was something more between Zak and you that, for whatever reason, you decided to ignore. But when he showed up here last year and I saw your reaction, I knew. I just knew whatever you felt for him hadn't died."

Evvie threw her arms around Stella and cried into the crook of her neck. Stella embraced her, stroking Evvie's hair. "Isn't it better for you to open up to me so we can talk about it?"

Evvie broke Stella's hold on her. "I am a poor excuse for a human being who has no fucking idea how to let myself fall completely in love. I fucked it up beyond repair and there's nothing I can do to fix it."

"I don't believe that's true. Call him."

"Even if I could bring myself to, I have no idea where to find him. He could be anywhere."

"Did you Google him? Or look him up on Facebook?"

"Of course I did. Apparently, a comic book he drew just got published." She flopped down on the float and covered her eyes. "It's what he always wanted to do. I'm happy for him and I'm sure that by now the … other parts of his life have worked out too."

When did this happen? Stella laughed inwardly. Evvie had always been the sensible, strong cousin with all the answers for her. Now, it was Stella who was meting out advice.

"I wouldn't assume anything," Stella said. She leaned over her cousin and pried her hands from Evvie's eyes. "You won't know until you find him and talk to him. Did it ever occur to you that he thinks you're already married?"

"I'm sure his mother mentioned to him that the wedding was off. My mom had invited them."

"Maybe it wasn't something she thought he'd be interested to know." Stella hit her forehead with the palm of her hand. "What's wrong with us? Your mom is friends with his. We can find out where he lives from her."

"And how do I explain why I'm suddenly looking for him?"

Stella hopped off the float and flipped it over sending Evvie tumbling out of it.

"Come on! Out of the pool. It's time for complete transparency."

Chapter 52

Evvie

July 2011

"Oh, Evvie," Sophia said. "You've been holding onto this all this time?"

"I couldn't sort my own feelings out. How was I to explain them to anyone else?"

"I'm not anyone else, I'm your mother and I only want your happiness." Sophia looked at her niece. "How long have you known about this?"

"I didn't really. Not all of it," Stella answered. "I had my suspicions, but I didn't know for sure."

Stella had summoned her aunt to Evvie's bedroom. Sophia and Evvie were seated, facing each other, while Stella rested her back against the headboard.

"I'm trying to understand your motives, Evvie, but I'm struggling." She handed her daughter a tissue from the nightstand. "After what happened in Greece, shouldn't that have been a sign Ryan wasn't the one for you? It wasn't fair to him to let this go on for so long. And honestly, it hasn't been fair to you either."

"I didn't break up with Ryan because I had feelings for Zak. I'm not sure that I was consciously aware I did when I broke it off. I did this for me. We would have never been happy together long term."

"But Ryan got in the way of your true emotions," Sophia stated, trying to make sense of it.

"No," Evvie said. "Fear got in the way."

"Fear of what?"

Evvie covered her face with the tissue her mother had handed her, pressing it tightly to her eyes. In seconds the paper was soaked with tears. "Afraid of the intensity of what I felt for him, and that if something happened, it would break me. I can't go through that kind of pain again," Evvie admitted.

Sophia latched onto her daughter, rocking her. "Oh, my sweet girl." Now Sophia was crying along with her daughter. "Don't shortchange yourself from the most exquisite moments life has to offer. I can't promise you heartache won't find you one day, but I can assure you that what precedes it is worth fighting for."

"Pappou said something like that to me once."

"And as you know," Sophia smiled, "he's a very wise man."

Evvie agreed as mother and daughter put their foreheads together. "So what do you do now?" Sophia asked.

"That's what we need your help with, Aunt Sophia," Stella said. "We need you to ask Mrs. Maryiatos where Zak is."

"I think that would be odd coming from me. I'll be happy to give you her number so you can call or meet with her yourself and ask her."

"Oh, Mom. I don't know that I can do that," Evvie said. "I don't know what she knows, if anything at all."

"If Zak is important to you then you can approach his mother," Sophia said. "You'll find out soon enough what she does or doesn't know. Glika hasn't mentioned a word to me so there's a good chance Zak hasn't shared any of this with her." Sophia rose from the bed, resting her hand on her daughter's shoulder. "I'll get my phone and text you her number," she said as she left the room.

A few minutes later there was a knock on the door. "Come in," Stella said.

"Girl talk?" Nicky asked, not wanting to intrude.

"I'd never turn you away," Evvie said. "Girl talk or not."

"What are you reading?" Stella asked, pointing to the softcover book in his hand.

"That's what I came to show you!" Nicky answered. "Ev, you have to see this." He wiggled his eyebrows. "It seems you've unknowingly become an artist's muse."

Evvie scrunched her nose. "Huh?"

Nicky flipped the book over for Evvie to see. A female superhero graced the front cover. "Tell me that doesn't look exactly like you."

Evvie snatched the book from his hands. "Oh, my God! Oh, my God! I can't believe this."

Stella crawled to Evvie's side. "Demeter, Battle of the Underworld," she read off the front cover. "Who's ZUM?"

"Zaharias Ulysses Maryiatos," Evvie said, stunned.

"No way!" Stella exclaimed, taking the book from Evvie to examine it closely.

"Let me see that," Evvie said, pulling it from Stella's hands. It was her face all right. Long, black flowing hair and large, brown eyes that mirrored the exact hue of hers. She stood fiercely, ready to take on her enemies, pointing a deadly, twisted, vine-like spear in her right hand. In her left palm, the she-warrior crushed a cluster of grapes. Evvie turned to the back cover. "Demeter, Goddess of the harvest and sacred law," she read aloud. "In a twist on Greek mythology, Demeter battles the underworld to save her child from Hades. Once won, Demeter vows to delve back into the underworld and fight for justice until every worthy soul is saved from evil destruction."

"Looks like your face is going to be the object of a lot of boys' fantasies," Nicky teased.

Stella ignored him. "Forget that! Ev, if that doesn't confirm what you should do, then nothing will."

"Talk to his mom. I'm sure she will lead you to him," Stella said.

Evvie fisted her hand to her chest. "I'll do it. I'm going to find him. I have to find him."

"What are you talking about?" Nicky asked.

"Come on," Stella said. "Let's give Evvie some time alone. I'll fill you in," she told Nicky as she pushed him through Evvie's bedroom door.

"Come in, Evvie," Mrs. Maryiatos said, greeting her at the front door.

"Thank you for agreeing to see me today."

"Of course, my door is always open to my friends and their children."

Evvie followed her into the living room and took a seat beside Zak's mother.

"So, what can I do for you, Evvie?" she asked, patting her hand.

Evvie's heart began to race as the knot in her stomach tightened. She drew in a deep breath to calm herself. "I was wondering if you could tell me how I might be able to get in touch with Zak?" She looked up at Mrs. Maryiatos for a reaction, but she remained unreadable.

"Zak?"

"Yes." Evvie nervously tugged at the hem of her skirt. "I'm not sure if he mentioned it to you, but we've been acquainted for some time. First in college and then again when we ended up on the same island in Greece."

"The same island?" Glika's eyes shone with curiosity. "It was my understanding that it was not only the same island, but the same vineyard. It seems our families share a connection we never knew existed."

"Did Zak tell you?"

"Yes, but only recently. I wanted to talk to your mother about it, but since she never brought it up, I assumed you never told her."

"I told her about going to the vineyard to visit my Yiayiá Sophia's friends, but I never told her they were related to you."

"Ah, that explains it."

"When did Zak tell you?"

"When your wedding invitation came in the mail." Zak's mother narrowed her eyes in thought. "I knew something was just not right with him after the party when your engagement was announced. Before that day, he had really pulled himself together. I thought to myself, finally, he'd stopped mourning his sister and was moving forward with his life."

Evvie took hold of her hands. "I am so sorry about Elpida," she said with genuine sorrow.

"It's the worst thing a mother can go through, losing a child. My worst fear was that I might have lost Zak too," Mrs. Maryiatos said. "I've seen him go through so many stages of despondency. The most recent one, however, was not related to my Elpida, and when I saw his reaction to your invitation, I decided to press him."

A groan escaped from Evvie's throat.

"Yes, he told me all of it," she said in answer to her groan. "Zak needed to accept that his feelings for you were not the same as yours were for him."

"No, that's not true," Evvie said, looking down at her clasped hands.

"Is my son the reason you called off your wedding?" she asked, her tone oddly somewhere between suspicion and hope.

Evvie played with a lock of her hair, thinking how to respond. "Ryan and I would have never worked. The closer we got to the date, the more I saw that. I think I stayed with him out of loyalty because we'd been together for so long." She leaned back on the sofa, covering her mouth with her hands in sorrow. "It's all so clear now. Ryan and I had been together for two years when Zak and I happened in Greece. I panicked, but I never meant to hurt Zak."

"Did it ever occur to you at the time that if you truly loved the other boy you wouldn't have been with my son?"

"Ryan was safe and familiar," Evvie whispered.

"Safe?" The woman truly looked confused. "Safe from what?"

"Devastating loss."

Assessing the anguished expression on Evvie's face, Mrs. Maryiatos smiled insightfully. "You and my son share the same soul."

"Does Zak know I called off the wedding?"

"No."

"How come you didn't tell him?"

"He's been hurt enough. You made your choice and whether or not you married your fiancé, Zak was not the one you chose. I didn't want to give him false hope."

"Will you tell me where I can find him? Please."

"Do you love him?" his mother asked.

Stella's yiayiá would say, 'the eyes don't lie.' Evvie fixed her gaze on Mrs. Maryiatos so she could reach inside her soul for the answer. "Yes, more than my own life. I love him so much."

Tears streamed down Evvie's face. Zak's mother circled her arms around her and kissed her cheek.

"Go get my boy," Mrs. Maryiatos said. "Go to him."

Chapter 53

Evvie

July 2011

Evvie rounded the corner and drove the rental car up the gravel driveway. She had barely said a word to her pro-yiayiá for the entire ride. Her thoughts were on what she would say to Zak and how he'd receive her. It felt as though all the butterflies in Europe were flapping their wings violently in her stomach. Her limbs were like jelly and her head felt as though it just might explode from the tension.

"*Stamata pethi mou,*" her great-grandmother ordered. She patted Evvie's hair. "*Ola tha eínai kalá.*"

She tried to smile in agreement, but although she thought of her as a wise, old woman who held all the answers of the universe, her pro-yiayiá had no way to guarantee her that this would work out.

Evvie stepped out of the car and a blast of hot, dry air nearly took her breath away. With not one cloud in the sky, the sun blazed down upon them like a burning laser, the black pebbles beneath her feet absorbing the light and intensifying the heat. She helped her great-grandmother from the car and walked to the front door of the house, one that held unforgettable memories for both women.

Zak's grandmother, Maria, couldn't contain her excitement when she answered. Taking Evvie's cheeks in her hands, Maria kissed her and then took Yiayiá Sophia by the waist, repeating the same greeting before helping her up the landing.

"*Éla mesa*," Maria said, guiding them into the house.

It had been exactly three years since Evvie had visited Kefalonia and this magnificent vineyard, but it was as if no time had passed at all. This piece of land was just as she remembered. Evvie had requested Zak's family not clue him in on her surprise appearance for fear that he might leave once he learned of her visit. For all she knew, he was done with her, and she wouldn't blame him. Too many times, she'd hurt him. She had to wonder if she even deserved another chance.

"Where's Elias?" Yiayiá Sophia asked. "I want to see my old friend."

"I'm afraid you won't find him as well as he was the last time you saw him, Sophia," Maria answered. "His old bones are not as strong as they once were."

"Where is he?" Sophia asked, her voice thick with worry.

Maria cocked her head toward the sitting room where the family gathered to watch television. "He spends most of his day in the recliner. It takes much effort for him to move around."

"And his mental state?" Sophia asked. "Will he remember me?"

"Yes, I believe so. He gets confused at times, but at one hundred years old it's to be expected."

Evvie began to follow her great-grandmother but Maria stopped her. "Let them have this time alone," Maria suggested. "You can see him later."

"Okay," Evvie nodded.

"Besides," Maria said, cupping Evvie's cheek with her palm, "isn't there someone else you came to see?"

"Yes." Evvie looked at her imploringly. "Where is he?"

"He has a favorite spot in the vineyard when he likes to be alone. I'll show you where it is."

"No need. I think I know exactly the spot you're talking about." She kissed Maria on the cheek and headed out the front door.

In the farthest corner of their land was a section of grapevines that were fuller and higher than the rest. As children, Zak and Elpida would chase each other down the narrow rows between the plants, play hide and seek, or lay a blanket down and read to each other.

Evvie knew this because Zak had not only told her about it, but he had also brought her to the little corner of heaven he'd shared only with his sister once before. Only at the time, she didn't know it was their secret place and she'd been puzzled by the momentary sadness etched across his face. It wasn't until the day they'd made love that he told her about Elpida.

Quietly, she stepped through the rows and rows of vines until she caught a glimpse of Zak seated in a portable camping chair, one leg slung over the armrest. With his sketchpad resting on his bent knee, his concentration was focused on his artwork. Evvie breathed deeply to steady herself, admiring his face in profile—the square lines of his stubble-covered jawbone, his fine straight nose, and his thick, dark eyelashes that many women would envy. He wore no shirt on this scorching day, just a low-slung pair of cutoff shorts, and Evvie couldn't take her eyes off his defined biceps as his hand moved swiftly across the drawing pad.

Evvie savored the moment, observing Zak in a relaxed and seemingly content state. Tightness constricted her chest as she silently prayed that her presence would only add to his peace and not disturb it.

As if Zak had sensed her, he turned. Frowning, he stood from the chair, looking at her with curious, angry eyes. Setting the drawing pad down, he shook his head, speechless to see her standing before him.

Evvie swore she'd caught a twinkle of brightness in his eyes before they faded to steely animosity. She kept repeating Stella's yiayiá's words in her mind. 'The first glance of the eye will tell you all the truth you need.' A drop of hope thrummed in Evvie's heart.

"Of all the fucking places you could have gone, you had to choose this island to take your honeymoon?" Zak's voice was laced with such bitterness it cut through Evvie like a blade.

Evvie thought she might cry, but she fought to hold back the tears threatening to overwhelm her. She took a step toward him. "No." She lifted her hand to show him she wore no rings. "No wedding, no honeymoon."

Zak blinked back his surprise but stood stiffly in place. "What are you doing here then, Evvie?"

"I—" She looked down at her sandals. He wasn't happy to see her. Should she crawl into a hole and hide? Turn around and walk away? But she had come so far to see him. "I came to speak to you," she said, crossing her arms protectively over her chest.

"I don't think there's anything left to say." He ran his hands over his stubble. "I jumped off that merry-go-round and I'm not getting back on."

"I understand and I don't blame you. But I came all this way and I'm asking you to hear me out."

"Go ahead," Zak said, his tone unforgiving. "Say what you have to, but before you begin, I have no intention of being anyone's second choice."

Evvie winced but she dared to take another step closer. "You're not. You're my first choice," Evvie said.

"Pfff!" Dismissing the sincerity in her voice, he continued angrily, "Did you leave him for me?"

"I left him because he wasn't the one for me. And I called off the wedding as much for his sake as for mine. A marriage between us would have never worked out. I stayed out of loyalty because we'd been together so long. Ryan was reliable and it was easy between is. We both fell into the comfort of the familiar."

Evvie moved in as close to Zak as she could without touching him. She wanted to though. Oh, did she ever. Her body craved contact with his, but Zak gave no indication that he wanted or desired her.

"God help me for saying this out loud, because I might be the most wretched person on the planet, but I'm going to finally admit what I've been burying for way too long. With Ryan, my heart was safe from ever having it broken."

Zak's eyebrows drew together and Evvie could see he was trying to process what she'd said. She had to make him understand before he came to the wrong conclusion.

"Safe from being smashed to smithereens if the worst ever happened to him. Naturally, I would have been terribly sad, I'm not heartless, but I would've survived."

"Are you saying you didn't love him?" Zak asked, with a little less coldness in his tone.

"Not in the way I should have. No," Evvie said, her heart galloping at a rapid pace. She looked up into his eyes and was certain she saw a fissure in his armor, be it ever so minute. "Not in the way I know with every breath in my body that it's you I love."

Zak clutched his stomach as if he were about to double over from a blow. He searched her face, seeking the truth of her words.

"You don't trust me and I deserve nothing less. All I can say is that I've been so wrong and so, so stupid." Evvie wiped away a tear before the salty liquid reached her lips. "I'm truly blessed to be loved by so many people in my life and I'd be crushed to lose any one of them. Two of them were taken from me far too soon. There's a hole in my heart that will never fully heal and, as a result of that pain, I've done everything in my power to avoid the possibility of going through that again."

"Evvie ..." Zak whispered.

"Let me get this out," Evvie cried. She kept brushing away the tears that were rolling down her cheeks, but the flow was continuous. "You'd think I'd have the mind to bring a tissue," she chided herself.

Zak went to his camping chair and ripped a paper from his sketch-pad. "Here, use this," he said offering it to her.

"Thanks." Evvie blotted her face. "I'm such an idiot for thinking I could never allow anyone into my heart. Three years ago, I knew I'd lost that battle but I kept fighting it anyway." Her bottom lip quivered and she took in a sharp intake of breath before she went on. "The truth is, you own my heart, and if anything happened to you it would completely destroy me."

Evvie saw the tears beginning to well in Zak's eyes. It gave her the courage to finish what she had to say.

"But I'm already dying a slow death without you. I shatter a little more each day with the weight of what I've done born from some deluded need to protect myself. And I know you said you're done," Evvie said, struggling to get the words out, "but I'm going to say what I came to tell you anyway, even though you no longer care for me."

Evvie looked deeply into his eyes. She wanted him to see the truth reflected in hers.

"I don't simply love you, I'm in love with you. Hopelessly and eternally in love with you."

Evvie closed her eyes and sighed. When she opened them, Zak stood, immobilized by her words. If she stayed in place a second longer, with no reaction coming from him, her humiliation would amplify. Afraid she'd completely break down in front of him, she panicked. Briskly, she pivoted, balling her hands into fists, and ran.

"Evvie!" Zak was jolted out of his stunned silence. Chasing after her, he caught up with her, grabbing hold of her wrist. "Wait, where are you going?"

"I've embarrassed myself enough for one day. I'm leaving."

Zak pulled her close, pressing her body to his. Cupping her cheeks, he bent down, a fire sparking in Evvie's belly when his lips met hers. He slid his hands down her shoulders, grazing her back until he circled her tiny waist with his fingers, leaving no space between them. "Evvie," he moaned into her mouth.

Evvie sighed as she ran her hands over his back. When she broke the kiss, she rested her head on his bare chest, taking comfort that his heart was beating at the same rate as hers.

Together, they stood tightly in each other's arms, soothed by the body heat between them. Evvie was swept away by the rise and fall of his chest against her cheek as he breathed. When he pulled away and held her at arms length, her body rebelled.

"Evvie, I need to know you won't ever leave me again." His eyes bore into hers. "I have to know this is real."

Evvie rested her palm on his cheek and ran her thumb over his lips. The corners of her mouth curled up with affection and her eyes sparkled. "Real," she assured him. "Nothing has ever been this real for me." She claimed his mouth and he responded with hunger. "I'm ready to stop living half a life. I'm ready to admit how much I love you. And I'm ready to stop living in fear."

"Courage is knowing what not to fear."

"Did you get that off a fortune cookie?" Evvie teased.

"You always have a comeback." He pressed his forehead to hers. "Plato."

"Of course it is!" Evvie laughed. "My Greek boy is alive and well."

"Isn't this how we began?" he asked, breaking his hold on her to cross his arms in mock annoyance.

"That was a long time ago," she answered.

They had soon relaxed into a playful banter but there was no joking in her regard for him. She took Zak's hand in hers and pressed it against her breast. "But then you plucked my heart from its ravaged vine and, like a fine wine, blended it with yours to let it age until it reached just the right amount of fermentation."

"What happened after that?" Zak asked, grinning.

"New life was breathed into it—a unique and extraordinary union with a flavor and soul all its own—ready to be savored and appreciated."

"I love you, Evvie," Zak said, emphasizing each word with conviction. "I've woken up in the middle of a dream, I'm afraid. I'd given up all hope."

She ran her fingers through his lush, brown hair. "I want to be your hope."

"Elpida," Zak said, mystified.

"Yes, *elpida*—hope. Zak? What is it? You look as though you've seen a ghost."

"Not a ghost, but definitely a spirit," he said. "Right before I met you I had a dream. Well, maybe it was more like a visitation. Elpida was standing before me, begging away my sadness. She promised she'd send someone for me. 'Someone like us,' she said, imploring me to understand her meaning." He shook his head slowly. "I didn't. When I met you, I was taken with you from the start, but when I discovered you were a twin like me, I was sure you were the one my sister had sent to me." Zak turned his back on her and snapped a leaf off a vine. "After everything that happened with us, I figured I'd let my imagination run away with me ..." Absently, he twirled the leaf by its stem between his fingers. "... and I convinced myself it was nothing more than a dream." He turned to face her and flung the leaf over his shoulder. "That same dream reoccurred two nights ago, so when you said you wanted to be my hope, my *elpida*, I—"

"I would have loved your sister," Evvie said, touching her fingers to the tattoo that rested over his heart.

Zak took her hand, kissing the inside of her palm. He fixed his gaze on the design inked on the underside of her wrist. Running a thumb over it, he eyed her with curiosity. "What is this?"

Intertwined in an elegant, fluid design were the Greek letters alpha and omega linked together. Nestled within the alpha was the lowercase epsilon and in the middle of the omega sat the lowercase zeta.

"You once told me that I was your alpha and your omega. I wasn't ready to face it at the time, but now it's etched on me permanently—on my body as well as in my soul." She closed her eyes when he ran his lips over her testament. Tears caught onto her lashes, blurring her vision. "You're my beginning and end and everything in between. Even if you didn't want me anymore, I wanted to do this as a reminder of my greatest mistake."

"Oh, I want you," he pulled her between his legs and pressed a smile against the hollow of her neck. "And now I can finally tell you how much I love you," he whispered.

Garlic, freshly picked oregano and lemon pleasantly pervaded the house. Evvie and Zak walked in the front door, following the aroma to the elderly ladies preparing dinner in the kitchen. Zak brought a finger to his lips, silencing Evvie before she announced their return. With rapt amusement, he enfolded his arms around her, pressing her back against him as they watched their grandmothers unknowingly put on a show.

Maria poured wine into two glasses that had obviously been drained of their contents. "*Yámas*," they said, clinking glasses. Chattering as they stirred, they added herbs and tested the seasoning with the famed wooden spoon that had dished out many whacks on the behind over the years. Another gulp of wine, a cackle over a funny anecdote and out came the plates.

"Should we take bets if they'll throw them or set the table?" Evvie laughed. Her pro-yiayiá was ninety-five and Zak's grandmother was in her seventies, but a bunch of college co-eds had nothing on the energy of these two old ladies.

"They're a force to be reckoned with," Zak whispered.

"We know you're there," Maria said. "Is something funny to you?"

"No, you're both so adorable," Evvie said.

"Adorable!" Yiayiá laughed. "Not us, but …" There was a twinkle in her eye. "… look at the two of you. *Eísate haroúmene, pethia mou*?"

Zak and Evvie peered into one another's eyes before answering. "Yes, very, very happy," Zak answered.

After that, there was a lot of cheek kissing and toasting. Evvie heard Maria say something about exchanging *stefana* soon and Yiayiá waved her finger at Evvie when she mumbled a protest under her breath.

"I tell you, *moro mou*, why. Because we want to be here to see it and time is running out for us."

"Zak is going to take me to the hotel to get my bags after dinner," Evvie said, changing the subject.

"I told you not to bother renting a room. Yiayiá knows everything," she bragged. Handing Evvie a stack of linen napkins, she declared, "You need to have faith."

Zak took the key card from Evvie and unlocked the hotel door. "Well, that's the shortest stay in history," Zak said. "You paid a night's rent for nothing."

"Maybe not," Evvie said, a slow smile lighting up her face. She tunneled her hands under his t-shirt, brushing her fingers over the smooth skin of his back.

"Did you have something in mind?" he teased with an impish grin.

"Me?" she asked, with the face of innocence. "What would make you say that?" She lifted his shirt over his head, discarding it over her shoulder and feathered kisses from his chest down to his abdomen.

"That's it!" Swiftly, he picked her up off her feet, throwing her onto the bed. "I've waited far too long for you." Zak pinned her body beneath his and peeled off her clothing, little by little.

Evvie shuddered at the kisses pebbled to each new exposed bit of flesh. Zak took his time, as if he was savoring his favorite meal, but Evvie grew needy and impatient for more. While he feasted on her body, she explored his—every curve and muscle—the firmness of his bottom and the strength in his arms. She read his body like a book of Braille and it was one she planned to read many times over.

Evvie had never forgotten the love they'd made on this island three years prior. It was a delicious, secret memory she treasured but had buried deep inside her. Making love to him now was even better. So much better than she'd remembered it to be. The burdens and commitments that had prevented her absolute appreciation of him were gone. Now, she could revel in his body, as it expressed to her what words could never reveal. And when he entered her, she looked deep into his eyes and swore she could touch his soul in the same way his had burrowed into hers.

He moaned her name and she replied with his. And there it was. Spontaneous combustion exploding within her. Evvie's eyes clouded over until bursts of orange and red dissipated to golden stardust. White hot stars—flickering, flickering, flickering.

For a long time, they laid stretched out, facing each other, Evvie running circles over his hip, Zak playing with a lock of her hair.

"Maybe we should keep the room," Evvie said. "I wouldn't mind doing that over and over again."

"Me too," Zak agreed, stroking her cheek with his knuckle. "Every day for the rest of my life. Marry me," he said.

"Sure! There's a church a few miles away."

"I'm serious. I'm so in love with you and … you did tell me you love me too." He pulled her into a sitting position on his lap.

"You're not joking," Evvie said, surprised. "It's too soon, isn't it? We've been apart more than together. We've only had stolen, guarded moments before today."

"We've had more time than you realize. If you're still not sure we'll last—"

"No!" she stopped him. "That's not it at all. I can't picture myself with anyone but you." She ran her finger over his pillowy lips and sighed. "Please trust what I feel in here for you." She brought his hand to her heart. "But we've been apart for so long. You're ready to be engaged?" Evvie asked.

"No," Zak said. "No engagement. I want to marry you right away, while we're here."

"You have to be kidding. How would we pull that off?"

"What's to pull off? We go to church and have a simple party afterward." He pulled a self-deprecating face. "I'm an ass. You want the whole big thing. All the bells and whistles."

"That's not what I was thinking," Evvie said. "I don't care about any of that stuff. But I can't get married without my family."

"If they were here would you be open to it?"

"Yes, I would marry you this second." There was a tenderness in her voice. "This is a special place for us."

Zak jumped off the bed to find his scattered clothing. "Come on! We have a wedding to plan for three weeks from today. That should give our parents enough time to get here. And whoever else can come will be a bonus."

Light from the full moon illuminated the night sky. Evvie leaned back on the trunk of the car, committing the moment to her memory. Silently, she thanked the moon, the stars and God in his heaven.

"Daydreaming?" Zak asked. "Let me get your suitcase out."

Evvie stepped aside to allow Zak access to the trunk. "I was just thinking that once we step inside those doors, nothing is going to be the same."

Zak's ebullient laugh was contagious. Evvie slapped her palms on his chest and giggled alongside him.

"They're going to go from ecstatic to frantic in three seconds flat when we tell them how much time they have to plan a wedding," Zak breathed though the laughter.

Hand in hand, they walked to the door. At the threshold, they stopped and took in a deep breath. "Let the happy chaos begin," Evvie said.

"Everyone is like a butterfly. They start out ugly and awkward and then morph into beautiful, graceful butterflies that everyone loves."

—Drew Barrymore

Chapter 54

Evvie

August 2011

Loud music echoed beyond the vast, open space surrounding the yard to the Maryiatos home located on the vineyard. Thousands of white lights, woven through the lattice pergola, glimmered above the stone patio. The youngsters had taken over the dance floor, singing in unison at the top of their lungs to one of the top Greek pop hits, '*Mia Nihta Mono*' – 'Only One Night.'

It was the night before the wedding and the celebration had been underway for two days, and that wasn't counting all the preparations that had been happening for the past week and a half. Evvie and Zak's mothers, along with Demi, had arrived before everyone else. And just as Zak had predicted, a whirlwind of chaos had soon ensued.

"You call that dancing?" Petros shouted to the crowd. "What is this bouncing and jumping? *Saklamara!*" He waved them off. He turned to the men sitting at the weathered wooden table. "Grigoris, Demos!" he summoned. "All of you, *éla!* We can show these kids what it means to dance from the soul."

A collective groan of protest reverberated when the music suddenly changed from Euro top forty to a traditional Greek zeibekiko. With his arms spread wide, the silver-haired, barrel-chested man looked like an eagle about to take flight. Both of his sons followed him as he began to snap his fingers, dropping his head and closing his eyes to soak in the essence of the music. One by one, Dean, Michael, and the other men formed a circle around Petros, clapping their hands and cheering. "*Opa!*" the men roared as one.

Clicking his heels in rhythm to the music, Petros pivoted, bending down to slap the floor and then jumping up and hitting the side of his shoe. Soon, everyone surrounded him, hooting and hollering. With a leap, Grigiros joined his father and Demos followed behind, spiraling gracefully to the floor. With his knees to the ground, he leaned back until his head touched the sole of his shoes. Petros continued his sweeping steps, making every beat of the music count by losing himself in the melody and the words.

Petros inched his way to Michael and Dean, pulling them into the circle to take their turn. Soon the dance became a competition for who could kick the highest or bend down lowest to the ground. This was the spirit and the soul of Greece, imbedded in their DNA for thousands of years—a love and appreciation for life as it was meant to be enjoyed.

Not to be outdone, the younger generation took the floor. Kristos, Nicky, Paul and Sam hit the dancefloor. Zak led the pack, drawing Adam and RJ into the fold. But their go at zeibekiko looked a lot more like a poor attempt at break dancing rather that the fluid moves of the men commanding the floor.

When the song was over, Zak removed the CD in the player and selected a slower song. Smiling, he narrowed his eyes and crooked a finger in Evvie's direction. A chill ran up her spine as she went to join him on the dance floor.

Zak was damp with sweat and she couldn't help but make a joke of it. "You just had to show them up on the dance floor, didn't you, *Hellas*?"

"Not them, *agapi mou*. It's all for you," he answered.

Evvie wrapped her arms around his neck, nuzzling her head into his chest as they danced.

Zak began to sing along with the music, loud enough only for Evvie's ears. '*Mono Esí*' oozed with emotion. The song spoke of souls communicating without words, vows of lifelong love, and confessions of desperate need.

Evvie's mind blissfully drifted, forgetting everyone around them. For all her teasing and mock indifference to her heritage, she'd come to embrace all of it. With this man, she wanted it all—every tradition and each custom. Even the *Krevati* ritual she'd found so archaic at Sam and Naomi's wedding she willingly embraced. Three times the bridal bed was made and re-made, and three times Zak came in the room to inspect it and finally nod his approval. Evvie ran her hands through Zak's hair as they swayed to the music. Her mind went back to the way his eyes tenderly fell upon her once the bed making ritual had been completed. Rice had been scattered on the bed along with sugarcoated almonds. Stella arranged red rose petals to form a heart shape, symbolizing a beautiful life together, and all the women threw cash onto the mattress.

But when it was time to place a baby boy in the middle of the bed in the hopes that a male child will be born to her and her husband, Evvie waved an admonishing finger. "This is where I want to break tradition just a little." A distant cousin to Zak stood cradling her infant girl in her arms. Evvie extended her hands and the woman handed the child over to Evvie. "I want both a female and a male child on the bed." Zak had come from behind her, circling her waist, whispering, "I want her to look just like her mother," he said of their future child.

It had been a celebratory week and each moment had been precious from the second her family had arrived. From her Aunt Demi urgently delegating wedding plans and her mother breaking into happy tears just about every time she looked her way, to the assembly line they'd formed making *boubouneires*—the traditional wedding favors of sugared almonds wrapped in tulle. And now, as if by magic, her wedding was only a sunrise away.

When the song ended, Zak held Evvie by the waist and kissed her as if no one was watching.

"Save it for after the wedding," Dean said, cuffing a hand on Zak's shoulder. "She's still my little girl for one more night."

"Over protective much?" Evvie asked Dean.

"Always," he answered. "Everyone's starting to leave. You should say goodnight and we'll head back to the hotel."

"Okay. Give me a minute," Evvie said.

Dean nodded smiling, leaving Zak and Evvie alone.

Zak threaded his fingers through Evvie's. "Thirteen hours and fourteen minutes."

Evvie looked at Zak with curious amusement.

"That's how long it will be until I'm standing outside the church waiting for you," Zak answered her unspoken question. "Don't make me wait a second longer."

"I won't." Evvie formed an X over her heart. "Cross my heart. I may even get there before you do." Evvie kissed him one last time before her mother insisted it was time to go.

The next morning, Evvie was awakened by streams of light escaping through the slats of the window blinds. Jumping from her bed, she pulled on the cord inviting the sunshine to envelope her. Behind her, Evvie heard her sister stir.

"Is it time yet?" Even with the morning rasp in her voice, Cia's excitement couldn't be contained.

"Not yet," Evvie answered. "You have a few hours left to sleep if you'd like."

"Then come back to bed," Stella grumbled. "And shut those blinds."

"Late night?" Evvie asked Stella, arching a brow.

"After the party RJ and I took a walk through the vineyard under the moonlight."

Cia crawled out of her bed and slid into Stella's. "Tell us everything!" she said.

"She just did," Evvie said. "They took a walk."

"You know," Cia said, frustrated, "I'm not a baby. I want to hear the good stuff." Pouting, she added, "Better yet, I want to know when I'll get a hot boy of my own."

"Not for a while. You're only twelve!" Evvie said.

"I guess I'll just settle for Maid of Honor for now," she whined.

"If you have to settle I can ask—"

"No! I'm too excited! I can't sleep now that I'm up, can you Ev? No, of course you can't. Let's get something to eat and then Stella and I can help you get dressed." Cia jumped out of bed and shed herself of her father's decades old Led Zepplin t-shirt she'd claimed as her own nightshirt.

Her rambunctious little sister often amused Evvie. "Mention food or boys and that girl's enthusiasm propels like a launching missile!" she laughed to Stella.

After Evvie ate breakfast with her family, she wanted some time alone. She showered, wrapped herself in a lightweight robe and took a seat on the chaise lounge by the window. She typed out a text to Zak, her finger hovering over the send button. Superstition dictated that it's bad luck for the couple to see each other before the wedding. But writing out a message didn't count, did it? She hoped not because she couldn't resist. She leaned against the backrest waiting for a reply.

Zak: *I love you more. I'll be the one waiting at the top of the steps for you. Don't be late. My heart can't take it.*

A knock on her door drew Evvie from her thoughts. "Come in," she said.

"I thought I might be able to help my daughter with her hair and makeup," Sophia said, her eyes glistening.

"Mom, are you crying already?"

"It's not everyday my daughter gets married. Let me have my moment."

Evvie stood and hugged her mother. "We've had some interesting times, to say the least, Mom." Evvie sighed. Evvie placed a gentle kiss on her cheek. "I'm sorry."

"For what?" The tenderness in Sophia's tone eased Evvie.

"For being so difficult."

"That's what children do when they're trying to find their place in the world. They challenge their parents at times." Sophia asked her daughter to sit beside her. "But you and Nicky had more loss to deal with than the average child. I tried to protect both of you. Maybe too much." Sophia raised her chin and grinned. "That's enough of that! This is a happy day. One you should remember for the rest of your life with nothing but the sweetest of memories."

Evvie applied her cosmetics while Sophia read messages from well-wishers in the States. Cia came in to announce that the hair stylist had arrived and, after introducing herself, Evvie explained she wanted a simple, natural style with loose waves down her back.

Too many women were crammed into one hotel room, all of them doting on Evvie, but when it was time for Evvie to slip on her dress, Sophia shooed all of them out of the room. All but Yiayiá Sophia.

From the garment bag, Sophia carefully removed the pale pink, tea length dress she had worn when she'd married Dean. Her own mother, Anastacia, who had worn it for Alexandros on their wedding day, had given the dress to her, and now she was passing it down to her daughter.

Evvie put a hand to her neck as she tried to hold back the tears that were sure to flow. Swallowing the lump in her throat, she looked up at her mother, catching her tears with her forefingers. Sitting in a corner chair, Yiayiá Sophia held a tissue under her nose, sniffling.

Stepping into the dress, Evvie pulled it up by the sleeves and her mother began to fasten the delicate buttons that ran up the length of her back. When she was done, she retrieved the matching seed pearl crown with the attached veil from a hatbox and placed it carefully on Evvie's head.

"There's only one thing left to do." Sophia dug inside her bag and pulled out a familiar black velvet box. "I didn't forget to bring these with me."

"Yiayiá's earrings," Evvie murmured hoarsely. She took the box from her mother, opened it and put the diamond studs in her ears. "She promised that she would watch over me when the day came that I married. She said a piece of her would be with me if I wore these."

Yiayiá Sophia spoke through tears. "You're a part of her. Evanthia *mou*, you look just like her."

"It's almost time!" Sophia said. "But before we go I want to say a few words to you. I can see how much you love each other. It's written all over your faces. It fills me with joy to know you've found such happiness. It's all I want for my children because, in the end, all that counts are the people you love. That's the true gift. Possessions and achievements, that's the wrapping paper. Pretty, but you need to strip it away if you want what's beneath the surface. Focus on what's really important." Sophia took Evvie's chin between her fingers. "But marriage takes work. To keep the love alive, it takes communication. Listen and compromise. I had wonderful times with your father but, like all couples, we went through rough spots as well. And with Dino, life threw us some challenges, but our love was strong enough to survive it, because nothing can ever separate us. It's not always going to be easy, but it'll always be worth it."

"Can I come in?" Dean called through the closed door as he rapped on it.

"Yes, I'm dressed," Evvie said.

Dean did a double take. "Who is this beauty? Surely it's not the girl who's usually knee deep in grapes and dirt?" With a couple of quick steps, he was standing across from her. He took her hands in his. "You look just like your mother did the day we got married," he smiled softly.

"Except I was almost twice her age," Sophia corrected him.

"And you looked half that," he said, turning to brush his lips against hers. "Can I have a few moments alone with Evvie?"

"Of course," Sophia said. "Yiayiá, come with me."

When Sophia shut the door behind her, Dean reached into his suit jacket pocket. "I have something for you, and I'm hoping you'll want to wear it today." He held out a red velvet case and opened it. Inside was a white gold, heart-shaped pendant encrusted in diamond chips.

"It's gorgeous. Of course, I'll wear it." She hugged her stepfather and pressed her cheek to his.

"It's a locket," Dean said, removing the necklace from its box. He opened it and showed her the pictures he'd inserted. Evvie looked up at him with more tenderness for the man than she'd ever felt before. On one side was a picture of himself and, on the other, one of her father, Will.

"When I married your mother, I told you and Nicky that I could never replace your father, but I could help him do what he could no longer do for you. Evvie, I have loved you from the moment you were born. I was the first person to see you come into this world. I knew then that you had the spirit of a Greek warrior and the beauty of a goddess." Dean cupped her cheek with his hand. "I held you before anyone else and I placed you in your mother's arms. My heart bursts with love for you, not just because you are hers, but because you're you." Tears began to well in Dean's eyes. "There's a special place in my heart reserved only for you and I know I can't take the place of your father but there's one thing I do know. When I walk you to the church today, I'm as certain as I am of my own name that, while I'll be the proudest father on earth, your dad's spirit will be right beside you too."

Dean took the necklace from the box and clasped it around Evvie's neck. She touched the heart as though it were her most precious possession.

"So wear this in honor of him, he who will always be with you, and I who am blessed to look after you when he was no longer able to."

"It's not fair, you know, to make me cry like this," Evvie blubbered. "I must look like a mess now."

"You look beautiful, but I'll give you a few minutes to freshen up before we leave."

He started to walk away, but Evvie ran to him, clinging to Dean as though he were her lifeline.

"I love you. I hope you know that," she said.

"I do, angel, I do," he said, pressing a kiss on her forehead.

A procession of cars drove uphill along the winding roads until they reached a narrow street that ended where a path of stone steps led to a small chapel overlooking the water. From this point, with most of his family following behind, Dean walked Evvie to meet her groom.

Turning to Alex, Dean said, "I think this honor should go to you as well."

Filled with pride, Alex kissed his granddaughter's cheek and laced his arm through hers. "You're a vision, *Engoní mou*," he whispered.

Escorted by both, Evvie began her ascent up the winding stairs to unite her soul with the man who'd been chosen for her either by destiny or some kind of unexplainable magic cast by a mythical Greek god.

When they reached the top, Evvie wanted to take in the splendid blending of sea and sky. She wanted to admire the magnificent yet simplistic beauty of the ancient church standing proudly on the cliff. How she would have loved to see the expression on the faces of the guests lining the stone barrier on the platform leading to the shrine.

But she noticed very little of it. Surrounded by family, friends and the clergyman, her Zacharias waited. She glanced at him and at the moment his eyes drank in hers, nothing else mattered. Slowly he strode toward her holding a simple bouquet of white jasmine flora, the green stems secured tightly by white satin.

Handing it to her, he dropped to one knee. "I didn't do this three weeks ago, so I'm asking you today, formally, in front of our families and friends, if you'll take me, this man who loves you, and trust me with your heart."

"Nothing would make me happier." Evvie took Zak by the hand, urging him to his feet. "It's me who should be begging you for that trust. I will always love you."

Zak leaned in for a kiss, but a priest, cloaked in white and gold vestments, separated them with his large, golden bible. "After the wedding," he admonished gently.

Evvie kissed Dean, her mother and her pappou on each cheek. Zak, as a sign of respect, did the same, murmuring promises to Evvie's family. Turning, they bestowed the same affection to Zak's parents. Together, the priest led them into the chapel with the guests following closely behind.

There was a simplistic beauty in the structure's antiquity. Life-sized icons hid the altar from view. The luminous gold paint in the sacred images had dulled from candle smoke and time, but it only added to the mystique of how many before them had stood on this ground and made an oath of love.

The stone floor was uneven and no pews had been provided for the guests. At best the room could hold forty people, and it was just about that many who surrounded the couple. Two four-foot candles adorned with satin and tulle flanked either side of an ornately carved, wooden table.

After the priest began reciting the prayers, he asked for the rings. Evvie handed Cia her bouquet. Nicky and Stella, as *koumbari*, stepped up for the betrothal. The priest took the rings from Nicky and placed them atop the large bible. Three times, the rings were placed on Zak and Evvie's fingers and three times removed and alternately crossed back and forth between them.

Evvie had been to many Greek weddings, so right before the time had come to exchange the *stefana*, a rush of emotion flooded her. On the table, a silver tray holding two white wreaths connected by a single ribbon waited to unite them. Evvie's mother and yiayiá had both been crowned to their husbands by the same ones used by Alex's parents, Evanthia's and Nicholas' namesakes. But the *stefana* had yellowed and crumbled from age, making it impossible to use them one more time. Wearing Anastacia's earrings and bridal dress, she felt her yiayiá's spirit surround her. But even a tiny silk flower from the age-old *stefana* would tie her to the ancestors who paved the way for her. Attached to the ribbon bonding the crowns was a single yellowed flower wound around each wreath.

Thrice the *stefana* were crossed over Evvie and Zak before the priest placed it on their heads. Then the couple drank from a golden goblet, representing the miracle at the wedding in Cana.

Evvie savored every single moment. Her senses exploded with joy, and there was a lightness her soul hadn't felt in many years. The smell of bee's wax and jasmine would forever remind her of this day. The sight of her mother and Dean as he held her while she happily cried was imprinted permanently in her mind. The sound of the chanter's voice, Evvie had faith, could be heard by her loved ones in heaven. And the feeling of Zak taking her by the hand, to take their first steps as husband and wife, was branded in her heart forever.

The priest led the newly married couple around the table for the 'Dance of Isaiah.' Stella and Nicky followed, holding the ribbon that attached the wreaths, bonding the couple for life. Three times they circled and each time the guests threw rice at them. Evvie and Zak couldn't help but laugh. By the third revolution they were being pelted with *koufeta*, sugar-coated almonds, along with the rice.

Finally, the crowd shouted, *'Na zizete,'* a wish for a long, happy life, and with that came their first wedded kiss, a kiss that seemed to go on for longer than propriety allowed. But Evvie didn't care and she was certain Zak didn't either.

"I love you," he said.

"Hmm, I might need a little more proof," Evvie teased. She fisted her hands in the lapel of his jacket and pulled him in for another kiss. "I love you so very much."

Immediately following the ceremony, the wedding couple and their guests celebrated at a nearby restaurant overlooking the water. Lush greenery hid the limestone patio from view. White linen covered each of the tables arranged on the perimeter of the open space, leaving more than a sufficient amount of room for dancing. In each corner, three-foot glass vases held puffs of white chrysanthemums, while pink rosebuds floated in glass bowls situated in the center of each table.

Demi had come to Kefalonia like a cyclone forging its way to shore. It was she who had designed the floral arrangements and chosen the linens, while managing, in a very short time, to coordinate the church, the photographer, and the caterer. At the bride's request, it was to be a small, casual affair—nothing ostentatious or complicated, and it turned out just as Evvie had imagined.

The band Demi had commissioned played a mixture of the traditional Greek music, old love songs and the latest in Greek pop. What they didn't know how to play were songs sung in English which presented a tiny but solvable problem.

Evvie and Zak had been mingling from table to table when her stepfather strode over and patted Zak on the back.

"What do you say?" Dean asked him.

"Say about what?" Evvie asked.

"It's time for our dance," Zak said, leading her to the middle of the open space.

"We never agreed on a song." Evvie wore an impish grin. "Are we using the one I suggested?"

"Oh, no. It's a nice sentiment, in a strange way. But we are not dancing our wedding song to 'My Life Would Suck Without You.'"

Before he could say anything more, Dean took the microphone from the bandleader.

"I want to thank everyone who pulled together to make this day possible. We couldn't have done it without your love and support. The groom has a special song request that was unfamiliar to the band."

Evvie looked at Zak, bewildered. "What song?" she whispered.

"So if you'll bear with me, my son and I will attempt to play it for them while our wedding couple takes to the floor for their first dance."

With his guitar in hand, Nicky climbed onto the platform and slung the strap over his shoulder.

"So the story goes that when Evvie and Zak had first met back in their days at Cornell, they attended an on-campus concert together. When Ben Folds sang this song, Zak felt as though the songwriter must have channeled his thoughts and emotions for him and Evvie alone."

Nicky played the intro and Dean began to sing the melody to 'The Luckiest.'

The wedding couple stood motionless until Zak pulled Evvie into his arms. "You never told me," she said. Looking deep into his eyes, she could see the affection and the raw emotion. Why hadn't she seen it sooner? He had always loved her, even back then.

Zak pressed his forehead to hers. "I wanted to, so many times." He kissed her and the crowd went wild. Suddenly, the guests encroached upon them, showering the couple with money as they swayed to the music. When the music changed to a lively *kalamatiano*, everyone circled the couple and danced around them.

"I think we should have a bite to eat. After, let's dance once or twice more and then make our escape," Zak said. "They'll be here all night and I want you to myself."

"Me too. It was hard to sneak off alone this past week with all the relatives around," Evvie said as they made their way back their seats.

After eating a few bites of food, Zak was ready to move the afternoon along.

"RJ," Zak motioned him over, "what do you say we take our ladies to the dance floor?" he asked with a wink.

"Perfect timing!" RJ said. "Here she comes now."

"Perfect timing for what?" Stella asked crossing over to the table where RJ sat chatting with Zak and Evvie.

"A dance," RJ said, sweeping her into his arms.

"But wait!" Evvie called out. "First I need to do this." She lifted her bridal bouquet from the table and, without warning, flung it in Stella's direction.

"Oh!" Stella exclaimed. "I wasn't expecting that. Shouldn't you have asked all the other girls to come up?"

"No," Evvie said grinning, "this one belongs to you."

Zak signaled for the band to begin a slow song and he took to the floor with his bride as RJ and Stella danced alongside them.

RJ held Stella tightly as they turned slowly to the music. Other couples had taken to the floor, including Sophia and Dean, Michael and Demi, and Zak's parents, Glika and Demos.

The day had been absolute magic. Stella couldn't have been more pleased for her cousin, but as she settled her head against RJ's chest while he held her, it was only he she thought of.

"*S'agapo*," RJ murmured in her ear. "That's the song. Did I say it correctly?"

"Perfectly," she cooed contently.

"And it means I love you." RJ dug his hand into his pocket.

"That's right! You're learning." Stella was impressed. Even the accent sounded good to her ears.

"I practiced saying that, because I do love you, and I wanted to tell you in the native language of this beautiful island on this special day."

"*Kai s'agapó pára poly.* And I love you very much," Stella translated.

RJ took one of her hands draped around his neck, bringing her fingers to his lips. "How much is very much? Enough for forever?"

"Yes, unless there's something longer than forever," she sighed.

RJ's eyes brightened. "In that case, maybe you'll wear this?" He pulled his hand from his pocket, pulling out a princess cut diamond ring and placed it on her finger.

"RJ," she said barely audible. Her eyes glistened nearly as much as the brilliant gem on her hand. She held his face in her hands and kissed him.

"I want to be your protector just as you've been my savior. You brought color to a world that had gone black for me. With you, I'm at peace and I want for nothing as long as I have you. I'm all yours—body, mind and spirit—every part of me there is to have. Say you'll be mine. Say you'll marry me, Stella Angelidis."

"Yes, yes!" Stella found her voice, raspy from tears. "I can't imagine my life without you. You're my friend, my family, my love."

RJ shot his hand in the air. "We're engaged!" he shouted.

The guests applauded. "*Syharitíria!*" they shouted their congratulations.

Evvie and Zak were the first to approach them, the four hugging in a circle. "What a perfect day!" exclaimed Evvie, tearing up.

"In every way," Stella added.

"It's about to get even better," Zak said. He slapped RJ on the back. "This show is all yours now. Ev and I are sneaking out while we have the chance. Thanks for the distraction, man." Zak took Evvie by the hand, waved a kiss goodbye to their families and headed for the exit.

"I didn't do it for you!" RJ corrected Zak.

"I know, but thanks anyway. The spotlight is on you and Stella now!" Zak said before disappearing with his bride.

Within seconds, family and friends descended upon Stella and RJ, kissing, congratulating and tugging at Stella's hand for a closer look at her ring. But she didn't care. The day had proven beyond her wildest dreams. With all they had both been through, she and Evvie were now happy. So very, very happy.

Chapter 55

Sophia Papadakis

Present day

I t was a comfortable seventy-two degrees on this Easter Sunday in Aegina. It had been a dream of Sophia's for years to gather the family for a traditional Easter in Greece. Too many work-related obligations and the lack of time always seemed to get in the way but Sophia was determined to make it happen, and it took a full year of planning and balancing schedules to assemble everyone in one place, but it proved to be worth every bit of her time and effort.

Anastacia had often shared precious memories with her daughter of her childhood holiday celebrations. It was the only time she had seen a faraway look in her mother's eyes that Sophia could interpret as a fleeting sense of homesickness.

Holy Week in the States always held a special place in Sophia's heart. Her mother would cook and bake, dye red eggs, and attend services that delivered spiritual renewal. She had kept those traditions alive and now her children held dear the customs that generations before them had fought to preserve.

Good Friday had been just as her mother had described it. Thousands of worshippers, walking in a procession holding vigil candles followed the *epitaphios*, a flower adorned sepulcher. They'd strolled along the harbor, dazzled by the illuminated boats moored there, weighed down with waiting onlookers aboard. Sophia was moved when they reached their destination. Throngs of people convened in the town square chanting the lamentations. Representation from three churches united, each one carrying a more beautifully ornate *epitaphios* than the next. Her mother hadn't exaggerated.

But it was the *Anastasi* service Sophia dreamed of. Parishioners filled every corner of the church, others waiting outside for news of Christ's resurrection. The aroma of heady incense billowed while the only sound that could be heard were the bells on the censer chiming as the priest rhythmically blessed the icons. The young boys wearing white and gold vestments extinguished the glass-encased candles, which had been set down in front of the holy images by the altar to venerate the Lord and his saints in heaven. Darkness shrouded the room, but only for a brief time.

Everyone waited in silence until the priest emerged from behind the gates of the altar holding a single candle adorned with white satin ribbon. A flicker of light revealed his face as he sang out, "Come receive the light, from the unwaining light, and glorify Christ, who is risen from the dead." One of the altar boys lit his candle from the holy flame and passed it to the others to spread amongst the congregation. From candle to candle, mother to child, brother to sister, and neighbor to friend, the light was shared by communal unity, lending hope for the world.

The crowd beyond the church doors crossed themselves, some genuflecting and many others touching the hem of the priest's garments as he exited the church, a procession following behind. It wasn't long before the night sky was alight. Candles shot upward as the worshipers sang out with joy, "*Christos Anesti*! Christ has risen!"

Fireworks exploded in the sky, and when the sound startled them, the smaller children began to cry.

Evvie and Zak held their three-year-old twins, Hope and William, to their chests, covering the children's ears. Stella and RJ's little one, Soula, had been fast asleep until the first thunderous crackle. It was now Sophia's turn to play the overprotective, indulgent yiayiá, and she reveled in every cherished moment. "Let's take them home," she said to her daughter.

The next day, Sophia found herself deep in thought as she looked on at the merriment of her friends and family. Dean snuck up behind her, wrapping his arms around her.

Tracing kisses along her neck, he murmured, "What's on your mind?"

"I'm thinking about how lucky we are."

A gentle breeze whipped through Sophia's hair and a shiver ran up her spine. She looked out onto the water, sparkling from the golden rays of the sun reflecting off it. It was a cloudless day, but for one pillow of white and she wondered if it was beyond there that heaven began.

"Do you think they can see us?" Sophia asked. "I wonder if heaven for them is the ability for their spirit to watch our lives unfold happily and to take joy in knowing it was the result of the impact they had on our lives," she pondered.

"We have no way of knowing for sure," Dean said, "but I'd like to believe that when we think of them, through a memory or a feeling, it's their souls touching ours."

Turning to face her husband she said, "I like that." She kissed him. "We're very blessed," she said. "Evvie has the life she's always wanted and Nicky is doing what he loves." She looked at her son and his girl-friend searching for Easter eggs with the children.

"He's going to propose any day now," Dean said with a sly smile.

"Is that knowledge or assessment?" Sophia grabbed her husband's face between her fingers. "Look into my eyes, Konstantinos Papadakis. What do you know that I don't?"

"He told me last night." Dean laughed at his wife.

"So that's it! Our children are grown and settled, leaving only Cia to worry about," Sophia said.

"I know you better than that. There's no end to your worry when it comes to our children," Dean said, brushing the hair from her shoulders. He planted a kiss just under her earlobe. "As for Cia, I think that spirited teenager is going to give us a run for our money."

Sophia groaned her amusement. "And the next chapter begins."

*"You have nurtured them, watched over them, prayed for them.
Now it's their turn to spread their wings and soar ..."*

—Aphrodite Papandreou

Epilogue

Evanthia Giannakos

The Heavens

I'm not sure why my life took the direction it did. On earth, we ask many philosophical questions, understanding full well that we were not meant to know the answers, but within the recesses of our minds we have faith that, someday, all the answers will be adequately revealed when our souls move closer to God's realm.

The truth is, I don't have too many more answers than I had before. And maybe it's not for me to discover the full scope of the mysteries in life and death. I only know that my existence on earth meant something—that my actions and those of my husband, Nicholas, and my brother, Vasili, had an everlasting effect on our loved ones for generations to come.

I watch them as they come together as one united family—not all by blood, but by a common bond greater than they know. Happy tears fall from the sky. My tears of joy. The sun is shining brightly down on them, and the momentary droplets of my emotional rain will evaporate within minutes.

"Look at what we've created, Nicholas," I say to my husband as he comes up beside me. "And you, Vasili, come see what we've done, my brother."

The sight of Samuouél and Naomi amongst the family makes my spirit soar. Amy scoops up the youngest of her three grandchildren, peppering him with kisses. David and Revekka are there as well; an impossibility had it not been for our conviction in justice and value for life.

"It all turned out as it should have and, given the chance, I would do it all over again," I say.

"Oh, but *agapi mou*, you did," Nicholas says. "We all did. Our son, Alexandros, stood by and pledged his love to Anastacia and her daughter. Sophia has honored us in her children, and her children will teach the next generation what we stood for."

"Through us and by the grace of God, we bestow our love, guidance and protection," Vasili added. "We are in their hearts and they are imbedded in our souls for all of eternity."

Sunbeams, as brilliant as spotlights cutting through a fog, pierced through the clouds, casting a mystical glow as though it were an apparition from the heavens. Puffs of pure white floated above as if convening for a nebulous assembly. It was so inexplicably beautiful that the loved ones in their watch looked up, admiring the celestial site.

I look behind me to find Anastacia and my Alexandros, united once again. The sun shines brighter as they approach, and brighter still when more souls who've passed into this blissful state of being gather near.

"That's right, my dear ones," I whisper a message below. "We will be with you for all time."

The end

The Gift Saga

Evanthia's Gift
Waiting for Aegina
Chasing Petalouthes

If you enjoyed *Chasing Petalouthes* please consider leaving a review for this book or any of the books in The Gift Saga on Amazon and Goodreads

Feel free to connect with Effie Kammenou on social media

Twitter - @EffieKammenou
Facebook - www.facebook.com/EffieKammenou/
Instagram - www.instagram.com/effiekammenou_author/
Goodreads - www.goodreads.com/author/show/14204724.
Effie_Kammenou

Sign up for Effie's newsletter to learn about promotions and events
http://eepurl.com/bIoJl1

For additional recipes follow https://cheffieskitchen.wordpress.com

Printed in Great Britain
by Amazon